THE PERSONALITY SURGEON

A Novel by
COLIN WILSON

MERCURY
HOUSE™

Mercury House Incorporated
San Francisco

Copyright © 1986 by Colin Wilson
First published in Great Britain in 1985 by
New English Library

Published in the United States by
Mercury House
300 Montgomery Street
San Francisco, California

Distributed to the trade by
Kampmann & Company, Inc.
New York, New York

Manufactured in the United States of America

Library of Congress Cataloging in Publication Data
Wilson, Colin 1986
The Personality Surgeon

Library of Congress Catalog Card Number 85-62423
ISBN 0-916515-04-4

ACKNOWLEDGMENTS

Many friends have helped in the writing of this book. Where computers are concerned, my friend Alan Radnor went to enormous trouble to obtain the information I needed, and it was through him that I contacted Dr. Howard Kahn, of Manchester University, who in turn put me in touch with Frazer Sim, of Micro-Consultants Ltd., who provided me with information about the Quantell Digital Paintbox.

Many medical friends also provided me with invaluable information: Dr. Andrew Crawshaw, Drs. Raymond and Jennifer Pietroni and Dr. James Rentoul. I also owe a considerable debt of gratitude to my editor, Colin Honnor, for his kindness and patience. Finally, I wish to thank the painter Robert Lenkiewicz for drawing my attention to Lavater's books on physiognomy.

Gorran Haven, June 1985

Dedication

For Karen Arthur
who suggested it

CHAPTER ONE

THE SEQUENCE of events that transformed Dr. Charles Peruzzi from an overworked general practitioner into one of the most remarkable medical discoverers of our time began in a corridor of the Park View Hotel in central London, on a mild Friday afternoon in late September 1978.

Peruzzi, preceded by a porter, was walking a few steps behind a blonde airline hostess, whose shoulder-length hair bounced gently on her back as she walked. He was experiencing the usual male curiosity about whether a girl's face is as attractive as her rear view. So when his porter stopped to insert his key in the door, and the girl halted a few feet away, he sneaked a cautious sideways look at her. He found her, on the whole, rather disappointing: pretty enough, but somehow lacking in vitality. She went into her room without even glancing at him.

When Peruzzi had unpacked his bag, used the bathroom, and explored the drinks cabinet—whose prices made him wince—he wrenched open the window and stood there enjoying the view over Kensington Gardens. It was his first experience of a five star hotel, and he was feeling slightly overawed. In the autumn of 1978, Charlie Peruzzi was just twenty-nine years old, and for the past four years had been the junior partner in a South London medical practice. He was spending the weekend in the Park View Hotel at the expense of the Pacific University of San Diego. His cousin, Professor Roberto Peruzzi, had been scheduled to deliver a paper at a psychological conference, but had been obliged at the last moment to fly back to California. Since the hotel accommodation had been paid in advance, it seemed pointless to waste it; so Charlie Peruzzi was there to represent his cousin and to deliver his paper on "The Role of Enkephalins in the Treatment of Mental Disorders."

Having arranged his clothes in the wardrobe, Peruzzi tried the handle of the door next to it. The door opened, and he found himself looking into the next room. A case was blocking the doorway, and an airlines jacket and skirt were draped over the back of a chair. The girl herself was nowhere in sight, her absence being explained by the sound of a shower running in the bathroom. Relieved that he had

3

not surprised her in the act of undressing, he closed the door quietly.

The telephone rang; a voice said, "Dr. Peruzzi?"

Taken unaware he said, "Yes."

"This is Erik Topelius. Feel like joining me for a drink?"

"Yes, but . . . " Before he could explain himself, the man hung up.

A glance at his lecture program informed him that Professor Erik Topelius, born 1928 in Kajaani, Finland, was chairman of the Department of Applied Psychology at the University of Uppsala. He was also chairman of the weekend conference.

When the chambermaid came in to turn down the bed, Peruzzi told her about the unlocked door between the rooms. It appeared that a family had occupied them both on the previous nights, and she promised to report it to the supervisor. As she was leaving, a tall, well-dressed man appeared in the doorway.

"Professor Peruzzi? I am Erik Topelius. You are younger than I expected."

He had the very blue eyes and faultlessly handsome face that is characteristic of so many Scandinavians.

Peruzzi hastened to correct the misunderstanding.

"I'm not Roberto Peruzzi. I'm his cousin Charlie. Roberto had a phone call from San Diego last night to say his son had broken his neck in a skiing accident. He decided to catch the first plane back."

Topelius looked shocked. "My God! Is he dead?"

"No. With luck he'll be all right. But Roberto felt he had to go. He asked me if I'd deliver his paper. Will that be in order?"

"But of course. We would be delighted."

It was still early evening and the bar was almost empty. Topelius suggested dry martinis, and Peruzzi, who was unaccustomed to hotel bars, agreed. He observed with admiration the natural ease of Topelius's movements as he crossed to the bar; Charlie was young enough to admire people who seemed to be completely at home in the world.

As the barman mixed the drinks, Topelius exchanged a few words with a tall man who was sitting on a bar stool. Peruzzi found the lean, sunburned face familiar, but was unable to place it. When Topelius came back with the drinks he asked, "Who is that man you were talking to? I seem to know him."

"I've no idea. But I can tell you the reason he looks familiar. He resembles the film star Gary Cooper."

Peruzzi snapped his fingers. "Yes, of course he does!"

The martini made him cough. Topelius said, "I hope it's not too strong for you? I prefer my martinis made in the American manner. I have a friend in New York who even refuses the shaving of lemon peel—I once heard him tell a barman, 'My good man, when I want lemonade I'll ask for it.' "

Peruzzi found the Scandinavian immensely likeable. He had charm and perfect manners, and the slight foreign accent seemed to give him a touch of wry humor. Peruzzi could imagine that women found him irresistible.

Topelius had reason to be grateful that Charlie was going to read his cousin's paper. It was one of the most eagerly anticipated items on the agenda. In 1978, the endorphins and enkephalins—the brain's natural "pain killers"—had only just been discovered, and were causing enormous excitement in the scientific community.

Like all good stories of scientific discovery, this one has the quality of detective fiction. In the 1960s, the American government decided to fund research into drug addiction, and Roberto Peruzzi was placed in charge of the Addiction Research Unit at San Diego. His starting point was an apparently useless piece of information: that the morphine molecule has two different forms, one of which is an exact mirror image of the other. And that while the morphine molecule is a powerful drug, its mirror image is completely inert. This seemed to imply that it is the *shape* of the morphine molecule that makes it active. In other words that, like a front-door key, it fits into a keyhole in the brain. But since morphine does not occur naturally in the brain, then the "keyhole" must be there to receive some other molecule which is almost identical to morphine. The search for the mystery chemical began.

Roberto Peruzzi's team located the site of the "keyholes" in the synapses—the terminals where nerves exchange chemical messages. They were among the first to realize that the mystery chemical was a peptide, a string of amino acids. And in due course, Peruzzi's team synthesized the most important of the brain opiates, met-enkephalin, in the laboratory—running neck and neck with a team from Aberdeen University. Once this was done, it was realized that it was possible to create other artificial brain opiates in the laboratory, such as Vasopressin, the "memory drug," and that curious relative of Aldous Huxley's "soma," ACTH, the "happiness drug." In the autumn of 1978, psychiatrists all over the world shared the same hope: that some of the most intractable mental illnesses, like schizophrenia, might be cured by these peptide-based drugs. An article on the subject by Roberto Peruzzi appeared in *Scientific American* and caused a sensation.

Topelius asked Charlie Peruzzi what he thought of his famous cousin's ideas. Peruzzi said, "Of course, we're all very proud of him. But I sometimes wonder whether he's not being a bit crude and wholesale."

He caught the gleam of interest in Topelius's eyes.

"Please explain what you mean."

"All right. Could I tell you about something that happened to me the other day?"

Topelius said courteously, "Please."

"I've got a patient—a retired businessman—whose skin came up in an awful rash, so he looked as if he'd been stung by a swarm of bees. I did a blood count, and tested him for the usual food allergies—eggs, shellfish and so on—but he seemed normal. Antihistamines had no effect, and after weeks he was as bad as ever. If anything, the urticaria was spreading. Well, four days ago, he came to see me in surgery. I'd begun to suspect that the root of the problem was psychological, and I wanted to get him talking. My surgery's next to the canal, and at the moment, it's being dredged. As we were talking, we heard a lot of shouting from outside, and I looked out of the window. I'm on the first floor, and I could see that a car had fallen into the water. It was yellow, and the top showed just below the surface. When my patient saw it, he nearly had a heart attack. It was his daughter's car, and she'd just driven him to the surgery. She'd lost control as she was backing—she'd only just passed her driving test—and gone into the canal."

"Was she drowned?"

"Fortunately, no. She'd got the window closed. There was a crane nearby, and it took about twenty minutes to get her out. She was perfectly all right—a bit worried and frightened as the water seeped in, but unharmed. She could see the daylight a few feet above the car, and she knew there were plenty of people around. So she just sat tight until they got her out."

"She was lucky."

"But here's the amazing thing. By the next morning, my patient's rash had disappeared. How would you explain that?"

"Did you tell your cousin about it?"

"Of course. He thought the shock had released some kind of brain chemical that cleared up the rash."

Topelius shook his head. "For me, that explains nothing."

"How would you explain it?"

Topelius said thoughtfully, "I see it as a problem of identity. You say your patient is a retired businessman. He has spent his life working hard. And his business has given him a sense of identity. In other words, if you were to say to such a man, 'Who are you?' he would reply, 'I'm a businessman.' But now he is retired, he is no longer a businessman. The main support of his identity has been removed. He has become a kind of nobody. I presume he has no hobbies?"

"A little golf, that's all."

"Quite. Nothing he can take seriously. The problem is that he has nothing to do with his energies. So he is rather like a man who is permanently constipated. The poisons remain in his system, and his body reacts by producing a rash. Then suddenly, his daughter's life is in danger, and he no longer has any doubt who he is. He is a father who wants his daughter to stay alive. He has been given a sense of identity. His energies begin flowing in their proper channels and the rash disappears."

Peruzzi said, "If you'd been me, how would you have set about curing his rash?"

"Ah, you ask an unfair question, because I don't know your patient. All I can say is that your problem is to give him a sense of purpose, a sense of identity. Every individual is different."

Noticing that Topelius's glass was empty, Peruzzi suggested another drink. As he stood up Topelius said, "I can give you a practical example of what I mean. When you go to the counter, say a few words to the man who looks like Gary Cooper. Tell me your impressions of him."

So while the bartender was mixing the drinks, Peruzzi turned to the tall man on the bar stool.

"Are you here for the psychiatric conference?"

"Lord no!" The man had a Yorkshire accent. "I'm a civil engineer."

They exchanged a few more words as Peruzzi waited. It struck him that the tall man was lonely and glad to talk. Back at the table, Topelius said, "Well?"

"He's a civil engineer. Seems rather lonely."

"Does he still remind you of Gary Cooper?"

"No."

"Why not?"

"He's simply not the same type."

Topelius pressed him to be more specific. Peruzzi said finally, "To

begin with, he doesn't have the kind of self-confidence you'd associate with a film star. He seems rather unsure of himself. For
example, he asked me what psychiatrists talk about at conferences,
and when I said theories of mental illness, he said, 'Oh, that's all a
bit above my head, I'm afraid.' But mental illness isn't above
anybody's head."

Topelius said, "Quite. He is a good-looking man. He has an
interesting appearance. Yet the moment you speak to him, you lose
interest, because his personality doesn't live up to his appearance.
Now suppose he could make a few slight changes in his personality:
get rid of his local accent, learn to speak in a more relaxed and
casual way, develop a few gestures and expressions . . . "

"You'd have to send him to a drama school."

"Not necessarily. He could learn a great deal merely by studying
himself in a mirror, or listening to a tape recording of his conversation. Haven't you ever noticed that when people hear their voices
for the first time, they always say, 'That's not me, is it?' They
obviously have no real idea of what they look like and sound like."

A couple came into the bar and sat in the corner. As the man went
to the bar to order drinks, the woman took out a mirror and applied
a touch of lipstick. Topelius said, "Look at her. She wants to see
what she looks like to her boyfriend. Imagine what the world would
be like if there were no mirrors. A woman would never realize that
she had smeared lipstick on her front tooth, or that she had a spot
of mascara on her cheek. But where our personalities are concerned, most people *are* living in a world without mirrors. Most of us
have no idea of what we look like to other people. How many times
have you met a girl with a serene, lovely face, who spoils everything
with a silly giggle, or a girl with a tall, slender figure who walks like
a crippled cow? Or a man like our friend at the counter who could
easily be a Don Juan, yet who sounds like a music hall comedian as
soon as he opens his mouth?"

As Topelius spoke, Peruzzi became increasingly excited. Like all
doctors, he had quickly come to realize that about a half of all
illnesses are due to psychological causes: the woman who develops
back pain when her husband no longer wants to make love to her,
the man who gets palpitations of the heart because his moth-
er-in-law has moved in with them . . . It had often struck him that
there ought to be basic *methods* of curing these complaints, as a sore
throat can be cured with antibiotics, or high blood pressure lowered

with beta-blockets. What Topelius was now saying seemed to give him a dazzling glimpse of such methods.

Topelius indicated a group of people who had just sat down at the next table. "Tell me what you make of them."

A middle-aged man was helping a woman off with her fur wrap. A younger woman, already seated, was taking a cigarette out of a cigarette case. Peruzzi moved his chair slightly so he could study them without seeming too obvious. The man, who had a clipped, upper-class accent, asked them what they wanted to drink. The elder woman said a gin and tonic, the younger asked for a lager and lime.

Peruzzi felt rather like Dr. Watson, being asked by Sherlock Holmes to give his opinion of a man walking down the other side of the street. Topelius reassured him.

"Don't try to jump to conclusions. Just look at them carefully and tell me what you see. Describe them for me as if I was blind."

"All right. The man is slim, rather good-looking, late fifties. He looks like a stockbroker, with his pin-striped suit and bow tie. The woman with the fur wrap is probably his wife. She's rather younger than he is—early forties—but I'd say she dresses in a style that's too young for her. That red dress doesn't really suit her, and neither does her eye makeup." Topelius nodded approvingly. "I'd guess the other girl is their daughter. She looks rather like a librarian or a schoolmistress. She's quite pretty, but doesn't make the most of it. She shouldn't be wearing her hair pushed up on top like that—it doesn't suit her face. And those glasses are awful. I also notice that the top button of her dress is undone at the back. She doesn't take enough care of her appearance. I'd say she's not as self-confident as her mother."

Topelius said, "That's very good."

Peruzzi was, in fact, rather pleased with himself.

"What do *you* think of them?"

Topelius said, "To begin with, I doubt whether they are mother and daughter. The girl looks like the man—they have the same nose—but she is nothing like the older woman. Besides, she doesn't look old enough to be the girl's mother. She can't be more than ten or fifteen years her senior. But that is not the only reason I don't believe they are mother and daughter. You have noticed that the older woman has a certain air of self-confidence—look at the way she is lighting her cigarette—always a good index of character, by the way. And, as you say, she dresses in a style that is too young for her. That is because she was pretty when she was young, and she is sure she is still attractive. Now daughters usually imitate their mothers. Yet the younger woman doesn't seem at all self-confident. She is quite pretty, but she spoils it by dressing badly. And she drinks lager, although she probably knows it is fattening. I think we can safely infer that the man has been married twice, and that the girl has an inferiority complex about her stepmother."

The man on the bar stool glanced casually around the room, and his eyes rested on the girl for a moment. Topelius said, "You see, our friend at the bar glances at the younger woman. The lone male on the lookout for a female. But she doesn't really interest him. On the other hand, I think he interests her—look at the way she just glanced at him while pretending to do something with her handbag. She also thinks he looks like Gary Cooper." Topelius chuckled. "Can you imagine what would happen if they were introduced? She would instantly lose all interest because he has no self-confidence. But if she could stop thinking of herself as unattractive, I think he might well be interested in her."

Peruzzi said, "You sound like a kind of psychiatric Sherlock Holmes."

Topelius shrugged. "When you begin to study the sense of identity, you begin to notice these things all the time. I have a friend in the Stockholm police who can walk along the street and recognize the criminals at a glance. He says it is something about their behavior, the way they look around them. Ordinary people hardly seem to notice their surroundings. The criminal is always on the lookout for a pocket to pick, or a car with the keys left in it. My friend says it has become second nature to observe this. And it has become second nature to me to see how people see themselves."

As he spoke, another couple came in. Peruzzi immediately recognized the girl: the airline hostess from the next room. She was now wearing a blue evening dress, and the shoulder-length hair looked soft and shiny, as if it had just been washed. She was followed by a tall, good-looking man in a gray suit. Peruzzi said, "What do you make of these?"

Topelius said, "You first."

The couple sat near the bar. The man offered her a cigarette, then leaned forward and lit it for her, looking into her eyes.

After watching them for a few minutes, Peruzzi said, "My impression is that she's in love with him, or ready to be. She has no eyes for anyone else in the bar. She doesn't even glance at Gary Cooper. Yet I don't feel the man is interested in her. He's too good-looking. He probably has a different woman every night. He lit her cigarette as if he always did it the same way. It's the same with the way he touches glasses. He's only interested in one thing, and she probably knows it."

Topelius was impressed. "That is very good."

"What do you think?"

Topelius said, "I don't have a great deal to add to what you say. She is a pretty girl, yet for some reason she is unsure of herself. There is something about her that I am trying to place. A kind of authority, or at least an air of being used to dealing with people. She might be anything from a schoolteacher to an assistant in a jeweler's shop. The man also has a kind of natural authority, as if used to giving orders. He could be a company executive, but I think not. He doesn't look the office type. He could be a racing driver."

"How about an airline pilot?"

"Yes, you could be right."

"In which case, the girl might be a stewardess."

Topelius studied them carefully. "Yes, I think you could be right. That was an excellent piece of observation."

Peruzzi felt obliged to own up.

"I'm afraid I cheated. I saw her walking down the corridor as I came in, and she was wearing a stewardess's uniform."

"Your honesty does you credit, but it is still an excellent guess about the man. It explains their relationship. She sees him every day in a position of authority, so she falls in love with him. But for him, she is merely another attractive stewardess."

As they were speaking, another couple joined the first. The girl was a striking redhead, and her split skirt drew the eyes of every man in the bar. The man with her was short, dark and distinctly ugly. The airline hostess's companion jumped to his feet and placed a chair for the girl. He said something that made her laugh.

Peruzzi said, "He's already going to work on her. Did you notice the way the blonde girl looked up at her?"

Topelius said, "But this second couple is even more interesting than the others. The girl is beautiful, the man is ugly. That argues that he is rich."

"Or influential. He could be a film director and she could be an actress."

"No. If he was a director, she would take more trouble to please him. Instead, she accepts the attentions of the pilot in a way that must make him jealous. Now he is looking into her eyes as he lights her cigarette." Watching them, Peruzzi caught the flash of irritation in the eyes of the airline hostess. "But beautiful women have no respect for mere riches."

Peruzzi said, "You ought to write a book about it."

Topelius made a deprecating gesture.

"Other people have said so. But what would be the point? What I have to offer is not new. Every good psychiatrist knows that mental health depends on the sense of identity. When people don't know who they are, they become confused and distressed. But how could you *make use* of such a theory? Freud believed that all neurosis has a sexual origin, so he asked his patients about their sex lives, and told them they were in love with their fathers or mothers. I think he was talking nonsense, but I do not have any better suggestion to offer. You ask me what I would have done in the case of your patient with the skin rash. The answer is that I do not know. Fate cured him by making his daughter fall in the river. But it is dangerous for a doctor to try to play the part of fate. I would not have known what to suggest."

They were still discussing the point half an hour later when it was time to go in for dinner. And by that time, Peruzzi had made an interesting observation. He was not used to spirits, and the third martini left him feeling distinctly drunk. Yet as he and Topelius continued to observe people who came into the bar, he noticed that the alcohol actually sharpened his observation by narrowing the field of his perceptions. He found that he could only focus on one person at a time, and that it was hard to pay attention to what anybody else was saying or doing. Yet in his slightly drunken state, he seemed to notice far more about those individuals on whom he focused his attention. It was an observation he filed away for later consideration.

For Charlie Peruzzi, the remainder of that evening is indistinct. He recalls sharing a bottle of claret with Topelius at dinner, and sitting next to the American Indian psychologist Jerome Seneca, with whom he discussed the identity problems of American Indians on reservations. In the coffee lounge he was introduced to a great many people of whom he has not the slightest recollection. And at about ten-thirty, ashamed of his attempts to disguise his yawns, he slipped quietly back to his room.

For the next hour or so, he slept heavily. Then he woke up and went to the bathroom. The room was very dark—he had drawn the curtains—and he had to grope his way. As he climbed back into bed, he heard the door in the next room close, and the light came on under the connecting door. The airline hostess had a man with her, presumably the one he had seen in the bar. They talked in low voices. Being a normal male, Peruzzi was curious about whether the man would achieve his object. Five minutes later, it was clear that he had. There was the sound of a moan of pleasure, followed by gasps and sighs that left no doubt as to what was happening. He experienced a twinge of envy for the tall man in the gray suit.

Finally, all was silent. Then someone struck a match. He could imagine them lying there smoking. Ten minutes later he was on the verge of sleep when the gasps and moans began again. He pulled the continental quilt over his ears and buried his face in the pillow.

The next time he drifted out of sleep, he dreamed that someone was quarreling. Then he woke up and realized that the sounds were coming from the next room. The man's voice was suddenly raised, and the girl said, "Please don't shout." The man's voice said, "Why the hell not?" He looked at the luminous dial of his watch. It was three in the morning. He could hear someone moving around the room, and more angry exchanges. Suddenly, the door slammed. There was a silence, succeeded by the sound of a woman crying. He found this upsetting, and was even tempted to go and speak to her. But this would obviously have been absurd. It took him more than half an hour to get back to sleep.

He was jerked awake by the sound of a telephone. Imagining he was on call, he reached out automatically for his bedside table. Then consciousness returned and he remembered that he was in a hotel bedroom, and the ringing noise was coming from the next room. He cursed under his breath, and lay there waiting for it to stop. When it went on, he pushed himself up on one elbow. There was still a light showing under the door, so she was presumably awake. The ringing continued for more than five minutes. And as he lay there, he reflected that it was unusual for a girl to ignore such a summons after a lover's quarrel. Finally, he began to experience a kind of premonition. He slipped out of bed, tiptoed across the room, and placed his ear to the door. Then, very slowly and cautiously, he turned the handle and pushed it open.

She was lying across the bed, face downward, one arm hanging down. She looked as if she was leaning over the edge of the bed to be sick. She was wearing a dressing gown over her nightdress. He took her under the arms and placed her on her back with her head on the pillow; her face was flushed and her breathing was heavy and irregular.

He knew of no standard procedures for an attempted suicide. If she had been awake, he would have tried to make her push her fingers down her throat, but while she was unconscious any attempt to make her vomit might choke her. He raised her eyelid; the pupil was dilated. He lightly slapped both cheeks, but it made no difference.

He dialed the desk, and, when the man finally answered, asked to be put through to the casualty department of the nearest hospital.

When the ambulance had been summoned, he went back into his own room and put on his dressing gown and slippers. In the girl's bathroom he found the empty pill bottle; the name of the general practitioner was on the label. Her clothes, he noticed, lay in an untidy heap by the bed, the underwear on top of the blue evening dress; they gave the impression of having been removed in haste.

As far as he could see, there was no suicide note.

There was a knock at the door. It was the hotel under-manager, together with a doctor, summoned by the telephonist. While he was still explaining the situation to them, the ambulance men arrived with a stretcher. Within seconds, the girl was being taken out, covered with a blanket. He asked, "Which hospital is she going to?"

"St. Mary Abbots."

Then he was alone in her room. He turned off her light, went back into his own room, and closed the connecting door. He felt it was a symbolic gesture, terminating the night's events. He was unaware that it was, in fact, a beginning.

CHAPTER TWO

In spite of loss of sleep, he woke up the next morning feeling relaxed and refreshed, with that feeling of happy anticipation that children experience at the beginning of the holidays. Since joining the practice four years ago, he had worked hard and continuously, and this was his first real break. He intended to make the most of it. The opportunity to have breakfast in bed seemed too good to miss, so he dialed room service and placed the order. Then, thinking about the girl in the next room, he decided to phone the hospital. It struck him that he had no idea of her name, so he went into her bedroom and looked at the label on her case. It was Sharon Engstrom, and her home address was in Reigate.

The hospital switchboard put him through to one of the wards. The sister who answered asked, "Are you a relative?"

"No. Just a friend . . . "

"And are you in London?"

"Yes."

"Would it be possible for you to bring her clothes along to the hospital?"

He was slightly taken aback. "I suppose so. When?"

"About an hour?"

It sounded as if they were anxious to get rid of her. He knew that many hospitals were impatient about attempted suicides, regarding them as a bid for attention that could divert medical resources from real emergencies. Some of them even administered unnecessary stomach pumps as a discouragement to further attempts.

After breakfast, he took his empty case into the girl's bedroom. The request for clothes caused him mild embarrassment; he could hardly rummage through her wardrobe. He solved the problem by making a bundle of the heap of clothes by the bed and pushing them into the case. As he was closing it, he noticed on the bedside table a red ballpoint pen. It had struck him as odd that the girl had left no suicide note. In his own small experience of suicide attempts, there had always been a note. He looked under the pillow and under the bed, then he saw it under her dressing table. She had evidently placed it against the wall, and it had slipped down a narrow gap.

The note read: "I have decided to end it all because I am sick of being a freak. I am sick of being treated like an object. I am sick of being alone."

There was no signature. This seemed to him unusual. So did the lack of expression of regret. In the few suicide notes he had seen, there was usually some expression like, "I wish there was some other way" or "Tell my parents I am sorry." And what did she mean by "I am sick of being a freak?" Physically speaking, she had struck him as perfectly normal. He decided to find Topelius and ask his opinion.

But he was too late. When he arrived downstairs, the proceedings had already started, and Topelius was on the platform, making the opening speech. He pushed open the door slightly. To his surprise, Topelius was telling the story about the businessman with the rash on his face. He would have liked to stay to hear more, but was already late for the hospital.

The hospital was less than a ten-minute walk from the hotel. The porter at the gate directed him to the casualty ward. He handed the case over to the sister, and was told to wait in the corridor. There he stood looking down into the gloomy Victorian courtyard, watching the porters unload a stretcher from an ambulance, and wondering what he would say to the girl and whether she would be embarrassed or resentful at his interference.

Then the ward door opened and Sharon Engstrom came out, looking slightly absurd in the blue evening gown. He realized with embarrassment that he had forgotten to bring her coat. She looked bewildered and confused, so he tried to smile reassuringly.

"I'm Charles Peruzzi, and I brought your things along. How are you now?"

He saw at once that she was neither resentful nor embarrassed—only tired and defeated. It made no difference whatsoever that it was a stranger who had brought her clothes. He took her arm.

"Would you like me to get you a taxi, or shall we walk back to the hotel?"

"I don't mind."

Her face looked so pale that he felt an irrational impulse to take her in his arms to comfort her. At the same time, he recalled her moans of pleasure, and felt an acrid tang of desire mingling with the pity.

Fortunately, it was a sunny autumn morning, so the lack of a coat made no difference. He had been afraid she would be embarrassed to walk through Kensington in an evening gown with bare shoulders, but she seemed indifferent. Neither did she seem in the least curious about how he came to be there. He deliberately refrained from telling her, waiting to see how long she would take to ask, but by the time they reached the hotel she had still not raised the question.

As he walked beside her, Peruzzi experienced a powerful impulse of curiosity whose compass was far wider than the problems of this defeated girl. His own senses were tuned to a high degree of awareness. The mild air, the falling leaves, the eggshell blue of the sky, filled him with a brimming vitality. This girl was surely seeing the same trees, feeling the same air against her cheeks, breathing in the same autumn smells? She was not in a different universe. So how could she behave as if she was in a prison cell? The few words they exchanged were about her job as an air hostess. It seemed she knew India, America, even Australia. In richness of experience, her life was far more interesting than his own. Peruzzi again found himself trying to understand the mystery of psychological illness, whose fundamentally absurd nature suddenly seemed so obvious.

As they stopped outside her room in the hotel, she said suddenly, "My key! I forgot to collect it!"

"It's probably still in your room." She tried her door; it was locked. "But it doesn't matter," he opened his own door, "you can get in through my room."

He opened the connecting door, and explained how he had found it unlocked the day before. Then he went on to tell her how he had come to find her. As he talked, her face changed. For the first time that morning, she seemed to be aroused to some kind of spontaneous feeling. He said nothing about hearing the lovemaking, but when he spoke of being awakened by the quarrel, she said, "Oh, my God!" and sat on the bed and buried her face in her hands. When he described finding her and sending for the ambulance she said, "I feel like a bitch."

"Oh, don't worry, I'm a doctor. Anyway, it's lucky that door was left unlocked. Otherwise, you might not be alive now."

She stared into space, and it came to him that she was wondering whether she really wanted to be alive. Again, he experienced the maddening sense that there was some sort of invisible wall between them. He switched on the electric kettle. "I'll make some coffee."

"Thank you."

He indicated her dress. "I expect you want to change?"

She glanced down indifferently. "Yes, I suppose I'd better." She went into the bathroom.

Peruzzi went back into his own room and closed the door. He wondered whether to tell her he had found the note, but decided against it. He wanted to show it to Topelius. When he went back five minutes later the kettle had boiled and she had changed into a skirt and blouse. He noticed that she had also applied some lipstick and brushed her hair. That seemed a good sign. As he poured the water she said, "Could you hear what we were quarreling about?"

"Good God, of course I couldn't! I wasn't listening against the door!"

She said in a controlled voice, "When he'd finished making love to me, he told me I was the thousandth girl he'd had."

"My God!" Peruzzi was genuinely shocked. The girl began to cry and he went and sat beside her on the bed, putting his arm around her shoulders. From that position, he could not help noticing that she had beautiful legs. She said through her tears, "Can you imagine why any man should want to say a thing like that?"

"I suppose it's a kind of boasting. He looked that type."

She looked at him with surprise. "Have you seen him?"

"Yes. I noticed you with him in the bar last night."

"Then you must have seen Moira—the redhead?"

"Yes."

She said grimly, "She's going to be the thousand and first."

"Does it matter?"

She sighed. "Not now, I suppose."

"Drink your coffee." He handed it to her.

"Thanks." She managed a smile. "You're very nice."

"Glad to help." Compliments always made him feel awkward.

"I suppose I must seem pretty stupid to you, but I just can't understand how men can be such bastards."

"They're not all like that."

"No. I just seem to fall for the wrong type. Do you think there's something wrong with me?"

"Of course not." But it was not entirely true. He could see precisely what was wrong. She was an attractive girl with a pleasant personality and a good figure. But she was carrying around a burden of depression and defeat. If men treated her like an object, it was because she saw herself as an object, a victim.

To get her mind off her own problems he said, "Who was the other man—the one with the redhead?"

"That's Chris, her future husband."

"Wouldn't he object if she slept with someone else?"

"Moira wouldn't give a damn. She does what she likes."

"Then why is she going to marry him?"

"Do you really want to know?" Suddenly, she was animated. "They were brought up in the same village near Bristol. She was the prettiest girl in the place, and Chris was in love with her. But he didn't stand a chance; she had about ten other boyfriends. So he went off to California, raised the money to start an electronics factory in Silicon Valley, and became a millionaire. Then he went back to the village and invited her to come to California for a holiday. She said she'd go on condition he didn't make any passes. He agreed. So he took her over on the Concorde. Of course, when she saw his house on the beach and his factory and his private airplane, she stopped playing hard to get and jumped into bed. Now they've come to England to get married. But she's not in love with him. She just can't give up all that money."

Telling the story had transformed her. Her eyes sparkled with malicious amusement. She reminded him of a child who had been coaxed into laughing. He asked, "Doesn't he realize she's not in love with him?"

"I suppose so. But he doesn't care. Men don't when they really want somebody, do they?"

That struck him as an acute observation. He asked, "Do you think he's attractive?"

"No. He's too slavish. He'd be more attractive if he didn't give a damn."

What surprised him was that she made no attempt to apply it to herself, that she failed to see *she* would be more attractive if she didn't give a damn. He thought of saying so but the words stuck in his throat. They could only make things worse.

Her watch beeped on the hour. He said, "I have to go. I'm supposed to be attending a conference on psychiatry."

"Are you a psychiatrist?"

"No. But all doctors have to be psychiatrists to some extent."

"I'd like to be one of your patients."

"We'll talk about it later. Why don't you come to the next lecture?"

"No thanks. I think I'll get some sleep."

"All right. See you later."

As he was about to leave his room, he thought he heard her voice. He opened her door a few inches. "Did you call?"

She was in bed. "I just wanted to say thank you."

He could see she was unwilling to be alone. He went and sat on the bed. "Glad to be of use."

"I'd like a chance to talk to you properly . . . "

"Of course. Why don't we have a drink this evening? There's someone I'd like you to meet."

"All right."

"Get some sleep." He was sorry to leave, but felt guilty about missing the first lecture.

As he stepped out of the lift, a man with a yellow beard and moustache said, "Peruzzi! What are you doing here?"

Peruzzi stared at him without recognition. The man said, "Don't you remember? Bill Robinson."

"Bill! I didn't recognize you behind all that hair!"

"Are you here for this conference?"

"Yes."

"I didn't realize you were in psychiatry."

Peruzzi explained about his cousin's change of plan. Robinson said, "Listen, let's meet in the bar before lunch. I want to dash upstairs before the next lecture. It's this man Jerome Seneca, and I'm told he's terrific."

Peruzzi stood staring after him. As Robinson had said "Listen," he had experienced an elusive feeling of familiarity, as if listening to someone else. It was like hearing a tune that recalls another tune. He was still thinking about the problem when the bell rang for the next lecture.

He sat at the end of a row, and found himself sitting next to the family he had seen in the bar on the previous evening. The daughter was sitting beside him. He was just wondering how to open a conversation when she asked if she could look at his program. He asked her, "Are you a psychologist?"

"Oh no. I'm just here with my father. He's a plastic surgeon." She pointed to the program. Dr. Henry Morton-Jones was lecturing on the Psychological Effects of Plastic Surgery that afternoon.

Topelius was introducing Jerome Seneca, the American Indian psychologist Peruzzi had talked with the previous evening. His memories of that conversation were now blurred. Seneca was an impressive figure, well over six feet tall, with a handsome, hawk-like profile. From the moment he began to speak, the girl next to

Peruzzi listened with total attention, never moving her eyes from his face. Peruzzi thought he had never seen a plainer example of a woman in the grip of fascination.

Seneca was an excellent lecturer. He talked quietly, in a businesslike way, like a man who knows precisely what he wants to say. He outlined the history of the American Indians, the seizure of their lands by settlers, the destruction of their hunting grounds by the railways, with a cool objectivity that was more effective than any amount of emotionalism. By the time he had finished describing their reservations, there was no need to explain the problems of the American Indian. They were obvious: boredom, loss of motivation, a sense of being left behind by history. Seneca compared them to the mountain gorilla, designed for life in the treetops, and now confined to the earth, his enormous strength wasted in the search for bamboo shoots.

Seneca described his own childhood as the son of a successful lawyer, his training as a Freudian analyst, the lucrative practice he had built up in San Francisco before he decided to devote his life to working on reservations. "And the first thing I discovered was that Freud was irrelevant to the Indian. These people weren't suffering from sexual hang-ups. Most of them weren't even interested in sex. Like the gorilla, they'd come to regard it as one of life's less important activities. What they wanted to know was who they were and what they were supposed to do . . . "

Peruzzi found his thoughts returning to Sharon Engstrom. That was her problem too. Something had undermined her sense of identity. But how could it be given back to her?

As if answering the question, Seneca said, "I got my first glimpse of a solution in 1975. The Paramount film company decided to make a movie about the Indian wars of the 1860s. The director wanted authenticity, so he started searching for an actor who looked like the Sioux chief Red Cloud. They couldn't find one, but on a reservation in Montana, they discovered a man called Charlie Crow who bore a truly amazing resemblance to Red Cloud. He made a living carving miniature totem poles for the tourists. They'd signed him up and got him back to Hollywood before they discovered that he couldn't act. He was a quiet, modest little man, and the moment he opened his mouth it was obvious that he wasn't a famous chief. The director was in despair until an old cameraman came up with an idea. They were to try and make Charlie Crow *feel* like an Indian chief by treating him like an Indian chief. They were to address him as chief, stand up when he entered the room, treat him with respect. And it worked. Within a couple of weeks, Charlie Crow was behaving like a great Indian warrior. His finest moment came when he told the American general, 'God made me an Indian, not an agency Indian.' And he said it with such dignity that everybody on the set cheered him at the end of the scene. They made the movie, and it was a tremendous success.

"And then Charlie Crow went back to carving totem poles on the reservation. At first he was a celebrity, and tourists came for miles to take photographs of him. Then the publicity died down and he was forgotten again. But Charlie just couldn't get used to being a nobody again. That winter he blew off his head with a shotgun."

Seneca took a drink of water. There was total silence in the room, not even a cough. Peruzzi noticed that there were tears on the cheek of the girl beside him.

"That was when I came to realize that identity isn't just a matter for the individual. It concerns the whole community. Everybody gives everybody else a sense of identity. And as far as the American Indian is concerned, identity lies in the past, in the history of his race. The same is true of all nations, of course. When a nation is great, it doesn't need history, it's too concerned with the present. The time a nation needs its history is when it's being trampled underfoot . . . . "

Peruzzi found his attention wandering. He was thinking again of the girl upstairs. How could Seneca's insights be applied to her? His descriptions of his attempts to make the Indians conscious of their racial heritage—with history lessons, historical dramas, traditional ceremonies—seemed irrelevant. At the end of the lecture, some of the audience stood up to applaud. The girl next to him clapped frantically.

Peruzzi slipped out while they were still applauding. He wanted to see if Sharon was awake yet. He wanted to introduce her to Topelius as soon as possible. He went into his own room very quietly and listened at the connecting door. There was no sound. Very slowly, he turned the knob and pushed open the door. She was looking across at him, her cheeks stained with tears. He said, "Now, what's all this?"

She began to cry in earnest. He went over to the bed, pulled a wad of paper handkerchiefs out of the box, and handed them to her. "Come on now, blow your nose."

She blew her nose. "I'm sorry. I don't seem to be able to stop crying. I feel frightened."

He took the handkerchief from her and wiped her cheeks dry, smearing her lipstick in the process. He recognized the symptoms of someone on the verge of a nervous breakdown. She said, "You must find me a bore."

"Of course I don't. I just want to help you."

He let her take his hand, and stroked her hair with the other hand. Although he could see the nipples through her almost transparent nightdress, he felt no sexual excitement, only pity.

She said, "What do you think is wrong with me?"

"Nothing. You're tired and upset, that's all. And the stomach pump probably made you feel low."

"No. It's more than that." The corner of her eye twitched. He bent over and kissed it; it was a gesture of reassurance.

"Come on. Lie down now. Would you like me to get you a sleeping tablet?"

"No." She lay down and tugged at his hand. "Lie beside me."

"All right." He pulled the sheet over her shoulder and lay beside her.

She said, "I feel horrible. As if I'm going to be sick."

"Go and be sick in the bathroom. You'll feel better."

"No, sick inside."

To distract her, he stroked her hair, trying to soothe her as if she was a child. It seemed to work; she sighed and relaxed. Then, with her eyes closed, she said, "Would you kiss me?"

He leaned forward and kissed her lightly. The touch of her lips was a shock. They were very soft and warm, and their contact caused a spasm of desire. Once he had started, it was hard to stop. It struck him suddenly that if this continued for much longer, they would be making love. And although she was not his patient, he felt this would be unethical. He forced himself to pull his head back. She opened her eyes. "Don't you want to?"

"Not now." He smiled to reassure her. "I want you to go to sleep."

"Then get in with me."

He felt misgivings because it was precisely what he most wanted to do. But he felt that the alternative, to reject her, would be worse. He kicked off his shoes, pulled back the continental quilt, and slipped in beside her. She moved into his arms. When she turned her mouth to him again, he said, "Sshh," and stroked her hair. The warmth of her body and the feeling of her naked legs against his trousers, made his heart beat faster, but he resisted the temptation to allow his hand to move below her waist. She clung tightly against him and, little by little, her breathing became quieter. His own desire gradually subsided, and he felt glad that he had not made love to her. It would only have complicated the situation.

When he was sure she was asleep, he slipped quietly out of bed and tiptoed back into his own room.

CHAPTER THREE

THE BAR was crowded. As he peered in through the door, looking for Topelius, he saw the girl who had sat beside him in the lecture. She was pushing her way through the crowd. He started to say hello then noticed, to his surprise, that she had tears in her eyes. She hurried past him without seeing him.

At the bar he ordered himself a lager. From there, he could see Topelius seated at a corner table, together with Jerome Seneca and the Morton-Joneses. Mrs. Morton-Jones had her hand on Seneca's arm and seemed to be talking animatedly into his ear. Her husband, Peruzzi thought, looked uncomfortable. When Topelius noticed him standing by the bar, he stood up and maneuvered his way across the room.

Behind him, he heard a noisy laugh and a voice said, "That's precisely what I've been telling the idiot for months!" He looked over his shoulder, and recognized Bill Robinson. Suddenly, he knew why Robinson reminded him of somebody else. That voice was a reasonable imitation of Sir George Slessor, their professor of anatomy at Guys. Slessor was celebrated for his sarcastic wit and his lack of patience with fools. He was fond of the word 'precisely,' and was likely to refer to people as idiots, imbeciles and clowns. He also had a Victorian beard of impressive dimensions. Robinson's was still modest by comparison.

Topelius said, "Let's go somewhere quiet, where we can talk."

They found a table in the lobby with a view of the park.

Peruzzi said, "What's the matter with that Morton-Jones girl? I just bumped into her at the door and she was in tears."

Topelius gave a snort of disgust. "That mother of hers is a bitch. She's the kind of woman who ought to be flogged twice a day until she stops being so totally self-absorbed."

His anger brought out the foreign accent.

"What happened?"

"That woman, her stepmother, began gushing all over Jerry Seneca and asking him a lot of inane questions. She didn't give anybody else a chance to say a word. Finally the daughter—her name's Roberta—said something like, 'Oh, give him a chance to drink his whiskey, he's been talking for two hours.' And with a poisonous smile, that bitch said, 'But men love to talk about their pet subjects. If you'd realized that, you'd have found a husband long ago.' I could have slapped her face."

"How did Jerry react?"

"What could he do? He just had to pretend he hadn't noticed . . ." Topelius emptied his glass; he was drinking a martini. "I'm sorry to sound so irritable. Things like this infuriate me. That girl is more intelligent than her mother. She is more sensible. She is more sympathetic. Yet she allows herself to be bullied by her." He shook his head. "And there you have a perfect example of why Seneca's identity theory doesn't go far enough. It's all very well talking about the identity problems of American Indians. But what about the identity problems of middle-class English girls?"

Peruzzi seized the opportunity to change the subject. "That's just what I wanted to talk to you about." He took the sheet of folded paper from his wallet and laid it in front of Topelius.

"What is this?"

"A suicide note. You remember the airline hostess we saw in the bar . . ." Topelius put on his glasses. Peruzzi remained silent while he read it.

"What happened?"

He described the events of the previous night, from the time he returned to his room to the summoning of the ambulance.

"Have you seen her since?"

"Oh yes. They asked me to go and collect her from the hospital this morning. She's asleep in her room now."

"And did she tell you why she did it?"

"Yes. She said that when her boyfriend finished making love, he told her she was the thousandth girl he'd had."

Topelius grunted. "That sounds like the conceited stupidity of the Don Juan type."

He reread the note. "I can understand what she means by 'sick of being treated like an object' and 'sick of being alone.' But what does she mean by 'I am sick of being a freak'?"

"I suppose she means a misfit."

"But surely a freak is something in a fairground sideshow, like the bearded lady?"

"That's right."

"There is nothing obviously wrong with her physically?"

"Nothing that I can see."

"Perhaps she has some sexual problem—some internal obstruction?"

"It's not that either."

Topelius grinned with friendly mockery. "You have examined her?"

"No. But I heard her making love. It didn't sound as if there was any obstruction."

Topelius said, "I would like to meet her."

"I was hoping you'd say that. Could I bring her along for an early drink this evening?"

"Of course." Topelius handed back the note. "I feel the key lies in that phrase about being a freak. She is like a person who looks at herself in a distorting mirror and imagines that she really looks like that."

"But how could you make her see herself without the distortion?"

Topelius thought about it. "That is something I cannot answer until I have seen her. But I am quite certain the answer lies in finding out *why* she thinks she is a freak. Find that, and the problem will be solved."

"But how do I find out?"

"Use your eyes, my dear boy. Observe. Listen. Probe gently without appearing to probe. Sooner or later, she will hand you the vital piece of information."

In the dining room, two large circular tables had been reserved for the members of the Association of Humanistic Psychology. The Morton-Jones family were already seated. The only empty places were next to Roberta. Topelius said in his ear, "Sit next to her. Talk to her."

Peruzzi chuckled, "Probe."

"Of course."

She glanced up as he sat beside her, then returned to studying the menu. She seemed to have recovered her self-possession, but he thought she still looked subdued.

"Hello again."

"Hello."

"My name's Charlie Peruzzi."

"Roberta Morton-Jones."

She made an attempt to smile, and he liked her for it. She had the same clipped, upper-class accent as her father.

On the opposite side of the table, Mrs. Morton-Jones was still monopolizing Jerome Seneca. She had pretty eyes, and a habit of raising her eyebrows as she spoke, causing her eyes to widen with a look of innocent astonishment. Although her looks were now too faded to arouse male interest, she compelled admiration by sheer vivacity. Peruzzi sensed that Seneca was puzzled, wondering whether she was really offering herself, or whether this was mere flirting. On the other side of her, Dr. Morton-Jones seemed to be paying no attention.

Peruzzi said, "What did you think of the lecture?"

"Very interesting." She said it without emphasis. Peruzzi remembered her expression as she listened to the lecture, and realized that this casualness was a self-defense.

He said, "I thought it was one of the most impressive talks I've ever heard."

"Oh yes." She was still giving nothing away. "Of course, I'd heard most of it before."

"Oh, you already knew Dr. Seneca?"

"For a long time. We knew him when he was still a Freudian psychiatrist in San Francisco."

Suddenly, he began to understand. He asked, "Is your mother interested in psychology?"

"Not particularly." She said it dryly. After a pause she said, "Anyway, she's not my mother. She's my stepmother. My mother died five years ago."

"Ah." He tried to make it sound as if he was merely making polite conversation. "Have they been married long?"

"Two years."

He glanced across at Mrs. Morton-Jones, who was just widening her eyes at Seneca.

"She's very attractive."

"Yes, most men seem to think so." Her tone was flat.

Bill Robinson had come in late and taken the last seat, next to Topelius. Peruzzi introduced them. He could see that Robinson was impressed that he knew Topelius. Within a few minutes Robinson was launched on an account of his own work with deaf-mute children. Peruzzi ate his soup and tried to listen simultaneously to Robinson and Mrs. Morton-Jones. He was fascinated by the change in Robinson since their days at Guys. He remembered him as a rather diffident man with a wispy blond moustache. He had spoken, as far as he could remember, with the anonymous accent of the home counties and he had a nervous habit of qualifying everything he said. Now the beard had transformed him into the likeness of Sir George Slessor, and he had also adopted a touch of Slessor's Scots accent, he was transformed into an aggressive conversationalist who waved his knife to underline his points. Robinson was a perfect example of Topelius's identity theory.

In between courses, Peruzzi kept up a desultory conversation with Roberta Morton-Jones. Disposed at first to like her because he felt sorry for her, he soon realized there was a basic sympathy between them. She had a smile of singular charm, underlined by a certain shyness. She was also perceptive enough to see what he thought of her stepmother, and this made them feel like co-conspirators.

Her comment that she had known Seneca for years provided him with the key to the situation. A few years ago she had been a teenager, probably in love with Seneca, and more than half in love with her father. When her mother had died, she probably became the substitute wife. Then her father had married this brainless woman, whose chief attraction was a trick of widening her eyes with an air of innocence that was designed to excite a desire to deflower it. Her stepmother had taken her father away; now she was doing her best to take Seneca too.

What Roberta obviously needed was for a man to give her the same absorbed attention that Seneca was now giving her step-mother. For a moment he considered the idea of flirting with her himself, then dismissed it. She was not his type and he was not hers. They found it too easy to talk, which meant there was no sexual signal between them. It was Seneca's attention she really needed.

After lunch he joined Topelius in the lounge for coffee. Topelius said, "I found your friend rather exhausting. Does he always talk so relentlessly?"

"No. Only since he's grown a beard."

Topelius was interested at once. "Really?"

"When we were medical students together he was shy and nervous. Now he's grown a beard I hardly recognize him."

"Most interesting! You see, a beard conceals the mouth, which is the part of the face that betrays most of our emotions. So a person with a beard no longer feels vulnerable. There is a whole chapter in my book about it. And of course, that flow of conversation is another form of self-defense. It is when there is a pause in the conversation that our spontaneous emotions sneak out of their hiding place."

"Is that why Mrs. Morton-Jones talks so much?"

"Ah, that woman! She talks because it forces men to look at her." Peruzzi laughed. "And there's something else I noticed. If you watch her face when she's speaking, her conversation sounds intelligent. If you turn away and just listen, it sounds stupid."

"That is because she uses her face as a substitute for intelligence. If you watch her closely you will see that she is always doing something with her eyes and mouth." Topelius did a surprisingly good imitation of Mrs. Morton-Jones. "Above all, she looks at a man as if she finds him fascinating, and as if she is longing to invite him into her bedroom. So naturally . . . "

He broke off as Jerome Seneca joined them. Peruzzi thought Seneca looked relaxed and pleased with himself. Topelius said, "Tell me, Jerry, what do you think of the new Mrs. Morton-Jones? Had you met her before?"

"No, this is the first time. Martha's okay. She's a bit overpowering, but very pleasant."

"Is she interesting to talk to?"

"Oh sure. She's very intelligent."

Topelius and Peruzzi exchanged glances.

At half past two, Henry Morton-Jones lectured on the psychological effects of plastic surgery. Peruzzi sat at the back. The thought that he would be on the platform in less than two hours made him feel distinctly nervous. But Morton-Jones's performance helped to make him feel better. As a lecturer, Morton-Jones undoubtedly lacked charisma. He was a good-looking man in his late fifties, and his immaculate dress emphasized the trim, youthful figure. But there was a touch of vanity and self-satisfaction in the way he delivered his pronouncements in his precise, nasal voice. And the rather patronizing smile with which he underlined his points gave him the air of a headmaster addressing a prefects' meeting.

The lecture itself was another example of miscalculation. The subject was interesting enough, and in the hands of a speaker like Jerome Seneca, would have been fascinating. But Morton-Jones seemed determined to keep it on an abstract, scientific level, with the result that potentially exciting material became boring.

The main point that emerged seemed to be that people revealed their basic fears by the operations they wanted performed. A woman whose nose looked perfectly normal wanted it made smaller. By questioning her, Morton-Jones discovered that she was insatiably curious and that people disliked her for it. She felt she was too "nosey," and a nose operation was her way of trying to demonstrate that she wasn't. A middle-aged woman with a large bosom wanted her breasts injected with silicon so they would stand out. Morton-Jones discovered that she felt she was not assertive enough, and she believed that outthrust breasts would make people see her as a strong character, her bosom cleaving its way through life like the prow of a ship. Another woman wanted him to make her face thinner, although he assured her it was already thin enough. The reason, it emerged, was that she had been brow-beaten by her mother, who told her again and again that she was "cheeky," and that no one would ever love her while she was so impudent. Now what she really wanted was to make her cheeks less prominent, to reassure herself that she was lovable . . .

When the lecture was over, the chairman asked for questions, while Morton-Jones beamed encouragingly at the audience. When no one spoke, the chairman thanked Morton-Jones for a fascinating lecture, and closed the meeting.

Out in the lobby, Topelius was talking with Jerome Seneca. As Peruzzi joined them, Seneca was saying, "He's a nice man, but how can he be so bloody dull?"

Peruzzi said, "*Is* he nice?"

"Oh sure. Decent, generous, helpful. But he just doesn't seem to know how to put himself across."

Topelius raised his eyebrows but said nothing.

After the meal and the lecture, Peruzzi was feeling sleepy. It was now nearly four o'clock and he was lecturing at half past. He excused himself and went up to his room.

He let himself in quietly. There was no sound coming from Sharon Engstrom's room. He opened her door cautiously, and saw she was still asleep. He went and lay down on his own bed and picked up the typescript of his cousin's lecture, but his attention drifted. He closed his eyes and fell into a light sleep.

The ringing of the telephone woke him up. It was coming from her room. Then he heard her voice speaking. He looked at his watch; it was four fifteen. He yawned and stretched.

The door opened. Sharon Engstrom stood there in her nightdress. She said, "Oh my God!"

"What is it?"

"That was him . . . "

He could see her naked body through the thin nightdress, and it caused a shock of desire.

"Who?"

"Jeff."

"Your boyfriend?" She nodded. "What did he want?"

She came and sat on the edge of his bed. "He wants me to go out with him this evening."

"What did you say?"

"I told him to ring me back."

"You'd better go and put some clothes on." The sight of her disturbed him; he wanted to pull her down and make love to her, but could see that her mind was on other things.

She sighed. "Yes, I suppose . . . " She wandered back into her own room, oblivious of the light that shone through the nightdress and turned the V of her thighs into a wordless invitation. Peruzzi was left with the unsatisfying task of defusing his excitement. He went into the bathroom and took a cold shower. When he came out again, she was sitting on his bed, wearing a dressing gown and slippers.

"What do you think I should do?"

"Does he know what happened after he left last night?"

"No."

"Then he can't be ringing you because he feels guilty. Do you want to see him?"

"I don't know . . . "

He felt a flash of impatience, in which he recognized an element of jealousy.

"Why not?" He slipped on his jacket.

"I suppose I don't want to be hurt any more."

He looked at his watch; it was nearly twenty-five past, and he had to leave. He said, "Why worry about that? He obviously likes you."

She looked up hopefully. "What makes you say that?"

"He rang you back last night after you'd quarreled. Now he rings you again asking to see you today. He can't have lost interest. And if he's agreed to ring you back, it proves you've got him on a string." He picked up the typescript. "I have to go. I'm lecturing in a few minutes. Why don't you come?"

"Yes, perhaps I will. I'll slip in at the back."

She stood up and put her arms round his neck. "Thank you for being so nice." As she kissed him, her dressing gown fell open.

"I wish you wouldn't do that!"

"Why not?"

He was unable to resist putting his hands on her hips. "It makes me want to undress you."

She laughed with real gaiety. "There's not time now." The implication was clearly that she would have no objection.

"I have to go." He left her in his room and went downstairs with an obscure feeling that fate was playing games with him.

The lecture hall was crowded and he felt his heart sink as he mounted the stairs to the platform. Topelius was already sitting there. On the front row, Roberta Morton-Jones smiled at him reassuringly. Her stepmother was sitting beside her. Peruzzi poured himself a glass of water, and realized to his alarm that his hand was unsteady. He placed the lecture in front of him on the table, pulling the paper clip from the corner so he could remove the pages without having to turn them.

Topelius was introducing him. He explained why Roberto Peruzzi had been obliged to return to America at short notice, and how his cousin, Dr. Charles Peruzzi, had agreed to take his place. "And now, since you are all anxious to hear this paper, I hand you over to Dr. Charles Peruzzi."

Peruzzi cleared his throat, took a drink of water, and started to read.

"In 1965, I received a letter from the president of the United States. I hasten to add that it was a Xeroxed letter that was sent to everyone who was known for research into drugs . . . "

Unlike Morton-Jones, Roberto Peruzzi knew how to present his material in a lively and amusing way. After the first laugh; Charlie's nervousness suddenly vanished, and he began to enjoy himself. His cousin had produced a brilliant summary of the research into neuropeptides, and he never lapsed into scientific jargon. From the total attention of his audience, Peruzzi realized that most of them were making their first acquaintance with the subject. They were particularly fascinated by the case histories: the middle-aged Dutchman who lost his memory after an operation for neuralgia, but who was cured by doses of Vasopressin; the girl who had a nervous breakdown after being the victim of a gang rape, and who recovered with the help of Oxytocin, the memory inhibitor; the eye surgeon who was suffering from hypertension, and who was cured by a course of the "happiness drug ACTH." The paper ended with a spectacular case of the cure of a suicidal psychiatrist with doses of beta-endorphin. When he laid down the last page, Peruzzi was surprised to receive an ovation that was as warm and prolonged as the one Jerome Seneca had received that morning.

Topelius stood up and thanked him. He said that since they had another half hour, they could ask a few questions. He himself would try to answer any that Dr. Peruzzi did not feel qualified to answer.

In fact, the questions were easier than Peruzzi had expected. He and Roberto had spent three days discussing the new drugs, so he was able to expand the case histories and cite others. Topelius took a highly technical question about the structure of neuropeptides, and he had a chance to survey the audience. Sharon Engstrom was sitting on the end of the back row, but she seemed to be trying to avoid his eyes. When he glanced down at Mrs. Morton-Jones, he received a dazzling smile.

Topelius was explaining how endorphins can be released by electrical stimulation of the brain, and how they can alleviate severe pain. He went on to say that they are also involved in the "placebo" effect, when a patient suffering from pain is given a harmless pill that nevertheless reduces the pain. What happens is that the pain is reduced by the brain's natural pain killers.

An old man with iron-gray hair raised his hand and stood up. Peruzzi had been introduced to him the previous evening, and recognized him as Dr. Alvin Coogan, of John Hopkins University. He spoke briskly and dryly.

"When I was at medical school, we used to do an experiment to demonstrate the power of suggestion. We persuaded blindfolded patients that we were going to touch them with a red hot needle. Instead, we touched them with an icicle. The patient always yelled out in pain, and in some cases, I even saw a blister form. Now you tell me that the brain's natural opiates cause the placebo effect. Are you telling me that the brain also has natural anti-opiates which cause pain when there isn't any?"

He sat down, and there was a murmur of laughter. Topelius looked slightly uncomfortable. He glanced at Peruzzi, to see if he wanted to take the question. Peruzzi stood up.

"I take Dr. Coogan's point. He is asking whether my cousin believes that all so-called psychosomatic effects can be explained in terms of brain chemicals. Well, I have discussed this with Roberto at length, and I can tell you that his answer is a qualified Yes. But if you are asking me my opinion, I can say that my answer is an unqualified No. Let me explain why I say that. My cousin is a scientist, and he spends most of his days in a laboratory, working with mice and rats. I am a general practitioner, and I spend my days working with people. This morning, Professor Topelius told you about the case of the businessman with the rash, who was cured when his daughter's car fell in the canal. The businessman is one of my patients. And I have seen many similar cases: women with obscure back pains or headaches; men suffering from heart palpitations and sexual failure. At first, I used to put these patients through every kind of test, then send them for x-rays, then try out all kinds of treatments. And when they were still exactly the same after months of treatment, it gradually began to dawn on me that their problems were not merely physical in origin, they were psychological. The woman suffering from back pains was worried because her husband had lost interest in her, the man with palpitations was worried because he knew his teenage daughter was sleeping with several boyfriends. If I could get them to tell me about their problems, they started to improve immediately. I don't see how any theory about brain chemicals can explain *all* these cases. That's why I'm rather skeptical about my cousin's larger claims." He sat down. There was a ripple of applause.

A tall, elderly man with rimless glasses was on his feet immediately. Topelius pointed to him.

"Professor Gordon Roach."

The professor said, "Surely Dr. Coogan's example about the icicle can be explained in terms of behavioral psychology? After all, it is not so different from the behavior of Pavlov's dogs who were taught to salivate at the sound of a bell. Professor Peruzzi's findings seem to me to fit precisely into the framework of behavioral psychology. It is surely no criticism to say that they fail to explain *every* form of auto-suggestion?" He sat down. Topelius glanced at Peruzzi, who nodded and stood up.

"My cousin makes no secret of being a behaviorist. We have discussed the case of the businessman with the skin rash, and he agrees that he cannot explain its precise mechanism in terms of behaviorism. He seems to think that the answer lies in some form of chemical released by the sudden crisis." As he spoke, he found himself looking at Sharon Engstrom, and he suddenly realized exactly why he disagreed with his cousin. He leaned forward, his fingers on the tabletop. "But that seems to me to miss the whole point. I *saw* my patient before and after the accident, and one thing seemed to be perfectly obvious. When he retired from business, he allowed himself to lose his sense of purpose. That in turn meant that he stopped using his will. And when people stop using their will, they seem to lose all their energy. It's as if the will is a kind of pump that keeps us brimming with energy and vitality. We seem to have a cistern that fills up with energy, and when we're full of purpose and optimism, the cistern fills right up to the top. My patient had stopped using his will, and his cistern was almost empty. For some reason I don't understand, that caused his rash. When his daughter's car fell into the canal, he suddenly regained his sense of purpose, and his will roared into life like an engine. And within seconds, the tank was full up, and the rash disappeared. And now I can explain why I disagree with my cousin. He seemed to think that the whole process was mechanical: the businessman lacked his usual stimulus, so his sense of purpose drained away, then the emergency supplied a stimulus and his purpose came back again. But it seems to me that my patient developed the skin rash *because* he allowed himself to turn into a machine. And when his daughter's life was in danger, he stopped being a machine and turned into a human being again. And, as far as I can see, that's the basic answer to the whole problem of mental illness." He could see Professor Roach shaking his head disapprovingly. "People get sick when they let themselves turn into machines. They get well when they use their free will to take control of themselves. As far as I can see, mental illness is another name for failing to recognize that you possess free will."

He sat down. This time there was no applause, but he felt that he had carried most of the audience with him. Only a few people, like Professor Roach, were frowning. Several people raised their hands. Topelius looked at his watch.

"I'm afraid we're not going to have time for further questions, because we've already exceeded our time. So may I thank Dr. Peruzzi, both for reading his cousin's paper, and for his own stimulating comments."

The audience applauded loudly as Topelius turned and shook hands with Peruzzi. He said, "*Very* good, Charles. That was magnificent."

Peruzzi felt himself blushing, and took a drink of water to cover his embarrassment.

As he stepped down from the platform, he found himself confronting Martha Morton-Jones. Her eyes were bright with excitement and enthusiasm.

"What a pity they didn't allow you to give your own lecture instead of reading that boring old paper. You were absolutely marvelous!" He caught the look on Roberta's face. She was raising her eyebrows as if to say, "Here we go again." Mrs. Morton-Jones laid her hand on his arm. "There's only one question I want to ask. How can an ordinary housewife develop a sense of purpose when she's thinking about what to give her husband for dinner?"

He said, "If you've *got* to do something, you'd better try and make it interesting. Make your husband buy you a lot of expensive cook books."

She said quickly, "I'm not saying I don't like cooking. I'm just saying that it's not very important. That's why I envy men so much. They can go out and look for something important to do."

Topelius said smoothly, "I suggest we adjourn to the bar. It's about opening time."

CHAPTER FOUR

THEY WERE the first in the cocktail lounge; the barman was wiping the counter with a damp cloth. Topelius asked Martha Morton-Jones what she wanted to drink. She paused in the middle of a sentence and looked at him abstractedly, as if not quite sure who he was or how he came to be there. Then she said casually, "Oh, a dry sherry," and turned back to Peruzzi. When he glanced at Roberta, she avoided his eyes, but her ironic smile told him what she was thinking.

Mrs. Morton-Jones was full of questions, but she never paused long enough to give him time to answer. For the next ten minutes he listened to her monologue and waited for a point at which he could interject. This proved to be an impossibility. Then, instead of listening to what she was saying, he began to study the way she prevented herself from being interrupted by immediately qualifying every question, and then moving on to other subjects. Finally, he merely observed the play of her expressions. Two spots of color had appeared on her cheeks and he realized that they made her look rather pretty. With her childish smile and habit of widening her eyes there was undoubtedly something rather desirable about her. He realized with interest that she was deliberately setting out to fascinate him, and that she was succeeding. When he seized the occasional pause for breath to interject a few words, she moistened the lower lip with the tip of her tongue, and he found himself thinking that it would be pleasant to take the lip between his teeth and gently bite it. His response to her surprised him. He felt like a fly being wrapped in strand after strand of sticky silk.

Topelius said, "Excuse me, Charles, but is that the girl you were expecting?" He looked up to see Sharon Engstrom hovering uncertainly in the doorway. He thought she looked nervous and ill at ease.

"Come in and meet Dr. Topelius."

She said, "I'm not interrupting am I?"

"Of course not." He took her arm and led her over to the table and introduced her. Topelius stood up to shake hands. Roberta gave her a friendly smile. Mrs. Morton-Jones hardly acknowledged her. Her cheeks had flushed and she looked like a spoiled child who has had a toy taken away.

"What can I get you to drink?"

"A gin and tonic, please."

As he was standing at the bar, Mrs. Morton-Jones came over to him. She said in a low voice, "I'm going to get changed. I'd like to talk to you later."

He gave her his friendliest smile. "Of course."

"I'll keep a seat next to me at dinner." She said it as if she was making a secret assignation. As she walked away, he realized that she had somehow managed to put him in the wrong, to make him feel guilty about breaking off the conversation. He also observed that although it was a relief to see her go, he felt a pang of regret. Martha Morton-Jones undoubtedly made life more interesting.

As he gave Sharon her drink, Topelius was saying, "With a name like Engstrom you must be Swedish?"

"My father's Swedish, not my mother."

Roberta smiled at him as he sat down.

"You seem to have made a conquest."

"Is she always like that?"

Roberta smiled wearily. "She's usually much worse."

Sharon turned to Roberta. "Your mother didn't seem to like me much."

"She's not my mother. She's my stepmother. And she is the most utterly spoiled female I've ever known."

She spoke with a depth of feeling that made it clear that she had been storing it up for some time. Topelius said, "Why did your father marry her?"

"I can't even imagine."

Peruzzi said, "I can. She has a definite fascination."

Roberta grimaced. "She just knows how to get her own way with men."

"She's just told me she's going to keep a place for me at dinner."

Roberta groaned. "Oh no! I just couldn't bear it!"

Topelius's eyes gleamed with malicious amusement. He said in Roberta's ear, "Why don't you keep an empty seat next to you and offer it to Charles?"

"Oh God, I'd never hear the last of it."

"On the contrary, I think she'd understand perfectly."

"She'd understand all right," Roberta chuckled sardonically.

"Though I must admit, it's just the kind of thing she does all the time."

"Then why not?" Topelius was enjoying playing the tempter. Roberta and Peruzzi looked at one another, both smiling at the thought of thwarting Martha. He said, "You could beckon me imperiously."

She laughed. "I'll snap my fingers if you like."

Sharon said, "Surely she can't be as bad as all that?" It was the kind of thing people say when they want to provoke further revelations.

Roberta rose to it. "Oh, can't she! I'll tell you something that happened . . . "

Topelius gave a warning cough. Morton-Jones had come through the door. He came to their table.

"Mind if I join you?"

"Please."

Morton-Jones drew up a chair next to Peruzzi. "I'm sorry I missed your lecture. I'm ashamed to say I went to my room and fell asleep. My wife tells me you were brilliant."

Roberta said, "You are hopeless, daddy!" She looked at him with such protective tenderness that Peruzzi felt almost jealous.

Topelius introduced Sharon to Morton-Jones. Peruzzi thought she was looking tense and abstracted. He was not surprised when, a few minutes later, she said, "I hope you'll excuse me. I've got someone coming to pick me up at seven."

She finished her drink and when she stood up the men also rose. Peruzzi said, "Take care."

Their eyes met briefly, with understanding. She said, "Don't worry. I will."

When she had gone, Morton-Jones asked, "Who is the young lady?"

Peruzzi said, "She's an airline stewardess."

"I thought she might be, oddly enough."

Topelius said, "Really? Why?"

"I noticed that scar under her chin. It seems to be an occupational hazard with airline hostesses; they get thrown forward with trays in their hands. I've operated on two of them myself."

Topelius and Peruzzi exchanged glances. Topelius said, "Did you notice a scar?"

"No."

Morton-Jones said, "No, you wouldn't. It had been dealt with quite skillfully. But I have a professional eye for these things. They should have done something about her eyelid at the same time."

"Her eyelid?"

"Oh yes. Again, it's hardly noticeable. But she has a slight twitch there, a tic, possibly a result of the accident. It probably shows a lot more when she's tired."

Topelius said with astonishment, "And you noticed all that in the few minutes you saw her?"

Morton-Jones said modestly, "Ah well, it's my job."

Peruzzi said, "I didn't notice a twitch."

"It's not obvious. And besides, she tends to sit with her left profile turned away."

Peruzzi thought about it. "Yes, now you mention it, she does!"

He and Topelius looked at one another and laughed. Roberta asked curiously, "Why are you so interested?"

Peruzzi said, "She tried to kill herself last night with an overdose. I happened to find her. I asked Erik to meet her and give me his opinion."

Topelius said, "I am tired of being a freak."

Morton-Jones looked startled. Peruzzi said quickly, "That was a phrase in the suicide note." He frowned. "But do you think a mere facial twitch is enough to make somebody feel a freak?"

It was Morton-Jones who answered. "Oh yes, indeed. Especially in a pretty girl like that. She's probably convinced herself that everybody notices it. Very tiny defects can have a quite disproportionate effect on people. Do you remember what it was like as a child when you had a cold sore on the lip?"

Roberta laughed. "And it felt as if everybody was staring at it."

Peruzzi said thoughtfully, "I wonder if you could be right?"

Topelius said, "I am convinced he is. That *has* to be the solution. She probably thinks it looks like spasms of palsy."

Roberta said, "The poor girl!"

Peruzzi asked Morton-Jones, "Did you say it can be cured by an operation?"

"Oh yes, it's a perfectly simple one. With an unimportant muscle like that one, the spasm can be controlled by dividing the supply nerve."

"But wouldn't that stop the eyelid from functioning altogether?"

"Good Lord, no! It wouldn't even be noticeable."

Peruzzi said, "How much does this operation cost?"

"Not much. At most, a few hundred pounds."

"And could *you* do it?"

"Oh yes. Quite easily."

Peruzzi looked thoughtfully at Topelius. "You know, I think I'm going to tell her. I think she'd take it coming from me."

Topelius nodded. "It can't do any harm."

Peruzzi emptied his glass. "Would you excuse me?"

Roberta asked, "Are you going to tell her now?"

"I think so. She's going out this evening with her boyfriend. The one who made her attempt suicide last night." He asked Morton-Jones, "And I can tell her you'd perform the operation?"

"Certainly, if she likes. It's a very simple one."

"Thank you." He smiled at Roberta. "See you at dinner."

He hurried upstairs, afraid that Sharon might have left already, but when he knocked on the connecting door her voice called, "Come in." She was sitting in front of the dressing table mirror applying makeup. "Oh, hello."

He said, "Sharon, can I ask you something?"

Her face from the mirror looked at him with surprise.

"Of course."

He pulled up a chair beside her, so he could see her left profile. Now he looked closely, he could see the slight scar under her chin and running along the line of the jaw. He could also see the tiny pulse in the corner of the left eyelid. He reached out and touched her face.

"Is there anything wrong with that eyelid?"

Her face went pale. For a moment he wondered if he had made a mistake. She looked as if he had slapped her. Then she said, "I had an accident. Why?" For a moment he said nothing, wondering how to begin. She said, "Is it so obvious?"

"No. I hadn't noticed. Neither had Topelius. It was Morton-Jones who pointed it out. He's a plastic surgeon."

"I see." She was under control again, but he could see she was shaken.

"He also said it's very easy to correct. A minor operation costing very little."

"Really?" She looked at him quickly, with a gleam of hope. "What did he say?"

"It's a slight muscular spasm, due to a supply nerve. If the nerve is divided, the spasm stops."

"Oh." She picked up her powder puff, but made no attempt to use it. "Wouldn't it . . . show?"

"No. He says it wouldn't even be noticeable."

When he caught the relief in her eyes, he suddenly knew it was all right. It was as if someone had turned on a light inside her.

"Does your friend do the operation?" She was trying to keep her voice casual.

"Yes."

"And he's quite sure it would work?"

"He seemed absolutely certain."

She smiled at him. "I'd like to talk to him about it."

"I'll tell him."

Her watch beeped. She said, "Good God, it's seven already. I must hurry."

"He can wait."

He went into his own room, and changed for dinner. As he was knotting a bow tie, she came into the room. She said, "Is it true you didn't notice it?"

"Quite true." He looked round at her. "You look marvelous!"

It was true, but it was not simply the off-the-shoulder gown, or the gauze scarf. There was color in her cheeks and, for the first time since he had known her, she looked happy and relaxed.

"I feel marvelous."

They were both aware of how much was unsaid. He bent and kissed her on the forehead. "Have a good time."

"I will." She stood on tiptoe and kissed his cheek. "And thank you."

When she had gone, he sat in front of the mirror and looked at his face. There was a slight smear of lipstick on his cheek, but he made no attempt to wipe it off. It was somehow a symbol of what had just happened and it filled him with an almost unbearable excitement. His mind was seething with ideas and insights. It seemed preposterous that her problems should be due to something as unimportant as a facial tic. Yet to her it probably seemed a monstrous twitch that distorted her whole face. Because she was unable to see herself through other people's eyes, she exaggerated the problem until it destroyed the foundation of her self-confidence.

What seemed equally extraordinary was that a mere *suggestion* could apparently undo all the damage. He had merely told her that the problem could be cured with a minor operation. She had not yet even arranged the operation. Yet the knowledge that she could be cured was enough to fill her with self-confidence. The placebo effect. How could an "insoluble" problem yield to such a simple solution?

Topelius was obviously correct. It was a question of her "self-image." Roberta and her stepmother provided another example. Roberta was more intelligent than her stepmother, more attractive, and an altogether nicer human being. So why was she so much less sure of herself? Because her self-image was weaker than her stepmother's. Her stepmother saw herself as intelligent, attractive and desirable, and somehow she managed to impose this image on other people.

And what was the answer? His mind conjured up a fantasy of Roberta at a regimental ball, surrounded by admiring officers who were all drinking her health in champagne. It was like a scene from a Viennese operetta. *That* was what she needed: male admiration, the certainty that other people saw her as attractive.

On the point of leaving the room, he remembered the lipstick on his cheek. He looked in the mirror and wiped it off with his handkerchief. It reinforced the point. If he had gone to dinner with lipstick on his cheek, and found out about it later, he would have felt a fool. Why? Because people might have been smiling behind his back. We are always unsure of ourselves when we are unsure of the image we are presenting to the world.

As he walked towards the lift, he saw Roberta waiting there with several other people. He called to her, and she turned and waited for him. By the time he arrived she was alone. She was wearing her hair combed out over her bare shoulders and he was surprised how much this changed her appearance. The brown satin evening dress emphasized gently the curves of her figure.

She said, "What happened?"

"It worked. It was incredible. Your father was quite right."

She smiled with a touch of complacency. "He often is."

"Sharon's going to talk to your father about this operation. But I wouldn't be surprised if she didn't need it after all. It's like a stutter; it can vanish if you simply stop worrying about it."

As they went down in the lift she said, "I think we'd better skip this idea of sitting next to one another at dinner."

"Why?"

She shrugged. "I suppose I don't want to cause trouble. It's just not worth it."

"Why not. It's the kind of thing she'd do."

"I know that. But I don't want to put myself on her level."

They gravitated naturally to the bar but it was so crowded that they took their drinks out to the coffee lounge. This was empty.

He asked, "How did your father meet her?"

"She used to be a friend of mother's—well, an acquaintance. Mother didn't like her much. I think that she had her eye on Daddy even then. She turned up at the funeral and offered to help, and . . . you know how it is."

"Could you see what was going to happen?"

"I suppose so. But there wasn't much I could do about it, was there? Besides, I rather liked her myself. It was only later that I realized that she's completely self-centered. Not just self-centered, mischievous."

"In what way?"

She grimaced. "You know, for example, why she wants you to sit next to her at dinner? It's not your brilliant lecture—I doubt whether she even understood it—it's because you sat beside me at lunchtime and we seemed to get on well together. So she wants to show she can take you over. It's the same with Jerry. The moment she realized we're old friends, she decided to grab him."

"Why? Is she afraid of you?"

"In a way. With me there, it's as if there was a bit of mother still around."

Through the glass doors, he saw Martha Morton-Jones entering the bar with her husband on one side and Jerry Seneca on the other. He was suddenly struck by an idea.

"Listen, I'll tell you what I suggest. Let's sit next to one another, just as we planned—no, let me finish—and let's behave as if we've fallen in love."

She looked puzzled. "But why? What would be the point?"

"To make her realize that people find you attractive. Of course, the ideal thing would be for me and Jerry to sit on either side of you and both flirt with you." The way she colored confirmed what he already knew. "But one of us will do as well."

Her eyes twinkled. "I suppose it *would* be funny . . . "

"Shall we do it?"

She chuckled. "All right."

"But you've got to take this seriously, or she'll guess we're just pretending. No giggling or pulling faces. Promise?"

"Promise."

"All right. Come and sit here beside me."

"Why?"

"Because I want to see if you can keep a straight face."

She came and sat beside him on the settee. Because he found her so likeable, he felt completely at ease with her. Charlie had never thought of himself as a ladies' man. At medical school, he had almost become engaged to a nurse, but when she had transferred her affections to a newly qualified dentist he had been unable to convince himself that his heart was broken and had soon forgotten her.

As a general practitioner he had flirted mildly with some of his prettier patients, and with his partner's secretary, but nothing serious had ever developed. With Roberta, it was tacitly agreed that there was no question of flirtation; there was no sexual attraction between them. This is why he now felt as much at ease with her as if she had been a man.

He took both her hands. "Look into my eyes. No smiling." She canceled an incipient smile. "Now, I've just kissed you passionately in the lift. We've suddenly realized we're in love. Right?" She nodded. "We're both a bit shy about it and we don't want other people to realize."

She said dreamily, "But we can't help thinking about that kiss." She was entering into the spirit of the thing.

He gazed into her eyes. "Every time I look at you, I long to crush you in my arms and feel your heart pounding againt mine."

"That's impossible unless yours is on the wrong side."

"Don't make jokes. Try to imagine you're in love."

"I'll try." She looked at him with a yielding expression, which he found very attractive.

"I think I'd better kiss you, just for practice."

"All right." She said it with such mock-contrition that he had to make an effort not to laugh.

He bent down and placed his lips against hers. Her mouth was soft and warm. He broke off and glanced towards the door to make sure no one was watching. She said, "Am I supposed to hold my breath?"

"I don't know. Do you usually hold your breath?"

"I don't know, I've never thought about it."

They both laughed. He looked at his watch.

"Perhaps you'd better go and grab those seats. I'll join you in a few minutes."

She smiled demurely. "Yes, darling." She finished her drink and went out.

He stretched out his legs and sipped his martini meditatively. He was developing a taste for martinis, no doubt because they induced a pleasant light-headedness in a remarkably short time. He was also intrigued by an interesting recognition: that playing at being in love could generate a feeling that was not unlike the real thing.

At half past seven, people began to move out of the bar towards the dining room. He saw the Morton-Joneses among them. He waited until the queue had disappeared, then followed them. In the dining room, he saw that Martha Morton-Jones had placed her wrap and handbag on the chair beside her. Further along the table, Roberta was talking to Jerry Seneca. She was unmistakably ex-plaining that the chair beside her was already taken. When she saw Peruzzi, she waved. At the same moment, Martha Morton-Jones beckoned him over. She removed her handbag and wrap from the chair.

"Come and sit beside me."

He caught Roberta's eye and said, "Excuse me a moment."

Roberta said nothing; she merely patted the chair beside her. Seneca, he thought, looked rather taken aback. He returned to Martha Morton-Jones.

"Will you excuse me? Roberta wants to talk to me. . . . "

"So do I." She caught hold of his sleeve, and gave it an imperious tug. For a moment he felt she had won. He could hardly tear himself free by force. Then Roberta's voice called firmly, "Charlie," and Mrs. Morton-Jones made the mistake of letting go. He said quickly, "Pardon me," and went and sat beside Roberta. He took care not to look back towards Mrs. Morton-Jones. But when he stole a glance in her direction a few moments later, he caught her gazing towards him with a brooding and baleful expression. Bill Robinson had taken the chair beside her, but she seemed to be ignoring his attempts to make conversation.

During the meal, Roberta did not once allow her eyes to stray towards her stepmother. Instead, she behaved as if she and Charlie were alone. He found it hard to believe that she was the same girl who had sat beside him at lunch. She was amusing and delightful and she played their game of make-believe with far more skill than he did, treating him as if they had just secretly become engaged. When she turned to give the waiter her order, she allowed her bare shoulder to press against his. When he asked her if the smoked salmon was tender, she gave him some on her fork. When they toasted one another in Soave, she looked into his eyes, and only a gleam of mockery told him that she regarded this as a game. During the dessert course, he dropped his napkin and, as he picked it up, took the opportunity to kiss her knee, expecting her to jerk it away. Instead, she reached down and caressed the lobe of his ear.

Seneca had found a seat at the next table, next to Topelius. At one point, as Peruzzi was signing the bill, Topelius caught his eye, and gave him a brief but perceptible wink.

Roberta talked about her job. She was working as a receptionist and secretary for her father, but admitted that she found it boring. She had been offered a post as a secretary in New York but felt that this would be cutting her last link with her father. Peruzzi told her about his own work, about his dissatisfaction with the National Health Service and about the course in family counseling that he had started to take. But his thoughts were elsewhere. He was thinking how well it suited Roberta to behave as if she were in love. The thought of her boring job, her irritating stepmother and her unsatisfactory life filled him with pity.

After the meal, as he and Roberta were moving towards the coffee lounge, he caught Martha Morton-Jones looking at him. She ignored his smile, and looked straight past him. There were two bright spots of color on her cheeks. Peruzzi had not expected her to be amiable but her show of bad temper irritated him.

"I don't understand how women like that get through life. She's utterly self-centered, and she can't stop herself from behaving like a spoiled child."

Roberta said, "Oh, well, one of these days she'll get her come-uppance." He felt this was a distinct improvement on her earlier attitude.

Before they could say any more, Topelius and Seneca came into the lounge, followed by the Morton-Joneses. Seneca looked at them quizzically.

"Mind if we join you?"

"Of course not." Roberta made room for him beside her.

Seneca looked down appreciatively at her bare shoulders and the rounded glimpse of bosom above the brown satin.

"That's a pretty dress."

Martha Morton-Jones, who was lowering herself into a chair, thought he was speaking to her.

"Do you think so?" Then she looked up and realized her mistake. She scowled at Roberta. "*I* don't much care for that dress."

Roberta said casually, "No? Why?"

"It's a little too . . . obvious."

Peruzzi expected her to wince. Instead she looked at her stepmother's unrevealing dress and said mildly, "It certainly wouldn't suit you."

Seneca and Topelius smiled. Morton-Jones intervened quickly. "Would you like a liqueur with your coffee, my dear?"

Roberta took a brown and cream silk scarf from her evening bag and covered her shoulders. She smiled disarmingly at her stepmother. "Is that better?"

Martha Morton-Jones glared at her. "I don't much care for the scarf."

Roberta asked patiently, "Why, what's wrong with it?"

"I simply don't like your taste."

"It isn't my taste. It's yours. You gave it to me for Christmas."

Seneca gave a snort of laughter. "She has you there, Martha!"

Morton-Jones said diplomatically, "Perhaps I gave it to her."

Roberta said, "Yes, perhaps you did." Peruzzi caught the glance of sympathy that passed between them. So did Martha Morton-Jones. She flushed angrily.

The sound of a band came from the ballroom. Roberta turned to Peruzzi.

"Do you feel like dancing?"

"I'm not much good. I always trip over my feet."

Seneca grasped the opportunity, as Charlie had hoped he would. "Feel like giving me a turn?"

Roberta said, "I didn't know you could dance."

"Ha, you've never seen me with my tomahawk and scalping knife."

It made them laugh. Even Martha Morton-Jones was coaxed into a sour smile. As Seneca and Roberta went out, Morton-Jones asked courteously, "Would you care to dance, my love?"

She shrugged ill-naturedly. "I suppose I'd better."

As she went out, Topelius said, "She must be the worst behaved woman in London. Even that besotted fool of a husband is bound to see it sooner or later."

Peruzzi said thoughtfully, "Perhaps he does see it. Perhaps he doesn't care. You can never tell what people need."

"It was good to see Roberta standing up for herself. Incidentally, is she really interested in you, or was she just pretending?"

"Pretending. She's in love with Jerry."

Topelius said reflectively, "I hope she doesn't get more than she bargained for."

"In what way."

"Oh . . . just that she's a typical English virgin in search of a husband. His intentions may be more straightforward."

"Would that matter?"

"Perhaps not. I'd hate to see her get hurt."

Peruzzi said, "I've got a feeling Roberta can take care of herself." It was a conviction that had grown upon him steadily during the past hour.

He had been in bed half an hour and was on the point of switching off the light when he heard someone enter the next room. A moment later there was a very light knock on the connecting door. He called, "Come in."

Sharon said, "I wondered if you'd be awake."

"How did it go."

"Marvelously."

"Where's the boyfriend?"

"Gone home. He wanted to come back, but I said no."

"Where did you go?"

"Into Soho for dinner, then to the Playboy Club."

"Did you tell him about last night?"

"No." She sat on the bed. "And I'm not going to."

He patted her hair. "Good girl. You're beginning to learn."

"Learn what?"

"Never let a man feel you're a victim. He'll walk all over you."

"Yes, I know." She kicked off her shoes. "I learned that today." She swung her feet on the bed and leaned back beside him.

"Is he serious about you?"

"As serious as he can be. Which isn't much." She leaned her head on his shoulder. "I wish Jeff was as nice as you."

He took her hand. After a moment, she turned her face, and he kissed her. Her lips parted and he felt a pleasant tingle of desire. As they both began to slide into a more comfortable position there was a knock on the door. It made them start. She whispered, "My God, who's that?"

He laughed. "Perhaps it's Jeff, come to see if you've changed your mind."

While she pulled on her shoes, he slipped into his dressing gown and opened the door. It was Roberta.

"May I come in?"

"Of course."

When she saw Sharon she said, "Oh dear, I'm sorry . . . "

"Not at all. Sharon's just back from the Playboy Club. We've been exchanging notes."

"I won't stay long. I just wanted you to be the first to know. I'm going to marry Jerry."

He laughed with delight. "That's marvelous! Congratulations!"

Sharon said, "It must be proposal day for girls."

"Why, did you get one too?"

She said dryly, "Only a dirty one."

Roberta laughed. "Oh, so did I!"

"I thought you said he wanted to marry you?"

"He does. He proposed the other thing first. And after."

"What happened?" Peruzzi climbed back into bed. The two women sat on either side of it.

"Well, he couldn't dance, as I remembered from the last time I tried it. He nearly broke my toe. Then he danced with Martha and managed to stand on the hem of her dress and broke the shoulder strap. So we decided to move to somewhere where he couldn't do any damage, and went to the roof bar. There he told me the story of his life, and drank too much, and ended by asking me back to his bedroom. I must admit I felt tempted but I was afraid it was just the drink. So I said no. Then he asked me to marry him."

Sharon said, "And you thought that was the drink too."

"That's right. So I said no. But then he talked about it and said he wanted me to work with him on the reservation, so I said yes. Then he ordered a bottle of champagne to celebrate—I must say, it's terrifyingly expensive in this place—and asked me to go to bed with him again. But I could see he wasn't in any condition, so I went to his room and tucked him in, and when I left he was snoring like an oversize baby. And as I left his room, who should I bump into but Martha and my father. I'm sure they think the worst."

Peruzzi chuckled. "You've burnt your bridges now."

"Thank God!" She stood up. "I'll leave you two in peace. But I had to tell somebody or burst." She knelt on the bed and kissed Peruzzi on the side of the mouth. "And thanks."

When she had gone, Sharon said, "I bet you feel like Santa Claus. It must be nice to be so clever!"

He laughed. "I'm not. You know, something just struck me, and yet it's been staring me in the face all evening. Roberta and I decided to sit next to each other at dinner to annoy her stepmother. And at the last minute she decided to back out. Then I suggested that we should pretend to be lovers and she agreed immediately. I thought she was just being a good sport. It never struck me . . . "

"That she wanted to make her boyfriend jealous."

"Yes, that's right. I suppose you'd have seen it right away. I'm not that clever."

"If that's stupidity it's the kind I admire." She bent over and kissed him. This time it was as impersonal as a mother saying goodnight. "We both need some sleep. See you in the morning."

He was not surprised to see her go. The moment had passed when Roberta knocked on the door. He was not sorry either. He wanted to think about the insights that filled his mind. Like Roberta and Sharon, he felt that the past twenty-four hours had been a watershed in his life. But unlike them, he was not sure of the reason why. And when he closed his eyes and tried to think about it, he was overwhelmed by the tide of sleep.

CHAPTER FIVE

WHEN CHARLIE PERUZZI was ten years old, his grandfather read him most of Victor Hugo's *Les Miserables* in French. In spite of the Italian name, the Peruzzi family originates in the northern Pyrenees, and his grandfather spoke English with a strong French accent. Charlie was deeply moved by the book—which he later came to find unbearably sentimental—and for years afterwards had to repress tears when he thought of how Fantine had to support her illegitimate child by selling her hair and teeth. The novel excited a desire to relieve the sufferings of the human race, and he often daydreamed of handing wads of money to poor old tramps, or arriving at the home of some starving family on Christmas Eve with a huge basket of groceries.

His fantasies took a specifically medical direction when he was twelve years old. Until that time, the family had lived at Fleetwood in Lancashire, where Charles Peruzzi was born on February 2, 1949; his father worked for British Rail in Blackpool. Just before Christmas 1960, John Peruzzi was appointed station master at the small town of Copton Green, between Preston and Lancaster, and the family moved into the house that went with the job. None of them liked it, and Charlie loathed it. He missed the sea and his grandparents and his schoolfriends. That winter was wet and cold and the Peruzzi family gave way to gloom.

Towards the end of a bleak and snowy February day, Charlie came home from school and sat at the table, eating his tea, while his mother gave his three-year-old brother Roy a bath in front of the fire. Roy objected to immersion in water, and his mother allowed him to play with a rubber dog with glass eyes while she scrubbed his back. Suddenly, the child began to cough and his face went red. His mother snatched him up and began to pat his back, which made him gulp. The coughing stopped, and his face began to turn blue. Charlie looked on in horror as his brother's eyes began to bulge. His mother screamed at him to fetch his father. John Peruzzi was only a few yards away, helping to unload a guard's van. He realized immediately that Roy had swallowed something that was choking him and turned him upside down, patting his back. The child coughed, choked, and then seemed to stop breathing. Charlie was ordered to run and summon the doctor. He was fortunate; he recognized the doctor's gray Jaguar outside a house a few hundred yards away, and banged frantically on the door. Within minutes they were back at the station. John Peruzzi was walking up and down the room holding the child, while Mrs. Peruzzi was sobbing and the elder sister, Violet, who had just come home, was having hysterics.

The doctor, an old man named James Grimshaw, ordered the child to be laid on the settee, and felt his pulse. The heart was still beating. He pressed his fingers at the base of the throat and the child began to choke. Evidently the doctor had located the obstruction. He asked John Peruzzi, "Have you a sharp knife?" Peruzzi brought one from his tool box.

Mrs. Peruzzi asked, "What are you going to do?"

"A tracheotomy. It's the only thing that might save his life."

John Peruzzi asked, "What's a tracheotomy?"

"I'm going to have to cut his windpipe, so he can breathe direct into his lungs." The thought of her child's throat being cut brought louder sobbing from Mrs. Peruzzi and screams from Violet. Grimshaw said quietly, "Get the women out of the room."

Charlie, unnoticed, stood and watched as the doctor, with a single clean cut, opened his brother's throat. Suddenly, Roy began to breathe again. Grimshaw told John Peruzzi to summon an ambulance. Then, as Peruzzi left the room, he muttered to himself, "There's one thing we may as well try." From his medical bag he took a pair of forceps and told the child to open his mouth wide. He peered down the throat, then asked Charlie, "Do you have a torch?" Charlie fetched one from the kitchen. "Hold it for me," said Grimshaw, and, while Charlie stood above his brother's head shining the torch, Grimshaw reached down the throat with the forceps while he pressed the base of the throat with the other hand. There was a silence, during which neither of them seemed to breathe. Then Grimshaw gave a jerk and the forceps emerged, holding a glass eye from the rubber dog. Roy immediately began to cry and cough, while the blood from the incision trickled down the side of his neck.

It was all over in a quarter of an hour. Roy, obviously well on the way to recovery, was taken to the hospital to have the incision stitched. Dr. Grimshaw countered their congratulations and thanks with some irritable words about not allowing children to chew glass eyes, but he accepted John Peruzzi's offer of a glass of homemade wine. When, an hour later, the family sat down to supper, there was an atmosphere like a Christmas party. By that time they had heard that Roy was now well enough to leave the hospital in the morning. When his father had said, "He's stopped breathing," Charlie's heart had seemed to stop beating. And as he ran to find Dr. Grimshaw he had been weighed down by a stifling sense of tragedy. They all loved Roy who was fat, placid and good-tempered. To lose him like this seemed an incredibly brutal blow of fate. Charlie found himself thinking, "We should never have come to Copton," and loathing everything about the place. The town seemed to be permeated by a kind of shabby evil. When he saw the doctor's car, his mood lightened. This, at any rate, was an unexpected piece of luck. And when Roy began to cry and cough, Charlie experienced a sense of relief that made him feel that he was about to float off the ground. As they sat down to their meal of sausage and chips, the railway cottage no longer seemed bleak and damp. Rain gusted against the windows, and the wind howled down the chimney and it became a haven of warmth and security.

An ambulance brought Roy home the next day. The wound in his throat healed within weeks, leaving a tiny white scar. His mother and father seemed to forget the incident almost immediately, but Charlie had no desire to forget. What fascinated him was that the surge of relief had somehow changed his way of seeing the world. He no longer hated the grimy, red-brick Victorian school or the mean little shops and houses of Copton's main street. They now seemed to him more cozy, more intimate, than the wide streets and middle-class houses of Fleetwood. And when the spring arrived and the countryside became green and scented with warm earth smells, he realized that he no longer missed the sea. And even at the age of twelve, Charlie was perceptive enough to realize that it was the sudden crisis that had shaken him out of his negative and resentful attitude towards his new home. It followed—and this is what puzzled him so much—that the misery and boredom he had experienced during those first two months in Copton had been somehow *unnecessary*. He was not quite sure whether this insight was of any practical use, yet he knew it was something he would never forget.

Dr. Grimshaw became Charlie's hero. It was not because he had saved Roy's life, it was because he had dared to slit the windpipe with an unsterilized wood carving knife to enable the child to breathe while he groped down his throat with the forceps. This revealed that Grimshaw was not like other men who live their vague and inefficient lives from day to day. He held the power of life and death; he had a touch of the god about him. In imagination, Charlie could see him entering bedrooms where patients moaned or tried to catch their breath, taking their pulse and temperature, administering pills or medicines from his mysterious black bag, and instantly relieving their sufferings. These fantasies, in turn, became daydreams in which he himself was conducted into the sick room of Lilian Pike—the prettiest girl in the school—or Mrs. Jevons, the attractive blonde who ran the sweet shop, and in which a single teaspoonful of medicine administered by himself produced an immediate cure and expressions of gratitude from delighted parents and relatives . . .

The weekend after Roy's accident, Charlie knocked on Dr. Grimshaw's door and offered to clean the mud off his car. With the aid of a brush attached to a hosepipe he left the Jaguar spotless. Even the hubcaps were shiny. When Grimshaw offered him two shillings, Charlie shyly refused, explaining that he enjoyed doing odd jobs, and Grimshaw assumed Charlie wanted to show his gratitude. He was mistaken. Charlie wanted some contact, no matter how slight, with his hero.

The following Saturday, the first warm spring day, Charlie found Grimshaw in his garden, digging out last year's cabbage stalks. Charlie offered to do the weeding and hoeing. As dusk began to fall, Grimshaw invited him indoors for tea and cake. Since the death of his wife, Grimshaw had lived alone in the large, unattractive Edwardian house, devoting his spare time to chemical experiments. The house had a distinctive smell of chemicals and of methylated spirit and iodine. To Charlie, it was the most exciting and romantic smell in the world. It made no difference to him that Grimshaw's tea looked like Brown Windsor soup and that the seed cake was stale. All that mattered was that he was in the same room with a man whom he regarded with a reverence that a student of physics might have felt for Einstein. He was breathing in an atmosphere that seemed to symbolize another world, another kind of life.

When, the following weekend, Grimshaw invited him into his laboratory, Charlie was surprised to find bundles of flowers and plants covering the bench and the chairs and a wall full of shelves containing jars full of leaves, berries and strips of bark. Grimshaw, it seemed, was a student of a long-dead herbalist called the Abbé Kneipp who believed that nature provides remedies for every ailment. But Grimshaw had taken it a step further. In some old work on alchemy, he had come upon the notion that all plants have their individual essence, and that this can be extracted by a series of distillations. So with the aid of meticulously polished flasks and retorts and a Leibig condenser, Grimshaw attempted to extract the essences of elm, birch, fennel, mugwort, sloe, basil and shepherd's purse. The results of these experiments were kept in brown, glass-stoppered bottles in a locked cupboard. When Charlie arrived one day with a sore throat, Grimshaw gave him a hot drink made from essence of lungwort mixed with honey; the sore throat was gone by the next day. When his sister Violet was confined to her bed by menstrual pains, Grimshaw sent her a small bottle of essence of shepherd's purse, with instructions to take a few drops in distilled water; the pains vanished within hours.

For years now, Grimshaw's arthritis had prevented him from taking long walks in search of herbal remedies. Charlie's arrival solved that problem. On Sunday afternoons, Grimshaw and Charlie would drive out to the Bleasdale Moors or the Forest of Bowland or the slopes of Eagland Hill, and Grimshaw would sit in the car or on a camp stool in a field, while Charlie explored the woods and ditches and returned periodically with a haversack full of plants and berries. Then they would go through them one by one, with Grimshaw identifying them—"That's St. John's Wort, good for sciatica, . . . That's vervain, cures jaundice and congestion of the spleen, . . . That's basil, excellent sedative"—and sometimes sending Charlie back for more of the same. Within a few months, Charlie could identify most of them without Grimshaw's help. By the middle of the following year, his knowledge of botany was as wide as Grimshaw's own.

At the end of the afternoon they would return to Grimshaw's house for tea, and Grimshaw would unlock the glass-fronted bookcase and allow Charlie to look through his medical books. For Charlie there was a magic about medical terminology. He would repeat words like "subclavian artery," "lymphatic drainage," "anterior funiculus" as if they were poetry. One Monday, after a particularly successful weekend in search of herbs, Charlie arrived home to find a parcel containing a copy of *The Illustrated Family Doctor* (by a "General Practitioner") waiting for him. The pages were stained and corrugated by damp— Grimshaw had found it on a stall in Preston Market—and it was at least thirty years out of date, but for Charlie it was the most exciting book in the world. The Arabian Nights seemed unromantic by comparison. He read it until he knew by heart almost every entry from A.B.C. Liniment and Abdomen to

Zinc Poisoning and Zymotic Disease. The following Christmas, 1961, he persuaded his father to present him with a copy of the latest edition of *Gray's Anatomy*—an expensive item for a station master—and spent the remainder of the holiday browsing lovingly through its fifteen hundred pages.

Charlie had never known so much contentment as during this period of his life when he was teaching himself the rudiments of medicine. He was never bored, never tired, never at a loose end. Yet life was not entirely smooth for all that. His interest in medicine made him neglect his school work, particularly English and geography. (He enjoyed science and mathematics.) A school report dated July 1963 carries a comment by his headmaster: "I realize that your son is interested in medicine, but if he continues to neglect his school work, he will fail his School Certificate examination and so be unable to enter medical school." That warning was enough. His school report for the following July has the comment: "Has improved beyond belief."

For Charlie, the real lesson was that if he applied to geography and English the same concentrated attention he gave to medicine, he could pass exams like a race horse. It was also impossible not to realize that the rest of his schoolfriends seemed to be standing still while he galloped on towards new horizons of discovery. At first he used to enjoy peppering his conversation with medical terminology. But one afternoon, when cricket had been rained off, the fourth form sat around in the pavilion and told dirty jokes, and Charlie suddenly became aware of the abyss that had opened between himself and his contemporaries. It was not that he was prudish. On the contrary, he contributed a few well-worn medical jokes. (Professor: What part of the body is as hard as steel? Why are you blushing, Miss Jones? I was referring to the nails. I am afraid you are an optimist . . .) But the glimpse into their minds embarrassed him, as he might have been embarrassed if he had gone into someone's home and discovered that they were too poor to afford furniture. It all seemed so dull, so barren, so repetitive. He realized for the first time how much his medical studies had altered his life by giving him a sense of purpose. From then on, he deliberately played down his medical knowledge and did his best to appear like everyone else. This was due partly to a sense of shame, partly to innate modesty. He did not feel that he was cleverer than his friends, or that he possessed more will-power. It was just that he knew *what* to will, and they didn't.

From the day Charlie insisted on having *Gray's Anatomy* for Christmas, it became obvious to his family that he was destined for a medical career. Any financial worries caused by another student in the family were allayed to some extent by the death of Dr. Grimshaw on Christmas Day, 1965; he left Charlie three hundred pounds, as well as his library, a collection of medical instruments, and all his herbal remedies. Charlie was shattered by the death of his old friend and mentor—Grimshaw died quite suddenly of a heart attack—and made a vow to keep his memory alive, a promise he fulfilled in 1983 with the establishment of the annual Grimshaw Memorial Lecture at Guys.

In September 1967, Charlie entered Guys Medical School. He had developed into a tall, good-looking young man with dark curly hair of a wiry consistency and intelligent brown eyes. He was shy and his speech was hesitant, but his pale, rather serious face was transformed by a smile of radiant good nature. There was something about Charlie that made strangers like and trust him. Tom Creevey, a contemporary at Guys, said that it took six months before anyone in the class noticed Charlie Peruzzi, but that by the end of the year there was no one who didn't like him.

That first year at Guys was a difficult period. Charlie lived on his meager student grant in an attic near the Elephant and Castle, and since medical text books were terribly expensive and work came first, he usually ate only once a day. Social life was restricted because he had no money to spend in pubs or the Students' Union.

In the spring term of 1968, he took a job working behind the counter in a workman's café for five evenings a week. This helped him eke out his grant and allowed him to eat; he could even afford the occasional pint of beer. But he found it exhausting. One day, his professor took him aside and told him sternly that his written work was deteriorating, and that he looked as if he was spending too many late nights in the pub. Charlie lacked the courage to tell him the truth. Instead, he began to stay up until the early hours of the morning, copying up his notes. The result was inevitable; the strain began to undermine his health. Just before Easter, a bout of flu forced him to stay in bed for a week. He wrote and told his family that he was working too hard to come home for the holiday, then spent a miserable Easter living off eggs and tinned tomatoes, and seeing no one for day after day.

That summer was the worst of his life. He had no idea that it was nervous fatigue that made life seem gray and futile. He believed that he was simply disillusioned with medicine. All those words which had once held for him a kind of sinister magic—anastomosis, haematoidin, phagedaena, angiology—were somehow reduced to banality by the daily drudgery. He could see now that his hero-worship of Dr. Grimshaw had been merely adolescent romanticism, which would have vanished instantly if he had actually spent a day at his hero's side, lancing boils, examining piles and doing urine tests. During the hot June of 1968, stifling in his attic where the temperature once rose above 90°, Charlie came near to despair.

Rescue came from an unexpected source. His sister Violet won a scholarship to the Royal Academy of Music, and in early July she came to London to look for lodgings. With the help of the Students' Lodging Bureau she found a large flat near the Gloucester Road tube station. It was less expensive than it might have been because the noise of trains made the windows rattle. She arranged to share with two girls, then she made her way to the Elephant and Castle to see her brother. She found him sitting by the open window, stripped to the waist, reading a book on diseases of the nervous system. She was shocked by his appearance. He was so pale that his skin had a greenish tinge, and he had lost so much weight that he looked like a concentration camp victim; he also had a boil on his chin. She telephoned his professor to say that her brother was ill and that she intended to take him back home. Then she paid his landlady a week's rent in lieu of notice and moved his few possessions over to the flat in Gloucester Road. That night she took him out for the largest meal she could afford, and watched with astonishment as he ate his way through two large steaks and a double helping of chips. The next day she took him back to Copton Green. Two months of good food and long country walks restored his health and optimism, and when he returned to London he moved into the smallest room in Violet's flat, paying the same rent he had paid for the attic. It took longer to travel to Guys, but Violet made sure that he ate regular meals. In the company of three girls, his shyness began to disappear. And, what was more important, the old idealism about medicine became stronger than ever.

Every young person in the grip of an enthusiasm believes that he is going to become famous. It was not a matter to which Charlie had given much thought until he discovered one day, on the bookshelf of one of his sister's flatmates, a novel called *Arrowsmith* by Sinclair Lewis. Charlie had never read a novel since *Tom Brown's Schooldays*; he regarded them as a waste of time. But in the mood of happy relaxation induced by his new life in Gloucester Road, he started to read *Arrowsmith* one rainy Sunday afternoon. He read on until he finished the book at dawn the next day. Lewis's story of a doctor who devotes his life to research made Charlie suddenly aware that he also believed he had a destiny to improve the lives of his fellow men. This, he now realized, was why he had become so depressed the previous summer. His sense of disillusionment had robbed him of his secret driving force.

From a book about Sinclair Lewis, Charlie discovered that he had been inspired by *Microbe Hunters* by Paul de Kruif. He borrowed the book from the local library. Once again he read it in a single sitting. Once again he became aware that he was driven by a devouring urge to make some vital contribution to medical knowledge.

In the final chapter of Glasscheib's *March of Medicine*, he came upon psychoanalysis. Up to that point, he had never taken much interest in psychology, regarding it as a pseudoscience lacking the precision of medicine. Glasscheib's chapter on Freud was a revelation. His first reaction was shock and incredulity. Glasscheib writes, "Freud asked himself in amazement where all these appalling perverse traits of his patients originated—traits that were so regularly to be found the nearer he got to their early childhood. The solution to the problem seemed to lie in that vague, nebulous early childhood . . . " Charlie found it almost unbelievable that anyone could suggest that babies were interested in sex. The idea struck him as preposterous and indecent.

That evening, a week before Christmas, 1971, they had a guest to dinner. He was Charlie's fellow student Tom Creevey, son of the well-known psychiatrist Roland Creevey. They had become friendly during the autumn term, and when Creevey mentioned that he loved music, it seemed logical to invite him back to the flat to meet Violet and the other girls. Creevey was the sort of person it is impossible to dislike; he had a highly developed sense of the ridiculous and irresistible high spirits. He made them all laugh so much that the food got cold. When Charlie raised the subject of infantile eroticism, Creevey found it unbelievable that Charlie had never really considered Freud before. Since the girls seemed to be equally ignorant of his importance, he explained why he considered Freud's theories to be the unshakeable foundation of modern psychology. Charlie listened with a kind of guilty absorption. It still struck him as shocking, but Creevey forced him to admit that there might be something in it. Charlie recalled something that had happened at his lodging in the Elephant and Castle. His landlady's four-year-old daughter was fascinated by a plastic skeleton that had been left by a previous tenant, and often asked if she could see it. On half a dozen occasions, Charlie allowed her into his room and made the skeleton "dance." One day, when he was writing up his notes, the child came in and asked him to make the skeleton dance; Charlie patted her on the head with one hand and went on writing with the other. She took hold of his hand, and Charlie suddenly became aware that she had trapped it between her thighs and was "riding" it like a hobby horse. It seemed a perfectly innocent gesture; he extricated his hand and thought no more about it. A few days later, she came in again when he was writing and, when he tried to send her away, again took his hand and jammed it firmly between her thighs. Charlie became aware that she was not wearing any knickers. He felt that this was simply her way of demanding attention, so he stopped writing and made the skeleton dance. The third time it happened was shortly before Violet came to see him. He was feeling irritable and rundown, so when the child closed her thighs tightly on his hand, he ignored her and went on to finish the sentence he was writing. Suddenly, his hand was warm and wet. He snatched it away, and the child shrieked with laughter at the pool of urine on the floor.

When he told Creevey about the experience, Creevey threw up his hands and said, "Of course! She was trying to seduce you."

"Seduce me! At four!"

"Not consciously, of course. But her unconscious knew exactly what she was doing." And he went on to explain that wetting his hand was her way of showing her exasperation that he was not responding to her invitation.

Now Charlie was fully aware that all small boys are interested in "dirty stories." But he had always assumed that this was something they picked up from older children. As a child he had been rather puritanical, and felt an instinctive revulsion for all the talk about "willies" and "fannies," and the sly suggestion that parents behaved like naughty children in bed. Now he was informed by Freud that babies experience sexual pleasure as they suck the mother's breast and go to the lavatory, and the idea startled and shocked him. He borrowed a biography of Freud from the library and learned that Freud's contemporaries had been equally startled and shocked, and that they had reacted by persecuting him. That finally convinced him; if Freud had been persecuted, he must be right. Charlie added Freud to the pantheon of his medical heroes, and when his brother

Roy, who, at the age of ten, was already fascinated by medicine, asked him for stories about the great doctors, Charlie told him about Ignaz Semmelweis, driven to despair by ridicule of his idea that infection is caused by germs, of Louis Pasteur, shouted down by the Paris Academy for suggesting that bacteria causes tuberculosis, and of Sigmund Freud, accused of insanity for daring to suggest that mental illness is caused by sexual repressions.

In the autumn of 1972, Charlie moved into a flat in the Camberwell Road which he would share with Creevey and a third-year student named Johnson. He was sorry to leave Gloucester Road but the situation there had become impossible. One of the original flatmates had left and her place was taken by a student nurse who fell openly and unashamedly in love with Charlie. She was quite uninhibited about it, and whenever she caught Charlie alone, would fling her arms round his neck and say, "Why don't you like me? Is there something wrong with me?" She made a habit of walking around the flat in her underwear or nightdress, and leaving the bathroom door unlocked when she had a bath. When Charlie began to feel that he could not hold out much longer—it seemed absurd for a man to have to lock his bedroom door—Tom Creevey's flatmate moved out and Charlie lost no time in moving in. He stayed away from Gloucester Road until he heard that the nurse had become engaged to a rich Nigerian student.

The first thing that struck Charlie when he moved from the classroom to the wards was that none of the doctors or surgeons he encountered seemed to be potential Semmelweises or Pasteurs. Some seemed more concerned with the accuracy of their diagnosis than with the recovery of the patients; these were usually the specialists. Some worked impossibly long hours and seemed to return home only to sleep. But all of them seemed to regard themselves as some kind of superior mechanic. The patient was like a car with some mysterious fault in the engine or transmission or electrical system. The problem was to pin it down and get the car back on the road. No one seemed to be very concerned with what had made it break down in the first place. Charlie found this attitude obscurely disturbing without quite understanding why.

Insight came through two cases that he encountered on the same ward. One was a skinny blonde teenager who suffered from muscular spasms that doubled her up and made her writhe in agony. She was in the ward for observation, her own GP having been unable to find anything wrong with her. Charlie overheard the sister tell a staff nurse that it was probably a demand for attention, but after he had seen the girl sweating with pain as she thrashed about on the floor he decided this was an oversimplification. Two weeks later, he was leaving the local cinema when he saw the girl sitting on a chair in the foyer looking pale and sick. She said she had just had a mild attack in the ladies' lavatory. When Charlie learned that she lived nearby, he offered to take her home. She lived in a slum street facing a builder's yard and the door was opened by a big, aggressive woman who asked Charlie what the hell he wanted. When the girl explained that he was a doctor, she became more polite and allowed him to come in. After the girl had been put to bed with a hot water bottle on her stomach, she even offered him a cup of tea.

The woman, he discovered, was the girl's stepmother. Her husband was a lugubrious taxi driver who suffered from ulcers. There were six children, three belonging to the stepmother, three to the husband. She began asking Charlie's advice about the health problems of the whole family, and when her husband had gone off to his evening shift, began to take Charlie into her confidence about her own sufferings and frustrations. Charlie pretended to listen sympathetically. In reality, he found her neurotic, selfish and rather horrifying. She seemed to him a kind of vampire, draining the emotional life blood of the whole family.

Soon after, he saw the girl in Casualty; she had a bruised cheek and a broken finger. She had told the doctor she had fallen downstairs. To Charlie, she admitted that her stepmother had hit her with a broom handle. Later that day, Charlie saw a social worker he had met at a party and told her about the case. The social worker had just left a girls' hostel where there was a vacancy. Within twenty-four hours, the girl had a room of her own in the hostel. Charlie and the social worker called on her two weeks later. The convulsions had stopped and she no longer looked pale and exhausted. The next time Charlie saw her was four years later when, as a houseman, he delivered her baby. After leaving home, her problem had never recurred. Charlie never made up his mind about the precise nature of her muscular spasms, but he had no doubt that they were in some way caused by the stepmother.

The second case involved a middle-aged woman, a doctor's widow, who was admitted to Casualty one morning with a severe burn on her forearm. She explained that she had been about to make herself a cup of Ovaltine before going to bed the previous night when the milk began to boil over. In her haste, she tripped over a rug and fell on the stove. Unwilling to call out an ambulance at that time of night, she had covered it in cold cream and bandages, taken a large dose of aspirin, and waited until the following morning before taking a taxi to the hospital. The doctor decided to keep her in the hospital for a day or two, in case of delayed shock.

Charlie had to dress the burn. He found her a lively and intelligent woman who talked a great deal about her late husband. Apparently she lived alone in a large house in a fashionable part of Camberwell. Before she left, she invited Charlie to her home to take his pick of her husband's medical books.

He went there the following day after leaving the ward. The house stood alone in a large garden that was overgrown with weeds and when the lady admitted Charlie, she was unmistakably drunk. But she was obviously delighted to have someone to talk to, and insisted on cooking him a meal. Then Charlie learned the true story. She had been drunk when she fell on the stove; so drunk that she was unaware of the severity of the burn until she woke up the next morning. And later, when he tried to leave, she told him the truth about her drinking. Her husband had been interested in spiritualism and he and his wife had made a pact that whoever died first should try to "appear" to the other. In fact, the idea terrified her so much that she made sure she was hardly conscious when she went to bed.

Charlie knew a midwife, Doris Brell, who had once mentioned that she had powers as a spirit medium. He told her the story and Mrs. Brell called on the doctor's widow. She explained that spirits seldom manifest themselves without the aid of a medium, and that she was fairly certain that the doctor would never make an appearance if he knew that it would terrify his wife. That was all that was needed. The woman stopped drinking and subsequently married a retired bank manager. Charlie was presented with her late husband's library, which included some expensive textbooks.

Both these cases gave him immense satisfaction because he felt he had gone to the root of the problem. *This* is what had always excited him about medicine—the idea that it is closely related to crime detection, and that the doctor is a kind of Sherlock Holmes. But all this remained an elusive ideal. In 1970, Charlie Peruzzi's image of himself was closer to Dr. Watson.

After the miseries of that first year, the remainder of Charlie's career as a medical student was relatively smooth and unproblematic. He took his second MB (Bachelor of Medicine) in his fifth term, and passed with excellent marks. (He was allowed exemption from the first MB because he already had the necessary A levels.) His performance in physiology and anatomy was so good that he was among the small number of students invited to spend an extra year of study to prepare for specialization. He decided against it because he was still intent on becoming a GP. The next three years were spent on the wards as a member of various "firms"—small groups of students—studying orthopedics, dermatology, pediatrics, neurology, anesthetics, obstetrics, psychiatry, ophthalmology and ENT (ear, nose and throat). His three-month period in obstetrics and gynecology was spent in the Mile End Hospital. Shortly before Easter 1972, he took his final exams and passed in all subjects, with distinctions in physiology and neurology. He applied for a houseman's job at Guys, but was not particularly disappointed to be appointed Junior House Surgeon at St. Ollaves. Then, suddenly, the post of Junior House Physician at Guys became vacant when the man who had been appointed fractured his leg and had to take six months leave of absence. Charlie was offered the post and accepted, so he spent his final year as a houseman at Guys and moved back into the Gloucester Road flat with his sister again.

In his final months as a houseman he applied for two positions in a medical practice, one in south London and one at Garstang, not far from his home. To his surprise, he was offered both jobs, but it was an easy decision to make. During the past six years he had come to love Guys and to love south London. For him, Southwark seemed full of memories of Dickens and Chaucer and the great surgeons of the nineteenth century. By comparison the north seemed raw and unappealing. In the autumn of 1974, he became a trainee in one of the largest practices in south London.

He described it as being like walking out of a sauna and plunging into an ice-cold lake. He realized suddenly that, for all his experience on the wards, Guys had been like a protective cocoon. While he was there he was learning, he had a purpose; the patients were a means to an end. Now, suddenly, the patients had become an end in themselves. All these cases of septic fingers and chest infections and sinusitis and asthma and psoriasis were no longer there to teach him to be a doctor, they were there simply to demand his healing skill. And the sheer quantity was overwhelming. On the first morning when he was allowed to take his own surgery without his trainer, Dr. Herbert Pike, he saw thirty-two patients whose complaints ranged from a cut finger and abrasions due to a car accident to myxoedema (a disease due to thyroid deficiency) and vaginal discharge. None of them were seriously ill, and he had a feeling that many of them were wasting his time. He was also dismayed by the sheer quantity of paperwork that seems to be involved in the National Health Service and for a long time found it difficult to memorize the numbers of all the various forms, a task complicated by the fact that most of them seem to have two alternative numbers. He soon began to recognize that a small percentage of patients—about a tenth of those registered in the practice, take up ninety percent of the doctor's time, returning again and again with all kinds of minor complaints. The seriously ill—those to whom he would have preferred to devote his time—hardly ever appeared in surgery and made few demands for house calls.

He soon came to recognize that most of these patients who demanded so much of his time had other problems apart from their minor ailments: stress, loneliness, boredom, domestic maladjustment. In the course of time, he became expert at sniffing out such problems and in encouraging the patient to talk about them. With women patients, the problem was often sexual in origin. One girl of twenty-two, pregnant for the third time, finally revealed that she suspected her husband of being homosexual and of having an affair with a schoolboy next door. It relieved her to tell him about it, and she cried for a quarter of an hour, but he had a frustrated sense of being unable to offer her the slightest practical assistance. When her husband came in with a sore throat and he tried to broach the subject, he was rudely told to mind his own business, and the girl appeared the next day with a black eye. But at least she was among the few cases in which he was able to get to the root of the trouble. Where most of the "chronics" were concerned, there was no specific problem, only inadequacy, inefficiency, a kind of boredom that drove them to demand attention as a bored child looks around for mischief.

He saw the problem in its most acute form in the South London Reception Centre. Known for some reason as the Wedge, this was in fact a temporary hostel for vagrants and down-and-outs. Charlie accompanied Dr. Pike there three mornings a week. What shocked him was that most of these men were not the rejects of society. Most of them were perfectly normal human beings, not so very different from the rest of his patients or, for that matter, his own family. It is true that there were a few alcoholics, a few hopelessly inadequate personalities, a few petty crooks and habitual tramps, but by far the greater number were the type you could meet in any south London pub any evening of the week. So how had they landed in this place with its drab corridors and its smell of sweat and dirty clothes? The answer frightened him. It amounted to this: that it was terrifyingly easy to slide down the social ladder and land at the bottom. Some of these men had been married and had families, then the wife had left them or thrown them out, and there was simply nowhere to go. This struck him even more forcibly when he accompanied Helen Pike, who was also a doctor in the practice, to the women's equivalent of the Wedge. Here there was a far greater age-range among the inmates, from girls of eighteen to old ladies of seventy. A large number had been prostitutes, either on an amateur or professional basis, although mostly amateur because professionals made enough money to afford flats. Whereas a male vagrant had nothing to sell— unless he was young and good-looking—a girl could always make a few pounds by offering her body. But for most of them, this was like putting on a convict's uniform. It seemed to confirm the feeling that they had landed at the bottom of the social ladder and would never climb back. Once again it struck him that these women were not basically different from the rest of his patients. (In fact, he discovered that a few of his female patients supplemented the housekeeping money by becoming prostitutes for a few afternoons a week, but these remained perched securely on the "housewife" rung of the ladder.) The only real difference was that these women now *saw themselves* as down-and-outs.

Geoffrey Elliotson, the senior member of the practice, had been a founder member of the London Anarchist Group, and was the author of a minor classic called *The Social Consequences of Anarchism*. When Charlie talked to him about the inhabitants of the Wedge, he replied that it was a consequence of capitalist civilization, and presented him with a copy of his book. Charlie found it unconvincing. It could be true that, in a better organized society, these down-and-outs might feel less sense of hopelessness. But no social change could eliminate them. They carried their own defeat around inside them. They felt like somebody who has been forced to resign from a club, and who accepts that he will never be allowed to rejoin. It was their self-image that had been damaged.

It would be untrue to say that Charlie became disillusioned with general practice. When the first strangeness had passed—that feeling of disorientation that every schoolchild experiences when he or she goes to a new school—he began to handle the problems with a certain mechanical efficiency, and life became as comfortable as it had been at Guys. A doctor is aware that he is perched on a fairly high rung of the social ladder—the equivalent of an officer in the army, or a priest in a Catholic community. Even if, like Charlie, he is of a modest and unassuming disposition, he still becomes accustomed to being treated with respect. He is a "somebody." By the end of his trainee year, Charlie was aware that a doctor's life is totally unlike anything he had imagined in his teens. Still it was pleasant enough and provided a soothing sense of financial security.

Yet there was something inside him that refused to be satisfied with respect and security. He could see that these endowed him with the authority he needed to be a doctor, yet he could never escape the feeling that this authority was, in a sense, a kind of confidence trick. The point was underlined by a case he encountered during his second year in the practice. One of his patients was a middle-aged woman who suffered agonies with arthritis in both hips. The obvious solution was an operation to replace the joints with artificial ones. The woman was a member of a medical insurance scheme which meant that she could go into a private nursing home with the minimum of delay. For some reason, she was adamantly against the idea. At first, Charlie was convinced that she was simply afraid of the operation. He went to some lengths to persuade her that there was no danger, and something like a hundred percent success rate. Then he became aware that he was encountering some deeper resistance.

When she fell and broke her wrist, he called on her several times and met her husband, a mild, bald-headed little man whose powerful spectacles made his eyes look small. Charlie tried to find an opportunity to speak to him about his wife, but he usually disappeared soon after Charlie arrived.

One afternoon, Charlie found her alone. She was exhausted with pain and had not slept for several nights. Sensing that she wanted to tell him something, he allowed long silences to fall in the conversation. And after one of these silences, she replaced her cup and saucer on the table and said, "You know he's a sex maniac, don't you?"

"Sex maniac?" Nothing seemed less likely. The husband looked as if he could be overpowered by a determined child.

She had first realized there was something wrong twenty-five years before when they were giving a children's Christmas party. Arnold, the husband, had disappeared from the room with his eight-year-old niece. Suddenly, the niece reappeared in the room with her father, who looked grim and angry. He told his wife, "Get your coat, we're going." That was the end of the party, but Arnold insisted that he had no idea why his brother-in-law was so angry. He claimed that he was sitting in the kitchen, telling his niece a story, when the father walked in and snatched up his daughter without a word. What he had failed to mention, as the woman discovered later, was that he had taken the child's knickers down.

Two years later, her husband was arrested for the first time for "interfering" with little girls, whom he met out of school and persuaded to go for rides in the car. A mitigating factor was that he never used violence.

At a certain point in these sex games, he would experience orgasm, and his interest in the children would vanish immediately. He would drop them off near their homes and hurry away.

The last time the patient had been in the hospital, for appendicitis, her husband came to visit her every day. But he was always late for the afternoon visiting period and she suspected that he was hanging around a local infants' school. The day she was discharged, he was arrested. This time he was sentenced to eighteen months, preventative detention. He explained that the temptation of passing the school as the children came out had been too much for him. He began accosting them quite openly. The surprising thing was that it took three weeks before one of the children, who had been a perfectly willing participant, mentioned it to her mother.

So now the patient was terrified about going into the hospital again, convinced that her husband would go back to his old tricks and spend the rest of his life in jail.

Charlie had to admit that this was probably an accurate assessment. He consulted a local probation officer about the case and was told that the man was too old to change his habits.

Six months later, Arnold was attacked by a wild cat he found in an old garden shed. It had seemed to be paralyzed, but when he tried to pick it up, the animal turned into a ball of spitting fur and he was badly bitten and scratched. A few days later he began to experience difficulty in swallowing and had spasms of the respiratory muscles. This was the year of the great rabies scare in south London when so many strays and wild animals were destroyed. It was a matter for instant decision, with no time for tests, so after a hasty consultation with his partners, Charlie began a course of injections with rabies vaccine. For twenty-four hours the patient was delirious. By the time Charlie was convinced the problem was blood poisoning, Arnold was on his way to recovery.

On the day it became obvious that Arnold was getting better, Charlie remarked to his wife, "Now it's time for your operation." All that he meant was that while her husband was convalescent, there would be no danger of further sexual offenses.

The woman said, "You mean he's cured?"

"Oh yes, he's definitely cured." He meant, of course, cured of blood poisoning. But from the expression of joy and relief on her face, it dawned on him that *she* thought he meant cured of his desire to assault children. Faced with the prospect of telling her this was not what he meant, he found that he hadn't the heart to do it. Pressed for further explanation, he told her that the rabies virus usually caused impotence. (He knew that the couple had ceased to have a sex life many years ago.) He admits that this was an indefensible thing to do, but says that the alternative seemed worse.

Two weeks later, the couple arrived at his surgery to tell him that she had decided to have the hip operation. The husband talked quite openly about his past record and told Charlie that the urge had vanished completely since he had "been sterilized." It was impossible to doubt his sincerity, or the atmosphere of relief and well-being that radiated from the two of them. When they left, Charlie found himself pondering the strange fact that a lie can be far more beneficial than the truth.

It was clear to him that, in this case, it was the wife's confidence that achieved the result as much as the husband's belief that he was "sterilized." For more than twenty years she had been looking at her husband with suspicion, diffusing a feeling of disapproval and mistrust. Now, suddenly, she was treating him like a favorite child. The result was that he ceased to see himself as an incorrigible little sex pervert. The relationship was reinforced by a new tenderness and mutual trust. His image of himself had changed and the problem had evaporated.

And while Charlie was still brooding on the implications of this insight, his businessman patient was cured of his erythemic rash when his daughter's car was rescued from the Surrey canal. For a moment, Charlie had a curious sensation, as if fate were taking him gently by the shoulders and forcing him to look steadily at the baffling mystery of the "confidence trick." He was still trying to understand it when he drove to London airport to meet his cousin Roberto from California. He told Roberto about it as they drove back toward Southwark, and was at first deeply impressed by his explanations about enkephalins and the placebo effect. But that night he lay awake for a long time and thought about the business-man, and the mild little pedophile, and about the woman who was afraid of seeing her husband's ghost, and suddenly he knew beyond all doubt that brain chemicals are not the answer to the mystery. It lay in the realm of something altogether more subtle and elusive, in a curious imponderable called optimism.

Thirty-six hours later, Charlie had to drive his cousin back to London airport to catch a direct flight back to California. And a few hours after that, he found himself walking along a corridor of the Park View Hotel, wondering how much he ought to tip the porter and observing with romantic curiosity the shoulder-length blonde hair of the airline hostess who walked a few yards ahead.

CHAPTER SIX

STARTING BACK to work, after his weekend at the Park View, was like waking from a pleasant dream and finding yourself in prison.

It was a cold, rainy day and the tree outside his window was shedding its leaves on to the wet pavement. It was a sign that the Indian Summer was over. He was slightly hung over, having arrived back at his lodgings at 2 a.m., and he took longer than usual to wash and shave. The result was that the yokes of his fried eggs were hard and the bacon was frizzled. Three days ago he would have eaten it stolidly, but after the Park View he found it irritating, and observed with interest how quickly one can become accustomed to luxury.

As he drove to the surgery in his secondhand mini, he thought back over the weekend. It gave him deep satisfaction to feel that he had been instrumental in solving Sharon's emotional problems and causing Roberta's engagement. Yet he was inclined to regard it as a fluke, a happy accident, and he found it almost impossible to see how Topelius's ideas could be applied to his own patients.

The practice was housed in one of those enormous concrete buildings, erected as a result of the Town and Country Planning Act soon after the war, in the innocent belief that Londoners would prefer to live in a kind of prefabricated beehive rather than in cramped but individual matchboxes. It had quickly been vandalized into a slum and reconverted into a mixture of old people's flats and council offices. Now, with its outside discolored with soot, rust stains and bird droppings, it was no more nor less depressing than any of the other remnants of that abortive planners' revolution.

It was ten minutes to nine; his surgery did not begin until nine so he went to their "recreation room," a kitchen and storeroom furnished with fold-up chairs and a large, bare table where a receptionist, a health visitor and the district nurse were already drinking coffee, and made himself a cup of Nescafé. Then, with five minutes still to spare, he opened his correspondence, mostly advertising material and reports from hospitals on patients he had sent for specialist opinions and tests. About sixty percent of these, he observed, were negative, suggesting that he was wasting the time of the hospital and the money of the National Health Service. This still

75

seemed to him one of the basic problems of general practice; the number of patients whose vague and indefinable illnesses seemed due to their mental states rather than to any physical cause. It was easy enough to see that they had difficulty coping with their lives and were compensating by becoming ill. But that made the illness no less real, it only made it far more elusive, like chasing a mouse round a room full of furniture. It was no sooner cornered behind an armchair than it made a dash under the sideboard.

The first patient that morning was a case in point. A young Irishwoman in her mid-twenties had brought her five-year-old daughter who was suffering from mouth ulcers and a sore throat. A few weeks earlier, Charlie had paid a home visit to see her seven-year-old son, who was having his first asthma attack. Their council flat, although poorly furnished, had been beautifully tidy.

Both children had been in and out of the surgery regularly for the past eighteen months, always with minor illnesses: earache, tonsilitis, conjunctivitis, bowel pains. The mother was a quiet, pale woman, efficient and hard-working, but in no way self-assertive. Apart from recurrent headaches, her own health seemed to be reasonable. During the home visit, Charlie had discovered that her husband was a builder's laborer who spent most of his time drinking with his friends. He was not an alcoholic, and had never struck his wife or beaten the children, but he paid them very little attention.

Charlie examined the child's throat and prescribed a mouthwash and some mild antiseptic tablets. He was unwilling to prescribe penicillin because the children were ill so frequently and he wanted to keep it as a last resort. Finally, feeling rather baffled he asked the mother, "How are you feeling?" It was a purely routine enquiry and he was surprised when tears came into her eyes and she said, "As well as can be expected." She turned away, as if to see what the child was doing, and when she looked back again the tears had been blinked away. Charlie pretended not to notice and went on writing the prescription. But he had recognized suddenly that the real problem in this family was not the health of the children, but of the mother.

"Problems at home?"

"No." But she hesitated before she said it.

Playing for time, he reached out and took her pulse.

"Do you have any health problems?"

"Only headaches."

"If you don't mind, I'll take your blood pressure."

As she removed her coat and rolled up her sleeve, he could feel her tension. He felt like kicking himself. Now he could see clearly that the patient, efficient exterior concealed misery and anxiety.

Her blood pressure was 160 over 110, far too high for a woman of her age. It was obvious that she was suffering from hypertension.

Now he recognized this, the picture suddenly became clear. She was alone in a strange country having been brought up in Ireland. Her husband neglected her and gave the children very little affection. Her response to these problems was to keep a firm grip on herself and work twice as hard. But the strain was building up and it was reflected in the health of her children. She needed help, yet was afraid to ask for it.

Anxious not to alarm her, Charlie explained that her blood pressure was a little too high and that the simplest way to get it down was to take more exercise. Make a habit of taking the children to the park once a day. (She admitted that she spent most of her time indoors.) Meanwhile, he would give her "water tablets" to make her urinate more often. When he suggested that she should come back after surgery the next day to discuss her problems, she agreed immediately, and he could sense her relief. And the child also seemed to sense it. As she left, she gave him a delightful grin.

That was a good beginning but it was not sustained. Of the remaining twenty-seven cases he saw during the next two hours, two-thirds were minor problems: coughs, colds, earache, boils and an ingrowing toenail. One man whose notes contained the words "personality disorder" kept him talking for half an hour about nothing in particular, and ignored every hint that he ought to leave, until Charlie was forced to take him by the arm and gently propel him to the door. A fourteen-year-old girl wanted to be put on the pill and admitted that she had lost her virginity at the age of twelve. He asked her to come back later in the week to give him time to discuss it with Dr. Pike. The only other case that gave him much satisfaction was his diagnosis of an abdominal tumor in a middle-aged Greek woman who said she had suffered from indigestion for the past month or so. Charlie made an immediate appointment with a surgeon, and when the woman asked him outright if it was cancer, he admitted that it was. He then spent ten minutes assuring her that it might well be a benign growth, and that even if it wasn't, the chances of a total cure were excellent. She went away looking much happier. It was Charlie who felt emotionally worn-out.

By the second post that morning he received a letter from a

specialist to whom he had sent a West Indian patient named Permesser. It said there was nothing wrong with the man and recommended that he should be sent to see a psychiatrist.

This case had been on Charlie's mind for the past week. He had taken an interest in the family ever since he had treated the mother for post-natal depression. She worked in an East End sweat shop and had returned to work the day after the baby was born. They lived in a block of grim high-rise flats and had trouble with their neighbors; racial slogans were often chalked on their front door. The husband had a withered right arm, the result of a childhood accident. Yet with everything apparently against them, they seemed to be a reasonably happy family. Mr. Permesser was a skilled cabinetmaker who earned a good wage. A few weeks ago he had even bought a secondhand car, in which he took the family for jaunts to Southend-on-Sea.

Then, two weeks earlier, the husband had picked up an electric sander which had been repaired by an incompetent electrician. It gave him a shock that knocked him unconscious. An examination at the local hospital established that there was no damage, but a few days later he came to see Charlie complaining of shooting pains in his chest and cramps in his arms and legs. Charlie had sent him to see the specialist. Now the result showed, as he had suspected, that the problem was mental rather than physical.

At lunch that day, Charlie joined Herbert and Helen Pike, and a new trainee called Johnson, for a bar snack in the pub next door to the surgery. They had these lunches once or twice a week and discussed their cases. Charlie had intended to tell them about his weekend in the Park View Hotel, but he began by mentioning the fourteen-year-old girl who wanted to go on the pill and they spent half an hour discussing the ethics of the matter. Charlie and Helen Pike felt that it would be sensible to give her the pill and say nothing to the parents. Herbert Pike felt the parents should be told. Johnson, to everyone's surprise, took the view that she should not be given the pill at all, because doctors should not contribute to the corruption of a minor.

Towards the end of the lunch, Charlie produced the letter about Mr. Permesser and asked their advice. All three were unanimous; the man should be told that his pains were the result of his imagination. The trainee seemed to feel that this would instantly cure him. To save further argument, Charlie agreed they were probably right, but he decided to leave the final decision until he had talked to his patient again.

In fact, the West Indian came to evening surgery. He looked exhausted, pale and miserable and told Charlie that someone had pushed a used piece of toilet paper through his letter box. He was still suffering from his chest pains, and now also had pins and needles in his legs. Looking at his sad, defeated face, Charlie suddenly realized that it would be impossible to tell him that his problems were all due to his imagination. That would only make him feel worse. The electric shock had convinced him that fate had turned against him; now Charlie could see a look of fear in the bloodshot brown eyes.

The patient asked whether he had received the specialist's report. Charlie admitted that he had, and that the specialist thought there was nothing wrong with him. As he said it, the man's shoulders drooped with an expression of weary hopelessness that was like a gesture of surrender.

Suddenly, Charlie experienced an inspiration.

"But that doesn't mean there's nothing wrong with you." The man looked up. "You say you experience cramp and pains in your muscles? You know what makes your muscles ache when you get tired?" The man shook his head. "It's a build-up of waste products, particularly a substance called sarcolactic acid. If you get really tired, these react on the central nervous system, and make you feel exhausted. Now I'll tell you what I think. I think this electric shock produced a build-up of sarcolactic acid, and it's making your nervous system react just as if you'd overstrained all your muscles."

Mr. Permesser was looking interested, almost cheerful.

"You mean I got to take a long rest?"

"Not necessarily. I think multi-vitamin tablets should do the trick. I'm going to give you a course of these, and a course of yeast tablets. I think you'll find that your pains will disappear within days."

"Hey, that's terrific!" Mr. Permesser's broad grin seemed to take years off his age. "And you really think the tablets should do the trick?"

Charlie said firmly, "I'm almost sure of it."

Mr. Permesser said admiringly, "Sercoleptic acid! That's one I never come across."

As he spoke, Charlie had a flash of *déjà vu*, the feeling that all this had happened before. Then he remembered. Sharon Engstrom had reacted in exactly the same way when he had told her that her twitch could be cured with a minor operation. Here again, in the case of Mr. Permesser, it was as if a burden had been lifted instantaneously, in the time it would take to snap his fingers. The vitamin tablets were superfluous.

Mr. Permesser was Charlie's last patient of the evening, a circumstance for which he felt grateful since it gave him time to reflect on the case as he drove back to his lodgings and to the cold supper his landlady had left in the refrigerator. As he passed a roundabout that he had passed on his way to surgery twelve hours earlier, he recalled the thought that had been in his head at the time: that it was impossible to see how Topelius's ideas could be applied to his own patients. Now he could see he was mistaken. Without conscious awareness, he had applied Topelius's ideas twice that day; to Mr. Permesser and to his Irish patient suffering from headaches. What he had done was to recognize that illness begins with a certain *inner* collapse, like letting the air out of a tire. A flat tire can be ruined in minutes by driving on it. A collapsed human being can be destroyed by almost any illness. Charlie had simply recognized that the first priority with these patients was to get some air back in the tire.

That evening, Sharon Engstrom rang him from the Park View Hotel. She was going to get an early night before flying to Bahrein in the morning. To Charlie, sitting in his small and depressing room with the gas fire burning, the Park View Hotel seemed a thousand miles away.

Before hanging up, she raised again the suggestion that she might become one of Charlie's private patients. He sidestepped the idea, pointing out that the airline already provided her with excellent medical attention, and he had the impression that she was disappointed. His reluctance was not due to unwillingness to see her again—the thought of her aroused a mixture of protectiveness and desire—but he knew that she wanted him as a kind of insurance policy, as a shoulder to cry on if new problems undermined her self-confidence again. And while she felt she needed an insurance policy, she would never learn to stand squarely on her own feet. As he said goodbye, rain suddenly began to hammer on the window and he experienced a wave of sadness that made him want to ring her back. But he resisted the temptation. He had a feeling that a closer relationship with Sharon would be a blind alley. And he already had an obscure conviction that the future was going to demand all the freedom he could hang on to.

CHAPTER SEVEN

THE PRACTICE covered an area of roughly four square miles, extending from the dockland and between London Bridge and Rotherhithe to Peckham and New Cross, and bounded on the east by Lewisham and on the west by Lambeth. Its fourteen thousand patients were under the care of five doctors, two trainees, four nurses and two health visitors. Socially speaking, they ranged from immigrants who, like the Permessers, lived three or four to a room, to businessmen, lawyers and estate agents whose homes were in pleasant little squares behind Guys, or tree-lined roads with a view of the Crystal Palace.

The oldest doctor in the practice, Sandor Kos, was a psychiatrist and, like Elliotson, a former anarchist. Born in Budapest in 1902, he had worked with Freud in Vienna, with Jung in Zurich, and with Reich in New York. Kos became a member of the practice because the others felt it would be a good idea to have a psychiatrist who was also a qualified GP. The idea had not been entirely successful at first, because Kos's flamboyant personality clashed with the other doctors, and also because he found the work load exhausting. Kos was not a prima donna but he was impatient, excitable and brilliant, and his attempt to keep these qualities in check had visibly wrecked his health. Now everyone accepted him as a privileged eccentric and a heart attack had forced him to confine himself to psychiatry, but he was still likely to shock his patients by asking them whether they had extra-marital affairs, or advising them to masturbate. Charlie found him charming and fascinating and spent as much time as possible with him surmising, correctly, that a combination of chain-smoking and an addiction to malt whiskey would sooner or later induce a fatal heart attack.

Kos's insistence that all mental problems were caused by sex at first made Charlie irritable, for it seemed so self-evidently untrue. Then he recognized that this view was an essential part of Kos's outrageous personality and he began to find it amusing. Besides, Kos could be remarkably acute. One of Charlie's patients was a beautiful girl who worked as the meals supervisor in a local school. Her pale face with its high cheekbones gave her a distinct resemblance to Marlene Dietrich, although the Irish accent somewhat spoiled the effect. Peggy was unmarried and, twice a year, in the spring and the autumn, developed severe peptic ulcers. When Kos met her leaving Charlie's surgery one day, he sighed disapprovingly and said, "That girl needs a good fuck." He pronounced "fuck" with a certain delicacy and finesse, as if saying, "That girl needs a good Tokay."

Charlie said, "I don't think she's sex starved. She's got two boy-friends." In fact, Peggy had been confiding in him that she felt she ought to have a baby by the time she was thirty, and that she was unable to make up her mind whether to marry a middle-aged sanitary engineer or a jaunty car salesman. She preferred the car salesman, but he was divorced and had to pay alimony to his ex-wife. Soon after this, Charlie read in the local paper that she had married the engineer.

Six months later she came to the surgery with her usual peptic ulcer, and raised the question of contraception. Her husband, she said, preferred the rhythm method but this made her anxious. Charlie recalled her previous statement that she wanted a child, but decided to say nothing. They discussed the relative merits of the pill and the Dutch cap, and he suggested that she should lie on the couch to be examined. As she went behind the screen to remove her underwear, Charlie said he would send for the nurse, since it was customary to have a nurse present for such examinations. To his surprise, the girl asked him not to send for a witness. "I'd feel embarrassed with someone else here." He decided she was not the type to make hysterical accusations of rape, and agreed.

She lay down with her knees bent and her legs apart, and he separated the labia with his gloved fingers. A glance inside the open vagina revealed immediately that she was still a virgin. The hole in the center of the hymen was too small to admit a finger, let alone a normal penis. He glanced at her face. She was staring woodenly at the ceiling, but the slight trembling of her legs revealed her tension. For a moment he was baffled. Why should she tell him stories about the rhythm method and interrupted intercourse when she knew he was bound to realize she was a virgin? Suddenly he understood. She was so innocent about the mechanics of sex that she had no idea that an unperforated hymen would reveal her secret.

For the first time since he had become a qualified GP, he felt a sudden acute awareness of his inexperience. No doubt the Pikes or Elliotson would have found some smooth, tactful way of telling her that they understood her problem but Charlie felt tongue-tied. The girl solved his dilemma by closing her legs and asking, "Can I get dressed now?" He recovered his poise.

"Yes, of course. In fact, I'd like you to come back tomorrow when I've had a chance to have a word with Dr. Pike. She's the expert on contraception."

At lunch that day he found Sandor Kos eating a chicken sandwich in the pub next door. When he told him about the girl, Kos said, "Ah. You should have sent her to me."

"To you?"

"Of course. I could advise her about her problem."

"But then she'd know I'd told you about it . . . "

"Why not? Confidentiality does not apply between doctors of the same practice."

"Er, no. I suppose not . . . " He could think of no tactful way of explaining why he felt it inappropriate to send a puritanical Irish girl to this forthright disciple of Freud and Reich. They dropped the subject.

The following day, as he saw a patient out, he observed Peggy sitting in the waiting room. She gave him a shy smile. Next time he looked she was no longer there. He asked the receptionist what had happened. "She's in with Dr. Kos."

He was horrified. "Did she ask to see him?"

"No. He came out and asked her to go in."

"I see." Since the waiting room was full of patients he had to make it sound the most normal thing in the world for one doctor to abduct another's patient.

For the rest of the surgery he was on tenterhooks. When he had only one patient left to see, he asked the receptionist what had happened to the Irish girl. "She left half an hour ago . . . " He repressed the urge to ask if she had looked upset.

At lunchtime he found Kos in the pub next door. He started to say, "Now look here, Sandor . . . " (for Kos went to a great deal of trouble to make sure that everyone, including his patients, treated him with informality) when Kos interrupted with a smile of dazzling Hungarian charm.

"I know what you want to ask me. Set your mind at rest. She is perfectly happy now."

"But what did you say to her?"

"I told her that you had told me about her problem—in strict confidence, of course. At first she didn't understand. I had to

explain about hymens. Then she had a good cry and told me everything."

It seemed that the girl's husband had reached middle age without
losing his virginity. On their wedding night, he had battered inef-
fectually against her defenses, then lost his courage and his excitement. That failure unnerved him, and subsequent attempts were
inept fumblings that led to mutual embarrassment and frustration.
He even confided to her his suspicion that nature had placed the
vagina in the wrong place, and that it would have been better
situated in the midst of the frontal pubic hairs.

Kos had examined her, inserted a gloved finger, and immediately
grasped the nature of the problem. Her buttocks were so small that
the normal position of intercourse was impractical. The problem
could be compared to a drunk trying to insert a key at the wrong
angle and wondering if the keyhole is blocked. The answer was to
place a pillow underneath her, and use a little cold cream to
facilitate entrance. Kos explained, and demonstrated with a
cushion.

"How did she take it?"

"Perfectly, of course. Why shouldn't she?"

"Well . . . she's a rather puritanical girl."

"Pooh." Kos waved contemptuously. "Most puritanical girls are
only shy. And why should she feel shy with a doctor? Anyway, she's
not in the least puritanical. When she left, I said, 'If you have any
problems, come back and I'll do the job myself.' "

"Good God!"

"I meant, of course, that I would make an incision with a scalpel."

"What did she say?"

"She gave me a roguish look and said, 'I'll think about it.' "

Three months later, Charlie had to admit that Kos had been right.
Peggy came to the surgery to report that she had missed two
periods, and was having morning sickness. Examination showed
that the hymen was now ruptured, her breasts were enlarged, and
colostrum could be squeezed from the nipples. A urine test verified
that she was pregnant. Charlie thought she looked healthier than he
had ever seen her. That autumn there was no recurrence of the
peptic ulcers.

The next time he joined Sandor Kos for a bar snack, Charlie told him
about his weekend at the Park View, and outlined Topelius's per-

sonality theory. But long before he had finished, Kos was pulling faces and shaking his head.

"The personality is no more than a mask. We change it a dozen times a day. When I talk to you, I am a different person than when I talk to my wife or my patients. But the sexual urge is far more powerful than the personality. Read *The Function of the Orgasm*."

"But you can't say that Sharon and Roberta were suffering from sexual problems."

"Why not?"

"Well, neither of them seemed to have any sexual hang-ups, as far as I could see."

Kos waved that aside.

"From what you have told me, I would say that the girl Roberta is in love with her father. And the same could be true of the other girl . . . " His brow furrowed in a way that usually preceded some outrageous generalization. "Most girls are in love with their fathers."

Charlie reminded him of the businessman with the skin rash, who was also one of Kos's patients. "You're not telling me *his* problem was sexual?"

Kos frowned judiciously. "My impression of Engledow is that he has sexual designs on his daughters."

Charlie threw up his hands. "Oh, come off it, Sandor! Be serious!"

"I am perfectly serious. Do you know his daughters?"

"Only Julia, the one whose car fell in the canal. She struck me as just a nice, ordinary middle-class girl."

Kos grunted. "Yes, Julia *is* rather plain. But the two younger ones are beautiful, and the youngest is a nymphomaniac. They had to send her to Switzerland to keep her out of trouble."

He went on to expound his view that, in primitive societies, fathers regard incest as their natural prerogative, and that the civilized taboo against it is unhealthy and abnormal. Charlie decided he was incorrigible, and changed the subject.

Precisely one week later, when Peruzzi was on night call, he was awakened by the telephone at two o'clock in the morning.

"Dr. Peruzzi. This is Bob Engledow. Could you possibly get over here right away?"

"What's happened?"

"It's my youngest daughter, Lesley. She's made a suicide attempt."

"How?"

"Cutting her wrists. She's in no danger, but she's hysterical. Could you bring a tranquilizer?"

He switched on his Ansaphone and checked Engledow's address in the London A–Z. It was slightly outside his usual area, on the "expensive" side of Camberwell Road. It took him only seven minutes to get there through the deserted, rain-drenched streets. The house stood on the corner of a tree-lined road, facing a park. Engledow was waiting for him at the gate, holding an umbrella. In the hallway, Charlie could see that his face looked gray and tired. He was obviously badly shaken.

"She's calmed down now. Her sister's in there with her."

Engledow's wife and daughter emerged from the sitting room; both were wearing dressing gowns. Mrs. Engledow was younger than her husband. She was slim and had enormous gray eyes; she also looked strained and depressed. Julia, the eldest daughter, was a tall girl with a healthy complexion. She looked as if she had been born to play hockey and ride horses.

It was Mrs. Engledow who showed him upstairs. A grandfather clock ticked softly at the head of the stairs; the carpets yielded softly under his feet. She said, "I'm so glad you were on duty. I've been meaning to bring Lesley to see you . . . "

"What's wrong with her?"

"She gets terribly depressed."

"Then perhaps she'd better see our psychiatrist, Dr. Kos."

"Oh no!" It was a cry of protest. "She's seen him and he didn't do any good at all. I think he made her worse."

"I'm not a psychiatrist."

"But my husband says you're a wonderful doctor. He swears by you. I don't know how you cured that rash so quickly."

He started to say, "I didn't," but she placed her finger to her lips, and quietly opened a bedroom door.

A towel had been draped over the bedside lamp so that its light did not disturb the girl who lay in the single bed, her face to the wall. The room seemed to be full of dolls, teddy bears and golliwogs, arranged along the mantelpiece and on the spare bed. A girl was sitting in the windowseat, looking out into the darkness. She stood up as they came in. She was a strikingly pretty girl with her father's controlled mouth and firm chin. Mrs. Engledow whispered, "This is Marion, Dr. Peruzzi. Is Lesley asleep?"

"No." This came from the girl in the bed. She looked at Charlie with hostility. "Why did you send for a doctor?"

"Darling, he had to look at you to make sure you're all right."

"Of course I'm all right! I'm alive, aren't I?"

Marion said sharply, "Don't be rude to mother!"

"I just want to be left alone. I don't want to see anybody."

Charlie said quietly, "Perhaps you'd better leave me with her." The two women went out without a word.

Charlie pulled up a chair close to the bed. "Could I look at your wrists?"

The girl pulled them from under the bedclothes and pushed them toward him with a gesture of resignation. Both were bandaged. Charlie removed the towel from the light, and started unwinding the bandages.

Lesley Engledow was very like her mother; she had the same enormous eyes, but they were green, not gray. She also had the same soft, vulnerable beauty. There was something about her that reminded Charlie of a small animal. She aroused an instant protective instinct. In her white cotton nightgown, embroidered with blue and yellow flowers, she looked as if she had stepped out of a fairy tale. When the bedsheets fell back he saw that the nightgown was stained with blood, and it made his heart contract. It was as shocking as seeing a slug on a rose.

The cuts on the wrist had started to bleed again. They were not deep, and he knew instantly that she had not really intended to kill herself.

He soaked one of the bandages in warm water at the sink and used it to wash away the dried blood. When the cuts were clean he could see two tiny white scars below them.

"This is not the first time you've done this?" He had to look at her before she shook her head.

"Do you want to tell me why you did it?" He decided to cover the wrists with bands of sticking plaster.

"Why should you care?"

"I'm your doctor."

She looked at him with interest. "Are you?"

He placed antiseptic pads on the cuts, then held them in place with adhesive tape. She said, "You're the one who cured Daddy?" He started to deny it, then changed his mind. "Do you think you can cure me?"

"It depends on what's wrong with you."

"I'm a bitch."

It was so unexpected that he laughed, and she was coaxed into laughing too. She had beautiful teeth, very white and regular. He realized with mild alarm that he was attracted to her.

He finished taping her wrists. "Shall I give you a sleeping tablet?" She nodded. He gave her a strong one, and she washed it down with a glass of water, holding the glass in both hands like a child. When he stood up she said, "Don't go yet."

He sat down again. She pulled the eiderdown up to her chin and sighed deeply. He switched off her lamp; the only light in the room came through the partly opened door. She said sleepily, "If you're my doctor, when can I see you again?"

"Any time you like. If you want to talk to me, the best time is after evening surgery, around eight o'clock."

"Any evening?"

"Yes, any evening."

She gave another sigh, and burrowed her head deeper into the pillow. A few minutes later, her regular breathing told him she was asleep.

Downstairs, the family was still in the sitting room, drinking cocoa. He declined Mrs. Engledow's offer to make him a cup.

"It's not serious. The cuts are only superficial. Who found her?"

Bob Engledow said, "I did. She'd gone into the bathroom I generally use. When I couldn't open the door, I burst it open."

"She'd done it in the bath?"

"Yes."

"What did she use to cut her wrists?"

"An old cutthroat razor of mine."

Mrs. Engledow said, "I always told you to keep that in a locked drawer."

"Any idea what caused this?"

"No. She came back from Switzerland last July; she'd been to a finishing school there. Now she's taking a secretarial course. She seemed perfectly happy."

"Did anything unusual happen today?"

"No. Nothing at all. It's been raining, so she's been indoors all day. She took the dog for a walk in Ruskin Park."

Charlie said, "Well, whatever it was, she seems all right now. I've given her a sleeping tablet. Call me again if you feel there's any problem."

Engledow saw him to the gate. Charlie said, "Are you sure you've no idea what caused this?"

"None whatever. It's been a perfectly normal day. She trimmed Marion's hair in the kitchen this morning and seemed quite happy. But she seemed depressed at dinner."

"Any idea why?"

"Can't think. I had an old business associate of mine to dinner. Otherwise it was the same as it always is."

As Charlie drove back, the moon was coming out, silvering the remaining rain clouds. He thought of the irony of a beautiful girl who lived in a luxury home and suffered unaccountable depressions when her father had business friends to dinner. He lay thinking about her for a long time before he fell asleep.

The next day, at evening surgery, he wondered if she was going to arrive and felt a pang of disappointment when he looked into the waiting room and saw that his last patient had gone. The following day, he had to make a house call only a few minutes away from her home and was tempted to call in, but he recognized that his motives were not entirely professional, and decided against it.

Life was too busy to waste much thought on Lesley Engledow and in less than a week, other cases had pushed her to the back of his mind. There was a middle-aged woman with thyroid problems who told him in confidence, and with every appearance of robust common sense ("I know you'll think I'm nuts"), that she was in telepathic contact with aliens in a flying saucer. There was a case of an old lady who claimed that her bruises were the result of falling downstairs, but whose domestic background suggested "granny bashing." And there was an *au pair* girl, six months pregnant, who admitted that she was not sure whether the father of her child was her employer or one of his two sons. He had spent an exhausting session with this girl, trying to persuade her that the best course was to have the baby and then send it for adoption—to which she finally agreed—when he saw Lesley sitting alone in the waiting room.

She said, "Hello."

"Hello. What can I do for you?"

"You told me to come and see you if I wanted to talk to you."

He looked at his watch; it was ten past eight, and he was hungry and tired. Tonight was his landlady's bingo night, and he was looking forward to buying himself a meal in a local workman's café.

"The trouble is, it's rather late . . . "

"Oh." Her disappointment was so obvious that he said, "Have you eaten?"

"Yes."

"Well, would you mind talking to me while I eat?"

"No, of course not."

She was evidently taken aback by the café on the corner but she received admiring looks as she sat down. Her cheeks were pink from the cold and she looked dazzling. Charlie ordered his egg, beans and chips at the counter, then joined her. They sat at a long table made by joining three smaller tables together. At the other end, two very scruffy old women were sitting over empty teacups. Opposite them, with his back to the steamy window, a vagrant was reading the *Daily Mirror*. A woman came and mopped their tabletop with a wet cloth.

She asked him, "Do you always eat here?"

"Quite a lot. The food's reasonable, and it's cheap."

The place obviously fascinated her, and he guessed that she had never been inside a workman's café in her life. Her idea of a cheap restaurant was a small Italian bistro with the menu in the window.

While he ate, they made small talk. She told him about her family. She thought Julia was "not especially bright," and said that Marion was "Okay but bossy." When Charlie said, "You seem more like your mother," she said, "Oh, God, I hope not."

He asked with surprise, "Why not?"

"She's not really the right type for daddy. She's rather vague and weak. When things get difficult she threatens to have a nervous breakdown."

"Has she ever had a breakdown?"

"Oh yes, that's how she got him. He was going off to South Africa to get into the diamond business. She had a breakdown, so he married her and took her with him."

Charlie was beginning to get a picture of her problems but he felt that a café, with someone sitting a few feet away and listening to every word, was no place to ask probing questions. So to keep the conversation casual, he asked, "Who was the business friend your father had to dinner the other night?"

He saw the shock in her eyes, and her face flushed. He looked back at his plate to give her time to recover. When she spoke, her voice was trembling.

"Who told you?"

"Your father."

"He knows, then?"

He could have said, "Knows what?" Instead he said, "No, I don't think so."

After a pause she said, "How did you know?"

"I didn't"

She said, "Could we go now?"

He had finished eating. He went to the counter and paid, then they left.

"Do you want to come back to the surgery?"

"All right."

The alternative would be to take her back to his lodgings. He had the use of the sitting room, but his landlady's son would probably be watching television.

The building was locked up but he had keys. He felt it would be too formal to sit at his desk, so he sat her in an armchair and pulled up his swivel chair to face her.

Without waiting to be questioned she said, "Desmond seduced me when I was twelve."

She wanted to talk, and he only had to be silent and keep his eyes on her face.

Her story astounded him, and it took a great deal of self-control not to show how much it shocked him. His own family background had been typically working class, and there had been a kind of natural prudery that was probably a legacy from the nineteenth century. There were no jokes about sex, and the boys and girls did not show themselves to one another in a state of undress. Charlie had always assumed that upper-middle-class families would observe the same rules, but even more rigorously. To learn that Lesley and her male cousins had exposed themselves to one another at the age of six made him want to blush and look away. He found it astonishing that she could tell him these things in such a matter-of-fact tone.

Gradually, it dawned on him that she felt she could tell him her most intimate secrets because he was her doctor, and he had a right to know everything. At first he was inclined to believe that this was because she was convinced that he had "cured" her father. But as she talked, he realized that she had no need for a reason. She simply wanted to believe that he was a combination of doctor and priest, and that he could solve all her problems. She handed him her trust like a child. He was aware that if he told her to take off all her clothes and stand on her head, she would have done it without question. Like most human beings, she *needed* someone she could believe in.

She told him about her first "affair" with a precision of detail that made it sound like an extract from a pornographic novel. Her father's partner was older than her father and he had gray hair and a kindly smile. She adored him and grabbed his hand the moment he came into the house. He brought her presents and told her long stories. She loved the smell of his tobacco and would sit on his knee in the windowseat and hide her face under his jacket collar. On her twelfth birthday, she insisted that her father should buy her a "grown up" nightie, and the trouble dated from then. As she sat on his lap, she sensed a new kind of interest in her, and was delighted. She had known about sex since she was six, and her female instinct told her why his heart was beating faster when she hid her face inside his jacket. She was perfectly well aware of the nature of the swelling that pressed against her hip. One day, as she wriggled against him, his face became red and he suddenly squeezed her tight. Then he relaxed, and she could feel the pounding of his heart. Soon, they played the game quite openly. She wriggled gently against him, then pressed herself tight against his trousers as he reached orgasm.

Their relationship changed subtly. In some way, she began to treat him as a husband. He seemed to enjoy it when she gave him orders. Her father once told her sharply that she ought to apologize for her rudeness. The game remained an unspoken secret between them. There was never any overt sex play; part of the pleasure lay in the pretense of normality. But when she felt him relax, she experienced pleasure, like a wife who has satisfied her husband.

It all ended very suddenly. One day he came to the house when her father and mother were out. Her sisters were playing tennis on the lawn. She was wearing jeans and she felt that this lessened his excitement, so as she sat on his knee, she allowed her hand to slip between their bodies. For the first time, the pretense vanished as she caressed him. Then, suddenly, he was asking her to lie on the bed, unzipping her jeans, promising that it would not hurt. She experienced pain as he entered her, but also an immense feeling of pride and fulfillment. But afterwards he said, "I'm sorry. I shouldn't have done that."

"Why? I don't mind."

He made her promise that she would never tell anyone, and for the first time she sensed that something had changed irrevocably. They had ceased to be lovers who trusted one another. Now he was a fifty-year-old pedophile and she was his victim. She could feel that he was terrified.

He still came to the house, but began bringing his wife. The first time she asked for a bedtime story, he said, "I think you're getting a bit too old for that," and her mother quickly backed him up, confirming her feeling that her mother was jealous. She felt utterly rejected, like a naughty child made to stand in the corner of the schoolroom, yet could not see what she had done wrong. She had only done what *he* wanted. It was a long time before she realized that he was haunted by the fear of spending the rest of his life in jail. Six months later, he formed another business partnership in Cape Town, and moved there to live.

Her next lover was the gardener's assistant. Both her sisters admired him because he had broad shoulders and slim hips, and she knew that Julia referred to him in her diary as "X." Julia suspected that "X" preferred Marion. One hot day, wearing only a bikini, Lesley giggled and baited the boy until he grabbed her by the back of the neck and threatened to throw her in the ornamental pond. As they struggled, she squeezed the bulge in his jeans and he suddenly became still. He allowed her to unzip him, then possessed her on a heap of plastic fertilizer bags in the corner of the gardening shed. She remembered that they felt cold against her buttocks. But, like her previous lover, he also seemed to be upset and a little shocked by the experience. He avoided her and she had to throw herself at him to overcome his nervousness. As soon as her hand crept to his fly, he was lost. One day, Julia saw them coming out of her bedroom and reported it to her mother. She never saw the gardener's boy again. Her father never mentioned the episode.

She avenged herself on Julia by seducing her first serious boy-friend, a young cavalry officer with a beautiful profile and nothing in his head. At a Christmas party, she succeeded in getting him to kiss her twice during a game of postman's knock, and wriggled her pelvis against him. Sensing that he would be shocked if she tried the direct approach she had used on the gardener's boy, she took the opportunity to establish a little-sister relation with him, asking him for hints about her tennis and badminton. And one day, when Julia was back late from her shorthand class, she found him alone and sat on his knee, asking him questions about horses. She was wearing only shorts and a T-shirt, and when she felt the familiar quickening of his heartbeat, did instinctively what she had done so many times with her father's business partner Desmond. They made love behind the settee, and she was still searching for her shorts when she heard Julia's key in the front door. She had to slip out of the window into the garden, half naked, and get into her room via the kitchen. She retrieved her shorts the next day.

Her advantage was short-lived. He showed the same curious reluctance and embarrassment that had already spoiled her two earlier love affairs, and she never had another opportunity to be with him alone. She consoled herself by seducing her partner at the dancing class, then the boy next door. That summer—when she was thirteen—she also gave herself to half a dozen young men she met at discotheques. She became pregnant for the first time, and her family had no difficulty procuring an abortion at two and a half months.

At summer camp when she was fourteen, she experienced a triumph. The muscular youth in charge of ablutions was generally admired; he had a black moustache and black curly hair, and all Lesley's friends agreed he was handsome enough to be a film star. One day, when she went to his office to ask about towels, he blushed, and she realized with a shock that he was in love with her. This astonished her, for it was generally known that he was having an affair with an eighteen-year-old traffic warden. The next time she went into his office she asked for a map of local footpaths, and as he showed it to her she leaned on his shoulder. He reddened and his breathing became faster. He began to make excuses to come past the tent she shared with eleven other girls, and she soon had the delight of seeing that the other girls noticed his infatuation. For almost a month, she played him like a fish on a line, enjoying the game of stolen glances and casual touches far more than she had enjoyed sexual intercourse with the gardener's boy. But on the last evening she felt she wanted something to remember. They slipped away from a barbecue and kissed in the bushes. She encouraged his excitement without seeming to be aware of it, then, as he kissed her, she pressed her hips tightly against him and did instinctively what she had done so often: unzipped his fly and disentangled his erect penis from his underpants. Then, to her astonishment, he suddenly lost his excitement and ceased to desire her. She asked what was the matter. He said he was afraid they might be interrupted. She suggested going somewhere quiet, but this seemed to make it worse. Then he announced that he had to go and left her. She walked on the beach, feeling miserable and sick, and suddenly hating herself. She wanted to beg his forgiveness, but realized that it was too late. He now knew her for "what she was," a little tart who was willing to have sex within fifty yards of two hundred folk-singing campers. For the first time, she thought seriously about suicide, but the sea looked too cold and lonely. She went back to her tent and cried herself to sleep. The next morning she woke up feeling that she had been involved in some awful disaster. She still hoped to see him before she left, but when she knocked on the door of his hut, the traffic warden told her he had gone into town. She thought the girl looked at her with contempt. That winter, she made her first suicide attempt with sleeping tablets. Fortunately, she washed them down with whiskey and they made her sick.

When she became pregnant again, Mrs. Pike put her on the pill. She also had a course of psychoanalysis with Sandor Kos, who concluded that she was a nymphomaniac, but told her this was nothing to be ashamed of. On her sixteenth birthday she made her first attempt to kill herself by cutting her wrists. Her family decided to send her away to a Swiss finishing school for a year. The place was known for its strict discipline, but Lesley had no difficulty in evading it.

Before she left the school, she scored her ultimate triumph and had an affair with her German professor, a serious young man in his early thirties whose wife suffered from some wasting disease. It was her father who had insisted that she should take private German lessons because she was bottom of her class. Within a week or so, she was aware that her professor found her dazzling. When she tried to encourage him, he seemed to become even more stiff and controlled, and she began to treat it as a challenge. One day, as she leaned on his shoulder looking at a book, his resistance broke down and he said "Fraulein Inkledoo, I would like you to be my wife." When she laughed and pointed out that he was already married, he became very upset. For the next two weeks, he behaved impeccably. Then, with only two weeks to go before the end of her final term, he told her one day that he was thinking of killing himself to escape his misery. She caressed his hair and was appalled when he burst into tears. Half an hour later they made love on the carpet. Then he bored her by spending the rest of the lesson solemnly discussing how he could tell his wife that he wanted a divorce. She told him that was out of the question, but he insisted that it was a matter of honor, now he had "seduced" her. During the rest of her fortnight there, he made love to her every day and continued to talk about marriage. But when she left, she had a feeling that he was glad to see her go. Moral anguish was wrecking his health. For her part, she was sorry to leave him but glad to hear the last of the interminable discussions about his wife. For her first few weeks back in England, she had been afraid that he would write or try to telephone her—even that he might arrive on the doorstep— but when it became clear that he had no intention of contacting her again, anxiety gave way to resentment. She recalled their regular lovemaking sessions in his office and felt that he had used her.

She had been in a depressed state for several days when her first lover, Desmond, came back from South Africa and began coming to the house again. She was prepared to let bygones be bygones and treat him like an old friend; she was still fond of him. But at dinner that evening, she observed that he seemed quite determined to keep the relationship formal. It was as if she was tacitly accusing him of seducing her, and he was tacitly denying that he had ever touched her. "If he'd just been friendly, it would have been all right." But this aloofness made her feel unbearably lonely, like an outcast. She tried to cry herself to sleep, but found she had no tears. Something had hardened inside her. So she took the cutthroat razor from the cupboard in her father's dressing room, then ran a bath and climbed into it. As she watched her blood staining the bath water, she felt she was dying, and experienced a drowsy satisfaction. When her father burst in, she had fallen asleep, and the water was still warm. The drowsiness was almost certainly self-induced, for the cuts were too shallow to cause her to bleed to death.

As she sat in the armchair telling him all this, Charlie could sense that she was experiencing an enormous relief that someone knew the worst about her. It seemed to him astonishing that she should treat him as a father confessor, and it filled him with a disturbing sense of responsibility. But as she talked, this gradually passed away. He could see that all he had to do was listen and nod sympathetically. So long as she accepted him as a kind of priest, he was serving his purpose.

Now he could see with total clarity what was wrong with her. She was beautiful; she had a delightful, spontaneous personality; yet she was unaware of the advantages these attributes gave her. She craved affection so much that she flung herself into the arms of anyone who showed the slightest interest in her. But when a man achieves his end too easily, he feels there must be a catch somewhere. The summer camp episode was a case in point. The boy was obviously dazzled by her; he regarded her as a fairy princess. All she had to do was to allow herself to be pursued and surrender gracefully at the right moment. But as soon as she reached down to unfasten his zipper, his illusion collapsed. The fairy princess had revealed herself as an experienced little tart.

It was obvious that the problem originated with her father. As a baby, she had adored him, but he spent so much time in distant parts of the world that she saw very little of him. And when he was at home, he always seemed preoccupied. She was jealous of her mother who absorbed the few drops of attention he had to spare when he came in late from the office and collapsed into an armchair. Julia and Marion had been more fortunate; when they were children, he had returned every evening at six o'clock and spent the hour before dinner telling them stories. By the time Lesley was born, the business had a turnover of a million pounds a year and he had no time for children.

Charlie was struck by the phrase she used about the loss of her virginity. "It hurt, but I didn't mind. There was a marvelous feeling of fulfillment." She had acquired a lover who was also a father. Now she had no need to be jealous of her mother. And then, almost immediately, she had lost him again; suddenly, he was only a middle-aged coward who was terrified that she would tell on him. What shocked her was his lack of trust. Couldn't he *see* that she would have died rather than betray him?

The affair with the gardener's boy had been motivated by a kind of malice. Both her sisters were infatuated with him, but they were inexperienced virgins. By seducing him, Lesley was demonstrating that she was more adult then they were, and therefore more worthy of her father's attention. When she described inviting the boy up to her bedroom while her sisters were downstairs watching television, Charlie wondered whether it was recklessness or just stupidity. Then he realized it was neither. She wanted to be caught. She wanted to flaunt the loss of her virginity. More important, she wanted to make her father jealous. And when he failed to call her to account, she saw it as yet another rejection. (In fact, as Charlie discovered later, Bob Engledow heard about it in South America and spent many sleepless nights before deciding not to reproach her.)

As he listened to her, Charlie had a sense of *déjà vu*. Then he realized that it was because she reminded him of Sharon Engstrom, and his own reaction was the same: the recognition that her problem would vanish if only she could *see herself* as he saw her. But there was no mirror that could reflect back her personality and make her see what he saw.

It was after ten, and he was tired. When she saw him glancing surreptitiously at his watch she said, "I'm sorry, I'm talking too much."

He could see the fear of rejection in her eyes. He smiled at her.

"Of course you're not. But I'm on call tonight, so I've got to get back."

A thin, cold drizzle was falling, but when he offered to drive her home, she refused.

"There's no need. I feel like a walk."

It was impossible to leave her there with the rain blowing in thin sheets in the lamplight.

"Look, why don't you come back for a cup of tea at my place, then let me drive you back?"

She said submissively, "If you want to."

He had an arrangement with his landlady to use the sitting room when he had guests and it was the first time he had taken advantage of it. He was hoping it would be empty, but his landlady's son, Vic, was watching television with his girlfriend. Charlie introduced Lesley, and left her with them while he went to the kitchen to make tea. When he came back, the television had been switched off and the girlfriend looked cold and hostile. The reason was obvious—Vic was unable to keep his eyes off Lesley. She had removed her coat and was wearing a green woollen dress that showed off her figure to advantage; her breasts were small and firm, and she had long, shapely legs. The girlfriend, who was plain and overweight, made things worse by staring sullenly at the blank screen and refusing to speak. Again, Charlie was struck by the irony of the situation. The girlfriend had no need to be jealous. Lesley was unaware of the effect she produced, and even if she *had* been aware, it would have made no difference; she seemed to regard her beauty as a liability.

After ten minutes, Lesley said she had to go. Charlie helped her on with her coat. Without speaking, the girlfriend went and switched on the television and ignored them when they said good-night.

In the hall they encountered Charlie's landlady, a plump, friendly woman who was proud to have a doctor as a lodger. Charlie introduced her to Lesley, and the woman shook hands. Then, without releasing her hand, the landlady stared intently into her face. She said, "I'd like to bet you were born in August."

Lesley said with astonishment, "I was. How did you know?"

Charlie said, "Mrs. Gibbs studies astrology."

"But that still doesn't explain . . . "

Mrs. Gibbs said, "I can tell you're a Leo. It's just something I know. I'm very seldom wrong."

"What's special about a Leo?"

"They bring sunshine into people's lives."

Lesley said dubiously, "That doesn't sound like me."

"Yes it is. And they're generous, good-natured and good at organizing people."

"I don't think that's me either."

Mrs. Gibbs said firmly, "They're your potentialities. You've got to develop them." She patted Lesley's arm. "You just remember what I've said. I'm very seldom wrong."

During the drive back, Lesley was silent. As they passed street-lamps, he glanced at her face, wondering if she was tired, depressed, or merely thoughtful. As they turned into the road where she lived he asked, "How do you feel now?"

"I'm fine, thanks."

He pulled up outside her house. "Not upset?"

"Oh no. I feel a lot better since I've talked to you. Daddy said you're a marvelous doctor."

He was not sure what to say, so said nothing. He switched off the engine and the headlights. She said, "I wish there was some way I could say thank you."

"You don't have to. It's my job."

"I know. But thank you all the same." As she opened the door, she leaned over and kissed him on the side of the mouth. It was obviously a spontaneous gesture of affection, the kind of kiss she might have given her father. He sat watching her until the front door closed behind her, then he drove back slowly and thoughtfully. The kiss had brought a new insight. It was soft and warm, and he could still feel the pressure of her lips against his face. It told him more than anything she had said in the past three hours. Suddenly, he had an intuitive understanding of her basic problem.

It was, quite simply, that she was the perfect mistress. She had a soft, yielding quality that made her totally desirable and feminine. There was something about her that made a man's mouth water and sent a tingle of dominance through his loins. What her kiss revealed was that her body was capable of fulfilling the promise of her eyes. And, ever since she was twelve, men had been accepting that unconscious invitation and obeying the impulse to make use of her body.

The problem was that, from the male point of view, she gave herself too easily, and so robbed them of the excitement of the chase. After lovemaking, they would probably roll off her with a sigh of satisfaction and promptly fall asleep. And her lack of self confidence meant there was no challenge to renew the pursuit. In fact, it was almost an invitation to cast her off.

If she had been a different type of girl, the answer would have been to persuade her to play hard-to-get. But in Lesley's case, it would have been pointless. Part of her charm lay in that air of vulnerability, of being willing to yield submissively to the male who ordered her to remove her clothes. Playing hard-to-get would only arouse resentment and a desire to "teach her a lesson."

Did that mean she was bound to remain a victim of her own attractiveness? That seemed a hard conclusion. Yet he could see no obvious alternative. He tried to imagine what Topelius would have to say about her and concluded that he would be just as baffled.

At breakfast the next morning Mrs. Gibbs said, "That was a very pretty girl. Is she a patient?"

"Yes."

"Nothing seriously wrong, I hope?"

"Fallen arches."

"Oh dear! There's nothing worse than flat feet. Except smelly feet. I should know—my husband had both. She's got such a lovely voice too. And a pretty smile. It's a pity about the flat feet. She'd never make a go of it on the stage."

"What stage?"

"You know, the stage in a theater!"

He was often baffled by his landlady's processes of thought. This one struck him as particularly obscure.

"Why should she go on the stage?"

"Because she's a Leo. They're all born actors."

"Oh, I don't think she is."

"What does she do for a living."

"Nothing at the moment. She's doing a secretarial course."

"That wouldn't suit her at all. Unless she's on the cusp of Virgo. But she didn't strike me as the Virgo type. Definitely a Leo. And she's pretty enough to be a film star. Reminds me a bit of Olivia Newton-John."

He thought about it on his way into surgery. It had never struck him that Lesley was in the least like an actress. But now Mrs. Gibbs had raised the matter, he could see that the idea was not at all absurd. She had a pleasant, clear voice and a poised, graceful way of moving. In spite of her lack of confidence, she was not shy. Charlie had been vaguely conscious that a secretarial course was not the best way to keep her mind occupied. Now he could see why. It was too prosaic. She needed something that would involve her more, and allow her to make use of her natural charm. The more he thought about it, the more the idea appealed.

He recalled that Patsy, the hefty young girl who made house calls to bathe bedridden patients, had a sister at drama school. He found her in the kitchen after surgery and asked her about it. Patsy's sister was at RADA, the Royal Academy of Dramatic Art, and it seemed that she had gained a scholarship against stiff competition. Before that, she had studied drama at night classes at the Regent Street Polytechnic. Charlie decided to telephone them, then forgot about it.

The following day, he was climbing into his car when he saw Bob Engledow emerging from the prescriptions department. Charlie rolled down the window to say hello.

Engledow said, "Lesley tells me she had a long talk with you."

"Yes. How is she?"

"Oh, she seems all right. But I can't tell what goes on inside her head. I wish she had more to keep her occupied."

Charlie said, "That's what I intended to talk to you about. Did you ever think of sending her to drama school?"

"Drama school!" The idea obviously startled him as it had startled Charlie. "What made you think of that?"

It was too complicated to explain, so Charlie said, "She seems to keep her feelings bottled up. If she went to drama school, she'd learn to express them."

Engledow thought about it. "You could just be right. But I think I know what she'll say—that she can't act."

"She doesn't know until she's tried."

"I suppose you're right. I'll talk to her about it."

In the event, Lesley Engledow made no such objection. The mere fact that her father was taking an interest in her induced her to agree immediately. She telephoned him two days later to say, "I'm going to be an actress."

"Good. When?"

"I've enrolled already. I start next Monday."

"Let me know how it goes, won't you?"

"Of course I will. I'll come round and tell you all about it. I'm going to get myself a slinky black silk dress and a long cigarette holder."

But the next time she telephoned, all the euphoria had vanished.

"It's no good. I haven't told daddy yet, but I'm hopeless."

"What's wrong?"

"Nothing's wrong. But I just can't act."

"You sound all right to me at the moment."

She said ruefully, "Pig!"

"Listen, come and pick me up after surgery and we'll talk."

She was sitting in the waiting room when he saw his last patient out. She was reading a book.

"What's that?"

"*You Never Can Tell.* I'm learning my part."

This time they went to the pub across the road. It was mid-week and the lounge was almost empty. He ordered beef sandwiches, enough for two since she was also hungry, and they took their cider over to the fire. While she ate, he read some of the play. She had marked her part in pencil.

He said, "This looks all right to me. I can't see what's bothering you."

"I just don't seem to be able to act."

He read a few more lines and said, "You shouldn't have to act. Dolly seems to be a bright upper-class young lady, and you're a bright upper-class young lady . . . "

"Middle-class."

"All right. But you are. So you ought to be able to be yourself."

She thought about this as she ate, then said, "That's not really true. Anybody can be themselves because they don't have to think about it. But if someone tells you to be yourself when you're acting a part, you don't know what they mean because you can't see yourself."

He said, "Let's try reading a bit. I'll read the dentist."

They started.

Dentist: That was my first tooth.

Dolly: Your first! Do you mean to say that you began practicing on me?

Dentist: Every dentist has to begin with somebody.

Dolly: Yes, somebody in a hospital, not people who pay.

Dentist: Oh, the hospital doesn't count. I only meant my first tooth in private practice. Why didn't you let me give you gas?

Dolly: Because you said it would be five shillings extra . . .

He could see what she meant. She read rather awkwardly, with a subtle misplacing of emphasis.

She said, "*You're* much better at it than I am."

"That's because I'm not self-conscious."

"Yes, but how do I stop feeling self-conscious?"

He laughed. "Have another drink."

He bought her another cider. A group of people came into the lounge, so they could not continue the reading. Instead they talked. She told him about her relationship with her sisters, and he began to understand the subtle network of family rivalries and its effect upon the way she saw herself. Julia was good with horses, and there was something about her healthy, gym-mistressy manner that seemed to attract an endless train of admirers, usually rather stolid young men with public-school accents whose mothers were probably exactly like Julia. Marion, with her direct gaze and firm chin, had passed her secretarial course with top marks, and was now secretary to a tea importer in the City. Her boyfriend was a junior partner in the firm and she made no secret of the fact that they slept together. She made it sound like a calculated part of a sensibly planned future, like buying a house and taking out insurance policies. By comparison, Lesley seemed to be good at nothing, and her life was unplanned and chaotic. She was not even the black sheep of the family, with interesting vices. She was merely a liability, the kind of girl who was sure to end up in some hopeless mess.

As he talked to her, Charlie could see that this was highly likely. Yet not *necessary*. She was likely to make a mess of her life because she saw herself as the sort of person who made a mess. Charlie was beginning to develop an interesting conviction that certain personalities attracted certain kinds of events. He had noticed it among his patients, particularly the inadequate ones. They seemed to get into the same kind of trouble again and again. And this could not always be blamed on their ineffectuality. Sometimes, their disasters seemed to be genuine accidents, over which they could have no possible control or influence. They just seemed to *attract* that kind of accident. They were sure to be walking across a pedestrian crossing when a learner driver went out of control, or alone on an

Underground platform when a gang of thugs were looking for someone to assault. It was as if their *attitude* toward themselves attracted disaster.

The bar was beginning to fill up. He said, "Come on back to my place and have a cup of tea. Then I'll take you back."

"I hope that girl won't be there."

"She won't. Vic tells me she's chucked him."

The sitting room was a chaos of wires, and Vic was on all fours behind the television set. He said, "Can you pass me that aerial lead! No, the white one. Don't fall over that camera, it cost six hundred quid."

Vic was an expert in electronics and worked for a TV and hi-fi shop in New Cross. His was a highly skilled job, and at nineteen he was making more money than Charlie at twenty-nine.

"Is that your camera?"

"It will be when I've paid for it. Can you hand me that screwdriver?"

Then minutes later, when Charlie came back from the kitchen with the tea, Vic said casually, "Let's see what's on TV tonight." He pushed the button that switched on the set. A moment later, to Charlie's astonishment, Lesley's face appeared on the screen. She was saying, "Well, I had rice crispies, then egg and bacon and two cups of coffee. Then—Oh, I can't think of any more to say!"

Vic's voice said, "Okay, tell me what you did when you'd finished breakfast."

"Let me think. I cleaned my teeth . . . "

"Don't you clean your teeth before breakfast!"

"No. What for? I'd get them dirty again." They both laughed. Vic said, "Let's run it back." The screen went blank.

Charlie asked, "Is the film expensive?"

"Videotape? Eight quid for three hours."

Charlie looked at Lesley, and suddenly felt his chest tighten with a curious excitement.

"Could you film her reading her play?"

Lesley said, "He doesn't want to waste film on me."

Vic said, "It wouldn't be wasted. You can use it again." Charlie could see that he was entirely in favor of anything that improved his acquaintance with Lesley.

Charlie sat beside her on the settee, and handed her *You Never Can Tell.*

"You read Dolly, I'll read the dentist."

"Her brother comes in in a minute."

"I'll read him too. Vic, say when you're ready."

Vic said, "Okay, off you go."

In the quiet of the room, with no sound but the soft hum of the video camera, and Vic peering professionally from behind it, they both experienced a flow of adrenalin, as if they were stepping on to a stage before a silent audience. This time, Lesley read normally and naturally, with the emphasis in the right places. They began to warm to it. She read her first long speech with a breathless, bubbling spontaneity that seemed to transform her. As he read, Charlie experienced the same sense of exhilaration that flooded over him when he knew he had solved Sharon's problem. He felt that it was no coincidence that Vic had been setting up a video camera as he and Lesley walked into the room. It all had a sense of rightness, as if it had been prearranged. He was too cautious to allow himself to believe that he had solved Lesley's problem. Yet the way she was reading made him aware that fate had presented him with an important part of the answer.

Mrs. Gibbs came into the room while they were reading. Vic placed a finger to his lips and pointed to the armchair. Lesley, halfway through a speech, glanced up and went on reading. If anything, the audience improved her performance. When they reached the end of the first act, half an hour later, Charlie closed the book, and Vic said, "Good, *ve-ry* good."

Mrs. Gibbs said, "Don't she talk beautifully?"

Lesley blushed. Vic pressed the rewind switch.

"Let's hear it back."

Lesley said, "Could you really bear it?"

"That was the whole object of the exercise."

Vic and Mrs. Gibbs came and sat beside them on the settee. They sat and watched themselves. What fascinated Charlie was that, from the opening words, they both sounded like professionals. The occasional fluff made no difference; they recovered immediately, with a certain natural aplomb. Charlie was aware that being "on camera" produced a vital tension that raised them above the mere mechanics of intonation and voice production, and made them feel that they *were* the characters they were speaking. As he listened, it flashed into his mind: "*That's* what causes neurosis. It's a loss of vital tension!" That was what was wrong with Sandor's conception of neurosis. He thought it was due to one cause: sex. In fact, anything could cause it, any discouragement that produced the "sinking feeling." And the result was a "vicious circle" effect, the sinking feeling causing more discouragement, the discouragement producing more of the sinking feeling. Sharon had been rescued at a single stroke, by the knowledge that her tic could be cured by a simple operation. And Roberta, like Lesley, had been rescued by playing a game, acting a part. Play acting, he could now see, was a way of trying on a new personality, exactly as a woman might try on a new hat in front of the mirror.

He was aroused from his reflections by their laughter. It reminded him that he ought to be paying attention. What had amused them was some piece of naive impertinence, delivered by Lesley with a childish air of innocence. The part of Dolly obviously suited her; she obviously enjoyed playing the *enfant terrible*. It struck him suddenly that Lesley sounded more like Lesley when she was playing Dolly than when she was "being herself." And this insight opened up vistas of speculation. If she was more like herself when she was playing Dolly, it followed that she was less like herself when she was being Lesley. That sounded absurd, but it was obviously true. He could *see* it was true as he watched the screen.

And then the answer burst upon him and made him tense with excitement. He glanced at the Lesley sitting beside him, watching with amusement the Lesley on the television screen, and saw clearly that there were two Lesleys. Lesley as she thought she was, being herself, and Lesley as she would like to be: charming, naive, infuriating and serenely indifferent to rebukes. And as Lesley watched herself on the screen, she could see the kind of person she wanted to become.

So Topelius was wrong. He had said, there is no mirror in which you can show people their own personalities. But there was such a mirror. It was called the television screen.

And for anyone who could interpret its message, this television was broadcasting all Lesley's secret problems and anxieties. For example, when Lesley read the part of Gloria Clandon, Dolly's elder sister, she made her sound cold and unsympathetic, which clearly reflected Lesley's attitude towards her own sisters. When she read Mrs. Clandon, Dolly's mother, she made her sound a boring nonentity. But when Dolly spoke about her father, who had deserted the family when she was a baby, there was an unmistakable note of emotional involvement in Lesley's voice.

The television screen went blank as the tape ended. Vic said, "*Very* good. Very good indeed."

Lesley colored with pleasure. Charlie asked her, "Do you still think you can't act?"

Mrs. Gibbs said, "Of course she can act. All Leos can act."

Lesley said, "I didn't think I could . . . "

"Well, now you know better, don't you?" Mrs. Gibbs patted her on the head. "Anybody feel like a cup of tea?"

Charlie stood up. "I'm afraid we ought to go. I've got to drive Lesley back home."

He could see all three of them were disappointed, but he was impatient to get her alone.

As they drove down the Old Kent Road he said, "Do you still want to give up drama school?"

"Not if you think I shouldn't."

"I *know* you shouldn't." They had stopped at a traffic light, so he could look at her face. "And I can tell you something else. If you *did* decide to give it up, you'd upset your father more than you've done so far."

She glanced at him quickly. "How do you know?"

He let the lights change before he answered.

"Do you know why your father didn't get angry with you when you went to bed with the gardener's boy?"

"Because he didn't care, I suppose."

"No. Think again."

She said, after a pause, "I don't know."

"Because he knew you wanted him to be angry. He felt you were trying to gain attention by behaving like a naughty child, so his reaction was to refuse to give you attention. And that only made you behave worse than ever. So he sent you off to Switzerland. Your reaction was to attempt suicide. His reaction was to feel you were attempting emotional blackmail. Don't you understand? It's a kind of vicious circle. Every time you've made a bid for attention, he's turned his back on you, and your reaction is to try and go further still." He paused, to see if she wanted to interrupt. She said nothing. "Isn't that true?"

She said softly, "Yes."

He pressed his advantage. "Now, for the first time, you've broken the vicious circle. You've started at Morley College and you tell him it's something you really want to do. For the first time, you're beginning to behave like a responsible, grown-up person, somebody with ambitions and a mind of her own, instead of like a spoiled brat. And you're beginning to get the kind of attention you've always wanted, because he's beginning to see you as someone he can take seriously, instead of a naughty child. He *wants* to give you love and attention, but he doesn't want to feel he's being blackmailed into it. So can you imagine how he'd feel if you told him you'd decided to give it all up after a few days?"

She said nothing. After a moment, he glanced at her, and saw to his surprise that she was crying.

"What is it?"

"Nothing." Her voice was choked.

He let her cry; finally he said, "Have I made you miserable?"

She wiped her face on her sleeve. "No. You've made me happy."

A lump formed in his throat, and he had to make an effort to control the emotion that rose in him. By frowning and concentrating hard, he succeeded in repressing it. Suddenly, he understood what she was feeling. For eight years she had been trapped in a vicious circle and now, all at once, she could see how to break out of it. And it was his own words, chosen almost at random, that had shown her the solution. It was this realization, combined with relief and excitement, that had brought him close to tears.

He reached for the box of paper handkerchiefs on the back seat and handed it to her. She blew her nose, then, with an obvious effort to keep her voice level, she said, "Did *he* tell you all that?"

"No. He didn't have to. I saw his face the other night when you'd cut your wrists. He looked as if he'd had about as much as he could take . . . "

This time he let her cry. He could see she was crying away years of frustration. He stopped the car fifty yards away from her house and switched off the ignition and the headlights. She mopped her face with a wad of paper handkerchiefs.

"I suppose I look a horrible mess."

"A bit damp, that's all."

She looked at her watch. "They should all be in bed now, thank God." She blew her nose again. "You must think me an awful bore."

"You know I don't."

She reached for the handle of the door.

"Thank you for everything."

"It's my pleasure."

She put her arms round his neck and kissed him. This time, he turned his mouth towards hers. He felt he deserved that much. It confirmed what he already knew: that nature had designed her to give pleasure. He thought of the German professor who had made love to her on the carpet, and experienced a flash of envy. Then, as he watched her walk down the street and turn into her front gate, the excitement subsided to be replaced by the sour taste of frustration. But this also vanished as he drove home, composing in his head the letter he meant to write to Erik Topelius.

This letter remained unwritten. He arrived home to find a message from the employer of the pregnant *au pair* girl; she was suffering from violent stomach pains. Charlie immediately suspected an attempted abortion and this was confirmed when he drove to the house; the girl was bleeding from the vagina. She showed him the plastic tube she had inserted into the neck of the womb. He asked her how far it had entered and, when she showed him, concluded that it had probably ruptured the peritoneum. Before the ambulance arrived, she had started to abort and was screaming in agony. Charlie had to make a difficult decision: whether to send the ambulance away and wait until the miscarriage was over, or to risk moving her. Finally, in spite of her pleas, he decided to send her to the hospital. He had intended to drive behind the ambulance, but she begged him to stay with her. He delivered the fetus on the way to Guys—the baby was already dead. Then he had to take a taxi back to where he had parked his car. The next morning, he learned that the girl had developed peritonitis. It was almost a week before she was out of danger.

That night, when he climbed into bed, he fell asleep without giving further thought to Lesley Engledow and her problems. The life of a general practitioner allows little time for reflection.

CHAPTER EIGHT

ON THE morning of Monday, January 1st, 1979, Charles Peruzzi sat at his desk at ten minutes to nine, holding a mug of hot coffee in an attempt to warm up his fingers before he began prodding patients in sensitive areas of their anatomy. Outside, snow was thick on the ground, and the surface of the Surrey canal was a sheet of ice.

The telephone rang; the switchboard girl said, "It's Mr. Engledow."

"Put him through."

"Good morning, Charles." They had been on first name terms since Christmas, when Charlie had attended a party at their house. "I'm ringing to ask if you'd be interested in taking on a private patient."

He said cautiously, "I suppose so . . . if he's in my area."

"He's not, exactly. He lives in Denmark Hill, but I think you might find it worth your while."

"What's his name?"

"Ben McKeown."

"*The* Ben McKeown?"

"That's right."

Even Charlie had heard of the financial "whiz kid" whose name was always being associated with takeover bids.

"What's wrong with him?"

"Ah, that's the point. There's nothing wrong with him. It's his son Nick. He keeps getting into trouble . . . "

Charlie's heart sank. He knew Bob Engledow regarded him as some kind of miracle worker. So far, he felt, luck had been on his side, but he had a gloomy conviction that Engledow's next demand would reveal his limitations.

"What kind of trouble?"

"Trouble with the law. To be honest, if it wasn't for Ben's money, the boy would be in a reform school by now."

With a sense of being trapped, Charlie said, "He sounds as if he needs a social worker or probation officer more than a doctor."

"He needs a good psychiatrist."

"But I'm not a psychiatrist."

113

"Well, you did wonders for Lesley."

That was the problem; Engledow expected him to do wonders. He said, "Yes, but I was called in as her medical adviser."

Engledow said earnestly, "Charles, I believe in you. I don't think you realize how good you are."

Charlie looked at his watch; it was almost nine o'clock. He said resignedly, "What do you want me to do?"

"Could you ring him now, before he leaves home?"

"Wouldn't it do later? I'm just beginning surgery."

"I'd be grateful if you could manage it now. He's hoping to see you today."

"All right. I'll do it right away."

"Thank you Charles. You won't regret it."

Engledow preferred to call him Charles. To his generation, a "Charlie" meant a person of low intelligence with more than his share of accident-proneness. Charlie felt rather like that as he dialed McKeown's number.

A voice snapped, "Hello, what is it?"

"Mr. McKeown?"

"Speaking!" He sounded like a schoolmaster urging a backward pupil to get to the point.

"This is Dr. Peruzzi. Mr. Engledow asked me to ring you."

"Ah yes, of course, Dr. Peruzzi! Nice of you to call." The voice suddenly became caressingly friendly, as if he had recognized Charlie as a companion of his boyhood.

Charlie's recognition that he was talking to a multi-millionaire made him very nervous. He had never addressed so much money before. He said, "Bob Engledow said it was about your son."

McKeown sighed. "That's right, my boy Nick. He's really being a pain in the arse."

"What's the problem?"

"He's due to appear in the Camberwell Magistrates' Court at eleven this morning. He's charged with attacking a police car."

"How?" Charlie had visions of a juvenile delinquent with a machine gun.

"He emptied a pot of paint over the windscreen."

"That doesn't sound too serious."

"No, but he did it right after he'd been put on probation for breaking and entering. So they may feel he's due for the high jump."

"What do you want me to do?"

"I'd like you to meet him and talk to him. Bob told me about what you did for his daughter. Do you think you could meet me at the Magistrates' Court at a quarter to eleven?"

"I suppose so . . . Where is it?"

"D'Eynsford Road—that's right opposite Camberwell Green. You can't miss it. A big building standing on its own. I'll see you in the downstairs entrance hall, by the information desk."

"I'll be there."

"Okay doctor, look forward to it . . . "

He hung up. Charlie felt as if he had been talking to a Hollywood film magnate, or a general commanding the forces of NATO. On the telephone, McKeown's voice sounded a little like rapid gunfire, as if he was waiting to snatch up another telephone and buy a million shares in Middle East Oil.

To Charlie's relief, surgery was over shortly after ten. The deep snow had probably kept patients at home. He walked across the reception room and knocked on Herbert Pike's door. He knew Pike was a magistrate and wanted to ask his advice. But Pike still had a patient. Charlie went to the recreation room to make himself coffee, and there met the senior partner, Geoffrey Elliotson, a tall, quiet, modest man who was adored by all his patients because he hated to say no, and was inclined to give them whatever they asked for. He had even been known to finance down-and-outs from the Wedge.

Charlie said, "Do you know anything about Ben McKeown by any chance?"

"A bit. Why?"

Charlie told him about his telephone conversation and his appointment at the Magistrates' Court. Elliotson said, "Come back to my office."

In his office—the largest and untidiest of the practice—he fumbled among a pile of old magazines and newspapers for a few minutes, and finally produced a copy of *Freedom*, the newspaper of the London Anarchist Group. He opened it to a center page and handed it to Charlie. The headline said, "The Pirate King of Lombard Street." There was a photograph of a middle-aged man with a bald head and an unmistakably Jewish nose, apparently in the act of striking a photographer. The photograph made him look like some prehistoric monster lunging in for the kill.

The article that followed was less complimentary than the headline. It gave a brief biography of McKeown, beginning with the statement that he was born in the East End of London in the next street to the Kray twins. His father had been called Steinberg, but he had preferred to adopt the name of his mother's second husband, Jamie McKeown, a Belfast Irishman. As a teenager he had somehow acquired a stake in an East End gambling club. At the age of twenty-two, he had married a rich woman who was ten years his senior, and had subsequently used her money to make a fortune in property during the building boom of the early sixties. He had then acquired for himself an evil reputation in the City by buying up semi-bankrupt companies and "asset stripping," selling off the viable parts at a profit and throwing the rest away. As a friend of a Tory ex-minister, he had been pilloried in Parliament by the Labour government, with the aim of embarrassing the opposition. By a series of brilliant financial maneuvers, he had extricated himself from the property market before it collapsed, leaving a number of close associates in serious trouble. In 1971 he had been cited by a bandleader as correspondent in a divorce scandal, but had flatly declined to marry the lady whom he had compromised. His wife subsequently forgave him. The bandleader's ex-wife sued him for breach of promise, produced highly compromising letters in court, and won heavy damages. Like a rubber ball, McKeown bounced back, sold African grain to the Russians, bought heavily into oil shortly before the first price rise of 1973, successfully survived a government investigation that accused him of illegal dealings, and announced a fifteen million pound profit in 1974. The article concluded by saying that even among the ruthless predators of the City, Ben McKeown was the kind of man who gave capitalism a bad name.

Charlie said, "They don't seem to like him."

"I don't think that even his own mother likes him." From a man as mild as Elliotson, these were harsh words.

"What would you advise?"

"Find out what it's all about, but don't commit yourself. Remember that people like McKeown love to get something for nothing."

"But he's a millionaire!"

"That's why he's a millionaire."

The Camberwell Magistrates' Court was less than ten minutes away, opposite Camberwell Green. It was a big, gray modern building that stood alone facing the north end of the Green. He parked behind a cream-colored Bentley whose engine was running. A uniformed chauffeur was sitting behind the wheel, reading a newspaper.

Charlie was five minutes early, but McKeown was already waiting at the information desk. He was smaller than Charlie had expected, and younger. The picture in *Freedom* had done him an injustice; there was nothing fierce or belligerent about his appearance. The face was sallow, and he was almost bald. Rimless glasses gave him a studious appearance, and behind them, the eyes were mild and brown. The voice, with its slight cockney accent, had a pleasant, throaty intonation.

Charlie said, "Mr. McKeown? I'm Charlie Peruzzi."

"Ah, nice to meet you." McKeown gave him a vigorous handshake. "You're younger than I expected."

There seemed to be nothing to say to that, so Charlie only nodded.

"Come and meet Nicky."

The boy was sitting across the hallway, next to a gray-haired man in a pin-striped suit, who was obviously his solicitor. McKeown introduced them. The boy stood up and shook hands sullenly. Charlie got the impression that the solicitor had been telling him some unpleasant truths. The solicitor, whose name was Brookes, was an English public-school type: tall, rather good looking, with a pleasant, smooth voice and an upper-class accent.

Nick McKeown's handshake was loose and damp. He had his father's sallow complexion and large brown eyes, but his black hair was thick and wiry. He was taller than his father, and considerably overweight. The mouth was sensual and the face flabby and self-indulgent. Charlie's first impression was that he looked like what he was: a spoiled juvenile delinquent.

Mr. Brookes said, "I gather that you're a psychiatrist?"

"No, I'm just a general practitioner."

McKeown said impatiently, "We'll talk about that later."

Brookes looked at him reproachfully. "I'm going to have to tell the magistrates that Nicholas is under the care of a psychiatrist. Now I gather that he's not."

McKeown said, "Nicky doesn't *like* psychiatrists. Dr. Peruzzi's a good man. He was recommended by a friend I trust."

Brookes asked Charlie, "Would it be totally inaccurate to say you are a psychiatrist?"

Charlie felt that they wanted him to stretch a point.

"Oh no. In fact, I attended a psychological conference only last month. All doctors have to know something about psychiatry."

Brookes seemed relieved. "Good. We'd better go upstairs. The police officer in charge of the case will want a word with us."

The courts were on the second floor of the building. This was the first time Charlie had ever been in such a place, and he found it impressive and a little menacing. The concourse was crowded with policemen, solicitors, and a number of subdued individuals who were obviously defendants and their relatives. Brookes led them into a small, bare room. A few moments later, a police sergeant came in. He and Brookes obviously knew one another, and they got down to business immediately.

"You're not asking for a remand?"

"No."

"Pleading guilty?"

"Yes."

"Right. In that case we shan't ask for it to go to Crown Court. Of course, the magistrates might decide to send it there anyway."

Brookes said smoothly, "Oh, I shouldn't think so. Not if you put in a good word for him. He's been pretty cooperative hasn't he?"

The sergeant glanced at Nick McKeown, who was glowering at the floor. Charlie felt a flash of impatience. If the boy had any sense, he would have looked up and tried a disarming smile. This display of sulkiness was stupid. He noted the ironic expression on the sergeant's face as he said, "Yes, I suppose you could say that. Not that he had much alternative."

"No, no, quite. But we shan't raise any problems if you don't."

The sergeant glanced at Charlie. "Is this gentleman going to give evidence?"

"Oh no. He's the boy's doctor."

McKeown spoke for the first time; his tone was conciliatory.

"Any idea what he might get, Sergeant?"

The sergeant glanced at Nick McKeown and, for a moment, Charlie saw the dislike in his eyes.

"My guess is six months in a detention center."

McKeown said in agony, "Christ, no!"

The sergeant shrugged, said, "See you in court," and went out.

The boy had gone pale.

"Does he mean they'll send me to jail?"

Brookes said, "It's not a jail. It's more like an army camp."

McKeown said in sudden fury, "You get him off."

It was the wrong thing to say to a man like Brookes. He looked back coldly and steadily. "You can't manipulate the law as you can manipulate the City. He'll have to take whatever sentence the magistrates decide is appropriate."

McKeown's anger collapsed into a sullen resentment, and for a moment he looked curiously like his son.

"I'm paying you to do your best."

"And I'll do my best." Brookes was cool and suave. Although his eyes did not betray a flicker of triumph, Charlie could sense that it gave him a quiet satisfaction to put McKeown in his place. McKeown sensed it too; he reddened, and Charlie looked out of the window and pretended to be studying the traffic around Camberwell Green.

Brookes turned to Nick McKeown.

"Now, you'll be in court in a few minutes. Try to keep your head up and look at the magistrates. If you stare down at your hands, you'll *look* guilty." The boy scowled. Brookes tried a different approach; he said more gently, "You're an intelligent lad. Try to let them see it. If the police make any mistakes in their evidence, don't hesitate to say so. But do it politely and respectfully. Don't get angry or resentful."

McKeown said, "He's talking sense, lad. Pay attention to him."

The boy said wearily, "Yes." Charlie caught himself hoping he got the maximum sentence.

The case was called ten minutes later. Brookes preceded them into court. The public gallery was crowded. Nick McKeown glanced around nervously, but his father walked to his seat looking grimly ahead, like a man walking to the scaffold.

It was all over so quickly that Charlie felt cheated. He had expected drama, but this was more like a business transaction. Nick McKeown stood in the dock. The three justices were facing him on the bench: two middle-aged men who looked like tradesmen and a thin tired-looking woman with a beaky nose. The clerk of the court, who sat in front of the bench, asked the sergeant if he wanted a remand. The sergeant said no, he would like the case dealt with immediately. The defense solicitor was asked the same question. He said his client wished to plead guilty. The police sergeant took his place in the witness box and read his evidence. On December 9, at 11:30 a.m., Nicholas David McKeown had maliciously caused damage and defacement to a police car parked outside the Magistrates' Court, and had shouted obscene abuse at the police sergeant and woman police constable who had been inside. The first thing he had noticed, he said, was blue paint running down the center of the windscreen, then he saw hands smearing it all over. He jumped out of the car and grabbed the defendant, saying, "What do you think you're doing, you little swine?"

"Bastard," said Nick McKeown from the dock.

The magistrate in the middle looked outraged. "I beg your pardon."

"He said bastard, not swine."

"That is immaterial. Proceed."

The sergeant completed his evidence, and added that the policewoman was unable to be present because she was at present in the hospital, having been assaulted by a drunk. The magistrates nodded sympathetically.

The magistrate asked the boy if he had anything to say for himself. He shook his head and said, "No," then added "Thanks" as an afterthought. Charlie could see that he was recalling Brookes' advice to be polite, but it sounded like insolence.

"Any previous convictions?"

The sergeant said yes, the defendant had stolen a motorcycle when he was fifteen, and had wrecked it, and had been charged with stealing a car one year later, although on this occasion he received an absolute discharge. On the previous December 9th, he had appeared in the juvenile court in the same building on a charge of breaking and entering, committed when he was still under seventeen. A psychiatrist had convinced the magistrates that there were extenuating circumstances. McKeown was under emotional stress because of the temporary separation of his parents, who had considered divorce. He was found guilty, but sentenced to Community Service in a local youth club and adventure playground. On leaving the court, the defendant had noticed the large pot of blue paint hanging from a ladder and had seized it and emptied it over the windscreen of the police car waiting outside the juvenile court. He had made no resistance when arrested, although when the sergeant had ordered him to clean the paint off the windscreen, he had reacted by trying to smear his hands down the sergeant's uniform. He had been taken to the local police station and allowed out on bail.

Mr. Brookes now made a short speech, which he kept deliberately low-key. The present offense, he said, was obviously due to the same emotional stress which had been accepted by the juvenile court as an extenuating circumstance. His parents had still been separated at the time of the offense. Now they were together again, so the cause of his emotional stress had been removed and he, the defending solicitor, was reasonably certain that there would be no repetition of this type of behavior.

The woman magistrate asked if the psychiatrist was in court. The solicitor said that he was unfortunately not present but that the boy's doctor, who also had psychiatric qualifications, was in court. Charlie experienced a moment of panic as he thought he might be called as a witness. McKeown also looked worried. But the magistrates evidently had no time for general practitioners. They conferred with the clerk of the court in low voices, then the magistrate in the middle announced that, in view of the damage to the police car, the defendant would be fined two hundred and fifty pounds. He would also be granted a conditional discharge. As he said this, the boy looked up with an expression of delighted astonishment and, for a moment, the magistrate looked as if he was regretting the lightness of the sentence. He frowned sternly and told the boy that if he was charged with anything else during the next three years, he would also be sentenced for the present offense. Charlie observed with irritation that the boy allowed himself a slight smile as the magistrate was speaking, and again found himself wishing that the magistrate had imposed the maximum sentence. A few minutes later they were all outside the courtroom. Ben McKeown was smiling with obvious relief. Nick McKeown wore a sly, rather sullen expression. McKeown squeezed Brookes' arm.

"That was really great! Thanks."

Brookes smiled coldly.

At that moment, the police sergeant came out of the court. McKeown rushed over to him and said, "Sergeant, I want to tell you that I'm going to contribute a hundred pounds to the police fund as some small compensation for your car."

The sergeant said thank you then saw, to his horror, that McKeown was pulling a wallet out of his pocket. He said stiffly, "If you'd hand it to the lady on the desk downstairs . . . "

He hurried away, looking embarrassed. Brookes caught Charlie's eye and raised his eyebrows. McKeown said disgustedly, "For Christ's sake."

Brookes held out his hand. "I'll say goodbye now. I've got another case." He shook hands briefly with McKeown, nodded at Charlie, and walked away without glancing at Nick McKeown. It was obvious that he had no desire to spend a moment longer than necessary in the company of the two McKeowns.

In the lift, McKeown looked sternly at his son.

"Remember what the judge said, one more slip like that, and you'll be in real trouble. And next time I'm not going to hire an expensive lawyer to get you out of it!"

"Yes, *all* right." Nick McKeown sighed, as if he was being outrageously persecuted.

Charlie glanced surreptitiously at his watch. "I'm afraid I have to leave you."

McKeown looked at him with amazement. "Leave? We haven't talked yet. I thought we could talk over lunch."

"It's rather early for lunch."

"That's all right, I know a place where we can eat as early as we like."

For the first time, the boy showed signs of interest in the proceedings. "Great! I'm starving!"

McKeown eyed him sourly.

"You are going back home!"

"Aw, Dad . . . "

McKeown suddenly got angry. "Listen, what do you think this is? You made me waste a morning in the lousy courtroom. You cost me two hundred and fifty nicker, and another five hundred for a lawyer. Not to mention the police fund . . . " This jogged his memory; he turned and went back to the information desk, took out two fifty-pound notes from his wallet and laid them on the counter. "Miss, this is for the police fund. The sergeant said to give it to you." The girl looked bewildered and was obviously about to raise some objection. McKeown turned his back on her. He said over his shoulder, "Don't forget to tell him I kept my promise." He glowered at his son, and turned on the anger as if flicking a switch. "And then you think you can say, Dad, I'm hungry, how about something to eat? What the hell do you think I am?" His voice rose to a shout of indignation that made passersby turn and stare at them. Charlie felt like cringing.

He was surprised to see that Nick McKeown seemed genuinely upset. He looked like a small boy who has been smacked by his father and is trying hard not to cry. They had arrived at the chauffeur-driven car; the chauffeur climbed out and smartly opened the rear door. McKeown said, "Alec, take Mr. Nick back home, and then come and call for me at the River View at two o'clock. Okay?"

Nick McKeown climbed in with his face averted. Without giving him a further glance, his father said, "Come on. Let's find a taxi."

Charlie said, "We could go in my car." He pointed to it. McKeown looked at the grimy red mini without enthusiasm.

"I like to stretch my legs. Let's grab a taxi."

They found one at Camberwell Green. Charlie looked back with regret at his own car. It struck him as typical of McKeown's disregard of other people that he should force Charlie to return to Camberwell for his car, when it would have been perfectly easy for Charlie to have driven behind the taxi until they passed the surgery. He experienced a sudden urge of irritation that crystalized into intense dislike of Ben McKeown. As they drove towards the City, his chief concern was how to explain, as politely as possible, that he did not feel qualified to become Nick McKeown's psychiatrist. He now regretted not finding some excuse to decline lunch. It was precisely one hour since he had met Ben McKeown, and his one thought was how to terminate the acquaintance as soon as possible. Both the McKeown's struck him as wholly unlikeable, but the father was the worst of the two: crude, boorish, insensitive and totally self-centered.

He expected McKeown to talk about his son. Instead, he began to discuss Bob Engledow, then asked probing questions about Lesley. It was clear that he wanted Charlie to take him into his confidence about her whole case history. When Charlie explained that there were certain things he could not discuss because of medical etiquette, McKeown switched his line of questioning to Charlie's own background. Charlie was aware that he did this with some skill, making it look as if this was simply friendly interest in someone he liked. In fact, it soon became clear that McKeown wanted to know about him to discover how far he could manipulate him. Since Charlie was now quite determined to end the acquaintance as soon as possible, he answered openly and freely, feeling that it made no difference anyway.

The restaurant had a good view of the river from London Bridge to Blackfriars Bridge; they could hear the rumble of trains from Cannon Street station. The white rooftops gave the City a magical appearance. They were the first in the place. The manager asked them to wait in the bar until the waiters had finished preparing the tables; McKeown looked irritable, but agreed.

"What'll you have?"

Charlie asked for a dry martini. He had decided that if he was going to be forced to waste the next two hours with a man he couldn't stand, he may as well enjoy himself.

McKeown said, "Well, I'm going to break my rule and have a drink. I usually don't touch it during the day, but I feel I deserve one." He ordered himself a double tomato juice with vodka.

They took their drinks over to a corner table. McKeown said, "Now, about that kid of mine."

The taste of the martini brought back the weekend in the Park View. Suddenly, Charlie began to feel relaxed. He listened quietly as McKeown began to tell him about his problems with his son—for most of which he seemed to blame his wife, and other indulgent women in the family.

As he listened, Charlie found himself wondering what Topelius would think of Ben McKeown. "You know my methods, Watson; apply them . . . " According to Topelius, what a man didn't say was just as important as what he said. He began to observe McKeown with deliberate detachment, as if he were a specimen in a glass cage. The thought crossed his mind that McKeown was, in fact, rather like certain poisonous snakes and spiders that he had seen under glass in the zoo; perhaps a tarantula or gaboon viper. The difference was that he was allowed to wander freely in society, stinging anyone he liked. For a moment, Charlie found himself beginning to sympathize with Geoffrey Elliotson's radicalism.

He observed the way McKeown used his hands to drive home his points, how his eyes tended to wander round the room every time someone came in, how he wagged his forefinger to underline statements about which he obviously felt some misgiving. It struck him that McKeown was not as self-confident as he pretended to be, and that much of his air of self-assertion was designed to cover this up. And as he watched McKeown ordering the meal, it struck him suddenly that this man's whole world was based upon dominance, the need to impress himself upon other people. Deciding on what to eat for lunch was a game of dominance, like any other. When the waiter came the first time, he explained that he had not yet had time to look at the menu, and asked him to come back in ten minutes. But during that ten minutes, he ignored the menu, and made sure that Charlie ignored it by talking all the time. When the waiter came back a second time, he pretended to be surprised, glanced at the menu for several minutes, then asked the waiter to come back again. When he returned a third time, McKeown had still not decided what to eat. He studied the menu slowly, made several decisions and then changed them immediately, enquired whether the asparagus was fresh in a manner that suggested he knew he was going to be cheated, and then finally dismissed the waiter with a condescending wave of his hand. As the man was going away, he called him back by snapping his fingers, and asked if he could see the wine waiter. The whole performance seemed designed to inflict the maximum humiliation without ever stepping beyond a certain limit into downright rudeness.

Watching all this, it struck Charlie that the photograph in *Freedom* had managed to catch the truth about McKeown's personality. He *was* a predator. He felt he lived in a Darwinian world of survival of the fittest, a jungle world where he might be attacked at any moment. People were either his enemies or his servants, and even servants were not to be trusted. McKeown's world smelled of blood; its most basic emotion was fear. It was an oddly barren and dreary world, apparently devoid of emotions like generosity or affection. But what it seemed to lack, above all, was the quality of disinterested intellectual curiosity that had driven Dr. Grimshaw to study plants and herbs, and which had been the driving force behind Charlie's desire for a medical career.

He made another observation that struck him as interesting. There was a definite resemblance between Ben McKeown and Martha Morton-Jones. Both had the same manner of relentless, non-stop talking, pursuing a method of free association that made interruption difficult. But it was not merely the method that was the same; there was some curious underlying similarity in their personalities. Once again, Charlie Peruzzi was struck by an observation he had often made before but never tried to crystallize in words: that personalities seem to run in types, as if God had decided to take a shortcut when he was handing them out. People of completely different types would have one or two odd features in common; a way of raising an eyebrow, pursing the lips, narrowing the eyes. But in many cases, it was even subtler than that, as if the underlying *structure* of the personality was the same, like some basic family characteristic that you could recognize in fathers and children and aunts and nephews, even though they all looked quite different. He found himself thinking: it's as if personalities came in construction kits . . .

Halfway through the first course, McKeown said suddenly, "What do you think?" That seemed a fair question, since Charlie was eating his food and drinking his wine.

"About Nick?" McKeown nodded. "He's given you a lot of trouble, and an outsider like myself can see why. What you've got there is what the Americans would call a 'negative feedback situation'. I noticed the same thing with Lesley and Bob Engledow. She wanted attention and misbehaved to get it. That annoyed him, so he didn't want to give her attention—he felt she was trying to blackmail him into it. So, in effect, he turned his back on her. Then she'd do something even worse to force him to pay attention."

Now Charlie discovered that there was one important difference between Ben McKeown and Martha Morton-Jones. When McKeown wanted to know something, he could stop talking. He merely listened and absorbed, nodding and making interested noises to maintain the flow of information. And because he was still feeling basically irritable and hostile, Charlie spoke with a certain bluntness, not particularly concerned if it caused offense. In fact, if McKeown lost his temper and told him to mind his own business, so much the better. It would make it easier to extricate himself.

"You say the trouble began when Nick was nine." McKeown nodded. "Now if I remember rightly, that would be in 1971, the year you were involved in that divorce scandal?" McKeown looked startled, but nodded. "So that could have been the point when he began to feel he had to choose between his mother and you?"

McKeown said defensively, "I didn't see much of him before that."

"No, but he probably looked upon you as the father figure in the background, the person he ought to love and admire. And then, suddenly, he sees your name in the newspapers, cited as co-respondent. He can see that it's hurting his mother. The boys at school probably make dirty jokes about it." McKeown winced. "He can't imagine what you've been doing, but it must be very bad to cause all this fuss—bad and rather dirty, like the things the boys do behind the public lavatory. And then one day, you find that your bed has been filled with burnt matches . . . "

McKeown grimaced. "Dr. Sagamore thought that was very symbolic." Dr. Sagamore was the boy's previous psychiatrist.

"By the way, what happened to Dr. Sagamore?"

"He said he couldn't take any more."

"Why? What did Nick do to make him drop the case?"

"He removed the nuts from the front wheel of Sagamore's car." McKeown's face betrayed a gleam of satisfaction.

"Dangerous."

"Not so very dangerous. The wheel came off in our drive and went bowling off down the road. A car won't go far without a front wheel."

"All right, not so dangerous. Like filling your bed with burnt matches when he could have set it on fire. He doesn't really want to harm anybody, just to express his resentment."

"But *why*, for Christ's sake? I've given him everything he's ever wanted. I've offered to buy him a car when he's passed his test, and if that's not generous, I don't know what is, when he's wrecked my car."

Charlie returned to his steak; he found McKeown's problems depressing and uninteresting. McKeown also ate in gloomy silence for a while. Finally he said, "You tell me what to do and I'll do it."

Once again, Charlie was suddenly taken aback by the realization that he was regarded as a wonder-worker. It was flattering but frightening. It dawned on him that McKeown had treated him with a certain respect, and that this was because he believed that Charlie had some secret method of achieving miracle cures. He said, "I can't tell you what to do without talking to Nicky."

"All right. When can you talk to him? This afternoon?"

He realized that he was committing himself, and felt irritated that he was not sticking to his resolution to turn down the case.

"I can't do that. I've got several house calls to make."

"All right, make it this evening after surgery. I shan't be there, but I'll tell my wife to expect you."

He said cautiously, "I'd like to ask you a few more questions first."

"Go ahead."

"Does Nick have any hobbies?"

McKeown grimaced. "Reading Superman comics and watching videos!"

"Nothing else?"

"Not that I know of. He used to play a bit of chess."

"Does he still?"

McKeown shrugged with repressed irritation. "I don't know."

"Don't you think that might be the trouble—that he doesn't have enough to occupy his mind?"

McKeown shrugged wearily. "There's an old saying: you can lead a horse to water but you can't make it drink."

They were interrupted by the waiter, who said, "Your chauffeur is waiting downstairs, sir."

Charlie was surprised that the time had passed so quickly. McKeown said, "Tell him we'll be down soon." He asked Charlie, "Coffee and brandy?"

"No thanks."

Now, he felt, was the moment to tell McKeown that he could not accept the case. But before he could speak, McKeown had beckoned to the waiter and asked for the bill. Then he excused himself to go the toilet. When he came back, he paid the bill with a Diners' Club card. While Charlie was still trying to find the right way of putting it, McKeown looked at his watch and said he had a phone call from Buenos Aires coming through at two-thirty. A few moments later, they were outside in the cold air. It was snowing again. McKeown snapped his fingers and the car drew up in front of them. The chauffeur jumped out and opened the door. McKeown said, "Take the doctor back to his car outside the court." He turned to Charlie and held out his hand. "Nice to have met you. I'll ring my wife and tell her to expect you this evening. What time would suit you?"

Charlie said, "I have to get a meal after surgery . . . "

"Don't worry about that. My wife'll have something for you."

A few moments later, Charlie found himself being driven back toward Camberwell in McKeown's Bentley. He was feeling pleasantly warm and relaxed, full of good food and wine. The chauffeur said, "What time this evening would suit you?"

"Oh, don't bother. I'll drive myself there."

The man said respectfully but firmly, "Mr. McKeown gave instructions that you're to be picked up from your surgery, and taken back afterwards. And if I don't do exactly what Mr. McKeown tells me, he tends to get a bit annoyed."

Charlie sighed. "All right. About a quarter to eight, I should think."

"I'll be there at seven-thirty, sir, just in case."

"But I don't want to keep you waiting."

"That's what I'm paid for, sir."

As Charlie drove back to the surgery from Camberwell, he understood why McKeown had no love of minis. After the Bentley, it felt cheap, cold and cramped.

At six o'clock that evening, Bob Engledow rang.

"What did you think of Ben McKeown?"

"A rather overpowering personality."

"Oh, he's all right. You'll get to like him better."

When he came out of the surgery that evening, the Bentley was waiting in the concrete space reserved for doctors' cars. As he climbed into it, Helen Pike, who was just unlocking her own mini, widened her eyes and gasped, "Blimey, get *you!*"

The road had turned into a sheet of ice, but the Bentley moved over it as comfortably as over soft gravel. Charlie relaxed in a corner, his feet on a padded foot-rest, and amused himself by imagining he was a company director being driven to a board meeting.

It was a large Victorian house standing in its own grounds in a cul-de-sac overlooking Ruskin Park. The outside had been so carefully restored that it produced a slightly bewildering impression, as if a fragment of the London of Dickens and Wilkie Collins had been deposited in south Camberwell by some freakish time slip. The butler who opened the door looked as if he belonged to a slightly later period, but still only just within the twentieth century. The inside of the house preserved a careful balance between Victorian décor and modern comfort.

Mrs. McKeown shook hands with him. She was a willowy, soft-voiced woman whose accent was upper-class without being obtrusively genteel. This aroused Charlie's interest; both Ben McKeown and his son had a distinct Cockney intonation. This implied that, subjected to the influence of both parents, Nick McKeown had unconsciously chosen to model himself on his father.

Mrs. McKeown said, "Ben said you wouldn't have eaten, so there's a snack waiting in the dining room. Would you like to eat before you talk to Nicky?"

The dining room was enormous, and the "snack" laid on the corner of the great oak table was a three-course meal, with cold consommé, half a lobster with mayonnaise and a fresh fruit salad. There was also a cheese board. Charlie knew nothing about wines, so had no way of knowing that the 1966 Chateau Lafite he was drinking had cost Ben McKeown £30 a bottle at auction. But as he sat alone in the silent dining room, lighted by a chandelier, he had no doubt whatever that he was being deliberately spoiled. He found himself wondering how a man like Ben McKeown, with his crude and unsubtle approach to human relations, could have attracted a woman like Mrs. McKeown, and concluded that he must possess qualities that were not immediately apparent.

He was pouring the last glass of wine when Mrs. McKeown came in and asked him if he had enjoyed the meal. He said he had, and did not mention that it was the first time he had ever eaten lobster. She suggested that he should bring his wine into the next room. There was a log fire in the grate, and a single lamp over the rocking chair in which she sat.

"Before you speak to Nicky, is there anything you'd like to ask me?"

"Yes. Does he know I'm coming?"

"No."

"Has he ever had any physical problems—any chronic illness?"

"He suffers from asthma."

"In that case, I'd rather he thought you'd called me in about his asthma. I've got a feeling he doesn't like psychiatrists."

"He hates them."

"Has he had many?"

"Four, if you count the lady doctor who tried to help him when he was ten."

"What happened to her?"

"She got married."

"Did he like her?"

"Oh yes, he adored her."

"And the other three?"

"Dr. Raikes, Dr. Hubner and Dr. Sagamore. He hated all three. They finally had to give him up becaues he wouldn't talk to them. And of course, he tried to kill Dr. Sagamore."

"Do you think he wanted to kill him? Or was it just a practical joke?"

She raised her eyebrows. "If it was a joke it was a very dangerous one." She took a deep breath. "Let's be frank, doctor. I love Nicky because he's my son. But I'm not inclined to make excuses for him. I know perfectly well that if his father hadn't been a rich man, he'd be in a Borstal institution by now. And I'm not sure he wouldn't be better off there."

"Why do you say that?"

"Because I sometimes feel desperate about what's going to hap-pen to him. You know that he was sentenced to community service last month? He was supposed to work at the local youth club. He went there just once, and then announced he hated it. He had a violent attack of asthma—he seems to be able to turn them on at will—and his father went to see the organizer of the youth club and made a huge donation. Of course, they're delighted to have the money, and they're not going to report Nicky for failing to do his community service. When he went to court today, I was actually hoping they'd sentence him to a Borstal institution." Her voice started to break, but she controlled it. "Yet even so, I don't know that it would do him any good. It might just make him worse. I've no idea *what* might help. All I know is that at the moment, he seems to be bent on some kind of self-destruction."

Charlie could understand her frustration. He knew precisely what she meant. Nicky McKeown had devised his own way of coping with reality; to defy it, and then rely on his father to bail him out of trouble. With a slum boy, a "short, sharp shock" might have been the answer. But for someone who had been indulged as long as Nicky, it would probably only make things worse. He felt that the McKeown's were trying to saddle him with an insoluble problem. Yet there was something about Mrs. McKeown that excited an immense sympathy and a desire to help. As he listened to her, he could understand why Ben McKeown had married her. Her face was lined and pale, and her eyes look tired, but the mouth, which was full and gentle, expressed a quality of kindness and enormous patience. After speaking to her for ten minutes, he no longer saw her as a woman in her fifties. A younger personality seemed to be pushing out from below her skin.

As they were talking, Nicky came into the room. He was wearing a red track suit.

"Ma, do you know what that woman did with my head cleaner?"

She said patiently, "No dear, I've told her she's not to go near your videos."

He gave a deep sigh, as if tried beyond endurance, and started to go out again. She called him back.

"Do you know Dr. Peruzzi?"

"Yes."

It would have been impossible to say it with less enthusiasm.

Charlie said, "Could you spare me ten minutes, Nicky?"

He looked irritably at the clock. "Does it *have* to be now?"

His mother said firmly, "Yes, dear."

He shrugged with a bad grace. "Okay." He slumped into an armchair by the fire. Charlie said, "Could we go up to your room?" This obviously encountered some deep inner resistance. Finally, the boy said, "I suppose so," and dragged himself to his feet.

But as he followed the boy upstairs, Charlie was not unduly pessimistic. When two people speak to one another, there is an adjustment between their personalities that cannot be expressed in words. A thousand subtle pressures set up a system of interlocking balances. Even in their brief exchange, Charlie sensed that the boy did not see him as an authority figure. He was aware that most people found him likeable on first acquaintance. Nicky was suspicious because he regarded Charlie as a tool of his parents but he was not basically hostile.

The boy's bedroom was large and comfortable, with four huge loudspeakers in the corners and a thirty-inch television screen facing the end of the bed. There were gramophone records and cassettes all over the floor, and a shelf containing videotapes above the bed. The door into the bathroom stood open. It looked as luxurious as the bedroom, with a deep pile carpet and polar bear rug.

Charlie said, "This is comfortable." The boy grunted. Charlie moved a pair of running shoes from a chair and sat down. "It's about your asthma." Nicky glanced at him ironically, but said nothing. His disbelief was obvious. Charlie took his lack of comment to be a subtle form of politeness.

For the next ten minutes, Charlie asked medical questions. The boy showed him his nasal spray, a box of glass capsules of amyl nitrate, and a bottle of tincture of lobelia. It emerged that a series of tests had established that he was allergic to several kinds of pollen, horsehair and hamsters. The original attacks had been traced to pet hamsters he had been given for his birthday; these had to be taken away.

Charlie asked about the circumstances of the attacks. As he expected, they were most frequent when he was on bad terms with his father. When they approached the subject of Ben McKeown, the boy became tense and cautious, and Charlie could sense an underlying resentment. At one point, he thought he was about to be told to mind his own business. As soon as he steered the conversation into other channels, the boy answered readily enough. He never put more into a reply than the question warranted, but he showed no sign of boredom or irritation. Gradually, it dawned on Charlie that Nicky McKeown was lonely, and that answering silly medical questions was better than having nothing to do.

All the time they were talking, Charlie was asking himself how Topelius would have approached this problem. He would undoubtedly have studied the room, looking for clues to Nicky's personality. Charlie began to take a mental inventory. The bookshelf in the corner contained mostly comic books—Batman, Superman, Spider-man—and copies of *Private Eye*. The only two books were *The Lord of the Rings* and Golombek's *Championship Chess*. The videotapes above the bed were mostly comedies, with the Pink Panther figuring prominently. There were also three James Dean films: *East of Eden*,

Rebel Without a Cause and *Giant*. In a corner, between the wardrobe and the wall, there was a chess table that looked like an antique. The ivory chess men were obviously Chinese, with dragons in place of knights and chariots in place of rooks.

"Do you play a lot of chess?"

"No."

"Why?"

"Nobody to play with."

He tried another approach, "What kind of things make you laugh?"

Nicky thought about this carefully. "Batman, Inspector Clouseau, the Goodies . . . Lennie Bruce. Do you like Lennie Bruce?"

"I've never heard him."

The boy crossed the room, selected a record from the rack, and put it on the turntable. The track that followed was a sketch in which a father tries to convince his son that condoms are balloons. Nicky wore a faint smile. Charlie realized that this was designed to shock him. In fact, it was so like the humor he had become accustomed to at medical school that he found it funny. In any case, the room was warm, the wine had made him glow with well-being, and it was pleasant to relax and listen instead of asking questions. When the side came to an end, Nicky asked, "What do you think?"

"He's very good." He felt this was a pardonable exaggeration. He looked at his watch. "I suppose I'd better be going."

The boy said nothing, but Charlie could sense that he was unwilling to be left alone. To gain time, Charlie looked through the videotapes on the rack. He pointed to *East of Eden*.

"Is James Dean any good?"

The boy looked at him with amazement. "Haven't you ever seen him?"

"No."

"Christ!" He seemed incredulous. "Feel like watching some of it?"

"Well . . . I don't like to keep your father's chauffeur waiting." In fact, he was thinking about having to get up at seven in the morning.

"He's paid to wait. Anyway, Alec plays poker with George until two in the morning—that's the butler. When he's not screwing Mary—that's the maid who hides my videos."

The boy put the tape into the machine and switched it on. Then he climbed on to the bed, propped himself against the wall with a duvet round his knees, and switched off the light. Then, as a second thought, he switched off the video with a remote control device, and picked up the bedside telephone.

"Is Alec there? Alec, it's Nick. What time do you want to go to bed? Yes, I want to show him a James Dean movie. Okay? Thanks a lot, Alec."

The call showed a consideration that Charlie had not expected. Clearly, the boy was not as self-centered as he appeared to be. Charlie was beginning to find him likeable.

Nicky settled down again and switched on the video machine.

Charlie found the film revelatory. It took him precisely one minute after Dean's first appearance to recognize certain of Nicky's mannerisms—a way of glancing sideways, of wrinkling his forehead, of lowering his head as if walking into a rainstorm. He glanced cautiously across at Nicky; the boy was watching the screen with the absorption of a child listening to a fairy tale. Charlie could almost imagine him with his thumb in his mouth. When Charlie expressed bewilderment about the intricacies of the plot, he explained it with a precision that showed he knew it by heart. But he talked only when lesser characters were on the screen; as soon as Dean appeared, he watched with rapt attention.

Charlie's mind was only partly on the film. He was reflecting on what he had learned, and wondering how he could make use of it.

It was shortly after half past two when he left the house. The night was freezing. As the Bentley was about to turn out through the gateway, they were dazzled by oncoming headlights. A moment later, Ben McKeown climbed out of the taxi and came over to the car.

"How's it going, doctor?"

"Very well."

"Did you learn anything?"

"Yes, I think so."

McKeown leaned in the window. "Alec, would you mind leaving us alone for a few minutes?"

That, Charlie thought, was typical of McKeown. He was a man who wanted quick results.

The chauffeur switched off the engine and headlights, and climbed out of the car. McKeown moved into the front passenger seat, and switched on the interior light.

"Well, what do you think?"

Charlie took a moment to think about it, wondering where to begin. He said, "The most obvious thing is that he's lonely. Doesn't he have any friends?"

"No. I don't know why, but he doesn't seem to want to mix with boys of his own age."

"That's because he thinks of himself as a loner, like James Dean."

"Who the hell's he?"

"He's a film star who died in a car crash in the fifties. He used to be the idol of the young."

"Yes?" McKeown's tone of voice implied: so what?

Charlie said patiently, "I believe that James Dean is the key to Nicky's problems."

"How?"

"Ever since this morning I've been wondering about that episode with the police car. Why should he walk out of court and empty paint over its windscreen? Most teenagers feel intimidated in a courtroom. You'd expect them to behave themselves for a few days afterwards—especially if they've got off with a light sentence. Well, this evening I found out the answer. It wasn't Nicky who was being sentenced—it was James Dean. And it was James Dean who walked out of the courtroom, saw the pot of blue paint hanging on the ladder, and decided to show just what he thought about judges and police courts."

"Did Nicky tell you that?"

"Not in so many words. He didn't have to. He showed me a James Dean film, and it was obvious. He's identifying with Dean. He sees himself as the misunderstood rebel. He thinks nobody cares about him, nobody takes the trouble to find out what he's thinking. Especially you. He really thinks you don't give a damn."

McKeown said irritably, "Oh, for Christ's sake." Then he checked himself and took a deep breath. Charlie said, "Don't take my word for it. Borrow the films when he's not in. They'll tell you more about Nicky than I could."

McKeown said, "All right. So where does that get us?"

"I don't know yet. I've got to think about it."

"But you think you can solve it?"

Charlie realized he was being pushed into committing himself further than he wanted. But he gave the answer that McKeown obviously wanted to hear.

"I think so."

CHAPTER NINE

As HE was about to leave the house the next morning, he found a letter on the hall carpet and recognized Lesley's small, neat writing. He opened it in the car.

"Dear Charles (Lesley had adopted her father's mode of address): The bellated (sic) Xmas present just arrived, and daddy says I'm not to mess about with it until you can help me as you said you would. Is this evening any good? Cd you leave a message with yr receptionist? We can give you supper. Much luv, Lesley."

There was a PS: "We have all been wondering what happened to you since Xmas."

The "bellated Xmas present" was a video camera, which her father had promised; it was a week late because it had to be ordered.

He thought about it as he drove to the surgery. It had been clear since Christmas that Lesley had decided she was in love with him. He knew it was the usual "transference phenomenon," the patient falling in love with the doctor, but to call it by its Freudian name made it no less perplexing and disturbing.

It was Marion, the Engledow's middle daughter, who was really to blame. She had opened the door to Charlie on Christmas Eve, a glass of champagne in one hand, and still laughing at some joke. She helped him off with his overcoat, then gave him a push under the mistletoe, and kissed him. Her lips were still pleasantly cold from the champagne. After a long, hard day tramping through the snow, it was a delightful sensation to be kissed by a shapely girl who obviously enjoyed it. Her lips made his head swim, and he concluded that this must be a family characteristic. The sounds of the party came through the open door, but since they were alone in the hall, neither made any attempt to end the embrace. Then Lesley's voice said, "Hey you, put him down!" They broke apart, and before Marion had picked up her champagne glass, Lesley was in his arms, kissing him hungrily. To demonstrate a sporting attitude, Marion went out and closed the door behind her. The sounds of festivity

137

receded. Lesley's lips parted, so he could taste moistness, and she suddenly pressed her pubis hard against him, releasing a tingle of delight. This broke some kind of psychological barrier between merely kissing and preparing for the act of lovemaking, and his loins responded with masculine promptitude. Then the party noises suddenly became louder, and Lesley broke away. Charlie took another minute or so to remove an unwanted hankerchief from his overcoat pocket, and his heartbeat was almost back to normal when a slightly tipsy Bob Engledow, wearing a paper hat, said, "Hello doctor, come and join the orgy!" (Before the evening was over, all the Engledows were addressing him as Charles.)

That Christmas Eve, Charlie experienced the agreeable taste of success. The Engledow women—including Mrs. Engledow—flirted with him, and treated him as if he was in some way their discovery and their property, while other women regarded him with undisguised interest. Soon it became clear that Engledow had been talking about him before he arrived, and had given the impression that he was some kind of medical celebrity. A handsome, gray-haired old lady backed him into a corner and said, "Now tell me, what exactly *is* this discovery of yours?"

Charlie said cautiously, "Discovery?"

"Robert said you went to some medical conference and caused a sensation with some new idea." He tried a modest disclaimer, but she was persistent. "What do you call this discovery?" Charlie had an inspiration. "I call it personality surgery."

"What on earth is that?"

Charlie said, "Well, briefly, it's the recognition that the personality can be altered by a kind of plastic surgery."

A good-looking young man, whose hair was already streaked with gray and who had apparently been a business acquaintance of Bob Engledow, asked, "And how do you set about it?"

Charlie could sense an underlying resentment. The young man seemed to regard himself as engaged to Marion. Since he had just consumed his third glass of champagne, Charlie was inspired to improvisation and said, "You start off by breaking down the personality into its constituent parts."

"You make it sound like a motorcar."

Charlie, possessed by a sudden insight, replied, "So it is."

When he left, at two in the morning, Lesley came with him to the gate. She said, "Merry Christmas," and suddenly stood on tiptoe and kissed him firmly on the mouth, then turned and went indoors without looking back. The gesture said "I love you" as plainly as her earlier interruption had said, "Let him alone, he's mine."

It was interesting to receive practical confirmation of his theory that Lesley was intended by nature to be the perfect mistress. Her kiss was, quite simply, an invitation to possess her. As they stood in the hall, he had realized that if they had been alone, he would have raised her dress, pushed down the briefs he could feel through the thin cotton, and lowered her gently to the carpet. There would have been no question of asking her leave. There was a yielding quality about her that made a male feel she belonged to him.

And that was what was so dangerous. Once, when he was fitting a shapely fifteen-year-old with a contraceptive device, it had suddenly struck him that it would be perfectly natural to climb on the couch and penetrate her (it is a myth that doctors never experience sexual excitement under such circumstances,) and the realization of how easy it would be—and therefore how flimsy the barrier between respectability and professional disgrace—had defused his excitement as effectively as a bucket of cold water. But thinking about how pleasant it would be to make love to Lesley aroused no inhibitions, and was therefore far more perilous.

He was reasonably certain, of course, that her parents would not object if he became her lover. He had a feeling that her mother would even welcome it. Lesley needed to settle down, or, better still, to get married. And that was the problem; he had no desire to be anybody's husband. Ever since that weekend at the Park View Hotel, he had experienced an obscure but stubborn conviction that, like a bloodhound, he had caught the scent of an important discovery. Getting involved with Lesley would be pleasant but irrelevant. That is why he had made no attempt to contact her since Christmas.

He reread her letter while drinking his coffee before surgery. It was not true that he had promised to help her set up the video-camera. What he had suggested was asking Vic Gibbs to help. On the other hand, it could hardly do any harm to go to her house for supper. The important thing was to make it clear that he was her doctor, not her lover.

Halfway through surgery, Ben McKeown telephoned. The telephonist said, "I asked him to ring back later, but he said it was important."

"All right. Put him through." He asked his patient, an old lady suffering from arthritis, "Will you excuse me for a moment?"

McKeown said without preamble, "Could you go and see Nicky again this evening?"

"Why?"

"I had a word with him this morning. You're doing him a lot of good. He's taken a liking to you."

"Good."

"It's damn good. He hated the other three. My motto is, strike while the iron's hot. Will you give my wife a ring and tell her what time you'll be arriving?"

He started to say, "I don't know . . . " when McKeown interrupted him. "There's a call on the other line. See you later." He hung up.

The old lady's presence prevented him from cursing aloud. He relieved his irritation by picking up the telephone and telling the girl, "If Mr. McKeown rings again, don't put him through. That last call wasn't really important. Find out what he wants first." He banged it back on to the cradle.

In the kitchen afterwards, he met Geoffrey Elliotson. Elliotson asked, "How did you get on with the millionaire?"

"He was worse than you said."

"They always are. Coffee?"

Charlie was glad of an opportunity to talk.

"He's one of the most irritating people I've ever met. He seems to enjoy making people dance to his tune. Not for any reason. Just for the sheer pleasure of it."

Elliotson said thoughtfully, "I've met quite a few like that. They're born manipulators. That's their real driving force, the desire to manipulate people."

"Yes, but I wouldn't mind so much if he was an *efficient* manipulator. But he's not." He told Elliotson about the performance with the waiter in the restaurant. "That didn't serve any purpose at all. It was just a kind of sadism, like a boy pulling wings off flies."

Elliotson shrugged. "Of course. He's basically a criminal type, but he does it on such a big scale that he gets away with it." He went into a discourse on the evils of capitalism. Charlie nodded and pretended to listen, but his attention was elsewhere. Of course, Elliotson was right. McKeown *was* a criminal type. And his son secretly admired him, so his son was a criminal type too. What else could you expect? He wondered how McKeown would react if told that unpleasant home truth.

It was a busy day. There was a "flu" epidemic, complicated by some new stomach bug that caused diarrhea. By the time Charlie had finished his surgery that evening, he was so exhausted that he felt like going straight back home and climbing into bed. He had totally forgotten about Lesley, and it was not entirely a pleasant surprise to find her sitting in the waiting room. The only other occupants were two long-haired youths, who were eyeing her with undisguised lust.

She said, "I was just passing by, so I thought I'd come and collect you."

"I'm afraid I can't come. I've got a call to make."

The disappointment in her eyes made him feel a brute. He said, "Let's go and have a drink first."

He took her to the pub next door and they sat close to the fire with halves of cider. She was looking subdued and depressed, obviously suspecting that he wanted to avoid her. He asked her, "Do you know Ben McKeown's son Nicky?"

"Ugh!" She made a noise like a dog being sick.

"Don't you like him?"

"I can't stand him. He smashed my favorite doll and poured Julia's Chanel No. 5 down the sink."

"It's Nicky I've got to go and see this evening."

"I didn't realize you knew him."

He told her about his morning in court and his lunch with Ben McKeown, glad to see that she had ceased to be depressed. Talking about Nicky obviously aroused old resentments. She interrupted to say irritably, "What he really needs is six months in a reform school."

"That's what I thought at first. Now I'm not so sure. It might work if he was the son of a coalminer or taxi driver. Then he'd realize he's *got* to adjust to reality. But he'll never do it while he can hide behind his father."

"He couldn't hide behind his father in a reform school."

"It's my job to keep him out of reform school."

"Rather you than me."

But as he described his evening with Nicky, he watched her expression change from boredom and impatience to increasing interest. She said, "You're right about his father. Nicky always adored him."

"If you'd seen them after the court case, you wouldn't have thought so. You'd have thought they hated one another."

"How sad. . . . " From the expression in her eyes he could see that she was thinking about her own father. Suddenly, he was seized with one of his inspirations.

"Why don't you talk to him?"

She looked at him with surprise. "What could I do?"

"I don't know, but I've got a feeling he badly needs to talk to somebody."

"He can talk to you."

"That's not the same. I'm a doctor. You're someone he's known since childhood. Besides, you're a girl."

She smiled at him. "All right."

He said, "Look, why don't you come over to Nicky's place with me, and we'll take him back and sit him in front of the video camera?"

"All right." She looked so happy that he felt a brute again, this time for taking advantage of her.

As they drove to Denmark Hill, he reflected that this was an unorthodox thing to do, to involve one patient with another. Yet his instinct told him it was right, not only for Nicky, but for Lesley. She felt vulnerable and passive because she was accustomed to being used by men. It made her take her inferiority for granted. With Nicky, she would no longer be in the inferior position.

As they passed Camberwell Green she said, "What do you want to find out?"

"I don't know. That's the problem. All I know is that I've got to try to get inside his skin. I've got to try and understand the way he sees himself."

"But surely you know? As a kind of James Dean."

"No. That's only a small part of it. No human being is as simple as that." He tried hard to think of a way to express what was in his mind. "Look, suppose you'd never seen your face in a mirror and you honestly believed you were ugly. And suppose you were also shy and unsure of yourself, so you imitated some girl with a loud voice and a self-assertive manner because *she* seemed sure of herself. You can imagine you might get yourself thoroughly disliked, and you'd believe this was because you were unattractive. Now suppose someone made you stand in front of a full-length mirror and said, 'Look, you're pretty and graceful and you have a nice figure, you don't *have* to be noisy and self-assertive. Why don't you cultivate a shy, quiet manner instead. . .' Do you see what I'm getting at? You don't know what part suits you until you know how you appear to other people. You may think you're a misfit when you're only playing the wrong part. Now all I know about Nicky is that he's playing the wrong part."

"And how can you decide which is the right part?"

He laughed. "If I knew that I'd be the greatest doctor in the world. I'd be able to cure everybody with personality problems, which means just about every human being."

Nicky McKeown was lying on his bed, reading *Private Eye* and listening to his record player through earphones. He was wearing his track suit and dirty white plimsolls and had a box of chocolates balanced on his stomach. He was staring up at the ceiling, a set frown on his face, and outthrust lips. When he saw Charlie, he looked startled, then his face broke into a sheepish smile. He pulled off the earphones, and reached out to turn off the record player.

Charlie said, "Do you know anything about video recorders?"

"Depends what you mean."

"Would you know how to attach a video camera?"

"Sure, there's a socket in the back."

"Feel like helping me set one up?"

Nicky heaved himself to his feet. "Okay." It sounded indifferent, but Charlie sensed his pleasure.

From a clothes closet with a sliding door, Nicky selected a grease-stained duffle coat and an old woolen scarf. The closet, Charlie observed, was full of expensive clothes, most of which looked unworn. He experienced a twinge of pity. It struck him that, in his expensively decorated bedroom, with its thick pile carpet, this boy was as lonely as in a prison cell.

When he saw Lesley sitting in the passenger seat, Nicky looked suddenly unsure of himself. She had to get out to let him into the back seat. She said, "Hello. Remember me?"

Evidently he didn't. He stared at her with nervous suspicion, a half-smile making him look imbecilic. She said, "Lesley Engledow."

"Christ! Liz! You've changed. I wouldn't have known you!"

Charlie noted with interest the slight American accent. It sounded like "I wouldn't 'a known ya."

In the rear view mirror, he could see Nicky fingering his chin, evidently wishing he had shaved.

Nicky said, "Christ, it must be years since I saw you. You were a fat little kid."

"I was *not* fat!"

Immediately, they had taken up the roles of sparring partners, and this evidently relieved Nicky's embarrassment. Within a few minutes, the awkwardness had disappeared. This was evidently because one was in the back, the other in the passenger seat. Their personalities could interact directly, undistracted by appearances.

They parked outside the Engledows' house; Lesley produced a front door key and let them in. Charlie said, "Nobody home?"

"No. They've all gone to the theater."

In the hall there was a sealed cardboard box. She said, "That's the camera."

Charlie carried it into the television lounge and cut the plastic tape that sealed it. The folded delivery note fell on to the carpet. Charlie glanced at it and saw that it was dated December 29, the previous Friday. Today was Tuesday, yet Lesley's letter had said, "The camera has just arrived." He glanced across at Lesley who was helping Nicky lift the video-recorder on to the table, and noted the attractive dress, evidently new, and the absence of tights or stockings. She had waited four days, until she knew her family would be at the theater, before asking him to the house. He experienced a sense of relief, mingled with regret. He knew himself well enough to recognize that, if Lesley had kissed him as she kissed him on Christmas Eve, he would have ended up in bed with her.

Lesley said, "Would you like to eat now?"

He was, in fact, ravenous. "Thanks. If it's no trouble."

She wheeled in a trolley from the kitchen. It contained a cold chicken salad and a bottle of hock, already opened. He remembered her telling him that hock was her favorite wine.

She asked Nicky, "Would you like something to eat?"

He looked wryly at his stomach, which bulged under the track suit.

"No, I'm too fat already."

While he ate, Charlie watched Nicky set up the video-camera. He worked with the speed and efficiency of an electrician. He said, "You seem very good at that, Nick."

Nicky shrugged. "It's easy. All the wires and sockets are marked." It took him precisely five minutes to set up the video-camera. He said, "Okay. Ready when you are."

Lesley said, "Let him finish eating."

There was an awkward silence. Nicky strolled over to the sideboard.

"Still play chess, Liz?"

"Yes."

"I'll give you a quick game."

She laughed. "There's no such thing."

"Wanna bet?"

She glanced at Charlie, who said, "Yes, go ahead. There's no hurry."

He sensed that Nicky still felt nervous and awkward in the presence of this slim, beautiful girl who moved with such poise and grace. Chess was a familiar refuge.

Nicky moved the chessboard on to the drinks table. Charlie noted the neat, economical movements with which he set up the pieces. Lesley made the first move, pawn to king four. Nicky grinned at her and also moved pawn to king four. Lesley moved her pawn to king's bishop four. Nicky chuckled and said, "Oh, come on!"

She said, "Your move."

He sighed. "Okay, if you insist." He took her pawn. Lesley grinned and moved her bishop to bishop four. Charlie, who had moved closer to watch, said, "Why did you say, 'Oh come on?'"

Both Lesley and Nicky smiled at him. Lesley said, "We're playing a game called the Evergreen."

Nicky said, "Wrong. It's the Immortal Game. Anderssen and Kieseritsky, 1851. The Evergreen was Anderssen and Dufresne in 1853."

Charlie gaped with astonishment. "You mean you can remember a whole chess game?"

Lesley was obviously pleased at his amazement. "It's not all that hard. It's only twenty-three moves."

Nicky corrected her. "No, the Immortal is twenty-three moves. Evergreen is twenty-four."

Lesley, eager to make up for her mistake, said, "It was a famous come-on. Anderssen sacrificed a pawn and both rooks in three moves, and then sacrificed his queen. And he still won on the twenty-third move."

"But who taught you?"

She said, "Daddy taught us chess when we were children. He'd bring us special presents if we memorized one of the great games."

Nicky rearranged the board to the starting position. He said, "Come on. Let's do it for real."

The last time Charlie had played chess had been with Dr. Grimshaw, and Grimshaw had always beaten him. But he remembered enough about the game to recognize that both these teenagers outclassed Grimshaw and, as he watched them, he was struck by an interesting insight. As they played chess, they no longer seemed to be teenagers; they had the concentration and purpose of adults. Yet less than half an hour ago, Nicky's self-confidence had been as fragile as thin ice. What had caused the change? It was merely forgetting himself and focusing his entire attention on the game. Genuine self-confidence is based on a certain *inner pressure.*

And that, of course, was what was wrong with Nicky's father. He lacked the impersonality of real self-confidence and tried to substitute belligerence and pugnacity. Nicky tried to model himself on his father. The result was juvenile delinquency, yet now, as he played chess, the juvenile delinquent had vanished. The problem, clearly, was to find Nicky a sense of purpose as strong as his love of chess . . .

Nicky said, "Checkmate."

"What do you mean, checkmate?"

Nicky nodded at the board. "Look."

Lesley frowned at the board for a long time, then sighed. "Yes. I resign."

Nicky gave a sardonic chuckle and returned the chessmen to their box. Lesley said, "You're *very* good."

Nicky pretended to polish an imaginary medal on his chest. "Yeah, I'm pretty good."

Charlie said, "Where did you learn to play chess like that?"

Nicky contemplated the carpet, and twisted his lips into a cross between a James Dean pout and a James Dean scowl. He said with throwaway nonchalance, "Oh, I taught myself."

Charlie saw he was enjoying the game, so he said with astonishment and admiration, "Taught youself!"

"Yeah." Nicky could not maintain the scowl, and his face broke into an open and attractive smile.

Lesley said, "How did you teach yourself to play as well as that?" Charlie was glad she had caught on.

Nicky said, "Oh, it's easy enough . . ." Before he could launch into explanations Charlie said, "Hold on, do you mind if we start the video-camera?"

A few minutes later he was peering down the view-finder at Lesley's profile and at Nicky's grubby plimsolls, which seemed to be slightly larger than his head. He said, "Okay, Lesley, fire away."

Lesley, with the aplomb of a skilled television interviewer, said, "Nicky, would you mind telling us how you learned to play chess?"

Nicky stared broodingly into space, sighed deeply, ran his fingers through his hair, and said, "My mother taught me when I was seven or eight, but I didn't begin to take a real interest until the time of the Fischer–Spassky match in Iceland. I suppose I'd be about . . . ten at the time."

"Why did you find the match so interesting?"

"Well, I watched this late-night program on TV just before the match, and it was all about how Bobby Fischer would rather forfeit a match than give way on a point of principle—you know, with Reshevsky in 1960 or whenever it was, and again in Tunisia in 1967—and he was winning when he withdrew from that one. This program said how nobody liked him, partly because he was a Jew, and partly because he wouldn't take no crap from anybody. I thought he looked nice. Nobody liked him because he was too honest . . ."

"Honest?"

"Well, like, he said, 'Chess is a violent game—it's a kind of war.' And also, he didn't mind admitting he liked to win, you know, he said, 'I like to watch their egos crumble. . . .'" Nicky gave a snort of sardonic laughter. "So when he played Spassky in Iceland, I watched every game. They didn't televise the game finally, because Bobby wouldn't play in front of TV cameras. That cost him a lot of money. But he didn't *care* about money." A note of defiance came into his voice. For a moment, he lost the thread, but found it again before Lesley could interrupt. "Anyway, they did these—er—reconstructions on TV, and I watched every one of them. Then I bought that book about the tournament, and played all the games through, and . . . well, I guess that's how I really learned about chess."

Charlie was again fascinated to observe how the video-camera brought a sense of heightened participation to everyone involved. Lesley looked cool, efficient and controlled; Nicky had been transformed from a shy, inarticulate teenager into an individual with conviction and a sense of purpose, and Charlie himself experienced a new understanding of the problem, a sense of looking down on it from a bird's-eye view.

Lesley was obviously feeling the same thing. Her questions sounded casual, as if this were no more than a game, a convenient way of testing her new camera. But he noted how skillfully she led Nicky to talking about himself; about his home background, then about his sense of boredom, frustration and isolation. What excited him most was his increasing certainty that Nicky knew precisely what was happening. He was not stupid. He knew that Charlie was a doctor who had been hired by his father to try and keep him out of trouble. He probably guessed that Lesley was on Charlie's side. For all he knew, this was a preconcerted plot, arranged in detail before they came to collect him. But if he suspected anything of the sort, it was obvious that he didn't care. He was clearly delighted to be the center of attention, to be questioned by a pretty girl, and to have his words recorded on videotape.

They recorded longer than intended. When the tape clicked to a halt, they were all surprised; the hour had flown past. They were halfway through replaying it when the front door opened, and they heard voices and the sound of snow being kicked off shoes against the step. Nicky said quickly, "Could we turn it off now?"

Charlie pressed the "stop" switch as the door opened, and Julia and Marion came in. Marion said, "Oh hello! It's Light-fingered Louie. Pinched any strawberries recently?"

It seemed that Nicky had once sneaked into the greenhouse and eaten all the strawberries that Marion had been growing for her birthday party. Marion had never forgiven him.

With all the Engledows present, Nicky became silent and withdrawn, answering questions in monosyllables. But Charlie could sense that he was no longer mistrustful. He accepted Julia's heavy-handed banter about Chanel No. 5 with a shy smile, and showed no resentment when Marion told him he had a figure like Billy Bunter. In fact, he obviously enjoyed feeling like a member of a family. Watching them, Charlie thought, they are treating him like a child, so he feels like a child. But at least he doesn't seem to mind . . .

After half an hour, Charlie excused himself. His previous late night was catching up with him and his stifled yawns were making his eyes water. Nicky dragged himself awkwardly to his feet, mumbled his goodnights in an inaudible voice, and tripped over the doormat on his way out; Charlie had a feeling that James Dean was back.

As he was unlocking the car door, Lesley came running out, pulling on her anorak. "Thought I'd come with you for the ride."

Charlie was glad she had decided to come; she seemed to act as a catalyst between himself and Nicky. As they drove towards Dog Kennel Lane, there was a pleasant atmosphere between them, a sense of intimacy that was stronger because it had been interrupted by the others. Charlie was the first to break the silence.

"Do you still admire Bobby Fischer?"

"No . . . not as much as I used to."

Charlie asked with curiosity, "Why not?"

"Well, he stopped playing chess, and he got religion and all that."

Lesley said, "Did you ever think of becoming a professional chess player?"

Nicky said with incredulity, "Are you kidding?"

"Why not? You could be good enough."

Nicky gave a snort of embarrassed laughter. "It's a hard life."

Charlie said, "Would that matter?"

Nicky said thoughtfully, "I s'pose not."

Charlie quoted, "Chess is a violent game, like war."

Nicky laughed dryly. "That's true, it's a kind of war."

They had arrived at his front door. Two spotlights had been turned on, illuminating the front of the house, and showing the glossy green of the ivy. Nicky said, "Wanna come on in?"

"No thanks. I have to be up at seven in the morning."

They waited until they saw the outline of the butler through the leaded glass, then drove off. Nicky waved after them.

They drove in silence, and Charlie found it entirely free of strain. This evening had established a new kind of intimacy between them; the intimacy of collaboration.

As they pulled up outside her house, she said, "I wish I could understand why he's lost interest in chess."

"Oh, I can tell you that. He became interested because he watched that program about Fischer. He identified with Fischer and hero-worshipped him. He followed all the matches in Iceland, all that tremendous drama; even I can remember the Reykjavik tournament. But then, when it's all over, there's nothing to do but replay the games. It's not very exciting for an eleven-year-old boy to sit in his room playing games out of a book. Then his hero stopped playing chess, and Nicky stopped identifying with him. That's why he lost interest."

"So he really needs somebody to identify with?"

"He's got somebody, and unfortunately, it's James Dean."

She sighed. "It seems a pity."

He said jokingly, "Now if you could come up with a combination of James Dean and Bobby Fischer . . ."

"Does he have to be alive?"

"Well, preferably. Why?"

"I was just thinking of Paul Morphy."

"Who?"

"You know, he's supposed to be the greatest chess player of all time."

"I don't know much about chess."

"I thought of it because you said a combination of James Dean and Bobby Fischer. I think that about describes Morphy."

"When did he die?"

"Oh, at a guess, about 1900. If you want to come in for a moment. I think we've got a book about him."

He looked at his watch. It was after midnight.

"I don't think I'd better. I'll borrow it some other time."

She said, "Well hang around a minute. If Daddy hasn't gone to bed I'll get it for you. He keeps the chess books in his bedroom."

Before he could object, she had vanished into the house. He yawned and rubbed his eyes, then lowered the window and breathed in the cold night air to try to wake himself up. She returned carrying a plastic bag.

"Sorry to be so long. We had to search for one of them. Keep them as long as you like." She handed him the bag through the window.

"Thanks, Lesley. Oh dear, I'm sorry . . ." He was too late to stifle a yawn. "I'll ring you soon."

"All right. Good night, Charles." She turned and hurried indoors and he felt a twinge of regret that she had not offered to kiss him good night. Then, as he started the engine, he cursed himself for not knowing his own mind.

CHAPTER TEN

THE SOUND of a car engine woke him up. He looked at the illuminated dial of the clock and saw that it was only six o'clock. Although still tired, he was aware that if he went back to sleep he would feel worse by seven. He lay on his back in the dark, thinking about Nicky McKeown and experiencing a certain resigned sense of frustration. The answer to the problem still evaded him. Finally, he switched on the light, lit the gas fire, then climbed back into bed. The plastic bag of books was on the chair by the bedside. He emptied them out on to the eiderdown.

There were three of them: Golombek's *History of Chess*, a book called *Paul Morphy, A Sketch from the Chess World* by Max Lange, and a novel called *The Chess Players* by Frances Parkinson Keyes. He turned to the chapter called "The Advent of Paul Morphy" in the *History of Chess*, and experienced a prickling sensation in his scalp. The picture of Morphy bore an unmistakable resemblance to Nicky McKeown. Like Nicky, Morphy was somewhat overweight, he had the same swarthy skin, and there was a slightly spoiled look about the downturned, sensual mouth and brooding eyes. Charlie said aloud, "Incredible!," and found himself wishing that Lesley was there to share his surprise.

The feeling increased as he read on. As far as character was concerned, Morphy was a kind of nineteenth century variant on James Dean. From Lange, he learned that the dark cast of Morphy's features was due to the fact that he was a Creole. Born in New Orleans in 1837, Morphy had learned to play chess at the age of ten, and within two years could defeat all the local champions. At twenty, he was an easy winner at his first chess tournament in New York. He sailed for Europe, predicting that he would defeat all the European masters. In Paris, he sat blindfolded in an armchair, while eight of the best players in France sat with their chessboards in front of them. Morphy defeated them all. He was carried shoulder-high out of the restaurant, and became the most celebrated foreigner in Paris.

The next great challenge was the English champion, Howard Staunton, who was also a renowned Shakespeare scholar. But

151

Staunton was quite determined not to expose himself to defeat. He made a series of feeble excuses, including the insinuation that Morphy could not raise the five hundred pound purse. When Morphy deposited it in the bank, he shifted his ground and claimed that his literary work prevented him from finding the time to play. Privately, he went around telling people that Morphy was a "mere professional," implying that he was not a gentleman. Infuriated and humiliated, Morphy returned to America, but not before he had beaten the two European champions Harrwitz and Anderssen. Cheering crowds were waiting for him when the boat docked in New York, but when a member of the welcoming committee inadvertently used the word "professional," Morphy insisted on his resignation from the committee. He was already showing signs of the persecution mania that brought him to the verge of insanity.

Back in New Orleans, he fell in love with a beautiful girl, and was deeply hurt when she let it be known that she had no intention of marrying "a mere chess player." He became increasingly eccentric and paranoid, believing that people wanted to poison him and that his friends were in a conspiracy to steal his clothes. He was rude to anyone who dared to mention chess, although when he played the occasional game he showed all his old brilliance. He was only forty-seven when, after taking a walk in the sun followed by a hot bath, he died of congestion of the brain.

All this produced in Charlie an almost unbearable sense of excitement—the same excitement he had felt in his hotel room after solving the problem of Sharon Engstrom's facial twitch. As he pulled on his clothes, he tried to calm himself by reflecting that he might be allowing his enthusiasm to run away with him. After all, Nicky might already be familiar with Morphy's career. But as he thought about it over breakfast, he suddenly knew that this could not be true. If Nicky had known about Paul Morphy, he would have been a different person.

By the time he drove to the surgery, the excitement had settled into a calm inner conviction. He felt that this would be a "test case," a turning point. It would either prove that he was right, or that he was capable of a great deal of self-deception. Yet somehow, he had no doubt about which it would be.

At the surgery, he rang the McKeowns' home. The butler answered. He asked if he could speak to Mr. McKeown, and gave his name. A moment later, Mrs. McKeown's voice said, "This is Jessica

McKeown. I'm afraid Ben left ten minutes ago. He has to meet someone at London airport. Is there anything I can do?"

"I wanted to talk about Nicky."

"Ben will be out of his office all day. But I'll be available, if that would help."

He decided quickly. "Could I come and see you some time later this morning?"

"Of course. I'll be expecting you."

That morning, surgery was longer than usual. A man with delusions of persecution took up almost half an hour. Charlie lanced a boil, diagnosed worms in a baby by examining the contents of her napkin, and diagnosed syphilis in a girl of ten. He had to discuss the latter case with Herbert Pike, since it was fairly certain that the child had been infected by her stepfather, and Pike undertook to report it to the police. At 11:15, as he was about to leave the building, a girl from the restaurant across the road came in with a badly scalded hand—a coffee machine had overflowed. It was a temptation to send her to hospital, but she was in such pain that he dressed it himself. By the time he reached the McKeowns' house, it was after midday.

Mrs. McKeown invited him into the lounge and the maid brought in coffee and biscuits. He was glad of both. The morning had been so hectic that he had had no opportunity for a coffee break. He thought Mrs. McKeown looked tired and pale, but when she smiled, the underlying warmth came through and made him feel suddenly relaxed.

He decided to come to the point immediately. "I think I have the solution to this problem of Nicky's."

"That would certainly be good news."

He tried to choose his words. "You see, I've felt from the beginning that his problem is that he admires his father so much. And because his father doesn't pay much attention to the rules of the game, Nicky feels he ought to be allowed to do the same." He paused, hoping she was not going to be offended. She merely raised her eyebrows.

"You mean Ben rides roughshod over everybody?"

He temporized. "Well, you know him better than I do."

"But what you're saying is that Nicky's a juvenile delinquent because Ben's an overgrown delinquent?"

She said it with such good humor that he felt his inhibitions dissolve.

"Precisely."

Her eyes sparkled with amusement.

"To be honest, I'd reached that conclusion a long time ago."

They looked at one another, and he had a sensation that he had known her a long time. He drank some of his coffee. She said, "The problem is, what can we do about it?"

"I think I can answer that. Do you realize how much he models himself on James Dean?"

"Who is James Dean?"

As he explained, she listened with deep attention. In fact, she was such a good listener that he went on to tell her about Topelius and his "self-image" theory. It was at once apparent that she found it fascinating and he was so carried away by the subject that he almost forgot about Nicky. She brought him back to the problem.

"And how do you intend to change the way Nicky sees himself?"

He smiled, and tapped the books.

"Amazingly simple, really. I think the answer lies in here."

It was characteristic of her that she did not try to look at the titles of the books. She only asked, "How?"

"I didn't realize until last night that Nicky is a brilliant chess player. Did you know how much he admired Bobby Fischer?"

"Yes, but that was years ago. I thought he'd lost interest in chess."

"No. He lost interest in Fischer, because Fischer dropped out of chess." He opened the Golombek volume to the chapter on Morphy, and handed it to her. "And if I'm correct, he'll find Morphy as fascinating as Fischer. In fact, more so."

"I'm afraid I've never heard of Morphy."

"Neither had I until last night. Lesley Engledow told me about him; she said he was a cross between James Dean and Bobby Fischer. That describes him rather well. He's the tragic, misunderstood genius of chess."

She raised the question that had struck him earlier.

"How do you know Nicky doesn't already know about him?"

"Because if he knew about him, he'd talk about him all the time. It's simply not conceivable to me that he could know about Morphy and not be fascinated by him. And if he was fascinated by Morphy, he'd still be playing chess. And that's what I wanted to talk to you about."

"I don't quite understand."

He took a deep breath. It was not natural for him to be dogmatic, but he felt like a gambler who is placing all his chips on one number.

He said, "If I'm correct—if Topelius is correct—then reading about Morphy ought to produce a perfectly predictable effect on Nicky's way of seeing himself. It should be a kind of chemical reaction, exactly like adding hydrochloric acid to iron filings and getting hydrogen. I think I can even describe this effect in advance. He'll want to read everything about Morphy he can lay his hands on. He'll begin to play all Morphy's great games. Lange describes a game he played in a box at the Paris opera against two aristocrats, a game in which he made a famous sacrifice of his queen. *That's* the kind of thing that will appeal to Nicky. And when he's learned all Morphy's games, I suspect he'll go on to Steinitz and Capablanca and Alekhine . . . "

"It sounds too good to be true."

"I'm almost certain that I'm right. And that's why I wanted to speak to your husband. Do you really *want* Nicky to become a kind of chess-maniac?"

She shrugged. "I wouldn't object."

"Good. But before you make up your mind, you ought to read that chapter on Morphy, and then the chapter on Fischer. I don't think chess masters are the happiest people in the world. I once heard about some famous actor who said that acting made him feel ashamed because it wasn't really a man's job. It's not like being a soldier or an explorer, or even a businessman. I think some of the great chess players felt the same about chess, only more so. That's why Morphy came to dislike it so much. I can't guarantee that chess is going to be the solution to all Nicky's problems."

She interrupted, "I don't mind in the least. But are you sure he's that good?"

"I don't know how good he is. You could easily find out by getting hold of a professional chess player. In fact, I was going to suggest you get him coached by a first class player. I don't think it matters whether he turns out to be a Grand Master or not. All that matters is that he finds something that gives him a sense of purpose."

She looked up from the book. Her expression showed that she was torn between hope and the fear of being disappointed. She said, "All I can say is that, if you're right, we shan't be able to thank you enough."

He shrugged. "Thank Lesley Engledow. She put me on to Morphy."

She laughed. "You're always trying to place the credit elsewhere."

As usual, compliments made him feel awkward. He looked at his watch. "I'd better go now. I've got house calls to make after lunch."

"Why not have lunch with me? Alice always makes enough for two."

He could see no reason to refuse, although, being shy and socially unsure of himself, he was tempted to think up an excuse. In fact, his diffidence vanished as soon as he realized that she was lonely and wanted someone to talk to. They ate a light lunch, consisting of veal cooked in a wine sauce, with salad. Charlie also drank two glasses of Muscadet. He found her very easy to talk to; she seemed like a combination of mother and sister. He found himself again wondering how Ben McKeown had captured anyone so delightful. Because she was intelligent and perceptive and seemed to enjoy listening, he told her about his cousin Roberto and his work on endorphins, then about his weekend at the Park View and his meeting with Erik Topelius. Explaining it to her seemed to give him a wider grasp of the subject, so that he found himself speaking with a new conviction. Her absorbed attention was more flattering than any expression of agreement. It seemed to him that, for the first time, he was beginning to achieve a real insight into the theory of the "self-image." While he was selecting cheese biscuits, she said, "There's only one thing that bothers me. All this seems so sensible—so obvious, if you don't mind me saying so—that I can't help wondering why no one's seen it before. Surely, every psychiatrist realizes that neurosis depends on the way the patient sees himself?"

"That's true. But before now, there was no way of allowing the patient to see himself as other people see him."

"I don't understand."

"I'm talking about the video recorder. Now, for the first time, you can show a patient exactly how he looks to other people. Suppose someone had filmed this conversation between us and we spent the afternoon watching it played back. We'd notice a thousand little things about ourselves; tiny gestures, hesitations, movements of facial muscles. Quite apart from what we're saying to one another, there's a whole language of communication in our expressions and gestures. A scientist could spend a month studying the film and discover all kinds of new things about us. Now, my idea is that it ought to be possible to set up a laboratory to study these things, to break down the human personality into its component parts and see how it's put together. And when we'd done that, we could perform a kind of personality surgery—just like altering the shape of someone's nose or improving their teeth. But this would be a kind of spare-part surgery of the personality. You see a delightful girl with a pretty smile, but the moment she begins to talk she ruins the effect with a silly giggle that betrays she's unsure of herself, although she may have no reason to be. You could make her watch herself again and again until she becomes aware of the precise situations in which she giggles, and then show her clips from the film library so she can see how other girls handle the same situations."

She was staring into space, past his head, but the gleam in her eyes showed that his excitement had kindled her own. He said, "And the beauty of it is that people would learn to *change themselves*. It wouldn't be like psychiatry or plastic surgery where the patient is in the hands of a doctor. They'd be like sculptors, remodeling their own personalities. And the doctor would only be the man who shows them their own possibilities . . . "

She was biting her lower lip, and he paused, wondering if she wanted to raise some objection. She said, "You could become a very rich man."

He stared at her blankly, wondering what had led to such a bizarre reflection.

"Rich?"

"If you could really teach people how to change themselves, you'd have them queuing up for miles."

He laughed. "I'm not sure I want them queuing up. I get too much of that at the surgery."

She said, "I'm sorry. I expect that sounded trivial. But don't forget that I'm the wife of a businessman, and I can't help seeing things from a business point of view."

"I don't think I'd like to be a fashionable psychiatrist."

"What *would* you like?"

"To have my own laboratory, like my cousin Roberto, where I could really investigate these things." In the hall, the grandfather clock struck two. He said, "My god, I've got to go. I've got to see eleven patients this afternoon."

She saw him to the front door. Outside, it had started to rain, and the snow was turning into gray slush.

"The books . . . You'll give them to Nicky?"

"Of course."

That evening, he was on call. He returned home after a meal in the workman's café, lit the gas fire, and climbed into bed to keep warm.

He was feeling uncharacteristically depressed. Before he left the surgery, the local police sergeant had called in to see him to talk about the ten-year-old girl who had syphilis. Her stepfather was under interrogation and the police surgeon had confirmed that he had the disease. The child was still a virgin, but it was clear that some kind of sexual activity had been going on. The thought of the vulnerability of children gave rise to gloomy reflections. He took down a textbook on venereal disease, but before he had read more than a few pages, his eyes closed, and he drifted off to sleep.

He was awakened by the telephone; he groaned and swore under his breath.

"Hello?"

"Hello, doctor. This is Ben McKeown."

"Oh, hello." He tried not to yawn.

"Are you doing anything this evening?"

"Yes, I'm on call."

"Any chance of getting over here? They could call you at this number."

He was taken off balance. "Well . . . I suppose so."

"Good. See you as soon as you can get here." Before Charlie could ask further questions, he hung up.

Charlie splashed water on his face and put on a clean shirt and tie—not because he felt untidy, but to wake himself up. Although he was mildly irritated at McKeown's assumption that he could be summoned like a servant, he was not entirely displeased. Since he was on call, he was liable to be interrupted anyway. He rang the operator and had calls transferred to the McKeowns' number.

When he arrived, a quarter of an hour later, he was surprised at the number of cars parked in the drive. The front door was slightly ajar, so he was able to walk in. The McKeowns were giving a party. The dining room and sitting room doors stood open, and both rooms were crowded. The butler took Charlie's duffle coat. It looked out of place among the expensive overcoats and fur wraps in the hall.

Mrs. McKeown saw him from the dining room and hurried toward him. When the butler was out of hearing she said, "Listen, I'm sorry about this . . . "

"About what?"

"Dragging you here at five minutes' notice."

"Not at all. I'm Nicky's doctor . . . "

"I'm afraid this probably has nothing to do with Nicky . . . "

He was startled. "No?"

At that moment, the telephone rang. The maid said, "It's for you, sir."

It was one of Charlie's more difficult patients, an asthmatic who was convinced he was dying every time he had an attack. Between gasps his words were almost unintelligible, but Charlie was finally able to establish that he had a supply of his inhalant and tablets of isoprenaline. He told him that if the attack became worse he would give him an adrenaline injection, and to ring back if necessary.

The call took ten minutes and Mrs. McKeown had vanished in the meantime. Charlie decided to slip upstairs and say hello to Nicky. When he knocked on the door, Nicky's voice shouted irritably, "Who is it?"

"Me." He pushed open the door. Nicky was lying face downward on the bed, reading; the chess table was beside the bed. His face brightened when he saw Charlie.

"Hi. Thanks for the books."

"Find them interesting?"

"Really fantastic." Charlie could see that the other two books were lying open on the floor. He said, "I wondered if you knew about Morphy."

"Only his game against Anderssen. Isn't he terrific? Look at this . . . " He sat up over the chessboard. "Look, this is Morphy's fourth game against Harrwitz. He's using Philidor's defense."

He began showing Charlie the game move by move. Charlie interrupted to say, "You know my chess isn't all that good."

"Oh, anybody can understand this. It's a lot like Bobby Fischer's game against Spassky—the sixth. Do you know it?"

Ten minutes later, Nicky was still explaining the difference between the two games when Ben McKeown looked into the bedroom. He said with relief, "Oh, there you are! I was afraid you'd been called away. Nicky, would you mind?"

Nicky said, "No." Charlie observed how the bored manner came back when he talked to his father.

McKeown was wearing evening dress, with a black silk bow tie. The clothes were a perfect fit yet, in some subtle way, they looked wrong on McKeown, underlining the sallow, predator's face with its ruthless mouth. McKeown said, "Come on in here for a moment."

He led Charlie into a large bedroom that was obviously the one he shared with his wife. It was even more luxurious than Nicky's, with the look of the VIP suite in a five-star hotel. The counterpanes on the twin beds were of a heavy brocaded material. McKeown gestured at the walnut and damask stool in front of the dressing table.

"Have a seat." He sat on the end of one of the beds. "Do you mind if I call you Charles?"

"Of course not."

"Thanks. You call me Ben. Now listen, Charles, I have something I want to ask you."

Charlie was full of curiosity; he thought McKeown looked ill-at-ease.

"Jessica's been telling me about these ideas of yours—very interesting. Now, correct me if I'm wrong, but as I understand it, you find out what's wrong with people by watching the things they do and say, instead of all this psychological stuff about childhood and all that . . . " He waved his hand vaguely. "Right?"

Charlie said cautiously, "In a way . . . "

"Now you may not realize it, but that's also a sound business approach. You try and find out what the other man's thinking by watching for the little tell-tale signs. Let me give you an example. A few days ago I had dinner with a man who was trying to get me to back a show in the West End. And I noticed that he kept drawing train-lines on the tablecloth with his fork. And I said to myself, try to put yourself in his place. If you were trying to sell somebody a slice of a show, and you kept drawing lines with your fork, what would it mean? Then I saw the answer. It'd mean that I wanted to convince him that everything was straightforward and smooth, like a railway line, but I wouldn't be doing it unless I knew that wasn't true. So I said, 'Look, Jerry, be honest with me. Where's the hidden catch?' He said, 'What hidden catch?' I said, 'You're bothered about something. What is it?' And he said, 'Okay, I'll tell you what it is.' And he told me the leading lady's got a bad emotional problem and she may back out at the last moment. That's what I'd call psychological observation. Do you agree?"

Charlie was genuinely impressed. "Yes."

"But that's a kind of intuition. I'm not a trained observer like you." Charlie was about to utter a polite disclaimer, but McKeown went on quickly. "Now I've got somebody I want you to meet downstairs, and I'd like you to give me your assessment. What does he want? What is he after? What makes him tick?"

Charlie experienced a sinking sensation. "Who is it?"

"His name's Sir George Pettie, and he's chairman of the board of Hadley-Thomson. You've heard of them?" Charlie shook his head.

McKeown was obviously surprised. "They own the Vanguard Supermarket chain and three West End stores, and the Benson-Mayes Breweries, and the Sinclair-Plaskett merchant bank. My group wants to take them over."

Charlie said, "I don't know much about business."

"That makes no difference. You know what a takeover is?" Charlie nodded. "Now the main thing if you plan a takeover is to keep it a secret as long as possible, because if the news gets around, the share prices go up. So when we started to buy Hadley-Thomson shares, we did it very cautiously, through several brokers. They own textile mills and our group owns clothing factories, so at first we made it look as if we were interested in the mills. Then, two weeks ago, the Hadley-Thomson share prices rose from four twenty to four fifty-five. That meant there were rumors of a takeover. Which is where we decided to come into the open. Tomorrow morning I'm going to present our plan to their board.

"The only thing that's bothering me is this man Pettie. I've got a feeling he's got something up his sleeve."

"Doesn't he want your group to take over his firm?"

McKeown gave a humorless chuckle. "It's the last thing he wants. He knows it'd be good for Hadley-Thomson, but that doesn't interest him. It's an old family business—his family founded the brewery in Glasgow in 1870—and he wants to stay chairman of the board."

"Would you want to get rid of him?"

"Oh, sure." McKeown shrugged. "He'd be no use to a group like ours. In fact, there's no place in the business world for people of his type; old school tie and dinner at the Athenaeum and all that. Hadley-Thomson lost three million quid last year. Their methods are old-fashioned. If we don't take them over, they'll be bust in five years."

"So what's the problem?"

"Pettie. He owns eighteen percent of the shares, and the deputy chairman owns another sixteen. That's thirty-four percent. We've got forty-one percent, so we can't get a controlling interest without buying one of them out."

"How about this deputy chairman?"

"Lord Ormkirk. Nobody knows much about him. He's a nonexecutive chairman and he lives in Scotland. He'll be at the meeting tomorrow, but I don't know what he's like."

Charlie said, "What can I do?"

"Talk to Pettie. Tell me what you think of him. He's got something up his sleeve, and I want to know what it is."

"Do you think he'll tell me?"

McKeown said impatiently, "Of course he won't. But you're a psychologist. See what you can find out."

Charlie was about to say, I'm not a mind reader, but changed his mind. Instead he said, "I'll do what I can."

"Thanks." McKeown slapped him lightly on the arm. "We'd better get back downstairs."

At the door, McKeown paused, and gave him a grin that was at once friendly and cynical.

"I know what you're thinking: what's in this for me?" It was quite untrue, but Charlie said nothing. "All I can say is, you help me and I'll help you. Okay?"

"Okay."

Halfway down the stairs, McKeown stopped and pointed.

"That's Pettie—the one talking to the woman in green."

Pettie was a tall, gray-haired man, with the handsome profile of an actor. As if alerted by a sixth sense, he glanced across at McKeown, then at Charlie. Charlie said, "He reminds me of your solicitor—Mr. Brookes."

McKeown gave a dry chuckle. "Yes, you're right. I expect that's why I don't like the bastard."

Jessica McKeown joined them. She asked Charlie, "What will you have to drink?"

"Wine, please."

"Champagne?" She signaled to a waiter.

McKeown said in Charlie's ear, "Stay sober." He moved off into the crowd.

Most of the guests were sitting around the walls with plates on their knees, or helping themselves to food at the buffet table. Mrs. McKeown said, "Won't you help yourself?"

"Thanks, I ate before I came."

He felt awkward and embarrassed, surrounded by so many people in evening dress. He glanced furtively at his own light brown suit and hoped that no one noticed it was crumpled.

He drank the champagne thirstily and found that it made him feel better. The butler immediately refilled his glass. For want of anything else to do, he moved over to the buffet. It was laid out on the dining-room table at which he had eaten a few hours earlier. Now it was covered with a dazzling array of food, from oysters and cold lobster to enormous joints of ham and rare beef. A youth in chef's uniform was carving the smoked salmon. Charlie decided that he was hungry after all. He stood there, sipping his champagne, waiting for an opportunity to take a plate, and listening in a state of pleasant confusion to the upper-class voices around him. "But white telephones are so hard to keep clean . . . They're the first oysters I've seen this year . . . And she's convinced they've charged her twice for the same saddle . . . The enormous chandelier overhead looked like an explosion of crystallized ice, and gave the room an air of enchantment.

A gap appeared at the table; as Charlie moved towards it, he cannoned into another guest who was making for the same place. It was Sir George Pettie. Both apologized and offered one another precedence. A second gap appeared, and they moved to the table together. Charlie had only just set down his glass on the tablecloth when Pettie, reaching for the asparagus, caught it with his sleeve and knocked it over.

"I'm most awfully sorry. Stupid of me."

"It doesn't matter. It was nearly empty."

Pettie gave him a pleasant smile.

"It wasn't, but it's nice of you to say so."

The exchange established a rapport. They regarded the variety of food with an attentiveness sharpened by greed. Pettie said, "That lobster looks delicious. I think I'm going to risk it."

Charlie said, "I'm not sure I can manage it standing up."

"You don't have to stand up. Plenty of seats in the next room."

The next room was a billiard room that had been converted into a combination of lounge and art gallery. The works were mainly by modern American painters. McKeown was proud of his collection; he had talked about it at some length during their lunch two days ago. Pettie contemplated with distaste a painting of an American flag by Jasper Johns.

"Do you suppose he really likes this stuff?"

"I don't think so. He told me he bought it as an investment."

They sat at an antique table by the wall; Charlie pushed back a bronze statuette to make room for his plate. Pettie had taken two half lobsters, which were smothered in mayonnaise. Charlie had contented himself with rare beef.

As they were eating, Ben McKeown looked into the room. He saw Charlie, smiled, and went out again. Pettie said, "Are you one of McKeown's business associates?"

"Oh no. I'm his son's doctor."

"Ah."

The question struck Charlie as odd. He hardly had the look of a young City executive. It struck him that Pettie was fishing for information. This was confirmed by his next question, "Nothing much wrong with the boy, I hope?"

"Oh no. Just asthma."

"Ah." After a silence Pettie said, "Is that the one who was in trouble with the law?"

"Yes."

Pettie wiped a spot of mayonnaise from his shirtfront.

"Odd."

Charlie decided to rise to it. He was curious to know what Pettie wanted to know.

"Why odd?"

Pettie shrugged. "He's obviously allowed to have anything he likes. Why should he want to break into other people's houses?"

The question made it clear that he already knew a great deal about the family situation.

"Boredom, I suppose."

"Really? Do they accept that as an excuse in court these days?"

Charlie decided to treat this as a pleasantry; he smiled and concentrated on his food. Pettie said, "You say McKeown bought these pictures as an investment?"

Charlie felt he could be less reticent about this. "Yes. Apparently he attended an art exhibition in New York, and a critic told him they'd all double in value in a few years. So he bought up the whole exhibition. Now he's delighted because one of them is already worth more than he paid for the lot."

"Yes, I imagine he would be."

Charlie was beginning to find the tone of dry superiority rather tiresome. He glanced cautiously across at Pettie, and decided that the handsome profile was spoiled by the double chin, and a general air of self-indulgence.

Pettie pushed away his plate and wiped his mouth with his napkin. "Yes, that lobster wasn't bad."

Charlie smiled. "Are you an expert?"

"I should be—I bought a ton of it yesterday."

"A ton!"

"Yes. My group runs Vanguard Supermarkets." He emptied his glass. "McKeown wants to take us over."

Charlie said, "I know." There seemed no point in concealment. Pettie glanced at him ironically.

"Ah, you do?"

Charlie said, "How do you feel about it?"

"Naturally, I detest it."

"Could I ask you why?"

Pettie beckoned to the waiter, and held out his glass to be refilled. He placed it on the table and stared at it thoughtfully.

"Yes, indeed you could. Because our firm cares about quality. When my grandfather launched the brewery, his aim was to make the best beer in Scotland, and he succeeded. It cost more than other beers, but it sold because it was good. That has always been the principle behind our operations. Our supermarkets sell lobster and rainbow trout and Chateau Lafite. We're more expensive than some others, but we provide quality." He flicked his glass with his fingernail, causing it to ring. "That's why this recession has affected us more than some other businesses. And why McKeown thinks we're ready to be taken over."

Pettie stared somberly across the room at a painting that consisted of parallel bands of gray. Charlie wanted to express sympathy, but found it difficult. He said, "But if McKeown took you over, wouldn't it be in his interest to maintain quality?"

Pettie looked at him with irony and a touch of pity. His eyes took on a stubborn, almost brutal, expression. "He wouldn't try to maintain quality because he doesn't know what quality is. McKeown's interested in only one thing: money. He doesn't give a damn about quality." His voice became cold and emphatic. "And if he wants to know why I intend to fight him tomorrow, you can tell him that's the reason; because he doesn't give a damn about quality." He raised his glass and slowly drained it. "Excuse me."

He stood up and walked away. Charlie stared after him with mild surprise. He was not certain whether Pettie was being deliberately rude, or had merely gone to look for another drink. While he was still pondering, the butler said from the doorway, "Telephone for you, sir."

This time it was a woman whose baby had been knocked unconscious. Charlie said he would come over right away. He found his hostess and told her he had to leave.

"What a pity. Why don't you come back later and have some coffee or cocoa?"

"Thanks. I'll try."

As he left, he saw that Pettie had joined a group of people in the dining room. That seemed to settle it; the rudeness was intentional.

He thought about it as he drove back to Southwark. The likeliest explanation was that Pettie thought he was an emissary for Ben McKeown. It was his suggestion that McKeown might be interested in quality that had caused the outburst. It was a pity; he had found Pettie likeable enough, but he seemed to be a prey to his emotions. He and McKeown had that in common.

The woman lived in a multi-story block of flats, not far from the surgery. It seemed that the child, who was nearly two, was in the habit of diving over the side of his cot on to the double bed next to it, and making his way back to the sitting room where the television was situated. His mother tried to discourage him by moving the cot away from the bed. The child had dived on to the linoleum. When Charlie arrived, he was drinking milk from a bottle with a teat on it. There was a bruise and a small cut on his forehead. Charlie cautiously felt his skull and concluded that there was no fracture. He shone a torch into the child's eyes and tested his reflexes. These seemed normal. The child was sleepy, probably from shock. Charlie told the mother to take him for an x-ray in the morning, left some mild sedatives that were obviously unnecessary, and left.

He was tired, and tempted to go straight home, but he wanted to talk to McKeown about Pettie so he drove back to Denmark Hill. It was after midnight when he arrived, and most of the cars had left. The butler said, "They're in the sitting room, sir. Would you care for tea, coffee or cocoa?"

"Tea, thank you."

Half a dozen guests were seated around the log fire in Mrs. McKeown's sitting room. The atmosphere in the room smelled of woodsmoke and cigars, and was permeated with a sense of fatigue and relaxation. Pettie was sitting next to the fire, with a half-full bottle of champagne at his elbow. He seemed to be half asleep. Most of the others were drinking brandy or liqueurs.

Ben McKeown said, "Brandy?"

"No thanks. I've got a hard day tomorrow."

McKeown said, "So have I."

Pettie gave a dry chuckle. "Yes, I think I can guarantee you a hard day."

McKeown, who was standing in front of the fire, glanced down at him sharply. "Oh yes?"

Pettie stared back at him with the amiable smile of the half-drunk. "You can't expect us to go down without a fight, now can you?" He spoke with a certain finicky precision, as if determined not to slur his words.

A bronzed man with a white moustache said, "Oh come, Pettie, that's surely not the way to look at it?"

Pettie smiled at him. "Isn't it, Colonel? How do you think I ought to look at it?" As he drank from his glass, McKeown and the bronzed man exchanged glances. McKeown said, "Well I can tell you one thing. If our bid succeeds, your shareholders are going to be pretty pleased."

Pettie nodded slowly. "Oh, I'm sure they'd be delighted—for the first six months."

McKeown flushed. "What does that mean?"

The entrance of the butler with Charlie's tea created a diversion. Mrs. McKeown tried to steer the conversation into safer channels. "Would anyone care for more coffee?"

The woman sitting beside the colonel said, "I'm afraid we have to be going."

McKeown had continued to stare down at Pettie and as the door closed behind the butler he said, "What did that mean?"

Mrs. McKeown said nervously, "Isn't it rather late to talk business?"

McKeown said stubbornly, "I'm not talking business. I only want him to explain his remark." His Cockney accent had become more pronounced.

Pettie seemed to become more relaxed as McKeown became more irritable. He made an obvious effort to collect his thoughts.

"All right. I mean that if your group takes over, our share prices will rise, and I'm sure you'll declare an excellent dividend. Then the shares will begin to go down. In two years you'll be lucky to get two pounds a share."

McKeown said, "Why?"

Mrs. McKeown tried again. "Ben, wouldn't it be better if . . . "

McKeown snapped, "Yes. When he's told me why."

Pettie said, "The reason's quite simple. I explained it to your young friend here earlier. Our group has always been interested in quality for its own sake. Yours doesn't give a damn about quality."

The colonel said, "Oh, come. That's not fair!"

"Isn't it? I'm not saying your people don't understand quality. I'm just saying they don't make it a priority." He looked up at McKeown.

"As soon as it stops paying dividends, you'll drop it in favor of something with a quick turnover. And you'll wonder why you've lost your best customers."

The colonel said, "I can only say that I think you'll find you're wrong."

McKeown said irritably, "Of course he's wrong. I don't think he knows what he's talking about."

Pettie refilled his glass. "I'm sure *you* don't know what I'm talking about."

McKeown said, with heavy irony, "I trust you've no objection to the quality of the champagne." Charlie saw the colonel wince.

Pettie raised his glass, as if in a toast. "The champagne is excellent, thank you. So are your pictures."

McKeown was surprised and mollified. "Thank you."

Pettie said, "But I'm told you bought them because you thought they'd double in value in a few years."

McKeown said promptly, "That's right, and I don't mind admitting it. Is there anything wrong with people who make a profit?"

Pettie smiled blandly. "Nothing whatever. So long as they don't pretend to be something they're not."

McKeown's face darkened. "I don't."

"No? In that case, why do you hang them on your walls? Isn't it because you want people to think you know a good picture when you see one?"

"All right. So what?" McKeown's eyes looked dangerous.

"So you want it both ways. You want to make a profit, and you want people to think you appreciate quality when you don't give a damn about it. I'd say that's hypocrisy."

McKeown went pale. "You can't talk to me like that."

Mrs. McKeown squeezed his arm. "Ben, *please.*" She placed her mouth close to his ear and said something in an undertone. The last word, "drunk," was quite audible.

Pettie heaved himself to his feet and smiled tipsily at Mrs. McKeown. "Madame, I must apologize for being a little drunk. It's obviously time I left. I wonder if someone could order me a taxi?"

Mrs. McKeown said, "Our chauffeur can take you."

The others also rose, and there was a movement towards the door. The feeling of relief was perceptible. Pettie said good night to everyone with punctilious politeness, with the air of a drunk who is making a special effort to appear sober. But as he turned to the door, his eyes rested for a moment on Charlie's, and Charlie caught the gleam of amusement and malice. Suddenly, he knew with certainty that Pettie was as sober as anyone in the room.

Left alone as the McKeowns saw their guests out, Charlie sat by the fire and used the tongs to rearrange fragments of logs into a pile, where they burst into flame. McKeown came back and looked surprised to find Charlie there. It was obvious he would prefer to be alone. Charlie stood up. "I have to go. But I'd like a word with you first."

McKeown nodded. "Okay." But his manner implied, Hurry up.

"You asked me to tell you what I thought of Pettie."

McKeown gave a snort of unamused laughter. "You don't need to. I already know. He's a drunken bastard."

Charlie said, "He may be a bastard, but he wasn't drunk."

"No?" McKeown seemed to think the point was purely academic.

"He wanted you to think he was drunk."

Jessica McKeown, who had come into the room while they were talking, said, "Why?"

"He's determined that his group is not going to be taken over."

McKeown said grimly, "How's he going to stop it?"

"I think I can tell you. Now he knows he can needle you into losing your temper, he's going to try it again tomorrow."

McKeown's air of sullen boredom suddenly vanished, and he was alert. "What makes you think that?"

"I talked to him while we were eating. He's a determined man, and he hates you. He thinks you're going to destroy everything he believes in, but if he feels like that, why should he come here this evening? Because he wanted to find out more about you. He wants to know where you're vulnerable. Now he knows. When people needle you, you lose your temper."

Mrs. McKeown said, "He's right, Ben." McKeown smiled wryly.

Charlie said, "I think he's going to try it in the boardroom. He'll probably start off by sounding very civilized and reasonable. Then he'll start to needle. And he'll keep on until he's got you off balance. I think he might even try dragging your private life in—talking about Nicky, for instance."

"Does he know about Nicky?"

"Yes. He asked me about his problems with the police."

McKeown whistled. "The bastard!"

Charlie looked at his watch. "I have to go." He could see that he had said enough.

CHAPTER ELEVEN

JUST BEFORE dusk on the following afternoon, Charlie came back from his house calls with frozen fingers and an incipient sore throat. He made himself coffee in the recreation room, helped himself to two chocolate biscuits from the communal supply, and went up to his surgery. Outside, the wind was moaning as it blew from the river. The ice on the canal was so thick that children were playing on it.

On days like this, he envied his partners their comfortable homes, where they could snatch an hour in front of the fire when things were slack. Even if he went back to his lodgings, the room would take half an hour to warm up. Days like this led to daydreams of marriage and cozy domesticity.

The telephone rang. Instead of the voice of the girl on the switchboard, there were various electronic noises. Then a voice said, "Hello, Charles?"

"Who's that?"

"Erik Topelius."

"Good God, Erik! Where are you?"

"In Uppsala. I wanted to talk to you about this proposition."

"What proposition?"

"From your businessman friend—I didn't catch his name."

He took a deep breath. "Erik, I don't know what you're talking about."

"You don't? Hasn't he talked to you already?"

"*Who?*"

"He said he was a friend of yours. It sounded like a Scotch name—Mac-something."

"Ben McKeown?"

"That's it!"

"When did he speak to you?"

"About an hour ago."

"What did he want?"

"He wants to know if I would be willing to come to England to work with you."

Charlie began to feel slightly insane.

171

"I know nothing about it. Can I ring you back when I've found out what it's all about? What's your number there?"

When Topelius was off the line, Charlie tried to get the switchboard operator. There was no reply. The switchboard in the dispensary was unmanned, and the lines had been switched to Charlie's surgery. This explained why the call had come straight through. On the notepad beside the phone there was the single word "Topelius." While Charlie was scrawling a note, the girl came back. She had been to the kitchen to make tea. "Has anyone phoned while I was out?"

"Yes, this professor rang twice from Sweden."

"No one else?"

"There was a lady. When I said you were out, she said she'd ring back."

From the surgery, he dialed the McKeowns' number. It was Jessica McKeown who came on the line.

"I'm so glad you rang. I've been trying to get you. I wanted to tell you the takeover was a success."

"That's marvelous!" He was genuinely delighted. "Do you know what happened?"

"No. But Ben told me to ask you to dinner this evening. Can you come?"

"Thanks, I'd love to. But do you know anything about his call to Uppsala?"

"Uppsala?" She sounded blank.

"Topelius just rang me from Uppsala. He said your husband had made him some kind of an offer."

She said, "Ah . . . I see."

"Any idea what it's all about?"

"No, but I think I can guess. I told Ben about Topelius. I expect he'll explain it to you this evening."

"But have you any idea what he's got in mind?"

There was a pause, then she said, "You remember I told you that you could make a fortune?"

"Yes."

"Ben thinks so too. That's what he wants to talk to you about."

He experienced a nervous contraction of the stomach. McKeown seemed to spend his time pitchforking him into situations for which he was unprepared.

"All right. Thanks. I'll see you after surgery this evening."

For the next ten minutes he sat in his chair, his coffee still untouched, staring at the opposite wall with its posters warning against the dangers of smoking. Although it was becoming dark, he made no attempt to switch on the desk lamp. Now the news had time to sink in, the tension in his stomach had given way to a watery feeling of excitement, not unlike his feelings as a schoolboy on the last day of term.

As he arrived that evening, Mrs. McKeown was showing out a big man with a broken nose. She said, "Charles, I'd like you to meet Mr. Soper of the South London Chess Club. He's going to coach Nicky."

Mr. Soper, who wore a white polo-neck sweater under his duffle coat, looked like a large and friendly gorilla. Charlie asked him, "Do you think Nicky's going to be a good player?"

"He's already good." Soper had a rasping, throaty voice. "We'll see how good when he plays in the under-twenties tournament next week."

As they watched him squeeze himself into his mini and start the engine, Charlie said, "I'm glad he's big."

"Why?"

"Nicky needs someone he can respect. Somehow, I don't think he'd react well to a little man with a bald head."

For some reason, this struck her as funny, and she laughed with a lightheartedness that he had never heard from her before.

McKeown had still not arrived home. As she handed Charlie a sherry Mrs. McKeown said, "Are you all right? You're looking pale."

He laughed. "To tell the truth, I'm feeling nervous."

She was surprised. "Why?"

"Your husband's always springing things on me. I never know what it will be next."

"Oh, that's Ben's way. When he gets an idea, he has to carry it out immediately. He's terribly impatient."

"Does it always work?"

"Not always. But surprisingly often. He seems to have some kind of an instinct."

Charlie shrugged. "In this case, I wouldn't be surprised if it hadn't led him astray."

They heard the sound of a car outside. She said, "You don't have to make up your mind now. Tell him you need time to think." She went to the door. "But *I've* got a feeling you'll succeed at anything you really want to."

Charlie stared after her, reflecting that there were times when it is a disadvantage to inspire blind faith.

Ben McKeown had the air of a man who has been celebrating, and who feels that the world means well by him. He was followed by the colonel, and a large, pink man with steel-rimmed glasses.

"Hello Charles. Glad you could come. You know Colonel Vowles, don't you? And this is our accountant, Hugh Masson. Jess, would you get Hugh and Robert a drink? I want a word with Charlie. Excuse me, gentlemen."

He led Charlie across the hall, into a room lined with bookcases. Nicky was sitting at a desk near the fire, a chessboard in front of him. McKeown ruffled his hair.

"Hello, kid. How we doing?"

Nicky said with enthusiasm, "Dad, I'm going to play in the tournament next week, and a man called Soper's going to coach me. He's the champion for the whole of the south of England."

McKeown laughed indulgently. "That's marvelous. You'll be world champion one of these days. Listen, Nicky, I want to talk to Dr. Peruzzi. Do you mind leaving us alone for ten minutes?"

"Okay." It was the first time Charlie had seen him obey his father without reluctance or resentment.

McKeown pointed to an armchair. "Have a seat." He bit the end off a cigar and spat it into the fire. Charlie could see now that he was not drunk; only brimming over with confidence and well-being. McKeown puffed the cigar alight. "Charles, I've got a proposition for you. Jess tells me you've got some tremendous ideas, but you need backing." He pointed his cigar at Charlie. "I'm going to back you. To the tune of a hundred thousand a year."

Although he had been expecting something of the sort, Charlie felt winded.

"That's . . . very kind of you. But . . . what am I supposed to do with all that money?"

McKeown grinned. "I never met anyone who couldn't spend money."

"No, what I mean is . . . what do you *want* me to do with it?"

"Use it for research. Set up a laboratory."

It suddenly seemed to Charlie that this whole conversation was based on a misunderstanding, and he would have to make this clear.

"But what I'm trying to say . . . " He tried to find a way of putting it tactfully. "What do you hope to get from it?"

McKeown laughed good humoredly. "Okay, good question. I take your point. Let me tell you a story. Four years ago I bought the controlling shares in a company in Silicon Valley. When I looked through the accounts I found a hundred thousand dollars for something called 'A.I. Research.' I asked what that meant and they said, 'Artificial Intelligence'. I said, 'Okay, so what's all that money for?' And they said, 'It's a computer program called Forty-Niner.' They said, 'We're feeding in all the information we can get about geology and mining to see if the computer can tell us where to find oil or mineral deposits.' I said, 'What's the result so far?' and they said, 'Oh, none so far. We're still working on it.' Well, six months ago we acquired the prospecting rights on a hundred square miles in Oregon, and I sent the surveyor's report to the Silicon Valley project. The answer came back, 'There's no oil, but there's a chemical called molybdenum in the mountains.' I said, 'What the hell's molybdenum?' and they said, 'It's a stuff you use in making spark plugs and furnaces.' Two days ago I got the first report from the mining company that's drilling there. They reckon there's at least two *billion* dollars worth of molybdenum under the mountains. And we found it because somebody decided to spend a hundred thousand dollars on a computer program. You see my point?"

"Well, yes." All this had done nothing to allay Charlie's doubts. "But I don't think my ideas on psychology are ever going to be as commercial as that."

McKeown waved this aside. "Listen. Nicky's had four psychiatrists, and they were all useless. They talked about traumas and repressed hostility and God knows what, and they didn't do a damn bit of good. You did more for Nicky in two days than they did in two years. Well, Jess tells me you've got some theory about chemicals. About human beings being like chemicals you mix together. And that strikes me as good sense. Look at me and that bastard Pettie. We're like two chemicals that don't mix. It's not because we don't *want* to get on together, we just don't mix. It's like chemicals. And if you want to learn about chemicals, you've got to have a lab. Right?"

"Right." But he said it without conviction.

"So that's what you do. You find yourself a lab. You get this pal of yours over from Sweden—I'll pay his expenses—and the two of you decide what you need by way of equipment."

"But he's got his own laboratory in Sweden."

McKeown looked startled. "He has?"

"Yes."

"And he's already doing these experiments?"

"No."

"Why not?"

"Well . . . because that's my idea."

"Ah." McKeown nodded slowly. "And where does he come in?"

"He gave me the idea. He started me thinking about it."

"So do you want to work with him or not?"

"Well, yes . . . if *he* wants to."

McKeown slapped him on the shoulder.

"Okay, fine. That's settled then. We'll discuss the details when he gets to London." A thought struck him. "You're sure you want to work with this Topelius character? I mean, he might steal your ideas . . . "

Charlie laughed. "No, I don't mind. They're half his ideas anyway."

McKeown said dubiously, "Well, I shouldn't be too generous. Ideas are worth money. But that's up to you."

"There's another problem. Topelius has got his own department. He can't just throw up everything."

"We'll see. How much does he make a year?"

"I don't know."

"Twenty thousand?"

"Perhaps."

"We'll offer him twice that." The clock on the mantelpiece struck nine. "Come on, let's go and eat."

Charlie felt that this conversation had been like something from *Alice in Wonderland*. It had sounded logical, and he understood nothing whatever. But McKeown was already on his way back to the other room, leaving Charlie to follow.

He heard McKeown say, "It's all settled."

Jessica McKeown said, "I'm so glad."

Charlie reminded himself to ask her what she was glad about.

When they were eating their first course and the butler and maid had left, Jessica McKeown said, "Well, tell us all about the great boardroom battle."

Ben McKeown laughed noisily, and raised his wine glass.

"To the great boardroom battle." He emptied most of the glass. They were drinking Corton Charlemagne and even Charlie could tell it was good.

Vowles said, "You tell them, Hugh. You're good at these things."

"Very well." Masson was a big, gentle-looking man, whose steely blue eyes were somehow at odds with his pink complexion and white hair, but he spoke with the precision of someone accustomed to presenting facts in an orderly manner. "It was all very polite to begin with. We showed them the accounts and brochures and visual aids, and Ben gave an excellent summary of the group's activities over the past ten years. And we showed them that publicity film about our American subsidiary. They all seemed very impressed, particularly this nice old chap, Lord Ormskirk. He didn't look as if he understood everything . . . "

McKeown chuckled. "He didn't look as if he knew his arse from his elbow."

Masson, obviously accustomed to these interuptions, did not bat an eyelid.

" . . . but I think he was rather more astute than he looked. Finally, that part was all over, and we all answered questions from their board."

Vowles said, "When they asked about Capital Gains Tax, we knew they were interested."

"Yes, at that point I must admit I felt it was all more or less settled. We offered to buy their shares outright, or make a generous exchange deal with our own shares, to save CGT. They all seemed to like *that* idea. Then, finally, Pettie got to his feet. He said he could see that his fellow board members found our offer attractive, but he himself had certain misgivings. Then he went on to give us a history of his own group. I think he did that part rather well, I must say. How the firm almost went bankrupt in 1914, and how they were saved by the war, when the English started drinking Scotch whiskey instead of brandy. And how they expanded their chain stores after the Second World War."

McKeown said sarcastically, "With the emphasis on quality, of course."

"Yes, I felt he was rather overdoing the talk about quality. Ben didn't tell me until afterwards about the little argument last night . . . And finally, when he'd finished, Vowles said, 'You seem to be suggesting that your reputation for quality might suffer if you became part of McKeown Enterprises. Have you any solid reasons for that assumption?' And Pettie cleared his throat and said, in a very gentlemanly manner 'Yes, I'm afraid I have.' Then he turned to his own board and said, 'I don't know whether you gentlemen know about Mr. McKeown's earlier history, and how he became one of the

most talked-about men in the City of London . . . ' And he went on
to give a brilliantly malicious account of McKeown and Farmer, and
the dealings of High Rise Property Development . . . "

McKeown said with cold satisfaction, "That murderous little
bastard dug up every bit of dirt he could find. He even read out the
nastiest bits from *Private Eye.*"

Masson said, "I could hardly believe my ears. I've heard some
unpleasant things said in boardrooms, but never anything like this.
I'm sure half of it was slander. And what made it worse is that he
sounded so calm and objective about it. The poor old chap, Ormskirk, looked as if he wanted to hide under the table. But I must say,
I was lost in admiration for Ben. He didn't bat an eyelid. Just sat
there absolutely calm, as if the chap was singing his praises."

Vowles said, "It was a bad half hour, I can tell you. I was
expecting Ben to start throwing things at any moment. But he was
as cool as a cucumber. I've never seen him look so unruffled."

McKeown smiled wryly at Charlie, and winked.

Jessica McKeown said, "Then what happened?"

"When it was all over, Ben stood up. He said, 'Well, gentlemen,
I'm glad to have all the cards on the table like this. If we're going to
be partners, it's important to know one another. You all know how
easy it is to get a bad reputation in business, particularly if you're
very successful. Now I'd like to tell you the true story of McKeown
and Farmer and the High Rise Property Development Corporation . . . ' And within five minutes, he'd got them all on his side.
It was quite incredible. He didn't argue. He just talked business
common sense, and they seemed to find it fascinating."

Vowles said, "I don't think they'd ever come across anyone like
Ben before."

McKeown was doing his best to look modest, and not succeeding
particularly well.

Masson said, "They decided to take a vote on it. Some of the
oldsters were on Pettie's side, but Ormskirk was on ours. If he'd
refused, we'd have been sunk. And when we added up the vote, we'd
got seventy-seven percent—exactly one percent more than we
needed for the takeover."

Jessica McKeown laughed. "No wonder you're all looking so
pleased with yourselves." She put exactly the right amount of
female admiration into it.

Vowles placed his hand on McKeown's shoulder.

"We owe it entirely to Ben. When Pettie had finished his bit of character assassination, I was convinced we'd lost. It was amazing to see the way Ben talked them round."

McKeown said, "Spare my blushes." Charlie observed with surprise that he was, in fact, blushing.

For the rest of the meal, Charlie listened carefully and said nothing. No one noticed his silence; the men were too busy talking. At one point, McKeown was called to the telephone. He came back chortling and rubbing his hands.

"The New York Stock Exchange got the news an hour before they closed. At closing time, our shares were up a dollar eighty."

Masson said, "My God," and began doing calculations on a pocket calculator. Then he held it out and showed it to McKeown and Vowles. Vowles gave a long whistle. McKeown said, "Well, what d'you know?" And for the next few minutes they were quiet and thoughtful, apparently slightly stunned. When they began to talk again, the heady excitement had evaporated. They talked soberly about tax havens, tax avoidance schemes and foreign subsidiaries. For all practical purposes it had become a business meeting, and Charlie and Jessica McKeown were superfluous.

As he listened to the figures they mentioned, Charlie began to understand. For McKeown Enterprises, a hundred thousand pounds was not a wild extravagance; it was little more than petty cash. They could have subsidized a dozen such schemes without noticing it.

But why should they want to subsidize him? This was also not difficult to guess. Because he had been forewarned about Pettie, McKeown had pulled off an astonishing business *coup*. The offer of a laboratory was not a gesture of gratitude, merely an attempt to secure Charlie's services for the future. It was a modest business investment, like taking out travel insurance before a holiday. It might, of course, be a waste of money; but then, it could probably be written off as a tax loss.

Masson was saying, "I'm sorry to talk business, Jessica, but we didn't think things would move so quickly. There's a lot we've got to decide before the Stock Exchange opens tomorrow."

She smiled pleasantly. "I'm glad it's all going so well."

McKeown stood up. "If you'll excuse me, I've got to call our broker in Los Angeles. I won't bother with coffee." At the door he said, "You two want to listen in?"

When Charlie and Jessica were alone, she said, "Well?"

"He's offered me a hundred thousand pounds to set up a laboratory."

"That's wonderful. Aren't you pleased?"

He said, "I know this sounds stupid, but . . . I think I'm going to have to turn it down."

Oddly enough, she did not seem surprised. "Yes?"

The wine, combined with his tiredness and the incipient cold, made it difficult to put his thoughts in order.

"You see, I'm not a business consultant. I'm not even a psychologist. I'm just an ordinary GP."

"Not quite ordinary."

He smiled faintly at the compliment.

"Thank you. What bothers me is that if I took all that money, I'd feel I had to start worrying about results. I'd begin to feel rushed. And at this moment, I don't feel ready to start thinking about quick results. I want to let the ideas develop at their own pace."

"While you work as a GP?"

"I don't mind being a GP. It's hard work, but it's rewarding. And it pays me more money than I need; only this afternoon I was thinking about getting a new car. Besides, I wouldn't know how to start spending that much money."

"It won't go as far as you think."

"I suppose not. But I still wouldn't know where to start."

She said, "Could I offer a suggestion?"

"Of course."

"Go home now and think about it when you've had a good night's sleep. Then ring me tomorrow."

She was obviously right. He knew that his tiredness was distorting his perceptions. He emptied his wine glass.

"Thanks. I'll do that." He glanced at the clock. "But hadn't I better wait to say good night to your husband?"

"I shouldn't. I'll tell him you were called away by a patient."

"It seems rather rude."

"Of course it's not. Besides, if you told him you were thinking about turning it down, it might upset him. You do understand, don't you?"

He did, perfectly. What she meant was that McKeown had a streak of paranoia, and might interpret a refusal, or even a request for time to think it over, as a snub. So if he was going to refuse, he had to find a gentle and tactful way of doing it.

As far as he was concerned, that was another reason for turning it down.

His landlady had switched on his electric blanket. He slid into the warm bed with a sigh of gratitude and turned off the light. He tried to stay awake for a few minutes, staring at the shadow of the window-frame cast by the street lamp on the ceiling. It seemed a pity to fall asleep immediately on the day he had been offered a hundred thousand pounds. But the effort to keep his eyes open was counterproductive, and within seconds he was fast asleep.

He woke up with a shock as someone knocked on the door. The light went on. Vic Gibbs was standing in the doorway, wearing a dressing gown and pajamas. "Charlie, there's a lady called Perrin at the door. She says her husband's cut his throat."

He was instantly wide awake. "Oh Christ."

Maude Perrin was the mother of the ten-year-old girl who had syphilis. She ran the newspaper shop a hundred yards down the road.

"Thanks, Vic. Tell her I'll be down right away." It was almost one o'clock. He had been asleep about two hours.

As he dressed, he found himself wondering whether this could be a case of murder. When Charlie had diagnosed venereal disease, her first words had been, "I'll kill the bastard that did it." She was a big woman, and looked physically capable of murder. Charlie recalled a passage in one of his books on forensic pathology about the difference between suicidal and homicidal cut-throat wounds, but decided there was no time to look it up now.

Mrs. Perrin was sitting on the chair beside the hall telephone. She was wearing an old black fur coat over her nightgown, and had carpet slippers on her feet. Her eyes were red, but her face looked set and stony.

Charlie said, "How long ago did you find him?"

"Ten minutes."

"Is he dead?"

"I think so."

Neither spoke as they hurried back down the hill. It was necessary to tread with care on the icy pavement.

She had left the front door of the shop wide open, with the light on. Charlie followed her through the shop and up the narrow stairs. He asked her, "Where's Gertie?" Gertie was the child.

"They took her into care."

"Oh, I see."

The door of the back bedroom stood open, and he could see that the pillow was soaked in blood. The bed was about six inches from the wall, and George Perrin was lying with his head in the gap. A meat carving knife lay on the counterpane.

Charlie took hold of the shoulders, and pulled the man on to his back; he was not heavy. The throat wound was about four inches long, from left to right, with a slightly downward direction. The wound had divided the windpipe, but, as far as he could see, missed the carotid arteries. He took the wrist, and thought he detected a faint pulse. He said, "Quick, the telephone. He's still alive."

The phone was in the living room downstairs. He dialed 999, asked for an ambulance, and explained that it was an emergency.

Back upstairs, he confirmed with the stethoscope that the man was still alive. He asked Mrs. Perrin for a warm sponge. When she brought it, he carefully wiped away some of the blood on the throat. When this was done, he could see that there were two more superficial wounds on the left side of the throat. It was clear that the man had made two attempts to draw the knife across his throat before he worked up enough courage to make the cut. There was also, he noticed, a cut on the index finger of his left hand. He had evidently stretched the skin of the throat before cutting, and sliced a piece of flesh off the finger. All this made it clear that this was a genuine suicide attempt.

Realizing that blood was flowing back into the windpipe, he turned the body on its side. A mixture of blood and mucus immediately flowed out, and the man began to breathe. Charlie had to make a quick decision. The man could bleed to death before the ambulance arrived. From his bag he took a broad roll of adhesive tape, and tried to bring together the divided cartilage with one hand and stick on the tape with the other. The blood made this difficult, but he finally succeeded.

Maude Perrin was sitting in an armchair by the empty fireplace, watching him without comment. Her eyes looked dull and lifeless.

He asked her, "How did you happen to find him?"

"I heard this noise . . . "

"Did he normally sleep in here?"

"No. He slept in there with me. But I told him he'd have to move."

Her voice was so low that Charlie had to bend close to her. As he did so, he detected alcohol on her breath.

He said, "Why don't you go and make some tea? There's nothing more to be done until the ambulance comes."

"Do you want tea?"

"Yes please." It was not true, but he wanted to give her something to do. She went downstairs, moving slowly and heavily.

The ambulance arrived a few minutes later. The ambulance man looked at the bloodless face on the pillow and said, "He's a goner."

"No, he's still alive."

"But he won't be."

"Why not?"

"Because when they sew it up, he'll die of suffocation. I suppose they might *just* do it, but it's a hundred to one."

When George Perrin had been taken away, Charlie used the phone to notify the police. The man on duty asked if he wanted someone sent around immediately. Charlie said there was no point; the man was already in the hospital. The policeman sounded relieved, and said they would send someone in the morning.

The woman brought him in a cup of tea. She was moving heavily, like a sleepwalker. She sat on the other side of the table and stared into the dead ashes of the fire. The room was small, dark, and smelled of eucalyptus. Charlie tasted the tea, and found it was far too sweet. But he took another sip for the sake of appearances.

"How do you feel?"

She shrugged. For the first time, her face showed some expression. It was of pain and incomprehension, but it was better than the blank indifference of a moment before.

Charlie said, "I think he may live."

"No. He's better dead." She said it with deliberation, like someone who has thought out a problem to its conclusion.

He made a noise that indicated neither agreement nor disagreement, merely acknowledgment of what she had said. After a silence she said, "He couldn't stand prison, at his time of life." She looked at him. "That's why he did it. He knew they'd send him to jail."

He remembered the child's genitals, and felt a spasm of disgust. "Then why did he commit the crime?"

She said without emotion, "It was my fault."

"Why?"

"George doesn't drink. He's a teetotaler. I used to have a drink in front of the fire and fall asleep; hot rum punch. That's when he'd do it. When we was first married, Gertie used to cry a lot. My previous husband used to beat her. That's why I divorced him. George'd take her into his bed. That's how it all started." She seemed to read his thoughts. "It's been going on for years."

"Did you know he was a pedophile?"

"What?"

"That he liked children . . . sexually."

She shook her head. "Oh no. I don't think it was children in general. Just Gertie."

"How did he pick up . . . the disease?"

"I don't know. He says he doesn't know, but I don't believe him. Mrs. Ostridge—that's my neighbor on this side—told me she'd seen him with a woman up at the Elephant, but I thought she must have been mistaken."

She began to cry quietly. Charlie made no attempt to comfort her. He could think of nothing that would not sound artificial and forced. Besides, he could see that the tears were a release. This was a problem to which there was no solution. As astonishing as it seemed, he could see that she still loved her husband. All this struck her as unreal; she found it hard to believe that everything had changed so much. But she was right; her husband would almost certainly go to prison, and would be treated there with the bitter intolerance that is meted out to child molesters. If he somehow escaped prison, Gertie would remain in care. The simplest solution was for George Perrin to die. He must have known that too, as he made two unsuccessful cuts at his throat with the razor-sharp knife. Suddenly, with total clarity, Charlie imagined what it had been like—a little, bald-headed man with weak eyes who has steeled himself to the recognition that he has to die, although the thought terrifies him. Pity choked him, so that he would have found it impossible to speak.

He opened his bag. "I'll leave you some tranquilizers and sleeping tablets. You can take three of these if you think you'll need them."

"Thank you." In her misery and shock, she still made the effort to be polite.

Charlie said, "Try and get some sleep."

"Yes."

As she came to the door, he glanced at her face. It was stony and fatalistic. He was fairly certain she would not attempt suicide. Besides, there was the child.

She said, "I've got to clean up that bed."

"Why don't you leave it till morning?"

"No. The blood'll never come out unless I get it into salty water."

As he hesitated at the door, wondering if there was anything more he could say, she said, "It'll be funny not to have a man in the house."

"Yes."

He walked back quickly because of the cold. In his own room, he rang the Guys casualty department and inquired about George Perrin. The houseman was a doctor he knew. He said, "Sorry, he's dead. He suffocated when we tried to sew him up."

"Thanks, Fred."

He undressed, climbed into bed, and switched out the light. In the distance, he could hear early-morning traffic. When he closed his eyes he saw the face of Maude Perrin, crying quietly, her big, rawboned wrist sticking out of the sleeve of the dressing gown. He experienced again what he had felt perhaps a dozen times since he had started training as a doctor: a sense of helplessness, of ineffectuality in the face of suffering. He felt sorry for them all: for Mrs. Perrin, who no longer had a man in the house, for Gertie Perrin, who could not understand why she had been taken away from home, for George Perrin, who had probably slipped so gradually and gently into temptation that he had not even noticed it.

When he had talked to Grimshaw about his desire to be a doctor, he had often observed a peculiar smile, a mixture of fondness, sympathy and pity. Now he understood it. Grimshaw knew that Charlie's ideas about medicine were as romantic and unrealistic as a child's desire to be a cowboy or an engine driver. He knew that the life of a doctor is not particularly heroic: that the moments in which he saves the life of a child with one stroke of the knife are rare, and that the rest is routine and repetition, the daily struggle against an enemy who is as tireless as the sea as it erodes the land. Grimshaw knew that the GP has to learn to live without major victories, and be content with winning the occasional skirmish. In retrospect, Charlie could see that his hero-worship must have struck Grimshaw as charming and rather saddening.

It was at this moment that, by an association of ideas, the face of Lesley Engledow superimposed itself on that of Mrs. Perrin. As he had listened to Lesley's recital of random promiscuity and emotional disasters, Charlie had experienced the same sense of helplessness and inevitability. Yet in Lesley's case, the inevitability had proved to be a lie, since the disaster was averted. The same had been true of Sharon Engstrom and of Nicky McKeown. Now, with sudden clarity, he recognized that his chief enemy was his own tendency to concede defeat, to decline to take the risk of hope and optimism.

His heart contracted with a curiously mixed sensation of foreboding and exhilaration. It took him a moment to identify its cause; the recognition that, whatever the consequences, he had to accept Ben McKeown's offer. The real answer to the problem of Mrs. Perrin, and thousands like her, was not to administer tranquilizers and sleeping tablets, but to look for more general solutions.

And now he had faced it, he realized that this recognition had been lying dormant in his unconscious mind since that weekend in the Park View Hotel, and that it had been the source of the curious sense of expectation that he had experienced ever since.

It had been the recognition that his days as a general practitioner were numbered.

CHAPTER TWELVE

It was as he was driving to the surgery the next morning that the misgivings began to set in. It was an unexpectedly bright day, with a foretaste of spring in the air, and he drove with the car window lowered, enjoying the cold freshness of the air. He experienced a sudden glow of affection for the familiar streets, and the thought that he would soon be leaving them behind brought a sharp pang of regret. This was followed by a kind of panic. Was he insane to think of throwing away his security like this? How would the other doctors in the practice react? He could already predict how his parents would react, and the thought made his heart sink.

He was at the surgery by half past eight. The Pikes had not yet arrived and neither had Elliotson, but in the kitchen he found Sandor Kos, brewing himself coffee in a battered percolator that had accompanied him halfway round the world. Charlie accepted his offer to share it, and they went back to Sandor's surgery. There Sandor produced a flash of brandy and poured a generous measure into both cups. They drank the coffee black, without sugar.

Hesitantly, Charlie told him about Ben McKeown's offer. He was convinced before he began to speak that Sandor would advise against it, but Kos lived up to his reputation for unpredictability.

"Take it, my dear boy, take it! Ring him up before he changes his mind."

"But you told me you thought Topelius's personality theory was nonsense!"

Sandor gave his expressive shrug. "Pooh, what does that matter? At least it gives you the chance to be independent."

"Independent of what?"

"Of all this." Sandor gestured with casual disgust at his surgery. "Ah, believe me, Charles, there is no fate worse than spending a lifetime treating piles and gumboils. It's worse than being a convict. Now, if I'd seized my opportunity in Vienna fifty years ago, I wouldn't be here now."

"What happened?"

Kos lit a black, evil-smelling cigarette, and had to wait for a fit of coughing to subside before he could speak.

187

"When Wilhelm Reich was setting off for Copenhagen, he asked me to become his personal assistant. That was in—let me see— 1933, when he'd just been driven out of Berlin by the Nazis, and Freud was determined to drive him out of Vienna. So after a few months, Reich accepted an offer to go to Denmark, and asked me if I'd like to go with him. I admired Reich more than anyone in the world, so my first impulse was to say yes. Then I decided I'd better consult my wife—we'd only been married for six months—so I told Reich I'd give him my decision the next day. That evening, when I arrived home, I found Federn waiting for me. He was the head of the Psychoanalytic Association. Freud had sent him to warn me about associating with Reich. When I told him I was thinking of going to Copenhagen, he said, "I beg of you not to do anything so foolish. Reich is a marked man. His career is in ruins. If you go with him, you'll be ruined too." My wife was there, and she agreed with Federn. Besides, she loved Vienna, and enjoyed being married to a rising young doctor. So the next day I told Reich I couldn't go. I remember he gave me a strange look and said, "Yes, I understand." And somehow, I knew instinctively that our friendship was at an end. Less than a year later, after the murder of Dolfuss, I decided to get out of Vienna. But by that time, Reich had been driven out of Denmark and was wandering around Europe. Helga and I moved to Zurich. Five years later, I went to New York and called on Reich. He had already started to develop his persecution mania. He felt I'd betrayed him by refusing to leave Vienna. We tried to collaborate, but it was a failure from the start. After a few weeks we quarreled, and I never saw him again."

Sandor's cigarette had gone out while he talked. He relit it and snapped the match between his fingers, as if it symbolized his career.

"I've always regretted that I didn't go to Copenhagen. It would have changed my life. I would have stayed with Reich, and I would have carried on his work when he died. But I missed my opportunity because I preferred security—or rather, because my wife preferred it. And while we were living in Zurich, she left me anyway."

"But surely you wouldn't have been any better off if you'd gone to Denmark with Reich?"

Kos shook his head, and his face was sadder than Charlie had ever seen it.

"No. But I would have had a purpose. And I would have been independent. Perhaps life would have been difficult. But then, life is always difficult. Freud had to struggle for years to achieve recognition. So did Jung." His eyes wandered to the concrete block of high-rise flats across the road. "It is far better to struggle with a purpose than to struggle with no purpose."

For the first time, Charlie understood the sense of futility that lay behind the ironic, faintly malicious smile. He would recall it six months later, when he attended Sandor's funeral.

He looked at his watch; it was nearly nine. He said, "Thanks, Sandor," and meant it.

In his surgery, he dialed the McKeown's home. It was Jessica McKeown who answered.

"I'm afraid Ben is already at his office."

"I just wanted to leave him a message. I wanted to tell him I'd like to accept his offer."

"I'm so glad." The tone of her voice said more than words.

Charlie's main worry had been how the other doctors would take it. They had all treated him with kindness, and Helen Pike had gone out of her way to smooth out his difficulties. The thought of deserting them at short notice filled him with guilt and self-reproach.

This proved unnecessary. The Pikes seemed genuinely pleased at his good fortune. Elliotson expressed some misgivings about the wisdom of making himself reliant on Ben McKeown, but even he seemed to feel that it was a risk worth taking. Charlie's resignation posed no problem. Both trainees were close to the end of their training period, and another was due to start at Easter. The only question was when the resignation should take effect.

At eleven o'clock he was in Herbert Pike's surgery when Ben McKeown rang.

"Morning, Charles. Jessica gave me your message. Any chance of getting over here?"

"When?"

"Now?"

"Sorry, that's impossible. I'm just setting out on my house calls."

Helen Pike signaled to him and whispered, "We can take over." He shook his head. McKeown said, "Could you come over for lunch?"

"Yes, fine. Where are you?"

"The Dorchester. Grab a taxi. I'll pay."

"No need, thanks. I'll drive."

"By the way, I want you to talk to the board for ten minutes—present your ideas. Okay?"

"Yes." But he experienced the sinking sensation.

As he hung up, Helen Pike said, "That's no way to treat a man who's giving you a hundred thousand quid."

He laughed. "I can't drop everything when he snaps his fingers."

"For a hundred thousand pounds I'd drop anything. And I mean *anything*."

Her banter gave him a sudden insight into why they had taken his resignation so well. They were enjoying his experience vicariously.

That morning, most of his house calls were in places he normally found depressing: a dreary block of flats that was due for demolition; a slum street where cars were regularly vandalized. He was interested to observe that they no longer had the power to lower his spirits. The knowledge that he would soon be seeing the last of them made them somehow more bearable, even gave them a touch of nostalgia. He made a note of the observation that our perceptions are influenced by our feelings.

Heavy traffic in Southwark made him late. Attempting to turn right into a main road, he was forced to brake sharply as a woman made a right turn across his path. He had to back in order to let her through, and received a venomous glare in acknowledgment. He experienced a sense of irritated vulnerability, then, when he thought about it, realized it was unnecessary. The woman was in the wrong for not looking right before she turned. He was still thinking about this as he arrived outside the Dorchester. The sight of the Daimlers, Rolls Royces and Jaguars opposite the entrance made him decide to try and park his own car in a side street. But while he hesitated, Ben McKeown came out of the swing doors.

"Come on, Charles, you're late. Leave that here and come on in." He turned to the commissionaire. "Can you get that parked?"

The man looked dubiously at the mud-stained Mini. "Yes, sir." He accepted the keys as if taking a piece of limp spaghetti. If McKeown noticed the lack of enthusiasm he ignored it. "Thanks." He took Charlie's arm and steered him across the lobby.

"I wanted a quick word with you before we go in. Takeovers are always a bit dodgy, and I don't want anything to go wrong at this stage, so I'd rather you didn't mention Pettie . . . " He made a see-saw motion with his hand to indicate a delicate balance.

Charlie said, "No, of course I won't."

He understood what McKeown meant: that he was not to mention his own advice about Pettie. The hint was unnecessary; he preferred to allow McKeown to take full credit for his boardroom triumph.

McKeown had hired a suite on the third floor, with a view over the park. In the distance, Charlie could see the silhouette of the Park View Hotel, and for some reason, this struck him as a good omen.

About three dozen men, mostly in morning dress, were drinking and eating cocktail snacks. In a corner, an enormous television set displayed the latest stock market figures. Glimpsing himself in a mirror, Charlie made a mental note to buy a suit that would not look shabby in broad daylight. Someone waved to him from the far side of the room, and he recognized Hugh Masson, his cheeks looking pinker than usual, his eyes gleaming behind the steel-rimmed glasses. McKeown touched Colonel Vowles on the sleeve.

"Robert, would you mind introducing Charles around? I've got things to do." He disappeared through the door.

Vowles was also looking relaxed and happy. He gave Charlie a friendly smile. "Hello, Charles, nice to see you. What will you drink? Gin and tonic?" He lowered his voice. "I hope you're going to explain what all this is about."

For a moment Charlie failed to understand him, then he said with astonishment, "Hasn't he told you?"

"Not a damn thing. Ben told us an hour ago that he had some new tax avoidance scheme and it involved you. He says you'll explain everything."

Again, Charlie had the sensation that McKeown had pushed him in at the deep end. He tried not to sound nervous as he said, "I'll do my best."

After the gin and tonic he felt better. The people all seemed friendly and there was a sparkle in the atmosphere, a sense of high spirits, which seemed to be explained by the performance of McKeown shares on the Stock Exchange. There was a general air of self-congratulation and a sense that everyone present was counting his gains.

It was half past one before they went in for lunch. Charlie excused himself and called the surgery, leaving a message that he would not be back until late in the afternoon. The Pikes had already arranged to take over his calls.

As he sat down, McKeown banged the table with an ashtray, then stood up and raised his champagne glass.

"Gentlemen, let us drink to McKeown Enterprises and its continuing success."

They all stood and echoed, "Success."

On Charlie's left, Colonel Vowles and Hugh Masson talked about the Tokyo Stock Market and how far it would be weakened by a scandal involving a leading Japanese politician. On his right, his neighbors were discussing something called floating rate notes and the Eurodollar bond market. Charlie was glad to be ignored. He was hungry and wanted a chance to think out what he was going to say. The meal passed in a pleasant haze, and his responses to Masson's attempts at conversation were absentminded.

When the cheese and grapes were brought in, Vowles stood up and proposed a toast to Ben McKeown, the "architect of the merger." They all stood up and raised their glasses to McKeown, who stared down at his plate with an air of detachment, but Charlie was close enough to observe the faint smile at the corners of his mouth. Vowles then made a speech about the takeover, including a reference to the boardroom battle that made it clear they all knew about McKeown's clash with Pettie. Charlie stared out of the window in case his eyes met McKeown's. After Vowles had sat down, Masson took a sheaf of papers from his briefcase and gave a summary of the group's present financial position. Charlie's attention began to wander and he had to stifle a yawn by pretending to blow his nose. He was jerked into wakefulness at the sound of his own name.

"... Dr. Charles Peruzzi, who will no doubt speak for himself." He felt as if someone had emptied a bucket of cold water over him. A moment later Masson said, "I would like to introduce Dr. Charles Peruzzi," and sat down to polite applause.

Charlie found himself on his feet with no idea of how he intended to begin, but a glance around the table convinced him there was no need for alarm. Some of the shareholders looked as if they were dozing; none looked particularly interested. Masson's flat, droning delivery had the same soporific effect as the distant hum of traffic from Park Lane.

Charlie drank a mouthful of wine to moisten his throat. "I'd better begin by explaining that I'm not a psychiatrist—just a general practitioner. And the ideas I want to talk about are not my own. The man who thought them up is a professor of applied psychology in Sweden called Erik Topelius."

He took a deep breath, and made an effort to focus the insights that had been developing in him for the past few months.

"If you asked me to explain Topelius's basic idea in a single sentence, I'd put it this way. There's something rather absurd about neurosis. It isn't necessary. People are far stronger than they think. The doctor's problem is how to make them see this. That's what personality surgery is all about.

"According to Topelius, none of us really knows what we can do until we're forced to make an effort. In my first year on the wards, we had a case of a man with several broken ribs. He was brought in on a Saturday afternoon by his son. This man ran a junk yard and he'd asked his thirteen-year-old son to help him load some old tractor parts. While they were trying to tilt a heavy crate on the back of a lorry, the man's foot slipped and he went under the lorry with the crate on his chest. The boy screamed for help but there was no one around, so he picked up the crate—weighing a quarter of a ton—and heaved it off his father's chest. Then he picked up his father, who weighed fifteen stone, and lifted him on to the back of the lorry. Then he drove him to the hospital. When the man recovered consciousness, he asked how he'd got there, and they told him his son had brought him in. He said that was impossible because his son couldn't drive, and this turned out to be true. I saw the boy myself and he was rather small and thin. I should say he was half his father's weight. Yet in the emergency he'd lifted a heavy crate, carried a heavy man, and driven a lorry when he didn't know how to drive. He'd obviously observed his father's driving subconsciously, and in the emergency, his subconscious took over.

"This is what Topelius means when he says none of us knows what we can do under pressure. And this is because we don't really know what we're like. We don't know the kind of person we are. That's why people seek out challenges: dangerous sports, mountain climbing, single-handed yacht racing. We can learn more about ourselves in five minutes of action than in a year sitting still.

"And yet this is the point. There ought to be some easier way of learning about yourself than risking your neck. You don't put your hand on the hot plate of a stove to find whether it's switched on; you hold your hand a few inches away. You don't jump into a swimming pool to find how cold it is; you put a few toes in the water. There ought to be similar methods for finding out what you're really like.

"Topelius compares the problem to looking into a mirror. If you think you've got a smudge of dirt on your nose, you can look into a mirror to find out. But if you've got something wrong with your personality, there's no mirror you can look into. Other people act as our mirrors, and they react to the way you present yourself. In other words, to what you *think* you are. So it's a kind of vicious circle."

He could see from the attention of his audience that he had captured their interest. He leaned forward, his knuckles on the tabletop.

"Imagine the following situation. You're about to pull out on to a main road when another driver turns straight across your path, forcing you to brake, and as you sit there, he goes past you cursing and shaking his fist. You know that *you're* in the right, yet his anger somehow makes you feel guilty. There's a part of you that reacts to his anger with a sense of guilt. And this part is stronger than your rational self, which tells you it isn't your fault. I call this part the *false personality*. And most people spend their lives being dominated by this false personality; overreacting to problems, feeling upset or angry or vulnerable when it's quite unnecessary.

"You see, if only we could create a kind of mirror in which people could see themselves as others see them, we'd have the solution. And in the past few months, I've begun to understand how this might be done. That's why I'd like to set up a laboratory to explore these ideas. And I'm grateful to Mr. McKeown for offering to make this possible."

He turned to Ben McKeown as he said this. To his surprise, McKeown rose to his feet.

"Gentlemen, I'm going to interrupt Dr. Peruzzi at that point." There was an audible murmur of disappointment. McKeown smiled and raised his hand. "I think you can all see that Dr. Peruzzi has some revolutionary ideas. And in our business, we all know that ideas are the most important commodity of all. So I'm going to suggest that we simply give him a vote of confidence, and tell him to go ahead. And when he's ready to talk to us about his results, we'll invite him to another board meeting."

There were murmurs of "Hear, hear." A few people seemed bewildered at the abrupt termination of Charlie's talk, but no one seemed disposed to object. At board meetings, McKeown's suggestions obviously had the force of commands. McKeown smiled benevolently around the table.

"Good, carried." He leaned across and held out his hand to Charlie, who shook it.

Colonel Vowles said, "Well, gentlemen, if no one else has any business to propose, I suggest we adjourn next door for coffee and brandy."

McKeown came up behind Charlie and squeezed his arm.

"That was terrific stuff. You've certainly got a gift for putting things into words."

"Thank you. But don't they want to know what I'm going to spend their money on?"

McKeown chuckled and winked.

"That's none of their business. All they need to know is that it's allowable against tax." He leaned closer and lowered his voice. "Anyway, the less you say in public, the better. You don't want other people to steal your ideas."

Charlie said, "I don't mind. Ideas are public property."

"Oh no they're not. Not when I'm paying for them."

Charlie said, "Yes, I see."

McKeown grinned at him and gave him a friendly punch on the arm.

"No you don't. But you'll learn."

CHAPTER THIRTEEN

THE NEXT few weeks were hectic, confusing, exhausting and curiously satisfying.

Three days after the meeting at the Dorchester, the whole project came close to shipwreck when Charlie was asked to call at the offices of McKeown's lawyers, Rowsley, Fox and Skerrit, at Fen Court in the City. He was shown into the office of Mr. Skerrit, a tall, thin man with a bald head and sunken eyes, who reminded Charlie of his old headmaster. Mr. Skerrit had drawn up a document of agreement, and Charlie was delighted to learn that it proposed that he should receive a hundred thousand pounds to set up a laboratory, and then a further hundred thousand a year to run it. This agreement could not be terminated by either party until the end of five years. Charlie glanced through the ten-page document, produced his pen, and prepared to sign. Mr. Skerrit shook his head irritably and insisted that Charlie should read it carefully and make sure he understood every clause. For example, paragraph four guaranteed that Charlie's ideas infringed no already existing copyright. Charlie replied that, as far as he knew, there was no copyright in these particular ideas. How far, asked Mr. Skerrit, were they the intellectual property of Professor Topelius? Charlie said he couldn't answer that. Topelius had given him the original idea, but the notion of personality surgery was his own development.

It became clear that Mr. Skerrit found these answers tiresome and annoying, and that he suspected Charlie of trying to evade the issue. The more he frowned and tightened his lips, the more he reminded Charlie of his headmaster, and the harder Charlie found it to explain himself. Skerrit pressed Charlie for the details of the experiments he proposed to carry out, and when Charlie admitted that, at the moment, he had only the vaguest ideas, Skerrit began to look more and more like a prosecuting counsel who is breaking down a dishonest witness. Finally, Skerrit said, "If what you say is true, then it seems to me that you are preparing to waste Mr. McKeown's money."

Charlie shrugged. "That could well be so."

197

"In that case, I feel it my duty to speak to Mr. McKeown before he signs this agreement."

Charlie felt a surge of temper. This man was *not* his headmaster, and he was not a schoolboy. Neither was he proposing to cheat anybody. He stood up.

"I suggest you do that. Good morning."

As he walked out into the confusing roar of Fenchurch Street, he felt relieved that he could still withdraw his notice and continue to work in the practice.

An hour later, the telephonist said that Mr. Gordon Fox wanted to speak to him. Mr. Fox, it seemed, was another partner in the law firm, and he wanted Charlie to return to the office immediately. Charlie said that was impossible. He had patients to see. Mr. Fox said that in that case, could he come and speak to Charlie in his surgery? Charlie finally made an appointment for three o'clock that afternoon. As he hung up, he experienced a certain grim satisfaction. Ben McKeown was not the kind of man who liked to have his judgment questioned, and it seemed obvious that he had used some harsh language to Mr. Skerrit.

That was confirmed when Mr. Fox arrived sharply at three o'clock. Mr. Fox was large, damp and propitiatory. He explained that Mr. Skerrit had exceeded his instructions, and from his briefcase produced the agreement and a fountain pen. Charlie said he would like a few days to study the agreement and think about it. (This was Herbert Pike's suggestion.) At this Mr. Fox became very concerned. He offered to go through the agreement line by line, and explain anything Charlie felt doubtful about. Charlie said he would still like time to think about it. Mr. Fox's eyes showed unmistakable signs of panic. He smiled confidentially, and explained that Mr. McKeown had insisted that the agreement should be signed today, so Charlie sat back in his chair and read the agreement paragraph by paragraph.

"Why does it say that I'm not allowed to publish any account of personality surgery without the permission of McKeown Enterprises?"

Mr. Fox explained that if McKeown Enterprises was paying for the research, then they expected to have some control over publication of the results.

Charlie said, "And what does this mean? Any commercial exploitation of the ideas uncovered during this research shall remain in the hands of McKeown Enterprises?"

Mr. Fox explained smoothly that it merely meant that *if* the research should have commercial possibilities, then McKeown Enterprises would expect to recover some of the costs of the financing.

"But what if I decided I wanted to write a book about my ideas? Would that mean I wouldn't be allowed to do it?"

Mr. Fox explained that there was nothing to prevent Charlie writing a book at the end of the five year period, although he would still have to ask permission of McKeown Enterprises to publish it.

Charlie reread these paragraphs several times and decided that he did not like them, but while Mr. Fox sat looking at him pleadingly, he found it hard to argue. Finally, he took the fountain pen and signed all three copies of the agreement. Mr. Fox looked immensely relieved. He said, "Now we can go on to more agreeable matters. Have you decided on how much you intend to pay yourself by way of salary?"

"No."

"Mr. McKeown has suggested thirty thousand a year, indexed against inflation."

Charlie tried to do a quick mental calculation and was staggered by the result. As far as he could work out, it gave him about six hundred pounds a week, more than three times his present salary.

Mr. Fox said, "It seems that Dr. Topelius has agreed to act as consultant, spending at least six weeks of every year in London. We suggest that for this he be paid ten thousand pounds a year. That would leave sixty thousand a year for the running costs of the laboratory, including rent. Do you think that will be sufficient?"

"I . . . I think so." He was feeling slightly breathless, and these sums seemed unreal.

"Have you found anywhere that might be suitable as a laboratory?"

"The top floor of this building is empty. We thought we'd consider that."

"How much?"

"They want a hundred and fifty pounds a week."

"Seven thousand eight hundred a year." Mr. Fox seemed to have a calculator inside his head. "That sounds reasonable. Then I'll leave that to you. Tomorrow morning, we shall deposit two hundred thousand pounds in Martin's Bank in the City. That represents a hundred thousand pounds for the setting up of the laboratory, and a hundred thousand pounds running costs for the first year. If you would like to call at our office in the afternoon, we'll give you the checkbooks."

Twenty minutes later, Mr. Fox was on his way back to Fen Court, with two copies of the agreement in his briefcase. When he had watched the car disappear into the traffic, Charlie went back to his surgery and stood by the window, staring at the brown waters of the canal, feeling curiously stunned and drained of energy, and reflecting that good fortune can produce much the same effect of shock and bewilderment as disaster.

That evening, Charlie telephoned Lesley and told her the news. She was as excited as he had expected.

"My God, you're rich!"

"Not exactly." He had been doing some calculations and concluded that two hundred thousand pounds was not, after all, an inexhaustible sum. "Most of that will go to rent and equipment and overhead."

"I expect daddy can give you lots of useful advice. Why don't you come over now and talk to him?"

The idea appealed to him. With so much to excite him, it seemed intolerable to be alone.

"Are you sure he can spare the time?"

"Of course he can. He'll be delighted."

In fact, Bob Engledow was looking concerned and uneasy. He took Charlie into his study and carefully read the agreement from beginning to end.

"You realize you've practically sold yourself to Ben?"

Charlie said awkwardly, "I'm not sure I've got much to sell."

Engledow threw down the agreement. "Ben obviously thinks so. He never does anything out of charity. The word's not in his vocabulary. Why do you suppose he's doing this?"

It was a question to which Charlie had given some thought. "To tell the truth, I think he's got some exaggerated ideas about me. I talked to his wife about my ideas, and she seemed very interested. She's the one who talked him into it." He said nothing about Pettie and the takeover bid. That seemed to him a private matter between himself and McKeown.

"And it doesn't worry you that you've become one of his employees?"

"Yes, it does. But I don't see any alternative. It's a chance and I've got to take it."

Lesley peeped into the room. "Daddy, we've opened some champagne. Shall I get you a glass?"

"No, thanks. I can't stand the filthy stuff. But I'd like a whiskey." When she had gone, he stared thoughtfully at the contract, his forehead wrinkled. "I just hope you don't regret this. If you did, I'd feel guilty for getting you mixed up with Ben."

Charlie laughed. "For heaven's sake! I'm the one who feels guilty."

Engledow looked surprised. "Why?"

"In case I waste his money and let him down."

Engledow laughed dryly. "He won't miss it. A hundred thousand a year is the equivalent of two company cars."

"I still wouldn't want to waste it. You see, when I talked to Mrs. McKeown about personality surgery, it all seemed perfectly straightforward. I thought I'd know exactly what to do if somebody offered me a laboratory. And now it's happened, I'm not sure how to begin. I suppose I'd really like more time to think it over."

Engledow placed his hand on Charlie's shoulder. "You've got time. Ben's given you all the time you want. Just stop worrying about it."

Lesley came in, carrying a tray with drinks. She gave her father his whiskey and Charlie a glass of champagne. She raised her own glass.

"Here's to *enormous* success."

Looking at her glowing face, Charlie experienced a twinge of shame. It was obvious that she believed in him far more than he believed in himself.

But the act of confessing his misgivings to Bob Engledow had relieved his mind. He woke up the next morning with a sense of lightness and exhilaration, as if it was the first day of a holiday. After surgery, he went to the municipal offices—the trainees took over his house calls—and collected the keys to the upstairs flat. The Pikes went up with him to look at it. Until three years ago, it had been used as an annex to the Inspector of Taxes. Now it looked vast and bleak and depressing, with damp-stained walls and grimy floors, and neon lights that made a loud humming noise. But the view north, over the Old Kent Road and the railway line from the Bricklayer's Arms Goods Station, was panoramic, with a glimpse of Southwark Park and the gray expanse of the river stretching to Wapping docks and the King Edward Memorial Park. It was not beautiful but breathtaking nonetheless. It looked even better when Helen Pike had found a bucket of water and a dishcloth in the kitchen and wiped the dust of three years from the large windows.

Herbert Pike said dubiously, "Well, I suppose something can be made of it."

Helen said, "What are you talking about! It's going to be marvelous! You'd be amazed what a difference you can make with a broom and a bucket of soapy water. If I had time I'd do it myself." She wandered through the kitchen. "You know, you could turn these two rooms into a nice little flat, if they'd let you."

Herbert Pike said, "They wouldn't. Not if it's being rented as an office."

"That's stupid! He's got to live somewhere! I bet this man McKeown could fix it. He can fix anything."

She proved to be correct. The borough council was at first adamant that it was impossible that office premises should be used for private accommodation. The administrative officer of the housing department sounded so positive that Charlie decided to drop the idea. Then Messrs. Rowsley, Fox and Skerrit undertook the negotiations, and within twenty-four hours it had been agreed that Charlie could use two rooms as a flat in exchange for a further two hundred pounds a year, bringing his rent up to precisely eight thousand pounds.

Helen was also right about the effect of soap and water. When Charlie brought Lesley Engledow to see the place on Saturday afternoon, the floor was still damp, and the main office still looked as bleak as an empty picture gallery; but the walls were clean and white, the cobwebs had vanished from the ceiling, and the view through the newly washed windows was almost magical. Doris Cahill, the Pikes' cleaning lady, was still there, sponging down the kitchen walls with a mixture of washing-up fluid and ammonia. She pointed out to Charlie that he could enlarge the kitchen by knocking down the wall that separated it from the storeroom next door. She also advised him that the cheapest way of covering the floors would be with cork tiles. Lesley disagreed. She said that it would be cheaper in the long run to buy woolen carpet at twelve pounds per square yard. Charlie objected timidly that a carpet seemed an unnecessary luxury in a laboratory, and both women immediately assured him that he was totally mistaken. From then on, he listened while the women walked from room to room and discussed carpets, curtains, wall paints and whether they should be eggshell or matt, and the advisability of double glazing. He stood back as they succumbed to an urge as powerful as the instinct of motherhood: the nesting impulse.

It obviously gave Lesley so much pleasure that he ended by leaving the furnishing and decorating in her hands, making his only stand when she proposed to paint the ceiling of the laboratory midnight blue, with gold stars. But she overruled his counter-suggestion of white paint, and finally settled on primrose yellow. She hired builders to enlarge the kitchen, and painters and plumbers, and supervised the fitting of the carpets, which, according to her suggestion, were wool. Their only approach to a quarrel came at the end of a Saturday afternoon spent looking at furniture in Harrods, Selfridges, Habitat and Peter Jones, when Charlie explained that he was trying to set up a laboratory, not a bachelor's penthouse, and that he would like to spend some of the money on equipment. Lesley became silent; then he saw she was upset and felt like an ungrateful brute. By way of apology, he took her to an Italian restaurant in Soho, where two martinis restored her high spirits, and the dim lights and Chianti made them feel very close and infinitely tolerant. Lesley admitted that perhaps two thousand pounds *was* too much to pay for two armchairs and a bed-settee, and they agreed to spend Monday afternoon looking around less expensive shops in Southwark and Lambeth. In the event, Charlie was out on calls, and told Lesley to make her own choice. The furniture proved to be modern, made of unstained Finnish pine and a kind of coarse gray worsted, and when Helen Pike saw it she winced and refused to make any comment. As far as Charlie was concerned, it was something to sit on, and he was indifferent to what it looked like.

Helen Pike happened to be there when the furniture arrived. Lesley was away at her voice production class. After she had helped him to unpack and set up the bed, Helen looked around the bedroom, which was painted in shades of pastel blue, and said, "That girl has the instincts of a housewife." And when Charlie failed to rise to the bait, "Are you thinking of marrying her?"

"Good God, no!"

"I was only asking. *I* don't know what your relationship is."

"Perfectly innocent. After all, she's my patient. What are you smiling at?"

Helen shrugged. "My guess is that she intends to become rather more than that."

"Why do you say so?"

"No woman can help a man furnish his flat and remain perfectly disinterested."

Her comment disturbed him because the same thought had been at the back of his own mind.

That evening, Lesley arrived just as he was finishing surgery. He took her up and showed her the furniture. She examined the gas cooker, bounced up and down on the settee, and tested the bed. She lay there looking at him, her hands behind her head.

"I saw a lovely blue counterpane in Westminster Bridge Road."

He said, "Ah." Then, after a pause, "Do you feel like going out for a meal?"

"Yes, all right." She sprang lightly off the bed. "There's nothing to stay here for anyway, is there?" Her manner seemed quite impersonal, and Charlie felt ashamed of his suspicions.

They had steak and chips in the pub, with a bottle of Beaujolais. On his new income, Charlie felt no guilt about spending fifteen pounds on a meal. They sat watching the television set suspended above the Space Invaders machine. It was a holiday program, and a girl was being interviewed on the terrace of a hotel on the Costa Brava. She was embarrassingly bad. Her voice had a nasal, singsong quality and she answered most of the questions with, "Ooh yes," which she pronounced "Ooh yase." She also had a habit of wrinkling her nose, which gave her an unpleasant, bad-tempered appearance.

Lesley said, "I wish they'd turn the sound down. Isn't it dreadful?"

"I find it interesting. If you look closely, you'll see she's not a bad looking girl—nice mouth, attractive brown eyes. But she spoils it all by pulling faces."

"And saying Ooh yase." Lesley produced a cruel exaggeration of the girl's manner.

The interviewer was saying, "So you prefer this place to Clacton-on-Sea?"

She giggled. "Ooh yase. You don't see real film stars at Clacton. Ron an' me saw Sean Connery the other day . . . "

Charlie said, "If she's watching herself now she's probably cringing with embarrassment. And for the next six months her friends are going to say, "Ooh yase" until she's sick of it. What do you think of her husband?" The interviewer had turned to a skinny little man with a pointed nose and a huge Adam's apple.

"Horrible." She pulled a Quasimodo face. "What my mother would call gormless." She added uncharitably, "They probably deserve one another."

"Yet she could be quite attractive."

Lesley pulled a face. "It would take plastic surgery."

"No. Personality surgery. *That's* what it's all about. You're saying she's not appealing enough to get a good-looking man. But that's not because she's ugly. It's because she doesn't know how to make the best of herself. She doesn't see her own potential."

"And she doesn't want to either."

"Oh yes she does. She obviously daydreams about film stars. If she was going out to dinner with her favorite film star, she'd spend hours putting on her makeup and choosing her clothes. She'd probably be willing to have a face lift. Are you telling me she wouldn't have a personality-lift if she had the chance?"

Lesley giggled. "You ought to put an advertisement in all the women's magazines. Do you want to sleep with your favorite film star? Then come to Dr. Peruzzi's magic workshop and have a personality-lift . . . "

The steaks arrived. Both were hungry, and for the next five minutes they concentrated on eating. Then Lesley said, "Do you think I can see my own potential?"

"Well, you certainly understand it better than that girl on TV. That's because you're middle-class. So you've been taught not to pull nasty faces and talk through your nose."

She grimaced. "That's not saying much."

It was near closing time and the bar had become so noisy that it was difficult to hold a conversation. He said, "Would you like to come back and have some coffee?"

The flat was pleasantly warm. There was underfloor heating and he had left it switched on to remove the last signs of damp. When he brought in the coffee she was sitting on the white mohair rug, hugging her knees. She said, "Do you really think you could tell any girl how to get any man?"

The casualness of her tone did not deceive him. "Have you anyone particular in mind?"

"Well, not exactly . . . " She suddenly giggled.

"Who is he?"

"Well, there's this boy in the second year. He's really a terrific actor, and all the girls are in love with him. He's just got a place in RADA."

He experienced a flash of jealousy.

"Is he interested in you?"

"Oh no! I've only spoken to him a couple of times."

"But you'd like him to be?"

She raised her eyes to his and laughed. "Well, it *would* be nice to upset the other girls." He observed in her eyes the expression he had noticed on the evening she had told him about her love life. The gleam of someone who finds a challenge irresistible. His jealously suddenly seemed absurd.

"Why not ask him to come to my lab when I've got the video equipment set up? No actor could resist seeing himself on a TV screen."

"He'd guess I was up to something."

"Then why not invite some of the other students as well? I need some actors to practice on with the video."

"Could I?"

"Of course."

"You *are* marvelous." She placed her arms round his neck and kissed him on the mouth. The warmth of her lips produced the usual shock of pleasure and instant response. After a moment, her pelvis began to move rhythmically against him. As he kissed her, she sighed, and seemed to melt. Her right hand left his neck, went down to her waist, and unzipped the top of her skirt.

Charlie broke off the kiss and moved away from her. She opened her eyes and looked at him. It was a sign of her sexual humility that she showed no resentment. He said, "You asked me whether you could see your own potential."

"Yes."

"All right. Let me be honest with you." He sat up on the rug. "Your problem is that you underestimate yourself. What you don't seem to realize is that when a girl is as pretty as you are, men want to idealize her. Now you enjoy giving pleasure, so you give yourself without any fuss. And most men find that worrying. They're like fox-hunters—they like to have a good run for their money."

She sighed, "I know. But I was just born that way."

"But you don't have to let the man know that. Try and look at it from his point of view. Men expect to chase women, and when they find a girl attractive and they suspect she likes them, it becomes an interesting game, like chess. They want it to go on for as long as possible. So if she concedes defeat in the first five minutes, they feel disappointed and go and look for another game. But if it takes a week to get the first kiss and a month to get her into bed, they're hooked for life. They've got addicted to her by that time."

Her eyes had begun to gleam as he spoke. He pressed his point. "I'll tell you another thing. It's well known that a man's mother provides a sort of standard by which he judges other women. So if you really want to make this actor chap fall in love with you, the first thing you should do is try and meet his mother. Find out what she's like. That will give you an idea of what he expects from a girl."

"You ought to write one of those advice to the lovelorn columns."

He grunted. "I might be reduced to that one of these days."

She sat up and put her arms round his neck. "No you won't. You're too clever. You'll be a famous psychologist, and I shall be able to say I was your first patient." She kissed him, and again he felt the stir of response.

He said, "Remember what I just told you."

"Yes, but *you* already know what I'm like."

He submitted.

CHAPTER FOURTEEN

FRIDAY, MARCH 21, 1979 was the day Charlie Peruzzi ceased to be a member of the Southwark practice and became a research psychologist. At 6:30 that evening, weary after a long day, he moved into his new flat. It was an uneventful evening. There were no callers and he was in bed by 10:30. Yet he still remembers it as the true beginning of his career as a "personality surgeon."

After the cramped room in which he had spent his leisure hours for the past two and a half years, his new home seemed too big and impersonal, like a hotel room. Even when he had arranged his books and records, it still looked bare. The laboratory was even worse. Except for three large cardboard packing cases, it was empty. He found the place disconcertingly quiet, with only a distant noise of traffic and the occasional mournful hooting of a tug from the river. As he stood at the window and looked down at the Surrey canal, whose brown surface reflected the light of the streetlamps, it brought a sudden clear image of Julia Engledow's yellow car being lifted out of the water by a crane. It seemed incredible that so much had happened in a mere eight months. But instead of giving him satisfaction, the thought generated a vague sense of unease.

He decided to take a bath. Like the rest of the flat, the bathroom had been completely redecorated. The enormous green bath had been chosen by Lesley and matched the fitted carpet. The bathtub at his previous lodging had been too short, so that he had to sit with his knees bent if he wanted to immerse his shoulders. In this one he could stretch full length, his head resting on a plastic cushion. And it was as he lay there that he suddenly identified the source of his disquiet. It was the fear that all this would prove to be a mistake, that it would vanish like fairy gold.

For now he was alone, prepared to embark on a new career, he had to admit that he had no clear idea of what he intended to do. In the packing cases in the laboratory there was an expensive video camera, and a television set with a thirty-inch screen. Less than three months ago he had told Jessica McKeown that this was all he needed to begin work, now he was not sure where to begin. On Monday, Lesley would be arriving with half a dozen fellow students

209

from her drama class. He would spend the rest of the day filming them, yet he had only the vaguest idea of why he would be doing it. He was beginning to feel that he had taken Ben McKeown's money on false pretenses.

It would have helped if he could have discussed it with Topelius, but for the past two months, Topelius had been a guest lecturer at the Massachusetts Institute of Technology. He was not due in London until the first of April, the date on which he became officially an employee of the McKeown Enterprises Personality Research Unit. Until then, Charlie had to work alone.

After the bath, he again stood staring out of the window, and suddenly found himself wishing that he was in his surgery downstairs, talking to patients. It seemed absurd that on the day that should have been a landmark in his life, he felt like a nervous child who wants to burst into tears.

For want of anything better to do, he went and opened the packing cases in the laboratory. Vic Gibbs had promised to come and help him set up the video equipment on Sunday. The camera, which had cost five thousand pounds, looked formidably complex, with yards of cable, and plastic packages of wing nuts and screws. The video recorder was the latest model, with an instant freeze-frame and various devices for making the film run backwards or forwards at different speeds. The television set was the largest he had ever seen, and came complete with a metal stand that could be moved on large rubberized wheels.

With something of a struggle he succeeded in lifting the television set into place, then spent another five minutes attacking a three-pin plug and impaling his thumb on the screwdriver in the process. And then, since Vic Gibbs had installed aerials in every room in the flat, he wheeled the set into the sitting room and switched it on. Then he opened a bottle of Italian wine, bought at the local supermarket, and settled himself in the armchair with a bag of dry roast peanuts on the table beside him.

ITV was showing a history of Hollywood comedy. Charlie had switched on about ten minutes into the program, and found himself looking at a clip from a Harry Langdon film. With his white makeup and tightly buttoned jacket, Langdon looked like an overgrown baby. The narrator—a famous film star—explained that Langdon's career in films was brief because he refused to vary his style and insisted on doing everything in slow motion. After a commercial break, the program moved on to Buster Keaton. Keaton's career, the narrator explained, had also come to a premature end because his style of surrealistic slapstick had become outmoded.

It seemed to Charlie that this comment missed the point. He had never been able to come to terms with Keaton's films because he found that deadpan face disturbing. What was supposed to be going on behind it? In order to sympathize with a comedian, you need to see him as a human being, like Chaplin or W. C. Fields. If his "stone face" never shows emotion, half the fun evaporates.

This left him considering the question of why clowns wear white makeup. The answer seemed to be that clowns are intended to appeal to children. Children are overawed by adults; they find them frightening. The clown is an adult who is no longer frightening because his dignity has been removed by his baggy trousers and his absurd makeup. He is there to assure children that they don't have to worry about *his* authority. He gets into even more trouble than they do. If there is a banana skin around, he is sure to slip on it; if there is a bucket of water, it is sure to end on his head. The white makeup is to dehumanize him, to de-adultize him. But place the clown in a real-life situation, buying groceries or taking his dog for a walk, and the deadpan face becomes disturbing. The audience *wants* to see him react to the comic disasters.

Now, as he watched Fatty Arbuckle, Laurel and Hardy, Harold Lloyd, W. C. Fields, Charlie began to formulate the outline of a theory of comedy. It was basically about the defiance of authority. Chaplin is the little tramp who is always upsetting policemen and public dignitaries. Groucho Marx sings, "Whatever it is, I'm against it." Laurel and Hardy are funny because one is a bossy adult, doing his best to stay in control, and the other is a disruptive child who turns order into chaos. W. C. Fields is funny because he is the bossy adult and disruptive child rolled into one . . .

What struck Charlie, as the program progressed from the Marx Brothers to Abbott and Costello, Dean Martin and Jerry Lewis, Red Skelton, Danny Kaye, was the increasing expressiveness of the faces. The program included Skelton's Guzzler's Gin sketch, in which the humor consisted of the expressions of an announcer in a commercial radio station, trying to convince his audience that he is drinking a "smooth, smoo-ooth gin," when his facial contortions make it clear that it tastes like paint stripper. But the point emerged most clearly in the final section on Danny Kaye, which included the cinema lobby scene from *Up In Arms*. Here everything depended on incredible control of voice and facial expression. It was the furthest possible remove from the deadpan clown.

As the credits came up, he switched off the television with the remote control. Then, as he stared at the blank screen, the solution came to him. Charlie Chaplin, Harold Lloyd, Buster Keaton, had the physical control of acrobats. Later comedians, like Danny Kaye, were aiming at a kind of gymnastic control *of the personality.* And this defined one of the most important aims of human beings: personality control. Sharon Engstrom felt that her nervous tic destroyed the image she was trying to present to other people. It undermined her control. Roberta's subservience to her stepmother was like a ball and chain round her ankle. It undermined her control. The same was true of Lesley's vision of herself as a mere sexual convenience. In the same way, Ben McKeown's inability to control his agressiveness was a permanent threat to the image he wanted to present. His temper was like a horse that might throw him into the duckpond at any moment. In each case the problem was the same; control of the personality.

But it would be no solution to persuade Ben McKeown or Sharon Engstrom to practice Danny Kaye's type of "personality control." What was wrong with them was a rigidity of the *whole personality,* not just of the face. What was needed was some method of dismantling the personality, of breaking it down into its component parts.

Of course, the idea seemed absurd. A human being is not a machine to be broken down into parts and reassembled. Then the sight of the television screen gave him the answer. A personality cannot be broken into parts, but its screen image can be. So anyone who wanted to study Red Skelton's Guzzler's Gin sketch could slow it down and examine it frame by frame.

He started to pour himself another glass of wine, then decided against it. He was too sleepy to drink more, but now it was the healthy tiredness of relaxation. That underlying feeling of tension and anxiety had vanished. As he switched off the lights and went into the bedroom, he had a feeling that the solution to the problem was hovering on the edge of consciousness, waiting for the right moment to emerge.

He allowed himself to sleep late the next morning, then cooked a breakfast of eggs and bacon. It seemed strange and exciting to be in his own flat. After breakfast, he went out to the local shops and bought groceries for the next week, as well as a few household necessities like an electric toaster and kitchen utensils. He was surprised to observe how much pleasure it gave him to unpack the groceries and stow them away in the larder and refrigerator. There was a bubbling sense of excitement, a feeling of beginning a new life. He drifted again to the window and looked north toward the river. The vague optimism suddenly turned into a warm glow of inner satisfaction that was like a beam of sunshine. It struck him suddenly that the river he was now looking at was the same river that had been seen by Dickens and Shakespeare and Chaucer, and that this was *true*, not merely some thought or idea. All at once, he could see that *this* was the real problem of human beings; their narrowness, their inability to escape their trivial personal limitations. This was the real aim of all psychotherapy: to help people escape from their own limitations, to bring them a glimpse of that immense richness that lay out there in that world beyond the immediacy of the here-and-now.

The insight seemed so important that he tried to write it down in a large notebook he had bought for that purpose. But when he tried to express it in words, it eluded him, producing a feeling of intense frustration. And while he was still frowning at the crossings-out and chewing the end of his ball-point pen, Vic Gibbs arrived. It would be a long time before Charlie Peruzzi would succeed in relating that insight to his ideas about personality surgery. Yet it stayed with him as one of the most important perceptions of his life.

It took Vic less than an hour to connect up the video camera to the recorder and the television set. He did this in the sitting room, since the laboratory still lacked furniture, then he tuned in the television channels and recorded from each of them in turn. He showed Charlie how to play them back, how to freeze the frame, how to make them move backwards or forwards in slow motion or at double-speed. They tested the video camera, taking turns sitting in the armchair and answering questions. Again Charlie was fascinated to observe how being filmed produced a heightened sense of awareness, so that he answered Vic's questions about his childhood with care and precision, even though he knew that Vic only wanted to make him talk and would have been just as satisfied if he had recited the nine times table.

At two o'clock, Vic had to get back to the shop. Charlie drew the curtains and replayed his own interview. At once he noticed something that he had not observed before. He had always taken it for granted that he was familiar with his own face, having seen it hundreds of times in mirrors. He even amused himself occasionally by pulling faces in the bathroom mirror. But now as he watched his face in motion as he talked, it seemed the face of a stranger. This effect was partly due to the size of the TV screen. The expensive video camera gave an exceptionally clear image, in which even the pores could be clearly seen, and by blowing up the face to twice its proper size, it made it somehow too large to focus as a whole. Instead, he found himself watching the movements of the mouth, or the muscles around the eyes, or the contractions of the forehead.

Now he was interested to observe things about himself that he had never noticed—or, at least, consciously reflected upon. Helen Pike had once commented that he had the face of an overgrown schoolboy and he could now see what she meant. It was an open, good-natured face and the wiry brown hair with its natural curl, and the direct gaze of his widely spaced eyes, combined to create an impression of frankness and innocence. Watching the face closely he could see that he had only a few basic expressions. There was an expression of serious attention, an open smile, a puzzled frown and a quizzical look that involved wrinkling the forehead and pulling down the corners of the mouth. There was also a slight pursing movement of the lips, suggesting reflection, and a lift of the eyebrows indicating surprise. Using the remote control, he was able to slow down or freeze all these expressions and to recognize how often they occurred. It struck him that he was fortunate to have this pleasant, rather neutral face; it minimized his problems of personality control. Strangers were predisposed to accept him as a good-natured, ordinary young man, about whom their expectations were limited. So if, in fact, he proved to be more interesting or intelligent than they expected, this was a pleasant bonus. Nicky McKeown lacked this natural advantage. With his swarthy, rather fleshy face, and downturned sensual mouth, he presented a negative impression. If he frowned, he looked spoiled and bad tempered. This was why Charlie's initial response to him had been unfavorable; it was only when he knew Nicky better that he realized he was not as spoiled as he looked. Nicky's problem of personality control was increased by his intuitive awareness that people disliked him on first meeting.

When he studied the interview with Vic Gibbs he realized that Vic's range of expressions was even smaller than his own. With his short-cropped red hair and narrow, triangular face, Vic produced a ferretlike impression. His forehead was always crumpling into lines, and his mouth was thin. His voice had a monotonous quality, a lack of inflection, as if forced out under pressure. But he made up for these apparent disadvantages with a nervous enthusiasm that compelled attention. On the tape, he was speaking about the improvements in video recorders in the past ten years, and he managed to give the impression that he wanted to jump up and shout with excitement. His eyes occasionally had a curious glitter which, isolated on the freeze-frame, looked slightly insane, but which, seen as a total part of his personality, intensified the effect of driving nervous energy. Vic was attractive because he produced an effect of honesty and single-mindedness, and therefore reliability.

Charlie was intrigued by this excited gleam in Vic's eyes. The eyes, after all, are merely balls of gristle and should therefore be unable to express any feeling. The logical explanation was that the expression in the eyes is really inferred from the muscles of the face. But as he studied Vic's eyes, this answer failed to satisfy him. He took a sheet of brown paper, cut an oblong hole in it, and taped it to the television screen so that Vic's eyes peered out at him through the crack. The glitter of enthusiasm was still unmistakable. He studied his own interview, and noticed what happened when he smiled. Once again, the eyes seemed to "light up," and he could detect the smile even when they peered at him through the aperture in the paper.

As he studied these pictures, then some of the faces Vic had recorded from the television, Charlie became aware that he was beginning to build up a basic vocabulary of facial expressions. What he found frustrating was that, in order to compare one with another, he had to wind the tape backwards or forwards, then locate the precise spot. What he needed, clearly, was to be able to capture each frame permanently. The obvious solution was a polaroid camera, but he was not even sure whether a television screen would produce an image clear enough to be captured on a photograph. Still, it was worth trying. He drove down to a camera shop in Camberwell Green, and explained his problem to an efficient young assistant, who immediately set his doubts at rest by taking an instant photograph of the football match that was being shown on a portable television on the counter. Twenty minutes later, Charlie was on his way home with an expensive polaroid camera, complete with tripod, and a huge economy pack of film.

In the flat, he set out to capture his own basic expressions: the smile, the frown, the quizzical look, the pursed lips, the wrinkled forehead. Then he laid each photograph on the tabletop and looked slowly from one to the other. The definition was so good that it was impossible to see that they had been taken from a television screen. He labeled each one on the back: "smile of amusement," "smile of understanding," "smile of incredulity," "frown of concentration," "frown of doubt," "frown of incomprehension."

It was at this point that Charlie decided to make himself a cup of tea. There are certain moments in life when the whole future depends on an act or decision taken by chance. For Charlie, this was such a moment. Casually, without thinking about it, he collected all the photographs together like a pack of cards and went into the kitchen with them in his hand. Having switched on the kettle he turned towards the window and, holding the "pack" of photographs in his left hand, flicked through them with the thumb of the right hand as if riffling through the pages of a book. What he saw startled him, so he did it again. As he flicked through the photographs, he saw his own face smiling at him, then changing to a frown, exactly as if he was watching it on a television screen.

What intrigued him was that there was a curious element of *alienism* about his own face. Gradually, he recognized the reason. The dozen or so photographs in his hand were selected from a twenty-minute interview, so there was no continuity between them. Yet because his head was in the same position in each photograph— he had deliberately held it still while being filmed—the faces blended naturally into one another to form a moving picture. Since they were in some sort of order—the smiles at the beginning, the frowns at the end—the act of riffling through the "pack" produced an illusion of his own face in motion. But since there were not enough photographs to produce a connected sequence, there was something alien and slightly comic about the effect, not unlike the jerky motions of early silent films.

Thoughtfully, he went back into the other room and sat down at the table. He rearranged the photographs, placing the smiles at the beginning and end and the frowns in the middle. When he flicked through them with his thumb he noticed that the alien effect was increased. The person he was looking at was simultaneously Charlie Peruzzi and a stranger.

He decided to try a simple experiment. He arranged the video camera so that it was pointing at his armchair, switched it on, then sat in the armchair where he could see himself on the television monitor and mimed a seductive smile. Then he played back the smile at four times its proper speed. The effect was quite unlike that of flicking through photographs. It looked comic, but the alien effect had vanished. He tried playing the smile backwards. This looked rather more strange, but was still quite different from riffling through a "pack" of photographs.

During the next ten minutes, Charlie filmed himself miming a series of expressions. He scowled furiously, smiled with ecstatic delight, widened his eyes in horror, stuck out his tongue, grimaced like a demon, drooled like an imbecile, laughed maniacally, fluttered his eyelids seductively, pursed his lips with distaste. Then he spent almost an hour taking photographs of each expression. Finally, he once again held the bunch of photographs in his hand and flicked through them. Again, there was the curious effect of alienism. It was as if he was watching a comedian who had borrowed his face.

It was six o'clock and Charlie was feeling tired and hungry. He decided that he had done enough for one day. He made himself a ham sandwich, poured himself a glass of wine, and settled down to watch an old gangster film on television. During his years as a medical student and GP, Charlie had seen so little television that almost anything fascinated him. But during the commercial break he found his mind reverting to the problem of the photographs. *Why* did they produce this curiously alien effect when he flicked through them, when the same pictures on video looked perfectly normal, even when played at four times their proper speed?

He riffled through them again and saw the answer. It was because he was *editing* the photographs. He was deliberately selecting certain frames and joining them all together, eliminating the intervening frames. The result could be compared to selecting photographs of a man who was running, and then cutting out every one in which his feet touch the ground, so that it looks as if he is flying.

As he flicked through the photographs, turning them into a moving picture, he felt as if he was catching a glimpse of another Charlie Peruzzi, a Charlie whose character was altogether more flexible and mobile and volatile than his own. And this was not simply an effect of pulling comic faces; it went deeper than that. It was because the faces gave him a glimpse of other personalities, a whole range of Charlie Peruzzis living inside himself. When he glimpsed his face in the bathroom mirror he took it for granted that he was a particular type of person, the Charlie he had known all his life. And now, suddenly, he felt that this assumption was false. It was simply that the other Charlies had never been given a chance to express themselves. They were hanging about in the wings, like forgotten understudies, waiting for a chance to go on stage.

The commercial break ended and he turned up the sound with the remote control. But the idea lingered in the back of his mind. He was still thinking about it when he fell asleep that night, and when he woke up the following morning, he had already devised a new experiment. The aim was to put the photographs back on video, so he could play through them on the television screen. He placed a photograph on the table, propped up against a book, and focused the video camera on it; then he pressed the "start" button, followed immediately by the "stop" button. In this way, he was able to transfer three dozen photographs on to film. Then he played the tape back through the television. When speeded up, the effect was identical to riffling through the photographs with his thumb. He then placed the film in the video recorder, put a new tape in the camera and focusing the camera on the television screen, he re-filmed his own face. Then he wound the tape in the recorder back to the beginning of the sequence, and filmed it over again. He did this a dozen times so he could watch the whole sequence over and over again without having to rewind the tape. Finally, he played it all through from beginning to end. It lasted just over ninety seconds and this continuity enabled him to study the effect more closely. He found it a strange, slightly unreal experience watching his own face making a series of absurd grimaces, with the manic fluidity of a born clown.

He also noted, for the first time, something he later called "the magic effect": the way that watching an altered version of one's own personality on a television screen produces a breathless fascination. The kind of total absorption children experience when listening to a fairy story.

The ringing of the telephone produced a sense of shock. It was the first time it had rung that weekend. Ben McKeown's voice said, "Hello, Charles. How are you settling in?"

"Very well, thank you."

"Good. Listen, I've got somebody here I'd like you to meet. His name's Alvin Rinkler, and he's in charge of our American operation. He has to catch a plane to New York later this afternoon. Mind if we call on you on the way to the airport?"

"No, of course not."

"See you sometime after lunch."

For the next two hours, Charlie experienced a certain apprehension. McKeown was now his employer. He still had a feeling that this situation was some kind of absurd mistake and that when McKeown saw the "laboratory," with its total absence of equipment, he would suddenly realize this. So instead of continuing his experiments, or breaking off for lunch, Charlie spent the next hour writing up his results in a massive ledger purchased for that purpose. And as he wrote, the sense of anxiety slowly evaporated. His ideas about a "transformational personality surgery" might be inexact and undeveloped, but he had no doubt about their underlying reality.

McKeown arrived at half past two. He was accompanied by one of the largest men Charlie had ever seen. Alvin Rinkler was over six feet tall, but his waistline was so enormous that he seemed short. The domed head was almost completely bald, and the cheeks were so fat that it looked pear-shaped. The drooping eyelids made him look permanently sleepy, but the handshake was firm and hard.

McKeown said, "You may have heard of Alvin. He wrote *The Future of the Future*. It was a best-seller."

Rinkler smiled modestly. "It had a chapter on psychiatry that seems to anticipate some of your own ideas. Did you ever read it?"

Charlie admitted that he hadn't.

"I'll airmail you a copy. But what I really want to hear is how you got this idea of personality surgery."

Feeling rather nervous in the presence of this expert on the future, Charlie took a deep breath and launched into explanations. At least he had now done it so often that he had perfected a standard outline of his ideas. McKeown, who had heard it all before, stared out of the window. Rinkler listened with his head sunk on his chest, his eyelids lowered. In this position, Charlie thought he looked like a hanging judge.

As Charlie talked, it struck him that the camera, which was in the far corner of the room, was pointing directly at Rinkler. Cautiously, he reached out and switched it on with the remote control. It ran silently, with only a faint whisper of tape noise.

When he had finished speaking, Rinkler looked up and nodded slowly.

"That's very interesting. And surprisingly close to some of my own ideas."

"In what way?"

"Well, I pointed out that most people learn their behavior from other people. In previous centuries, most people only met people in their own social group, so there wasn't all that much to learn. Since the invention of the movie, all that's changed. People can get to know their favorite movie stars as well as they know their own family. And nowadays, a teenager can watch a movie or TV soap opera a hundred times on video, so he absorbs the unconscious behavior patterns of his favorite stars. In other words, they're reprogramming their mental patterns by studying the people they'd like to resemble. And since the aim of the psychiatrist is to reprogram the mental patterns of his patients, he ought to be able to do it by choosing the right videotapes and getting the patient to watch them over and over again."

Charlie said, "But how do you find the right videotapes?"

"Aha!" Rinkler's smile had a babylike quality that transformed his face. "That's a question I didn't really explore. But the obvious method is to find out about the fantasy life of the patient, and try to find a videotape to match it. They could even be made specially for the individual patient—fantasies made to order."

McKeown said dryly, "If they're rich enough."

"Sure, that goes without saying. But there are thousands of people who *are* rich enough." He turned back to Charlie. "Now let me throw your own question back at you. How do you intend to put their theories into practice?"

Charlie said, "I suppose my starting point is to show people what they look like on videotape."

"Fine. But what if they already know? I've seen myself on television quite a few times."

"But that doesn't mean you know what you're like. We've all seen ourselves in a mirror thousands of times. That doesn't mean we know how we appear to other people."

Rinkler frowned. "I'd have said it does."

Charlie said, "Let me try and show you what I mean." He went to the video camera and pressed the rewind button. Then he switched on the television set. Rinkler said, "Ha, you've been recording me!"

"Only for the last few minutes." He switched the tape to playback and Rinkler's face appeared on the screen. The camera was pointing slightly too low, so it missed the top of his head. Rinkler was listening to Charlie's explanation of personality surgery. His head was sunk on his chest so that his collar and tie were hidden by the enormous double chin. Charlie pressed the pause button.

"Notice an interesting thing? When I press the freeze frame, it

makes no difference, except that you stop breathing. Most people
nod slightly when someone talks to them to show they're listening.
You look as if you're asleep. That's why my voice sounds hesitant.
I'm getting no response."

McKeown laughed. "That's true, Al. I've seen you do that trick at
board meetings. It makes people nervous."

Charlie froze the picture. "Now notice what happens when you
begin to speak. You lift your face and raise your eyelids so you no
longer look as if you're asleep. But you still speak slowly and
deliberately, so it all sounds rather weighty—like a judge summing
up."

Rinkler chuckled, but said nothing.

"Now notice what happens when you smile. Your face changes
totally. You look like a baby who's been offered an ice cream."

McKeown gave a snort of laughter. "So your personality has at least
three gears. First gear, the great stone face. Medium gear, the
impartial judge. Top gear, the innocent baby. And then there are a
number of intermediate expressions. Like this one." He played the
tape back in slow motion until he found the frame he wanted. "Your
lips thrust out, one eyebrow raised, the forehead wrinkled, as if
you're being intentionally funny. And this one: the eyes suddenly
bulging as if in amazement. Then, a moment later, you lower your
eyelids completely, as if you feel you've given too much away."

McKeown chuckled. "He's got you there, Al."

Rinkler nodded seriously. "I agree. That's good observation. But
I still don't quite see how you can *use* it . . . "

Charlie said, "Do you have ten minutes to spare?"

"Sure. Plenty of time."

"Then let me show you a little experiment."

Using a second videotape in the camera he filmed Rinkler's face
in repose, the chin sunk on the chest. After that he filmed a series
of expressions, sometimes repeating the same one a dozen times, to
produce an effect like riffling through a pack of photographs. It had
dawned on him that the intermediate stage—using the polaroid
camera—might not be necessary. His own experiments had sharpened his eye for individual expressions, so he was able to freeze the
frame again and again to catch an unexpected grimace or flicker of
response. When it was over and he could see from the numerical
display that he had about two minutes on film, he wound it back to
the beginning.

"Now watch."

Even Charlie was surprised as he studied the playback. Viewed in the flesh, Rinkler's big face seemed singularly inexpressive; its fleshiness gave it a quality of immobility. What Charlie had succeeded in catching was a series of unexpected expressions, some of which lasted only a fraction of a second. But played back consecutively, they transformed the face like gusts of wind blowing across the still surface of a pond. After the initial immobility of the "hanging judge" expression, which Charlie allowed to continue for about ten seconds, the face seemed to explode into movement. And since it occupied almost the whole screen, the effect was far more alien, far more startling, than in Charlie's experiments on himself.

Charlie switched off the recorder. Rinkler expelled his breath. "Mmm. That's really something."

McKeown nodded, obviously impressed, but said nothing.

Charlie said, "It's basically a method of highlighting certain aspects of the personality. You could compare it to those photographs taken by Muybridge of a horse in motion. Before Muybridge, no one was sure how a horse moved because the horse is moving too fast for the eye to analyze its motion. The same goes for the personality. As you listen to me speak, you're following the words, so you don't really notice my expressions. That's why people look so odd in telephone kiosks when you can't hear what they're saying. You have a chance to study the expressions in isolation. This method does the same sort of thing, but it underlines the oddness by selecting certain expressions."

Rinkler said, "If I may, I'd like to see that again."

They watched it three times more. On the second viewing, Charlie observed something that had not struck him the first time. By chance, most of the expressions during the first ninety seconds of the tape were serious: frowns, manifestations of puzzlement, of doubt, of grudging agreement. During the last half minute, the face was transformed by a smile. The difference was remarkable. Alvin Rinkler seemed to be two different characters.

Charlie switched off the recorder. Rinkler said, "So what you're trying to do is to show people aspects of themselves they've never seen before."

Charlie shook his head. "That comes later. To begin with, I just want to show them how they appear to other people. Most people have no idea of how they look on film. You know what people are like when they first hear a recording of their voice. They can't believe that's really what they sound like. It's the same with a video. And if you can show someone how they look to other people—sometimes how awful they look to other people—you've taken the first step towards changing them."

McKeown said unexpectedly, "My God, you've got something there."

Both looked at him, waiting.

He laughed. "I was thinking of Mrs. Bonowitz." He explained, for Charlie's benefit, "She's the wife of the executive controller. She's just had an operation to straighten her nose and take the fat off her stomach. But it won't do any good because she's got the most godawful personality you ever came across. She's got a laugh like a hyena, and she screeches like a parrot."

Rinkler raised his forefinger, like one who has had an inspiration. "Why don't we find a good plastic surgeon to go into partnership with Dr. Peruzzi? You could charge a million dollars a time. Complete transformation, physical and mental!" He had a surprisingly high-pitched laugh for such a big man.

McKeown said, "You might have something there." He was looking thoughtful. Charlie had a disturbing vision of himself transformed into the head of a nursing home for rich women. He said quickly, "I don't have much to offer anybody until I've done a lot more research."

Rinkler seemed to read his mind. "No, of course not. You've got a long way to go yet. Still, all this is fascinating. I'd love to know how it's going to work out in practice. Do you think this technique would work for *any* patient?"

"No. Because no technique works for any patient. This is only a way of trying to gain an insight into the potential of the patient. Someone once said that inside every fat man there's a thin man trying to break out. I've got a feeling that we've all got several people trying to get out from inside us. When I was watching you just now, I had a feeling there were two distinct personalities. And when I was watching myself yesterday, I felt there were a half a dozen. Now suppose you could learn to pick out these personalities on tape, so a person could see the difference. After all, a plastic surgeon can show his patient half a dozen different noses and say, 'Which one would you prefer?' A personality surgeon ought to be able to show his patient half a dozen different personalities and say, 'Which one would you like to become?'"

Rinkler said, "You really think you could offer your patient a choice of half a dozen personalities?"

Charlie shook his head. "That's only a manner of speaking. You see, what we're really talking about is personality *control*. Most neurotics feel the personality is out of control. It's a basic human problem. An adolescent blushes all the time. An irritable person keeps getting surges of anger. An envious person can't control his resentment. A shy person can't control his timidity. What we're trying to do is to show them how to control the personality."

"And how do you go about it?"

"I've got a feeling that some of the basic answers lie in the face. Gain control of the face and you've gained control of the personality. A good actor can control his audience through the expressions on his face. But what's more important is that you can control yourself through the expressions on your face. The face is the gearbox of the personality. Think of the way a schoolboy pulls a face when he wants to concentrate, or bites his lip when he feels anxious, or scratches his head when he's puzzled. They all help him to control his energies. So the first thing I want to do is to build up a basic vocabulary of expressions, and try to understand how the gearbox works."

Rinkler snapped his fingers. "What you need is a computer."

"A computer?" Charlie looked blank.

"To store what you learn."

"Could a computer store photographs?"

"Sure. Why not?"

"I thought they could only store information."

"A photograph *is* information. You can reduce it to a series of microdots, like a newspaper photograph. In fact, that's exactly what a television screen does, projects the picture as a series of colored dots."

"How much do computers cost?"

"The kind you'd need, between four and five thousand dollars." He turned to McKeown. "But I reckon we could let him have one at cost?"

McKeown laughed dryly. "If it saves me money let's do it."

Charlie said, "Would I be able to work it? I know nothing about computers."

"You'd need a programmer to work out the basic programs." He looked at McKeown. "I suppose we could spare Boris for a day or two?"

"If you think it's a good idea."

Rinkler nodded. "I've got a feeling it's a damn good idea."

Charlie was altogether less convinced, but was too polite to show it.

Rinkler looked at his watch. "We have to get a move on or I'll miss that plane." He heaved himself to his feet. "Good to have met you, Charles. I'll let you know about that computer over the next few days. Keep working. I think you're on to something."

When they had gone, Charlie stood and stared out of the window at the river. He was experiencing a curious mixture of excitement and seriousness, of exhilaration and gravity. The excitement came from a sense of having glimpsed some enormous vista of meaning, some amazing general solution to the problem of mental illness. The sobriety was the recognition that it might take a lifetime to pin down the insight into scientifically testable results. But at least the doubts had evaporated. He knew now that there could be no turning back.

CHAPTER FIFTEEN

"Dr. Peruzzi?"

"Speaking."

"This is Sharon Engstrom."

"Sharon! Where are you?"

"In the Park View Hotel. But I'm just about to drive down to Reigate. I was wondering if I could come and see you on the way?"

"Of course! Do you know the way?"

It was half past eight in the morning and he was sitting in bed, drinking tea, and completing his account of the weekend's experiments in the enormous leather-bound ledger. He was delighted to hear from Sharon. In the past six months he had often wondered what had happened to her. Unlike Roberta Seneca, who wrote regularly from New Mexico, Sharon had not bothered to keep in touch. He thought of her as his "first case," and felt he owed her a debt of gratitude for the insight she had given him. Now, as he surveyed the bedroom, whose pastel colors seemed to reflect his feeling of excitement and optimism, he thought back on that weekend in the Park View Hotel with a certain nostalgia. It seemed to be part of an earlier existence.

When she called him over the intercom, he went down to show her where to park her car. The moment he saw her, he was struck by the change. It was not simply the color in her cheeks or the smart gray suede suit and red chiffon scarf which gave her the air of a fashion model, it was the indefinable air of confidence in the way she moved. As they were standing by the lift, Sandor Kos came into the building, and when he saw Sharon, he raised his eyebrows with a gesture of irony and congratulations. It was evident that he thought Charles was embarking on a seduction.

Sharon's eyes widened when she saw the flat.

"Is this *all* yours?"

"It's my laboratory too."

"What do you need a laboratory for?"

As he made coffee, he explained briefly about Ben McKeown's endowment and his partnership with Topelius. She said, "But what are you supposed to *do*?"

227

"Study human behavior. I'll show you."

He pointed the camera at her and pressed the start button, then he switched on the television set. Her face on the monitor was more than twice its natural size.

"My God!" She laughed at her own astonishment, reflected back at her from the screen. "Don't I look dreadful!"

"No, you look marvelous, better than I've ever seen you. Look, you're blushing!"

She laughed. "Turn the damn thing off." He switched off the television with the remote control and sat down facing her.

"Tell me what's been happening to you."

"All kinds of things." She wrinkled her nose. "I've just walked out on Jeff."

"Walked out?"

"We were living together. But it didn't work."

"Why not?"

"Because he's a typical male, I suppose. He wants to have his cake and eat it." He noted the bitterness in her voice and was disturbed by it. There was an underlying hardness that had not been there before.

"I'm sorry."

She shrugged. "I'm not. I suppose I had to learn the hard way. At least we don't have the hassle of a divorce. He wanted to marry me, but I wouldn't." She laughed suddenly. "It's all your fault, you know."

"Why?"

"You showed me what I was doing wrong. You made me see that men don't like women who adore them; they treat them like doormats. So I decided I'd be independent and treat him as if I didn't give a damn, and I suppose that must have intrigued him. He suddenly proposed to me."

"That must have been pleasant." He was deliberately feeding her comments to keep her talking.

"Oh, I was flattered!" Again he noted the bitter twist of the mouth. "I kept telling myself I was the first woman to pin him down. I told him I wouldn't marry him. But that night I stayed on in his penthouse, and I just went back there every day after that. He seemed to enjoy it at first. When we were both off duty, we'd spend the evening watching TV or cooking marvelous meals. Then I realized he was beginning to get restless. I asked him if he wanted me to leave and he said no. But one day when I'd been on duty and he hadn't, I found a woman's handkerchief in the bed. It turned out to be my best friend Barbara. So that was it."

He could see how badly hurt she was. At the same time, he could see that her misery was making her unattractive. Not physically, but on a deeper level. In women, bitterness exudes its own peculiar repellent.

He said, "He was never the right person, from the beginning."

Her smile was ironic. "I know. But that doesn't help if you're attracted to someone, does it?"

Suddenly, he felt the need to try to communicate to her what was in his mind, to make her see what he could see.

He said, "Listen. You say I showed you what you were doing wrong. But I didn't show you what I really wanted to show you, because I didn't know how. When I first saw you in the Park View, I thought: here's an attractive girl with a pleasant smile, a pleasant voice, a graceful walk, a good figure, marvelous hair; everything she needs to get any man in the world. But the one thing she doesn't seem to have is confidence, awareness of how attractive she is."

She said somberly, "Only a man can give you that."

"And he *has* given you that. He's done that for you at least. You've changed since I last saw you. You're far more sure of yourself. Yet you're *still* not aware of what you're really like."

"I suppose no one ever is."

"Oh, it's not all that difficult. Watch." While he had been speaking, he had used the remote control to make the videotape rewind. Now he switched on the television. Sharon's face appeared, saying, "My God! Don't I look dreadful!"

"You haven't been recording me!"

"Yes. Because I want you to look at yourself. Now watch."

The girl on the screen laughed and said, "Turn the damn thing off!" Charlie froze the frame, then wound it back a few seconds.

"Notice that beautiful laugh. It's completely spontaneous, a kind of gurgle. Look at the way your eyes sparkle as you laugh."

Sharon was watching herself with a mixture of fascination and alarm. As her screen image said, "Because he's a typical male, I suppose. He wants to have his cake and eat it," Charlie again froze the frame.

"Observe what you said—'Because he's a typical male.' But he's *not* a typical male. There are thousands of males who aren't in the least like him. I'm not, to begin with."

"That was just a manner of speaking."

"I know, but it's important all the same. You're allowing yourself to generalize about all males. Now watch."

He allowed it to play on. As she said, "Oh, I was flattered," he froze the image again. "Look at your mouth." He played it back again. "That little twitch of bitterness." He played on to the point where she spoke of finding the handkerchief in the bed, then stopped it again.

"Do you see what I'm trying to show you? You seem more confident, more alive, than when I saw you last year, but you spoil it all with that bitterness. Just as when you call Jeff a typical male." He saw from her eyes that he had made his point, and he pressed his advantage, speaking slowly and gently to compel her full attention. "When I first met you, you lacked self-confidence. You seemed to have a kind of hollow inside. Now that's gone, but you've filled it up with the wrong thing. You've decided you've got to be hard and mistrustful. You can watch it on the screen." He rewound the tape and played back the last fifty seconds. "Do you see what I mean? You seem to be saying that because Jeff's a bastard, you're never going to trust a man again, but that's even worse than lacking self-confidence. You're not allowing your natural personality to express itself." He had wound it back to the beginning. He switched on her laugh, followed by, "Don't I look dreadful!" That's the natural you, that laugh. Not all this disillusioned stuff about typical males."

She said, "Could I have some more coffee?"

"Of course." He went into the kitchen. She came in a moment later. Without looking at him she said, "I know you're right."

It made him feel guilty; he felt that he had imposed his will on hers. Then the telephone rang, and he was glad of the interruption.

Ben McKeown said, "Are you going to be at home all day tomorrow?"

"Yes, I think so."

"Good. I'm having that computer delivered. I don't know what time it'll arrive. It's being sent down from Newcastle. On Wednesday I'm sending a man to show you how to use it. His name's Boris Gorski. Okay?"

"Yes. Thank you very much."

But McKeown had already hung up. He was in one of his laconic moods. Charlie was accustomed to them now, and no longer wondered if McKeown was annoyed with him.

His watch beeped on the hour. He realized that it was already eleven o'clock.

"I'm afraid I have to leave in a few minutes. I have to collect some patients."

"Patients?"

"Well, subjects for experiments. They're drama students, in fact. I'm going to film them and then try to analyze their personalities."

"That sounds fascinating." He could see she was unwilling to leave.

"Why don't you stay? You won't be in the way."

"I'd like to. I don't have to be in Reigate until this evening."

He had arranged to meet Lesley in a café in Westminster Bridge Road. Although they arrived ten minutes late, there was still no sign of her. But a good-looking, red-haired girl caught his eye as he came in and said, "Are you Charles?"

"Yes."

"I'm Lucasta. Lesley told me to say she'd be a bit late. We're all coming back with you." She indicated four others who were sitting at the same table. "That's Jonathan and Norman, and that's Mandy and Pam."

Charlie introduced Sharon. They found chairs and sat down. Mandy, a pin-cheeked little girl with very blue eyes said, "Lesley's trying to persuade Duncan Baron to come."

Charlie said, "Oh." The name meant nothing to him.

The student called Pam said, "He won't, of course." She was a thin, dark-haired girl with an intense face.

"Why not?"

"He doesn't have time for first-year students."

Lucasta explained, "He's the best actor in the school. He's going on to RADA."

Charlie said, "Ah yes. Lesley told me about him."

Pam said, "I bet she did." When he looked at her curiously, she colored and looked away. There was, he sensed, rivalry here.

Lesley came in a few minutes later, accompanied by a tall, gangling youth with close-cropped hair and a loose-limbed walk. She said, "I'm sorry I'm late, Charles. This is Duncan Baron."

Baron shook hands. His manner was shy and withdrawn. He certainly didn't look like an actor, least of all a good one.

But as they drank cappuccino, Charlie observed that Baron seemed to have a natural authority over the group. He spoke in a quiet, hesitant voice, which had a peculiar timbre, and his comments revealed a quick, dry intelligence. The girls obviously re-

garded him with admiration, while the two males, Jonathan and
Norman, looked at him with the eyes of disciples. It was clear that
Lesley had scored a considerable triumph in persuading him to
come.

Back at the flat, the girls prepared the food that Charlie had laid
on. While he also offered them a choice of beer or wine, he himself
drank nothing. He was aware that it was his business to observe
them closely, to try to arrive at some estimate of their personalities.
So as they talked and ate, he tried to apply what Topelius had taught
him, and to study them as a zoologist might study animals in a cage
or fish in a tank.

He was interested to observe how Sharon's personality seemed to
expand and radiate self-confidence. It was partly, of course, because she was older than the other women, and had more poise and
sophistication. But it was also, unmistakably, due to her interest in
Duncan Baron. His curious, offbeat personality, with its mixture of
diffidence and sharp intelligence, clearly fascinated her. Lesley
watched all this with poorly disguised misgivings, and her vulnerability made Charlie feel strongly protective. The other girls, he
sensed, were unsympathetic. It amused them to see Lesley's prey
slipping away from her. The dark-haired Pam lacked sympathy
because she harbored designs on Duncan Baron herself. Lucasta, a
noisy, cheerful girl whose exuberant laugh made Charlie wince,
obviously felt that any girl who wore her heart on her sleeve was an
idiot and deserved whatever she got. As to the pretty, middle-class
Mandy, she knew better than to pursue any man. She relied on her
strawberries-and-cream complexion to attract males like bees to a
flower.

They made an interesting group, because they all had dreams of
fame and riches or, at least, a part in some long-running television
soap opera. Unlike the majority of Charlie's patients, they all had a
sense of the future as a delightful, rosy glow of expectation. With the
exception of Sharon, they were too young to have tasted disillusionment and the sense of anticlimax. So, without even being aware of
it, they exuded an atmosphere of optimism and excitement. None of
them gave him that feeling that he had experienced so often when he
looked at a waiting room full of patients, who all took their medi-
ocrity for granted. Was that because they were so much less medi-
ocre than an overworked housewife or an old man suffering from
chronic bronchitis? No. It was merely that they felt they had something to look forward to. Anything could happen tomorrow or the

day after. Most of Charlie's patients felt they knew exactly what would happen tomorrow and the day after, and if it was any different from today, the change would probably be for the worse.

When they had finished eating, Charlie suggested it was time to start work. He asked them to bring their chairs and stools into the laboratory, and with the help of the men, he moved the television and video equipment. He wanted the setting to be as formal as possible, to compel them to pay attention. When they were seated in a semicircle, facing the television, he explained briefly the purpose of the experiment. It could, he said, be regarded as an extension of what they were doing at drama school. There they had to learn to project their personalities towards an audience, which in turn meant trying to *control* their personalities—control the way they walked, the way they spoke, the way they signaled emotion. As actors, they had learned to do this instinctively, from inside, so to speak.

"What I want to do is to try to understand the personality by studying it from the outside. I want to study the way we unconsciously express what we're feeling, or try to hide it. If I could do that, I believe I could teach you many things about yourselves that you didn't know. But first of all, I need the raw material. That's why we're here.

"I'm going to ask each of you to sit in this armchair and be filmed as you answer questions. I'll begin by asking certain standard questions about your background, your parents, why you decided to study drama. But while that's going on, I want the members of the audience to think up some of their own questions and comments. And these can be as searching as you like—the more searching the better. They can even be downright rude or impertinent, because the aim is to try to get a reaction out of the interviewee." He paused to allow this to sink in. "All right, who's going to be first?"

They looked at one another, and the girls giggled. No one volunteered. Charlie pointed to Norman, who was sitting at the end of the row.

"Let's start with you."

Norman, a tall, rather good-looking youth with dark, wavy hair, took his place in the armchair, facing the audience. Charlie focused the camera so that his face, in half-profile, filled the television screen. After asking him to try to avoid moving his head as he talked, Charlie started the camera and asked the first question: "Where were you born?"

"In Stoke on Trent."

"Would you describe your parents and your background?"

"My father's an optician and my mother's always been interested in amateur dramatics. My father met her when she was playing Eliza in *My Fair Lady* . . . "

When he felt the ice had been broken, Charlie turned to the audience. "Has anyone a question to ask Norman?"

Jonathan raised his hand. "Yes. When did you last have sex?"

Everyone laughed, and Norman blushed. Charlie said, "Good, that was a joke, but it got a reaction. Let's see how it looks." He rewound the last thirty seconds and played it back, slowing down as he came to the end. "Notice what happens. He starts to smile, to control the embarrassment, but the embarrassment overtakes the smile." He turned to Norman. "By the way, when *did* you last have sex?"

Norman replied promptly, "At nine this morning, on top of a London bus."

Again, there was a laugh. Charlie stopped the tape and replayed it.

"Now observe what happens. This time he doesn't allow the question to throw him. Note the gleam of malicious amusement as he starts to reply. You can see that he has now *gained control*. When Jonathan asked the question, it took him off balance. But when I asked it, he'd watched himself on the screen, and he made everyone laugh. In other words, he was now controlling the audience reaction. And seeing himself on the screen helped him to do that. Any more questions?"

He soon discovered that the problem was not to persuade people to talk, but to stop them. They all wanted to see themselves on the screen, and everyone was fascinated by the slow-motion effect which revealed minute variations in expression. Charlie became adept at observing certain revealing expressions, and making a note of the reading on the digital counter, so he could relocate them later. With seven people to film, time passed so quickly that Charlie was finally obliged to restrict each interview to a quarter of an hour. But this awareness that time was limited generated a sense of urgency and excitement, so that some of the later interviews had the quality of a good game of tennis.

Again, he was struck by the difference between behavior on-screen and behavior off. Duncan Baron was the most obvious example. In private conversation he seemed almost self-effacing, and he occasionally hesitated or stumbled over a word. The moment he was being interviewed, he seemed to draw upon hidden resources. His eyes developed a curious, concentrated look, and all the hesitancy vanished.

With the others, the difference between on- and off-screen behavior was less marked, but still provided some interesting insights. Lucasta, who might have been expected to radiate confidence on the screen, became oddly subdued. Jonathan, with his comedian's face and natural charm, also seemed to become unsure of himself, and he blushed at any question that seemed remotely personal. Pam, whose intense gaze suggested an underlying aggressiveness, became calm and tranquil in front of the camera, with occasional gleams of humor that seemed to transform her eyes. The reserved Mandy was the biggest surprise. She began badly, blushing as she talked about her home and her parents. But when Charlie asked her about her earliest experiences of the theater, she began to describe a pantomime horse act, and suddenly became more animated. When she reached the climax of the story, with the horse trying to clean its teeth with a handbrush, she burst into shrieks of laughter that made everybody laugh. From then on, she seemed to become a different personality, sparkling with excitement. It was as if she had burst through some inner barrier. More than with any of the others, Charlie had a sense of a repressed aspect of her personality trying to burst out of its shell.

It was nearly six o'clock when he finished videotaping Mandy. Everyone was beginning to feel tired, and when Sharon said she had to leave, Charlie decided to bring the session to a close. Lesley went to the kitchen to make tea.

Sharon asked, "Anybody need a lift towards Reigate?"

Duncan Baron said, "I'm going to Mitcham."

"I'll drop you off."

They left together. Charlie was glad that Lesley was out of the room.

The others stayed for another twenty minutes, then Jonathan offered them a lift into central London. Finally, Lesley and Charlie were alone.

"Glass of wine?"

"No thanks."

He yawned. "I think that went pretty well."

She managed to summon a smile. "Yes."

He took the empty cups into the kitchen. When he came back she said, "Does she really live at Reigate?"

"Yes. Why?"

"I thought it was just another excuse to get him alone."

He said, "You don't have to worry about Sharon."

"No?" It was plain that she did not believe him.

"She's not his type."

"She made it pretty obvious *she* thinks she is."

"All the same, she's not."

It was what she wanted to hear. "Why not?"

"Watch." He pressed the rewind button. He had already made a note of the exact part he wanted to replay.

Duncan Baron's face came on the screen. Charlie was asking: "What sort of a person is your father?"

"I suppose he's what you'd call an extrovert. Rather noisy."

"And your mother?"

"Oh, she's . . . rather quiet."

"Would you say she's a strong person?"

"Underneath, yes. She's the kind of person who gets things done quietly, without making a fuss. Deep down, she's probably the stronger of the two."

Charlie switched off the tape. "You see? When he talks about his father, there's just a touch of contempt. He obviously admires his mother. His own personality is more like that of his mother. She's a quiet sort of person who doesn't say much. He uses the word 'quiet' twice in talking about her. If you'd decided to make a pass at him, he'd have run a mile. As it was, Sharon made the passes, and you behaved with dignity. You won hands down."

"You think so?" She tried not to smile, but it broke through.

"I'm sure of it. I told you the other day, a man tends to form his impression of women on his mother, particularly if he admires her. Now Sharon's a sweet girl, but she's definitely not the quiet, self-contained type. There's a slightly worrying feeling of underlying nervous tension about her. She's too concerned about the impression she makes on other people."

"So am I."

"Perhaps, but you don't show it."

"He's sure to find out sooner or later."

"No. You'd be surprised how little men notice. They believe what they want to believe. Once they've formed an impression, they stick to it in the teeth of all the evidence. So you're probably lucky Sharon was here this afternoon. It meant that you didn't make any attempt to impress him. You even did the right thing when you went out to make the tea—'the sort of person who gets things done quietly, without making a fuss.' You couldn't have done better if you'd planned it."

She laughed from sheer pleasure. "You *are* marvelous." She put her arms round his neck and kissed him.

"But I'll tell you something important. When you kiss him, don't do it like that."

"Like what?" She was genuinely puzzled.

"Look, do it again." She put her arms around him and kissed him, pulling herself up slightly to reach his mouth. He said:

"Hold still, don't move. Now look, you're kissing me as if inviting me to undress you. You've got to stop kissing as if you want to be seduced. Try to imagine you're a small girl having her first kiss at a Christmas party, and I'm the small boy next door. You're not sure if you're going to like this . . . " He removed her arms from round his neck, and pulled her against him. She was not used to holding back but she did her best. Her lips remained firmly closed, and her body was yielding without being inviting. "That's better. Remember that if a girl presses her thighs against a man, it's almost the same as saying, 'Come and get me.' Let *him* decide whether he wants to come and get you."

She said doubtfully, "It's awfully difficult."

"No, it isn't. Just remember that you're a quiet, self-contained girl who doesn't mind being kissed, but who doesn't invite it. *Think* of yourself that way until it becomes second nature. If you see yourself like that, he'll see you like that too. And by the way, when you go to college tomorrow, don't go and look for him. Let him come and find you."

"What if he doesn't?"

"I'll bet you anything you like he does."

CHAPTER SIXTEEN

THE FOLLOWING morning, Charlie drew the curtains in the laboratory and settled down to a careful study of the videotapes of the drama students. The knowledge that Topelius would be arriving in less than a week gave him a sense of urgency. He wanted to demonstrate that he had not been wasting his time.

As he had filmed the interviews on the previous day, Charlie had made a note of certain expressions, certain gestures, certain tones of voice, that struck him as significant. It was his intention to return to each one, photograph it with the polaroid camera, and then arrange the photographs in a large album that had already been labeled: "Personality Identikit." In fact, as he began playing the first interview on one of the tapes—it happened to be of Duncan Baron—he became so absorbed that he forgot about the camera. Instead, he found himself studying slight movements of the eyebrows, the changing lines of the forehead and the lips, the manner of emphasizing certain words. When he had played less than five minutes, he rewound the tape and played it again in slow motion, freezing the picture and moving it forward frame by frame when some expression or gesture intrigued him. When that happened, he studied the whole face, observing how the expression of the eyes, the mouth, the forehead, combined with the angle of the head into a single unified whole. He was already aware that when someone is speaking, we tend to pay most attention to the eyes and the mouth. Now he wanted to study the way that the rest of the face reacted, and what dawned on him as he studied Baron's face was that our facial expressions, gestures and tones of voice are all part of some highly complex code. What he was trying to do was to crack the code.

Baron's words about his father, " . . . he's what you'd call an extrovert. Rather noisy . . ." gave rise to the suspicion that his attitude toward his father was ambivalent, perhaps hostile. Now he played that part of the tape frame by frame, and tried to look below the surface of the face to the mind underneath. He studied the mouth as it closed momentarily after the words, "Rather noisy." The lips pressed together for a moment. There was almost a slight pout.

239

What did that mean? The movement of the lips drew attention to the mouth, and in so doing, removed attention from the last words spoken. It was a movement Charlie labeled a "distraction gesture." It usually denoted a desire to change the subject, to steer away from some topic that produced a sense of unease. It was usually accompanied by a brief drooping of the eyelids or "clouding" of the gaze. When, on the other hand, Baron talked about his mother, the gaze became "open," and there were no "distraction gestures." This was a subject about which he had nothing to hide.

Charlie was struck by the thought that in adults, the purpose of the face is not to reveal emotion but to hide it. Babies *want* their faces to show what they feel. They have not yet learned the use of language, so the face has to tell the mother when they feel uncomfortable or hungry or tired. For the adolescent, this expressiveness is a nuisance. His face is always betraying self-doubt and social insecurity. The adult has turned his face into a poker-player's mask. Tell him a piece of good news, and he allows himself a restrained smile. Tell him of a disaster and he frowns and raises his eyebrows. His aim is to convince the world that he is in control of his feelings, yet the mask is not rigid, and continually betrays the tensions below the surface.

All that day, Charlie sat in the darkened room and stared at the faces on the screen. Towards half past five in the evening, when he stood up to draw the curtains, his eyes felt tired and his limbs were stiff, but he knew that he had made a start on the task of understanding the secret codes of the human personality.

At ten o'clock the next morning, Charlie had already been seated in front of the television monitor for an hour when the telephone rang.

"Dr. Peruzzi?" The man pronounced it "Proozy."

"Speaking."

"My name is Gorski."

"Ah yes. Mr. McKeown said I'd be hearing from you. But the computer hasn't come yet."

"No, because it's been sent here." In spite of the foreign name, Gorski had an American accent. "That's what I wanted to talk to you about. I've never used this type of digital paintbox, so I'd like a couple of days to find out what it can do. Would it be okay if we delivered it early next week?"

"Yes, I suppose so." The delay was disappointing. "Would it be possible for me to come over there to look at it?"

"Oh sure, no problem. When would you like to come?"

"Is today possible?"

"Fine. How about three this afternoon?"

Charlie drove into the industrial trading estate near Acton at a quarter to three. Half an hour later, he was still driving through a labyrinth of identical-looking streets lined with concrete buildings that looked exactly like all the other concrete buildings. He had to find a telephone box and ask for further instructions before he succeeded in finding Pixell Electronics, and then he discovered that he had been past it half a dozen times.

He had pictured Boris Gorski as a balding middle-aged man. In fact, he was about Charlie's own age, with an uncombed mop of red hair and a skinny, angular body. His dirty jeans and oil-stained tee shirt looked as if they had been slept in continuously for a year, and Charlie made the logical inference that he was the equivalent of the office boy. It was only later that he discovered that Gorski was regarded as one of the most brilliant computer programmers in the country, and that his salary was enormous.

Gorski led him through a reception area that might have been a dry cleaners, an office with half a dozen typists and a chaotic and overcrowded workshop, into a glass-walled office. Gorski pointed to a bench against the far wall.

"There you are. Sixty thousand quid's worth."

Charlie stared incredulously. The bench contained a television monitor, beside which stood an upright control box with a few knobs and a small control panel like the keyboard of a typewriter. The main item was a large white screen lying on the bench in front of the television.

"Why is it so expensive?"

"Because of what it can do. It's virtually an artist's canvas. Look, here's the type of computer we normally use for television graphics." He indicated another machine with a keyboard and a monitor screen. "That only costs five thousand." He picked up a floppy disc and pushed it into a slot. A moment later, the screen filled with a picture of colored skyscrapers against a deep blue sky. They rushed forward at a vertiginous speed, as if being filmed by an airplane diving among them. "That's one of my advertisements for North Sea Oil." He switched it off. "But this thing doesn't need a program. You can paint direct on to the screen." From the bench he picked up a stylus with a wire running from it. He touched a button on the keyboard. On the lower part of the white screen there appeared a grid of squares, each one a different color. He touched the stylus point to one of the squares, then applied it to the screen. A dab of red appeared on the television screen. He dipped it in another color, and drew a figure eight on the screen—it appeared in green on the television screen. He dipped the stylus first in red, then in yellow, and made a smear on the screen. The two colors blended together into orange as if they were liquid paints. With a few strokes of the stylus, Gorski drew a matchstick man in black, then colored his eyes blue, his mouth red and his nose purple.

Charlie said, "It's fascinating, but I'm not sure it's what I wanted."

"Can you explain what you have in mind?"

"To alter photographs and videotapes. Alvin Rinkler said I'd find it useful."

"Well, if Al said so you can bet he knew what he was talking about. What exactly do you want to do with the photographs?"

Charlie took from his briefcase the album labeled "Personality Identikit." It's first page consisted mainly of photographs of Lesley Engledow. "Suppose I wanted to alter this first picture, 'amused smile,' to this one, 'bright smile.' How would I go about doing it?"

Gorski studied the photographs carefully.

"There are two ways. With an ordinary computer, you'd put the photographs on a floppy disc, then do a computer analysis of the two pictures to find out the exact difference between them. Then I'd devise a program that would do it. But with the digital paintbox, you'd transfer the photographs to disc, project them on the screen, then use the stylus, like an artist touching up a canvas."

"Could you do it with a videotape?"

"No problem. That'd save transferring it on to disc. Have you got a videotape?"

From his briefcase Charlie took the tape he had made with the students. Gorski loaded it into a slot in the control box. A moment later, Lesley's face appeared on the television screen. Gorski froze the frame, then, dipping the tip of the stylus in the palette, he applied it to the flat screen. On the monitor, Lesley's mouth became glistening and sensuous as Gorski traced the outline of her lips. A flickering black dot on the screen showed the precise position of the tip of the stylus. Another touch on the keyboard made the mouth expand until it filled the whole screen. This enabled them to see that the line was too thick and coarse. The expanded size made it possible to apply the color with more delicacy.

Gorski invited Charlie to try. At first he found it difficult touching the stylus against a blank white screen and watching the results appear on the monitor, but it took only a few minutes to become accustomed to watching the television instead of the stylus.

"Could we enlarge the eyes?"

"Sure." Gorski reduced the face again, then caused the eyes to expand, until one of them filled the entire screen. Using black pigment, Charlie carefully enlarged the pupil until there was only a narrow rim of iris. He knew that enlarged pupils make a person more attractive, and he wanted to test this for himself. When the other eye had been treated in the same way, Gorski touched the key that projected the image of Lesley's entire face. He said, "Hey, that's pretty neat."

The enlargement of the pupils and the lips had transformed her face. Somehow, it was softer and more alluring.

Gorski said, "I've got some things to do. Can I leave you here for a while to play around with this thing?"

"Yes, of course. One more question. Is there any way to transfer these changes to every frame on the film, without having to do it to each one?"

"Of course. It's fairly complicated, but it can be done. I'll explain it when I come back."

Left alone, Charlie amused himself by magnifying different parts of Lesley's face, to study them in detail, then used the stylus to make subtle changes. At school, art had bored him. This, he now realized, was because he lacked motivation. He could see no reason to try to capture a scene in watercolor when it was so much simpler to do it with a camera. But it was quite another thing to know exactly how to reproduce a reflection of light in the eyes, shadows at the corners of the mouth, the faint line of blue veins underneath the skin. As he studied these problems in detail, he realized he was teaching himself more about art than he had learned in four years at school.

It was simplest, he found, to work with a still-frame of Lesley's face in repose, listening to him as he asked her a question. Then, studying the photographs in the album, he tried to add different expressions. After a dozen or so attempts, he realized that the secret was to use the bare minimum of color. After that, the faces began to look less like a crudely painted clown's mask. Eventually, by luck rather than judgment, he created a subtle, enigmatic smile that reminded him of the Mona Lisa, but the eyes had a twinkling brightness that was quite unlike Leonardo. The combination was piquant. He was staring at it when Boris Gorski came back. Gorski said, "Is that the same girl?"

"Yes."

"She looks different somehow."

Charlie smiled. "That's what I'd hoped you'd say."

Gorski leaned forward and studied it closely. "That's damn good. It's hard to tell that it's been retouched."

"Is there any way of making the same alteration to every frame on the tape without having to do them one by one?"

Gorski shook his head. "No simple method. Think how complicated it would be when she's talking?"

"All right. But it *would* be possible when she's just listening?"

"Oh sure, that wouldn't be difficult." He drew up a stool. "The first step is to put the picture into the computer's memory." He touched a button on the keyboard. "Then we take the next frame," he touched another key, "and we press the memory retrieval and the repeat key . . . damn, what did I do wrong?" The picture vanished. "Sorry about that. I've got to get used to this machine."

For the next half hour, Charlie sat and watched while Gorski performed complicated operations with the keyboard, periodically consulting the bulky instruction manual. Occasionally Charlie asked questions, but the answers usually left him baffled. Finally, Gorski wound back the tape and pressed the playback key. The section that had cost him half an hour's work lasted only twenty seconds, but the effect was astonishing. For that brief interval, Charlie was watching a different Lesley, a fascinating stranger who looked at him in a way he found disturbing. Then she began to speak, and once again it was the Lesley he knew.

Gorski said, "Would you mind explaining what you're trying to do?"

"Certainly, it's very simple. Every doctor has had the experience of trying to talk a patient out of depression. Our headmaster used to do the same kind of thing before we played a football match against another school. He'd give us a ten minute pep talk, and we'd all go away convinced we could beat Manchester United. The formula's always the same; a little flattery and common sense, and a lot of optimism. Depressed patients have *allowed* their self-confidence to leak away, so life turns into a series of obstacles, and the doctor's approach is to say, 'How could someone as intelligent and resourceful as you allow these silly problems to get you down . . . ?' You could call it selling someone the confidence trick—except that it isn't a trick. The patient really has the power to overcome his problems, but he's not *aware* of it. The doctor has to change his way of seeing himself. The same thing happens to a girl if you tell her she's looking attractive or you like her new dress. It changes her image of herself. Now I reckon that the most effective medium of flattery is the television screen. You're not merely telling her she's marvelous, she can see it with her own eyes. This girl Lesley, for example, doesn't realize how attractive she is. Her self-confidence has been undermined so much that she'd believe you if you told her she was ugly."

Gorski said, "You're trying to create a kind of visual pep talk?"

"You could call it that."

"But how long would the effect last? I can see she'd feel pleased for an hour or so. But how about the next day?"

Charlie shook his head. "There's no earthly reason why it shouldn't last a lifetime. You see, you're trying to change the way someone *sees herself*, and once you've done that, she won't want to change. Look, watch this." He pressed the playback switch, but turned down the volume control, so they could see her lips moving without hearing the words. "Look at her eyes. There's something sad about them. . . . look, there. Do you see what I mean?"

Gorski said, "She has the look of a loser."

"Exactly."

But even as he spoke, her face broke into a delightful smile. For a brief moment it was dazzling. Charlie rewound the tape a few seconds, then turned up the volume. His voice was saying, "But you've always loved mischief, haven't you?" Her response was a smile that made her eyes dance. She said, "I used to be the worst girl in the class."

Charlie stopped the tape with a freeze frame. "Is there any way of capturing that smile as she talks, would you say?"

Gorski replayed the smile, then played it again frame by frame. Then he played it in slow motion.

"I don't see why not. It's essentially the same problem as before, but slightly more complicated because her lips are moving." He looked at his watch. "Christ, I've got to get moving. Listen, why don't you come back in the morning and we'll look at this thing again?"

Charlie looked at his own watch and was startled to see how late it was.

"Thanks. You're very kind."

Gorski replayed the last few seconds of the tape. "She's sure got a pretty smile." As they left the building together— they were the last to leave—he said, "Girls with smiles like that never seem to have problems getting themselves a man. It's nature's equivalent of fly paper."

Charlie thought about that comment as he drove through the heavy traffic towards Shepherd's Bush. Gorski was obviously right. Girls with attractive smiles never seemed to have any problem finding a husband or lover. He remembered a nurse called Barbara; a plump little thing, in fact, downright overweight, whose smile was so bright and spontaneous that other people smiled as soon as they saw her coming. She had married a good-looking anesthetist. Then there was a fourteen-year-old girl called Valerie, one of his patients. She had a spotty complexion and wore round glasses, yet she had such a sweet smile that she never seemed short of male admirers. Then there was that girl in the tobacco kiosk near the surgery, and that skinny electrician named Danny who always seemed to wear dirty overalls, and that youth with ginger hair in the garage near Tower Bridge. All had infectious smiles, and all seemed to be popular with the opposite sex.

What Gorski had made him realize was that the smile is the most basic and simple form of personality transformation. The trouble with Lesley's normal smile was that it reflected a certain wistfulness, as if she expected to be treated badly. Her smile signaled vulnerability, so it was almost an invitation to take advantage of her. And there was no obvious way of making her change this. A smile grows from inside, and nothing is easier to detect than a counterfeit smile. What Lesley needed was to *feel* more self-confident, and that was a problem to which he could see no answer.

Thursday March 27, 1979 was a memorable day in Charlie Peruzzi's researches.

He was out of bed by eight o'clock, ate a light breakfast, then spent an hour reading some psychological papers that had been sent to him by Topelius, and writing his comments about them in the ledger in which he described his experiments. At nine-thirty he left the flat with the intention of returning to Pixell Electronics.

As he stepped out of the lift he came face to face with one of his ex-patients, a young married woman called Rosemary. He started to say good morning, then saw that she was in tears. When he asked her what was wrong, she began to sob. Since other patients were coming out of the surgery, Charlie drew her into the lift and took her back up to the flat. There he lit the gas fire, sat her in front of it, and went off to make coffee.

He regarded Rosemary as one of his successes. When she first came to him, about a year before, she had been suffering from the condition known as vaginismus, spasmodic contraction of the orifice of the vagina when she attempted intercourse with her boyfriend. And on one occasion when he had succeeded in obtaining entrance, a sudden contraction had trapped his organ, causing them both some discomfort. They were inhibited about trying again, and she was afraid that he would find someone else.

Rosemary knew enough about her condition to realize that it was basically a psychological problem, and this made it worse. Through questioning, Charlie discovered that her father had died when she was a baby and her mother had married again. Her stepfather was a highly dominant man who bullied her mother and allowed no one to contradict him. When Rosemary began to have boyfriends, at the age of fifteen, she preferred quiet, weak young men, and had, at one point, become engaged to a man with a withered arm. Her present boyfriend was the first with whom she had attempted coitus, and the failure made her miserable.

Charlie had concluded that fear of her dominant stepfather led to her preference for non-dominant males. Her boyfriend was apparently a quiet, well-behaved young man, but his attempts to make love to her produced a sudden irrational fear, leading to the vaginal contractions.

Charlie had consulted his medical textbooks and discovered that vaginismus could be due to local inflammation of the vaginal passage. Internal examination showed that there was, in fact, a certain reddening of the epithelial surface of the mucous membrane, probably due to the upsetting events of the previous night. But, since he could see she was close to the brink of hysteria, Charlie decided to tell her that he thought the source of the problem was physical and could probably be cured by painting with an ordinary antiseptic. It was obvious that this diagnosis came as a tremendous relief. She went away perfectly happy, and a few months later, Charlie was invited to her wedding.

Now, he discovered, the problem had come back again. She had telephoned the surgery and asked for an appointment, and a receptionist called Mabel had asked her which doctor she wanted to see. She was not sure whether to ask to see Herbert Pike or Sandor Kos, and when she hesitated and stammered, the receptionist told her to come into the surgery the following day.

Charlie had received complaints about Mabel before. She was an overweight woman with a strong personality who was inclined to be a bully. With Charlie and the other doctors, she was always charming, if a little overpowering. With patients who were nervous or unsure of themselves, she often became bossy and irritable. That morning, Rosemary had arrived to find the waiting room crowded. When she explained she was not sure which doctor she wanted to see, Mabel asked, with only a token attempt to lower her voice, whether the problem was physical or mental. Paralyzed with embarrassment, Rosemary had been unable to say a word. Mabel had snapped, "Hurry up, please, there are other people waiting." And Rosemary, aware that she was on the point of tears, had rushed out of the surgery and bumped into Charlie.

He made coffee for both of them and made sympathetic noises. It was plain that she felt more at ease with him than with any of the other doctors in the practice, and she explained her problems at length. At Christmas, her husband had drunk too much at a party and tried to make love to her afterwards. She became frigid and unresponsive—"I think it was the smell of beer"—but from his point of view, the lovemaking was successful. But the next time, the old trouble began. What upset her so much was that she often *wanted* sex; but when it came to the point, her body refused.

Charlie said very little. He simply let her talk on. At one point she suggested that he might examine her. This revealed to him that she wanted to be told that the problem was again due to inflammation even though she knew, deep down, that this was not so. He explained tactfully that he was no longer allowed to examine her since he was no longer her doctor, but he encouraged her to go on talking. After nearly an hour she admitted what he had always suspected—that her stepfather had made sexual advances to her. She had told her mother about it, and her mother had begged her not to mention it to anyone else, because he could be sent to prison and they would lose their breadwinner. This gave an overwhelming sensation of helplessness and frustration. For years after that she locked her door every night and then barricaded it with the dressing table.

Charlie made her describe the attempts at assault. He was aware that this was necessary to enable her to get it out of her system. It seemed that he had never attempted rape, but often tried to fondle her, and on one occasion had backed her into a corner and succeeded in pulling down her knickers. Only the arrival of her mother had forced him to stop.

Charlie pointed out that none of these advances amounted to attempted rape, and she ended by agreeing with him. This seemed to make her feel relieved. He stood up to indicate that he had work to do, and escorted her to the door. When she asked if she could come and see him again, he suggested that she ought to send her husband along first. She agreed immediately, and he was touched by this evidence of her total trust in him. Her smile as the lift door closed made him feel that the last two hours had been well spent.

It was almost midday, and he realized he was hungry, so he grilled himself a pizza and made more coffee. While he ate, he thought about Mabel, and wondered if he ought to speak about her to the Pikes. It was a difficult decision. She had not actually been rude and the problem may have been due entirely to Rosemary's over-sensitivity. If Pike felt obliged to reprimand her, it might lead to more trouble than it was worth. Efficient receptionists were hard to come by.

In fact, he came face to face with her as he stepped out of the lift. She was probably on her way to lunch. She was a big-boned, dark-haired woman who had obviously been pretty in her youth. Now she was middle-aged, and about forty pounds overweight, but there were still signs of a striking attractiveness in the large, dark eyes and sensual mouth. They exchanged a few words as they left the building together. She seemed glad to see him and asked him how he was enjoying his new life. They stood and chatted for a moment before they went off in opposite directions, and her smile as she said goodbye seemed genuinely warm.

He thought about her as he drove to Acton. She had separated from two husbands, and plans for a third marriage had fallen through. Most of the nurses and midwives in the practice disliked her. The men seemed to find her tolerable enough, but none actually liked her. Then what was wrong with her? The trouble, he realized, was that she exuded a certain predatory air. Even as he stood talking to her outside the surgery, he had a feeling that she saw him as a potential lover, and this was clearly out of the question. She was not even remotely sexually attractive.

And this, he suddenly realized, was the root of the problem. She was strong-willed and highly sexed. If she had been rich, she would have hired healthy young gigolos. As it was, she knew perfectly well that she stood no chance of attracting the males she found desirable.

This created an attitude of resentment, which had engraved itself on the corners of her mouth, so when she talked to a pretty but nervous girl like Rosemary, the resentment bubbled over in the form of contempt. Why do men find this idiot attractive when she's obviously a fool . . . ? Her desire to captivate men led her to dress well, but an underlying sense of the futility of it all made her incapable of resisting the temptation to overeat. What she needed was a certain self-discipline, the ability to control her negative emotions, but she would never achieve it because she could see no reason to discipline herself. She was caught in a vicious circle.

For a moment, Charlie experienced something like despair. It was the sudden recognition that the world was full of people who were trapped in vicious circles, and beyond the help of any psychiatrist. To recognize that seemed an admission of failure. But then, medicine, like politics, is the art of the possible. That reflection, and his natural optimism, brushed away the momentary shadow of depression. As if to signal its approval, the sun came out as he drew up in front of Pixell Electronics.

The girl in the reception area said, "Mr. Gorski was expecting you this morning."

"I'm sorry. I got delayed."

"You know the way through, don't you?"

Gorski was at the far end of the laboratory, leaning over a bench. Beside him, on a high stool, sat a dark-haired man. They had moved the digital paintbox out of the office; it seemed to be connected up to various other items of electronic equipment. They were so intent on the screen that neither of them noticed him.

Lesley's face looked out at him with a frozen smile, her lips parted. The dark-haired man, who looked like a teenager, was using the stylus to draw on the tablet on the bench. The movements were so delicate that Charlie could see no change in the picture on the monitor; but after watching attentively for several minutes, he saw that the smile was becoming slightly broader, and that he could see the reflection of teeth where before there had only been the corner of the mouth. This gave the smile a lopsided appearance that was not unpleasant.

Gorski looked round and saw him.

"Hi. Glad you came. This is Dermot McCaffrey. Dermot, this is Charles Peruzzi." He still pronounced it Proozy.

"Call me Charlie."

McCaffrey shook hands without getting up. The small-featured face, with its pointed chin and black curly hair, was unmistakably Irish. Gorski said, "Dermot's our TV graphics man."

McCaffrey was already back at work, retouching the other corner of the mouth. To Charlie, it seemed incredible that he could work with such deftness when his eyes were focused on the monitor screen. He was also astonished that McCaffrey made no use of the magnification facility.

McCaffrey sat back. "Okay?"

Gorski pointed. "I think you need just a touch of shadow here."

McCaffrey added it with a delicate application of blue which, to Charlie's eye, was almost invisible.

Gorski said, "Let's go from the beginning."

He rewound the tape and turned up the sound. Charlie was asking, "How would you describe your social background?"

Lesley wrinkled her nose. "Boring."

"How did your mother and father first meet?"

"Mummy hit Daddy with a golf ball."

"How?"

"She took this terrific swing to get it out of a bunker, and heard a scream of pain from the next green. When she got there, Daddy was dancing on one leg, holding his knee. He said it hurt too much to play any more, so they went back to the clubhouse and got drunk."

Charlie had heard her tell the story several times, but now there was something subtly different. He asked Gorski, "Have you kept the original version?"

"Oh, sure. We re-recorded the tape."

"Could I see it?"

Gorski inserted another video-cassette into the machine. A moment later, Charlie's voice was asking, "How would you describe your social background?"

The difference was immediately obvious. In this original version, Lesley spoke with a touch of scorn. When she said "Boring," her face made it plain that she meant it. In the retouched version, the smile and the amusement in the eyes contradicted what she was saying. This could be seen even more clearly as she described the golf-ball incident. In the original version, it sounded as if she suspected her mother of doing it deliberately. McCaffrey's retouching had removed the element of scorn, so it all sounded far more good-natured. Yet the voice in both versions remained the same, and somehow the contrast between its tone and the dancing amusement in the eyes gave the interview a new zest. Charlie was fascinated. He insisted on replaying both versions half a dozen times. McCaffrey was obviously delighted with his praise.

This was another of those moments when Charlie knew, beyond all possible doubt, that his investigations had reached a turning point. Gorski and McCaffrey had spent the whole morning working on the videotape, feeding each small alteration into the computer's memory, then using the memory to feed back the change into subsequent frames. Since Lesley's mouth changed from moment to moment, it was seldom possible to produce more than a few seconds of videotape by this method. But as the memory built up a repertoire of changes, it became possible to alter many of the frames by a mere touch of a key. Gorski and McCaffrey had not concerned themselves with subtle changes. What they aimed for was maximum effect. The result was that there were moments when the contrast between the face and what was being said was almost absurd. This contradiction produced a curiously piquant effect, suggesting that Lesley possessed a remarkable control of her emotions. For example, at a point when Lesley said, "I don't think parents care much about children after they've reached their teens," McCaffrey had added a faintly amused smile, so she seemed to be mocking the stupidity of parents. It was all strangely exciting and stimulating, producing an effect that was oddly akin to poetry.

He quickly sensed that, in spite of their air of professional indifference, the other two were as excited as he was. What caused that excitement was the realization that, in a sense, the television screen was telling lies. The image looked like Lesley. Lesley's closest friends would have sworn that it was genuine. Yet it was another Lesley, a changeling. The great artists of the past had often managed to catch the living reality of their subject, but with the aid of the digital paintbox, Gorski and McCaffrey were *transforming* that living reality. What they were doing was almost godlike. As he stared at the screen, observing the changes that were like the growth of a living creature, Charlie experienced the sudden conviction that they were creating history.

At four o'clock, a boy in overalls brought them tea. Charlie and Gorski drank theirs; McCaffrey left his untouched. He was working more swiftly, with a new ease. The method was always the same. He played a sentence, sometimes half a dozen times. Then he went back to the beginning, froze the first frame, dipped the stylus in the "paintbox" on the screen, and made the first experimental transformation. Charlie was not surprised to learn later that he was a skillful cartoonist. It was obvious that he knew precisely what he was doing and exactly what he wanted. Occasionally he was dissatisfied, erased what he had done, and began again. In most cases, he achieved what he was aiming for the first time. When he had made the basic changes to the eyes and mouth, he sometimes used the magnification facility to add fine touches. When this happened, Charlie was able to see the individual dots—known as pixells—that made up the photograph. But he was usually baffled by the alterations McCaffrey made with the stylus; it was only when the picture was again reduced in size that he could see their significance. All this he studied intently. He was aware that in the future he would be working alone, and that this was his opportunity to learn from an expert.

In the last few seconds of the interview, Charlie had asked her, "Why do you want to become an actress?," and Lesley had wrinkled her nose and replied, "Because I don't like being me." McCaffrey transformed the rueful grin into an amused smile, removed the wrinkles from the nose and forehead, and gave the eyes a sparkle of humor. Again, Charlie experienced a certain doubt. Again, the replay proved that McCaffrey's instinct had been correct. The smile changed the meaning of the words, so they sounded like a joke.

It was almost six o'clock when McCaffrey threw down the stylus, massaged his eyes with his fingers, and said, "That'll do for today."

For Charlie, words seemed absurdly inadequate. He said finally, "I don't know why you should do all this for me."

McCaffrey said dryly, "It's not for you. It's for me."

"In what way?"

Gorski said, "We learn as much as you. If you'd told me yesterday about what I've seen today, I'd have said it was impossible."

McCaffrey ejected the cassette from the machine and handed it to Charlie. "What amazes me is the endless number of uses a computer can be put to, half of them dreamed up by people like you who know nothing about computers."

Charlie shrugged. "Perhaps that's why I thought it was possible."

But his casual air concealed an enormous excitement. As he drove back to Southwark, he put his hand to his pocket at least half a dozen times, to make sure the cassette was still there. For the first time since resigning from the practice, he had ceased to feel guilty about accepting McKeown's money.

As soon as he arrived home, he telephoned Lesley. Julia said she was not yet back from drama school.

He poured himself a glass of wine and played back the cassette. This was the first time he had seen the retouched version from beginning to end. It generated a peculiar excitement which sprang out of fascination. Once again, he recognized that this fascination was akin to the feeling produced by certain pieces of music; it caused a prickling sensation in the scalp.

This puzzled him at first, then he realized that this was because music produces a sense of *expectation*, of mysterious distant mountains glimpsed through clouds. And this film of Lesley created that same feeling of distant horizons of possibility. It was because he knew Lesley, and he knew that Lesley took a poor view of her own possibilities. She accepted herself as she was, as if any change was impossible. The Lesley who smiled at him from the television screen represented a breakthrough into a new realm of potentiality.

During the course of the next hour he watched it over and over again, as he might have listened over and over again to a piece of music that excited him. After several viewings, he became increasingly aware of its limitations. McCaffrey had made her smile too much, and so devalued her smile. And there were places where her smile was simply unsuited to what she was saying. Yet the overall effect was astonishingly convincing.

There was one place on the tape where McCaffrey had surpassed himself. Lesley was talking about a Batman doll she always kept on her pillow as a child. Charlie asked, "You admired Batman?" and Lesley replied, "Of course . . . I suppose I was in love with him." As she said this, she smiled with a radiance that he found breathtaking. He played back the original tape for comparison. Here Lesley spoke the words with a broad smile, but it contained an undertone of self-mockery. Studying the two versions side by side, Charlie could see that McCaffrey had used the basic structure of the smile, yet somehow eliminated the self-mockery, so the final effect was of sudden delight, as if she had remembered something that filled her with excitement.

The doorbell rang. He pressed the intercom button. "Who is it?"

Lesley's voice said, "It's me. Are you busy?"

"No. Come on up."

He met her at the lift; her coat was spotted with rain.

"I rang home and Julia said you'd called." She flung her coat on the settee and dropped into an armchair. "Ooh, I'm exhausted! That bloody Lionel made us do the last act twice."

"Wine?"

"Please!"

He poured her a glass of wine.

"Seen anything of Duncan?"

"Yes."

"Anything happening on that front?"

She shrugged. "Nothing much."

"Did you look for him or did he look for you?"

"Neither. He came up to me in Mike's café and bought me a coffee."

"That sounds promising. What are you complaining about?"

She took a deep breath in a way that was characteristic of her. It indicated she wished to unburden herself.

"I think he likes me. But it doesn't seem to be more than that. He treats me if I was his little sister. I think he thinks I'm just a child."

"That's a good beginning."

She said vehemently, "It's not! A girl can tell if a man's really interested in her . . . "

"Do you think he can tell you're interested in him?"

She considered this, thrusting out her lower lip.

"I don't think so."

"Then how do you know he's not interested in you?"

"Oh, I don't know. Men are so much more stupid than women. They don't seem to notice things."

As they had been speaking, Charlie had used the remote control to rewind the videotape. Now he touched the "play" button. Lesley said, "There's me!"

He said casually, "I was just going to play it when you came in."

Without comment, he turned up the volume. Then he pushed back his own chair a few inches, so he could watch her out of the corner of his eye. He was wondering how long it would take for her to realize that the tape had been retouched. To his surprise, Lesley showed no reaction. She sipped her wine, and stared at the screen with the passivity of a child in a cinema. When the tape had been playing for about a minute he asked, "Notice anything different?"

She looked at him with astonishment. "No."

"We've been using a kind of computer to retouch the tape."

"What, *that?*" She stared at the screen with perplexity.

"Yes. Don't you notice anything?"

"The lips are a bit redder."

He nodded. "Yes."

"But I thought that was just the TV."

It dawned on him that Lesley saw nothing unusual about the tape because she was not aware of what she looked like when she spoke. As far as she was concerned, she was simply watching herself.

When the interview came to an end, he turned it off.

"And you didn't notice anything different about it?"

"Apart from the lips, no." She was obviously puzzled and intrigued. "Can't you give me a clue?"

"All right. The tape's been doctored with the aid of a computer."

"You mean you've cut something out?"

"No, we haven't cut anything out."

She shook her head. "And you haven't added anything. . . . No, I give up."

"Don't give up. Watch it again."

This time she watched with intense concentration. At times she shook her head. When it finished, she said, "It's funny. I can *feel* something different, but I can't tell what it is. How about another clue?"

He shook his head, smiling at her. She smiled back at him. As she did so, he experienced a shock of surprise and pleasure. It was the smile he had seen on the tape as she talked about Batman.

"Try again."

"All right."

This time he moved his armchair so he was sitting where she could see his face. After a few moments she said, "Have you done something to my voice?"

"No, not your voice."

What he now observed, as he sat at a right angle to her chair, made him wish that he was recording it on the video camera. As she watched herself on the screen, Lesley was smiling in sympathy. And as he watched her face and that of her screen image, he became aware that she was imitating the smile of her image. Lesley's normal smile had an element of restraint about it, almost a touch of sadness. The result was that the smile on her lips often failed to reach her eyes. On the "doctored" videotape, McCaffrey had removed this element of constraint, so the smile spread across her face like a shaft of sunlight. And as she watched herself on the screen, Lesley was unconsciously smiling in the same way. When he caught her eye and smiled at her, she smiled back with a dazzling spontaneity that he had never seen before.

Suddenly, Charlie could understand why Archimedes had jumped out of his bath and run through the streets of Syracuse shouting "Eureka!" It came to him that he had solved the problem that had haunted him since that first evening with Topelius in the Park View Hotel. He had discovered the basic technique of "personality surgery," and this realization seemed to open up such vistas of possibility that he experienced a kind of vertigo. It was as if he was suspended in the air above the problem, seeing all its aspects at the same time.

It now seemed self-evident that the trouble with most human beings is a kind of modesty, a conviction of their own helplessness, and that this in turn is due to a failure to grasp their own potential. They feel passive, as if they were victims of fate or circumstance. This attitude means that they make no real attempt to control their lives. It is rather as if a driver insisted on sitting in the passenger seat and trying to control the car from there. Obviously, it would be ten times as difficult as sitting behind the wheel. In most human beings, the self is displaced, sitting in the passenger seat instead of the driver's seat. That was the trouble with Bob Engledow. Retirement had caused a displacement of the "self" from the driver's seat to the passenger seat. The accident to his daughter's car made him leap back into the driver's seat, and his problem vanished. The same was true of Nicky McKeown: the "displaced self" made him feel helpless and ineffectual. He felt that nothing he did could make any impression on the world. Why else should he do anything so stupid as emptying a pot of paint on the windscreen of a police car? As soon as he began to play chess, he developed a sense of purpose that moved the displaced self back into the driver's seat, and he ceased to be a delinquent.

And here was Lesley, making heavy weather of attracting Duncan Baron, when she could easily have done it with a single smile and the lift of an eyebrow. Now her twin sister on the screen was showing her how it could be done, and he could see that the lesson was not being wasted. Because her lack of self-confidence was so deep-rooted, it might be difficult to persuade her that her proper place was behind the steering wheel. But the evidence of his own eyes told him that at least he had stumbled on the correct method.

The videotape came to an end and the screen went blank. He pressed the "stop" button. Lesley said, "Come on, tell me the truth. What did you do to it?"

Suddenly, he experienced a sense of caution. It could be a mistake to reveal too much. He said, "We touched it up. Removed lines from the forehead, added highlights to the hair and the eyes, made the lips redder . . . "

"Do you still have the original interview?" In fact, she was looking at it, where it lay on top of the television set.

"Er no, unfortunately. It's back at the electronics factory."

"I'd love to see it, just to compare."

"All right, I'll get it back some time." He changed the subject. "Would you like some more wine?"

Half an hour later, as he was driving her back home, he said, "Can you describe the difference between that tape and the way you imagine yourself?"

"It's hard to explain. I suppose it seems somehow prettier. . . . "

"You are pretty."

"That's not really what I mean. It looks like me, yet there's something different . . . That's not how I see myself."

"That's how other people see you."

"Do they?"

"Of course."

She lapsed into silence. When he glanced at her out of the corner of his eye, she was looking straight in front of her, head tilted slightly as it leaned back against the headrest. Her eyes had the soft, contented expression of a woman who is relaxed after lovemaking.

He recognized the same contentment in himself. But it was mixed with a deeper satisfaction. The satisfaction of seeing his way forward.

CHAPTER SEVENTEEN

TOPELIUS ARRIVED at three o'clock on the following Sunday afternoon. McKeown's chauffeur had met him at London Airport. The chauffeur also conveyed an invitation to dinner for the two of them that evening.

Topelius, dressed in a light gray suit, was looking as handsome as ever, and the piercing blue of his eyes was emphasized by his suntan. He went to the window and stared out towards Tower Bridge. Even through the mist of a rainy afternoon, the view was still impressive.

"Very comfortable and spacious. How big is your laboratory?"

When Charlie showed him the next room, Topelius registered astonishment.

"But where is the equipment?"

"That's all in the other room at the moment. I'm afraid I've only got a video camera and a VTR. I've borrowed a digital computer, but that's still at the electronics factory."

"But that is absurd! You need more than that. Listen, I have a suggestion. On Wednesday I have to go back to Uppsala. You come with me and spend a few days in my laboratory. Then you can decide what equipment you need."

"Do you have a digital paintbox?"

"No. What is that?"

"It's something you said didn't exist. A mirror in which people can see their own personalities. Come and look."

Charlie had spent the whole of the previous day preparing a videotape for Topelius. It consisted of alternating extracts from the two tapes of Lesley: the original and the "doctored" version. For the first ten minutes, there were brief extracts from each version, each lasting for only a few seconds, so that Topelius could see precisely what McCaffrey had done. Then there followed the remainder of each interview, so Topelius could form an overall judgment. As Charlie had anticipated, Topelius became so excited after the first few minutes that he asked Charlie to turn it off while he explained the workings of the digital paintbox. Boris Gorski had simplified this problem by providing an illustrated brochure. Topelius said,

259

"This is a fantastic discovery. I congratulate you. Has the girl herself seen it?"

"Only the retouched version. I didn't want her to compare the two, in case it made her too self-conscious."

"And . . . ?"

"You'll have to meet her and judge for yourself. But my own feeling is that it's already had an important effect on her. Do you remember that airline hostess, Sharon, and how quickly it worked when I told her she could get rid of that twitch with a simple operation?"

"Yes, of course. What happened?"

"She didn't need the operation. As soon as she stopped worrying, the twitch vanished of its own accord. You see, it was just a question of *lifting a weight* from her mind. And it's the same with this girl Lesley. She'd got into the habit of seeing herself as a loser, a victim. And I think she's now realized that it's something she can stop worrying about. And once they stop worrying, the weight lifts, and they become different personalities."

"Incredible!" He looked at the brochure, then smiled with a gleam of malice. "This machine is bad news for the psychiatric profession. It is going to put them all out of business."

Charlie laughed. "Oh, I don't think so!"

"You don't?" Charlie detected a trace of diappointment in his eyes.

"No. Think of Bob Engledow, that businessman who was cured when his daughter's car fell into the canal. I don't think he'd have been cured by the digital paintbox. And the same thing is true with Ben McKeown's son Nicky. He's cured since he started playing professional chess. His coach thinks he'll end up as European champion. The best way of curing people is to give them a sense of purpose. But the paintbox is an important step in the right direction. Look at this woman, for example."

He inserted another cassette into the machine. It was an interview that he had made with the receptionist, Mabel.

"This is the receptionist from the surgery downstairs. She's overweight and sex-starved and nobody likes her. If I can cure her with the digital paintbox, I'll really feel I've achieved something."

"Where is this paintbox?"

"It's at a laboratory in Acton at the moment. I'll take you there tomorrow."

Topelius continued to study the face of the woman on the television screen. From his expression, Charlie concluded he was not optimistic about effecting any improvement. Then, to his surprise, Topelius said, "It may be less difficult than you think."

"Why?"

"I can tell that she is a good hypnotic subject—it is a subject I have studied. And if she is highly suggestible, we have won half the battle."

That "we" gave Charlie a deep glow of satisfaction.

Later, as they were drinking tea, Topelius picked up the volume labeled "Personality Identikit."

"What is this?"

"I'm trying to work out some kind of classification of facial expressions."

"For what purpose?"

"To use with the digital paintbox. If you want to alter someone's expression, you can look through that until you find exactly what you want."

Topelius went on turning the pages. Charlie had now filled more than a dozen.

"This could be important. Have you heard of the ancient Chinese science of *hsiang shu?*"

"No. What is it?"

"We call it physiognomy, but it is more than that. The Chinese believe that a person's character and destiny can be read from his face. I know a woman who practices it in Stockholm, and it is surprisingly accurate."

Charlie thought about this.

"I can see how a person's character might be written on his face. But surely not his destiny?"

"Why not? The two are interconnected. For example, you could assume that a weak and lazy person would be unsuccessful. "

"I don't see how that can help us."

Topelius continued to look through the pages of photographs. He said finally, "Do you know the history of fingerprinting?"

"Not really, no."

"It was known for centuries that everyone's fingerprints are unique. In the ancient world, they were often used as signatures on documents. But no one believed this was of any practical use, because there was no way of classifying them. Then Sir Francis Galton began to study them closely, and discovered that there *are* certain basic features—loops, arches, whorls—that can be measured and classified. As soon as he showed how to classify them, the police were able to use them to catch criminals."

Charlie looked down at the book over Topelius's shoulder. "You think expressions could be classified like fingerprints?"

"I see no reason why not. If there is anything in the science of *hsiang shu*, it should be possible to classify the basic characteristics of faces, and then feed them into a computer."

"I still don't see what use that would be."

"No? Suppose you are a personnel manager of a large factory, and you invite applications for a particular job. You ask every applicant to submit a photograph. And instead of having to interview two hundred people, you feed the photographs into your computer and ask which of them is most suitable."

"And you really think that would work?"

Topelius shrugged. "I am willing to find out."

The chauffeur arrived to collect them at seven. Charlie had pointed out that it would be just as easy for him to drive to Denmark Hill in the mini, but McKeown had insisted. It was either a strong sense of hospitality or a desire to impress. Since Alec was driving the Rolls, he suspected the latter.

When the butler showed them into the sitting room, Charlie was surprised to find Alvin Rinkler there. With his vast bulk clad in evening dress, and displaying an enormous expanse of starched white shirtfront, he was an impressive sight. Charlie was glad he had decided to treat himself to a reasonable suit.

As Jessica McKeown shook Topelius's hand, she said, "Alvin has been telling us how famous you are."

"Famous?" Topelius looked blank. He evidently thought it was a mistake.

Rinkler said, "I've been telling the McKeowns about your experiments with brain extract on the opiate receptors. That was a truly brilliant piece of work."

"Thank you. I didn't realize you were familiar with my work." Topelius was obviously gratified.

McKeown said, "Alvin is familiar with everything that's going on." Rinkler smiled modestly.

It established a pleasant atmosphere. McKeown was in a mellow mood. As they drank dry sherry, he talked about the recent defeat of the Labour government in a vote of confidence, and his certainty about a Conservative victory at the next general election. And when

Topelius congratulated him on the house, he delivered a brief lecture on the history of Denmark Hill, and took them on a tour of the picture gallery.

When they were seated at the dinner table, Rinkler turned to Topelius.

"There's one question I'd like to ask you."

"Please."

"You've spent ten years doing some classic research into brain chemistry. Isn't it rather a change of direction to move into the field of general psychology?"

"Ah, but I do not consider personality research a change of direction. May I tell you about an experiment I have just been conducting at M.I.T.?" He looked for permission to his hostess. Jessica McKeown said, "Please do."

"Stop me if I become too boring or too technical." He asked Jessica, "Has Mr. Rinkler explained to you about enkephalins?"

"A little." She looked doubtful.

"They are the brain's natural pain killers. And we have discovered that they tend to concentrate in the nerve endings in the spinal cord. So, for example, if you stick a needle in your finger, an impulse travels up your arm to the spinal cord, and a neurotransmitter is released that causes the sensation you call pain. Now at M.I.T., I heard about a Black woman who was an exceptionally good hypnotic subject—so good that when she burnt her hand badly, her doctor was able to make the pain disappear by placing her in a trance.

"We persuaded this woman, Fran Baker, to allow us to plant an electric contact in her mouth, attached to the gum, so that when the current switched on, it caused a pain like toothache."

Jessica said, "I hope you paid her adequately."

"More than adequately. Well, we placed her under hypnosis, and told her that she would feel the pain when the current was turned on, but that it would diminish and then disappear within a few seconds. When we switched on the current, she began to moan with pain. Then I told her, 'It is beginning to go away now. And now it has vanished completely . . . ' And she smiled and said the pain had gone. In fact, the current was still switched on.

"Next, we used a method I had developed to find out what was happening at the pain receptors in her spinal cord. And, just as I had suspected, we found that the pain was being neutralized by enkephalin neurons."

Topelius smiled triumphantly around the table, then saw, from the look on Ben McKeown's face, that he had failed to grasp the point.

"The experiment shows that hypnosis relieves pain by causing the body to produce its natural opiates. But if that is so, what is there to stop us doing the same thing every time we burn a finger or stub a toe on the bed?"

Rinkler said, "I suppose we don't know how."

"Precisely. We don't know how to trigger the unconscious mechanism that releases the enkephalin. When you burn your finger, you feel you *ought* to feel pain. If you were absolutely certain that you ought *not* to feel pain, then you wouldn't. In other words, it is a matter of self-belief, self-confidence. And self-confidence is a quality that springs from the personality."

McKeown was clearly unconvinced. "Are you telling us we could all stop pain if we wanted to?"

Topelius said, "I am saying that we all *possess the power* to stop pain. I am not saying we know how to do it. Let me give you another example of what I mean. Last year I investigated a strange case of a mentally subnormal girl who began to speak in Japanese when she had a high fever. A Japanese chef lived in the house, and he asked her questions in Japanese. She replied in the same language. The head of the local medical school heard about it, but by this time the girl had recovered, and her power to speak Japanese had vanished. But the chef had tape recordings in which they talked Japanese. Dr. Fogelqvist, the head of the medical school, conducted a careful investigation into the girl's past, and discovered that she had an uncle who owned a cinema that showed foreign films. As a child, she used to spend hours in there. She was particularly fond of Japanese films, although she made no attempt to understand the language. But she watched the characters on the screen speaking Japanese, and her unconscious mind somehow learned Japanese. And when she had a fever, she could suddenly speak Japanese.

"Now if you or I wish to learn a foreign language well enough to speak it, we have to devote about a thousand hours to it. Yet there is something in here," he tapped his forehead, "that can learn it in a matter of hours. If we could find how to activate this faculty—let us say, for the sake of argument, that we discovered some drug that could make it operate—you could watch a Spanish film with English subtitles, and come out of the cinema with a good working knowledge of Spanish." He turned to McKeown. "I hope that answers your question. I believe we have enormous untapped resources, and that they are being held in check by our belief that we are more limited than we are." He turned to Rinkler. "And this is precisely what personality surgery is about."

Rinkler said, "There's one question I would like to ask . . . "

Jessica McKeown interrupted, "Let him eat his soup, Alvin, or it will get cold."

"Your word is law, ma'am. But let me ask him the question anyway, and he can think about it while he's eating." He turned to Topelius. "What would you say is the basic difference between your theory of mental illness and those of the classical psychologists: Freud, Jung, Adler and the rest?"

Topelius flashed him a smile as he raised his spoon.

"I don't need time to think about that. I don't have any theories. I am only interested in results."

Charlie observed the look that passed between McKeown and Rinkler, and wondered what it meant.

Jessica McKeown steered the conversation on to more general topics. McKeown and Rinkler talked about American politics, and Topelius joined in. All three seemed to feel that President Carter's popularity was waning fast, and that the next elections would see a Republican in the White House. The food was good and the wine plentiful. Charlie found that it made him sleepy. So did Topelius. As they were drinking coffee in the lounge, he stifled a yawn, and immediately apologized.

"I'm afraid I am suffering from jet lag. For me it is now after midnight. I hope you will excuse me if I leave early?"

Again, a glance passed between McKeown and Rinkler. Rinkler said, "If I may, I'd like to go back to what you were saying earlier about self-belief. I've come across a rather interesting case recently."

Charlie was not deceived by the casual tone. Something inside him became instantly alert. Ever since they had arrived, he had experienced an obscure certainty that Rinkler was there for some purpose. The same instinct suggested he was about to find out what it was.

Rinkler said, "Have you heard of Roger Macy?"

Topelius nodded. "The astronaut?"

"That's right. One of the original eight astronauts, together with John Glenn, Al Shepard, Gus Grissom and the rest. He was one of the first men to orbit the earth, and the first man to step on to the dark side of the moon. Two years ago he left NASA and did some useful work for the Republican party in his home state. There was talk about running for Congress. Then he began to suffer from nervous depression, and at the moment, he's in a Swiss clinic."

Topelius said, "The depression is a fairly normal reaction in a man who has been under heavy stress for years, and suddenly goes into retirement."

"Except," Rinkler raised a finger, "that he's been busier in retirement than he was in the space agency. So how would you account for that?" The question was addressed to both of them.

Charlie said, "That's a question I couldn't answer without knowing a lot more about him."

Rinkler looked at Topelius. Topelius said, "I agree with Charles."

Rinkler said, "In that case, would you be willing to take a look at him?"

Topelius said, "I thought he was in Switzerland."

"He'll be in London on Thursday, on his way back to the States."

Charlie and Topelius looked at one another. Both knew what the other was thinking; that they had been hired to do research, not to deliver off-the-cuff medical opinions. Rinkler read their minds.

"I understand it's not fair to spring this on you at short notice. But let me explain why I think you can help. Ben told me about his friend Engledow, and the problem he developed when he retired from business. Now I reckon this is a very similar case. Macy's been examined and psychoanalyzed and given drug therapy, and none of it seems to have done any good. My feeling is that it's just conceivable that your approach might come up with an answer. If it doesn't, I'd quite understand, and nobody's going to blame you."

Topelius said, "Is Macy a friend of yours?"

"No. I've met him, that's all. But he's a friend of a friend. Governor Reagan of California, to be specific."

Topelius said, "The man who is hoping to become the Republican presidential candidate?"

"Exactly. He's stood twice before and lost. This time we all think he's got a good chance of winning. That's why we're so concerned about Roger Macy. He's a national hero, and he's going to be a valuable asset in the primaries."

"Which are?"

"Less than a year away, but as far as Reagan's concerned, the campaign has started already. He's been stumping the country for the past three years. He'd be glad of Macy's support right now."

Charlie and Topelius looked at one another. Charlie said, "Well, I suppose there'd be no harm in seeing him."

Topelius shrugged. "If you wish."

McKeown spoke for the first time. "That's great. That's what I hoped you'd say. I've deliberately kept quiet because I didn't want to influence you, but I have to admit, I'd have been disappointed if you'd said no."

Charlie said, "If Macy's a national hero, I take it that there's plenty of film archive material on him?"

"Plenty."

"Any chance of getting hold of some before Thursday?"

Rinkler said, "I'll have it to you by Tuesday morning."

As they were driven home half an hour later, neither of them said much. They were constrained by Alec's presence. But when they were in the lift going up to the flat, Topelius said, "I cannot pretend that I welcome this development."

Charlie shrugged. "Neither do I. But it doesn't worry me either. After all, it doesn't matter if there's nothing we can do."

Topelius said, "Mr. McKeown strikes me as a man who doesn't like failure."

Topelius slept on the bed-settee in the living room. The next morning, he awakened Charlie with coffee at half past seven. Charlie put on a dressing gown over his pajamas and cooked eggs and bacon. It was pleasant to have Topelius there. One of the problems of working alone was that new ideas often filled him with such excitement that he wanted to communicate them immediately, and writing them down was no substitute for a sympathetic listener.

Immediately after breakfast, Charlie played the videotapes of his interview with the drama students. He wanted to show Topelius how he had come to classify certain expressions in his "personality identikit." He found it exciting to work with a man as perceptive as Topelius, someone who had spent years training himself in the minute and accurate perception of individual differences. Charlie had studied these tapes half a dozen times, yet Topelius was able to point out things he had not even suspected. For example, when they were watching the interview with Mandy, the middle-class girl with the strawberries-and-cream complexion, Topelius commented, "Is she in love with somebody in the room? Who is sitting over there to her left?"

Charlie thought hard and said, "Duncan Baron, I think. . . . "

Then he closed his eyes and tried to visualize the room. "No, it was . . . what's his name? . . . a student called Norman. But there was another student called Jonathan sitting beside him. It could have been either. What makes you think she's in love?"

"Her eyes move more to the left than the right. But on at least two occasions, she looks away to the right, as if deliberately avoiding looking at someone. Could you play it back a few seconds?"

The moment he was referring to was when Pam called out the question, "Ever been in love?" Mandy replied promptly, "No," and her eyes swiveled to the right.

Now Topelius pointed it out, it seemed obvious. It is easy, said Topelius, to observe when someone is trying *not* to look at someone, or is trying to pretend that someone in the room means no more to her than anyone else. Small movements of the eyes betray it, even if her manner appears perfectly neutral.

At one point during the "free for all" questioning period, Jonathan's voice asked, "What do you think of sex before marriage?" Mandy hesitated for a fraction of a second, then snapped back, "I like it." Topelius said, "Who asked the question?"

"A boy called Jonathan."

"He is not the one she is interested in. He is trying to embarrass her. She takes pride in not being embarrassed. Such an attitude is possible only between two people who have no sexual interest in one another, like Shakespeare's Beatrice and Benedick. As soon as romantic interest develops—even if it is confined to one of them—there is a new attitude of deference, a desire not to offend or upset the other person."

Charlie said, "If it's not Jonathan, it has to be Norman. Do you think you might be able to tell from the interview with Norman?"

"Let us try."

They played the videotape of Norman, the first interview Charlie had made that afternoon. Within seconds, Topelius said, "You see. That same movement of the eyes. You can tell he fells sexually interested in someone in the room, someone to his right."

"That must be Mandy. She and Pam were sitting at the far end."

When Jonathan asked, "When did you last have sex!" and Norman blushed, Topelius gave a shout of triumph, and used the automatic control to stop the tape.

"You see. Watch that again."

It was true, and now Topelius pointed it out, obvious. As he blushed, Norman's eyes were drawn compulsively to his right, then instantly swiveled away. Topelius played it in slow motion, then frame by frame.

"You see that the camera is like a lie detector. When sex is mentioned, he immediately betrays that he has been in sexual contact with someone to his right. My own guess is that it was fairly recent, perhaps the previous night. They are both middle-class. They are determined to keep their secret to themselves for as long as possible. But the camera reveals it."

At ten o'clock, Charlie rang Pixell Electronics and asked Boris Gorski if he could bring Topelius over; Gorski told him to come immediately.

Although neither of them mentioned it, both were experiencing a sense of urgency. The thought of Roger Macy hung over them like a threat. The material would arrive the following morning. When that happened, they would have to give it their full attention. Both felt a vague resentment, accompanied by a desire to make the best of their freedom in the meantime. As they drove to Acton, the morning was bright and springlike and London seemed to sparkle. For the first time since he had retired from the practice, Charlie experienced a pure sense of delight in his new life.

It was one of those days when everything went right. They arrived at Pixell in time for the mid-morning coffee break. Boris Gorski took them to the canteen. He and Topelius took to one another immediately and within minutes, they were talking computer technicalities. Charlie was astonished at how much Topelius knew about the subject. Back in the workshop, McCaffrey joined them. Again, there was instant rapport between himself and Topelius. They opened the Personality Identikit album on the bench, and launched into a detailed discussion of the precise difference between one expression and another. Not simply between a happy smile and a sad smile, but between a shy smile and a diffident smile, a puzzled frown and a meditative frown. Once again, Charlie was struck by the quickness of Topelius's intelligence and his astonishing powers of observation. He also observed his power to bring out the best in people, to generate excitement and enthusiasm.

Charlie produced from his pocket the interview with the receptionist, Mabel. All four of them watched it from beginning to end, then McCaffrey selected a frame that showed her full-face with her mouth closed, and proceeded to make sweeping alterations with the stylus. Working with the ease of a portrait painter, he removed ten years from her age by narrowing the face, dissolving away fat from her chin and altering the shadows under the cheekbones. Then he made the mouth firmer and the eyes brighter, and altered the hair style. It was no longer the face of an overweight middle-aged receptionist looking at them, but that of an attractive, well-groomed woman who might have been the managing director's secretary. At this point, Gorski took over the operation, and transferred the alterations to subsequent frames. Before they broke off for lunch, they were able to play back almost two minutes of film. It was unbelievable. McCaffrey had not merely changed her face, but had somehow altered her personality. When the altered section came to an end and Mabel's normal face appeared on the screen, all experienced the same curious shock of outrage. It was as if the woman they had been watching had suddenly aged. All admitted to the same sensation. The feeling that the "transformed" Mabel was the real Mabel and that the older, wearier face was some kind of grotesque travesty.

Soon after lunch, McCaffrey had to leave them; he was doing some work for an advertising agency. Gorski retired to his office. Watching McCaffrey, both Charlie and Topelius felt they could continue the work alone, and it only took them a few minutes to realize how little they understood the techniques of the digital paintbox. Yet in a sense, it was more rewarding to make their own mistakes, to attempt various transformations and then to see precisely where their judgment had been faulty. Neither of them could believe it when McCaffrey came back and pointed out that it was after six o'clock, but they had no difficulty persuading McCaffrey and Gorski to look at the results of their efforts, and to make dozens of changes. When they left Pixell after seven, Charlie and Topelius were exhausted. Charlie had a hallucinatory impression of actually *knowing* the woman they had spent the day creating. It was hard to believe that she had no real existence.

Topelius insisted on taking Charlie to dinner. They went to the pub across the road. Over his T-bone steak, Charlie explained in detail all that had happened to him since he last saw Topelius at the Park View Hotel. He told the story of Lesley, then of Nicky McKeown and Ben McKeown. The story of Sir George Pettie and the Hadley-Thomson takeover required a second bottle of Beaujolais. Topelius's total attention told him more than any amount of comment or congratulation. And, without any feeling of conceit or self-importance, Charlie himself became suddenly aware of the significance of what he was saying. A calm, objective recognition that some instinct had guided him like a sleepwalker to his discoveries. His mind went back to the afternoon when he had read *Arrowsmith* in his sister Violet's flat, and that sudden conviction that he also had a destiny to improve the lives of his fellow men. It was strange to realize that he had already taken the first important steps along the way.

They were eating cheese and biscuits when he heard Duncan Baron's voice. He leaned across the bar and looked around the frosted glass partition. Baron and Lesley were standing at the bar counter. Charlie invited them to come and join him, and ordered another bottle of wine. As he introduced them to Topelius, he stole a sidelong glance at Lesley, and she met his eyes. The warm glow in her cheeks told him what he wanted to know. He also noted the protective way that Baron's hand rested briefly on her waist as he offered her a chair.

Baron explained that they were on their way back from the cinema, and had decided to ring Charlie's doorbell as they passed. Receiving no reply, they had decided to go for a drink. As they talked, attempting to make themselves heard above the din of last-minute orders, Topelius's eyes rested on Lesley with speculative interest. Charlie knew what he was thinking. That it was inconceivable that this beautiful, shy-looking girl, whose skin was as delicate as a porcelain shepherdess, could be the nymphomaniac who had lost her virginity at the age of twelve. In fact, Charlie had never seen her looking so desirable. Contentment had given her a curious inner peace and relaxation.

Lesley declined the invitation to come up to the flat. Charlie guessed that she wanted to take Baron to meet her family. They said good night outside the surgery. She leaned forward and kissed Charlie on the side of the mouth and as usual, her warm lips triggered a flash of sexual voracity. As he watched Baron's rusty Ford Cortina drive away, he had to repress a twinge of envy.

When they stepped out of the lift, Charlie saw a brown paper parcel outside the flat. The label said, McKeown Enterprises, New York, and large red stickers announced it was a special delivery. Charlie took it into the flat and placed it on the table next to the telephone. Both of them knew what was inside it. Neither had any desire to open it. The problems it contained could wait until the next day.

CHAPTER EIGHTEEN

THE FOLLOWING morning, as they ate breakfast, they continued to ignore the parcel. Charlie felt as if he was making some importunate visitor wait his turn. They talked about other matters: about Lesley, and Mabel, and Topelius's friend in Stockholm who practiced *hsiang shu*. And when the breakfast things had been cleared away and the moment could be postponed no longer, Charlie used a breadknife to cut the plastic tape around the parcel, and tore off the paper.

It contained videotapes, books and several manila folders full of press cuttings. The books included a history of rocketry by Werner von Braun, and Norman Mailer's *Fire on the Moon*. Charlie selected a cassette labeled simply "Astronaut Documentary," and inserted it into the machine.

He was immediately gripped by the sheer visual magnificence of the opening shot, of the flames bursting from the base of the rocket, creating a tide of fire, out of which the rocket rose slowly, like some monstrous bullet fired out of a volcano. Then there was the superb, curving flight into the blue, the sense of a tremendous power defying gravity and spurning the earth, like a god determined to return to his own realm. Charlie's attention was so totally concentrated that when the second explosion came, and the command module separated from the rocket, his heart also exploded with alarm, assuming for a moment that some accident had occurred. The whole experience was like a symphony rising to a climax at the beginning. He felt as if pinned in his armchair by some force. From that moment there was no longer any question of boredom.

The credits over, the film went on to present archive material on the history of rocketry. The first methane-oxygen rocket that rose to an altitude of a thousand feet above Dessau in 1931, the Soviet liquid-propellant rocket that reached three and a half miles in 1936, the V-2 rockets that destroyed so much of London in the last year of the second world war. Von Braun described his flight from Peenemünde with the secret documents and drawings of the German rockets, and their surrender to the Americans at Reutte, in the Tyrol.

The result of von Braun's move to America was the first Viking rocket, which rose to a height of fifty miles in May 1949. Viking 4, fired from a ship at sea, reached a height of a hundred and five miles. By the mid-1950s, Viking 12 had reached a height of a hundred and forty-four miles.

Then came the shock that galvanized the American government: the Russian Sputnik that went into orbit in October 1957. If the Russians could put a rocket into orbit, they could also wipe out every American city with ballistic missiles. Suddenly, the American space program went into top gear. By the time the Russians sent up their second Sputnik, containing a dog, American scientists were working frantically on Explorer 1, which finally went into orbit in January 1958. And in the following year, eight men were chosen to be America's first astronauts. They included Roger Macy.

Macy, like most of the others, had been a test pilot. Born in Mapleville, Oregon, in 1927, son of a wealthy furniture manufacturer, Macy had entered the U.S. Navy in 1944 and fought in the Pacific. After the war he trained as a test pilot and a stunt flier. In January 1948, he was the second man in the world to fly an airplane faster than sound. For the next ten years he tested rocket planes, and in December 1958, he was selected from among five hundred other military test pilots to attend a secret meeting at the Pentagon. The thirty or so young men who attended with him were told that the National Aeronautics and Space Administration needed volunteers for Project Mercury, whose ultimate purpose was to put a man into space. Macy volunteered, and a few months later, knew he had been selected. Then came the day when the eight men appeared at a nationally televised press conference. The following morning, they were all famous.

The video showed the training of an astronaut, the endless exercise to keep him in peak condition, the hours spent in a simulator, being whirled around at high speed to accustom them to the build-up of gravitational pressure, or being subjected to strange switch-back maneuvers in jet planes to get them used to the sensation of weightlessness as the plane went over the arc of a parabola. It made Charlie feel exhausted merely to watch it. The take-off was simulated over and over again, until every single action became a reflex. The astronaut was trained to become a part of the machinery.

In April 1961, the Russians again deflected some of the glory by putting the first man into space. Yuri Gagarin was launched into a single earth orbit. During the next two weeks, two American attempts to launch orbital rockets with dummy astronauts were failures. Both had to be blown up. But three weeks after Gagarin's flight, astronaut Al Shepard was hurled into space from the coast of Florida, rose to a height of a hundred and sixteen miles, and landed back in the ocean near Bermuda. Two months later, Roger Macy followed the same course, experienced five minutes of weightlessness out in space, and splashed down within three miles of the recovery ship. But this triumph almost ended in disaster when the capsule turned upside down and began to sink. Macy had to release himself under water and cling to the capsule until he was rescued by a helicopter. As he looked down from its cockpit, he saw sharks circling the capsule.

In 1966, Macy was selected to be one of the three astronauts to make an orbital flight round the earth, but he had to be dropped when he picked up a stomach virus a few weeks before scheduled take-off. On January 27, 1967, the three men actually selected for the mission—Gus Grissom, Ed White and Roger Chaffee—died as a result of a fire in the cockpit of the spacecraft.

The greatest moment in the early history of space flight was the first landing on the moon on July 20, 1969. Macy was not selected for that flight, nor for the subsequent six Apollo missions. But on April 17, 1973, he had his supreme moment of glory when, in the last of the Apollo missions, he stepped out into the great unnamed crater between Tsiolkovsky and Jules Verne, on the dark side of the moon. Together with Ed Volkov, he drove seventeen miles in a lunar roving vehicle, and brought back invaluable samples of volcanic rock. The crater in which he landed was subsequently named after him.

The final sequences of the documentary showed the three astronauts being received by Richard Nixon in the White House, and Macy opening the new Roger Macy Hospital in his hometown, Mapleville, Oregon. The credits went up over pictures of the far side of the moon, taken on that final mission.

The screen went blank. For several moments, neither of them spoke. Then Charlie said, "I can understand Macy feeling depressed after he left NASA. The sheer sense of anticlimax. What I can't understand is why it took two years. Bob Engledow was already feeling at a loose end when he'd been retired two weeks."

"The circumstances were different. Engledow retired into private life, with nothing to do but play golf. Macy went into state politics."

"In that case, why did he have the breakdown at all?"

"Perhaps he doesn't know the answer himself."

Charlie went into the kitchen to make coffee, and to give himself a chance to clarify his ideas. When he came back, carrying a tray, he said, "Look, here's how I see it. Macy goes into the navy when he's still a teenager, and he sees the fall of Japan. All discipline and excitement. Then he goes home and becomes a test pilot. More discipline and excitement. Then he becomes an astronaut—still more discipline and excitement. Then, after thirty years in uniform, he becomes a civilian again. He must have felt like a fish out of water."

"Or a homesick child. I call it 'the homesickness effect.' A child spends years in the same environment, then he goes away on holiday and feels lost and frightened, and longs to get back home. When Macy left NASA, he probably experienced the homesickness effect, and that can undermine a man's sense of values. He may end by feeling that it is not worth getting out of bed in the morning."

Charlie sighed. "But that still doesn't explain why it took two years." He emptied the contents of the parcel on the table and began to examine them one by one. "Look, this sounds interesting. It's a television program made by the local station in Eugene, Oregon. Feel like watching it?"

"Of course."

By comparison with the previous documentary, this one was distinctly amateurish. Much of it consisted of interviews with relatives and friends of the astronaut: the minister of his local church, his headmaster in high school, even the woman who ran the local candy store. But it also contained some useful background information. Both Macy's parents and grandparents had been "achievers" and pillars of the local community. His grandfather had come west with the forty-niners. He had failed to find gold in California, but had found copper in Oregon and become a rich man. He and his wife had built the Reformed Episcopal Church in Mapleville. Macy's parents had been deeply interested in education, and had founded Mapleville College to introduce the Montessori system to their fellow citizens. The father, Cunliffe Macy, had been mayor of Mapleville three times; his wife was president of the Women's League and honorary dean of Mapleville College. Macy's grand uncle, General Cunliffe, had led the American forces to victory in the battle of the Argonne in 1918, and had twice been a candidate for the governorship of the state, being defeated on both occasions.

While the tape was playing, Charlie made notes, and kept a record of the numbers on the digital display. When it was over, he rewound the tape to an interview with Macy's sister Samantha. She was telling an interviewer, "It caused a lot of bitterness when Roger volunteered for the Navy instead of going to college. My parents were pacifists. But when he came back from the war with a chestful of medals, they decided they'd better forgive him. They even organized a civic reception . . . "

Charlie switched off the tape. "That's interesting, don't you think? He obviously didn't share their religious views."

"From which you infer . . .?"

Charlie shrugged. "Well, to begin with, that he didn't have any ambition to build a church."

Topelius nodded. "Anything else?" Charlie glanced at him sharply. His tone of voice implied that he had noticed something that Charlie had missed. Charlie thought about it.

"Only that it makes it more puzzling than ever. His parents and grandparents were 'achievers,' so he felt he had to be an achiever too. And he was. He became the all-American hero of his generation, and the moon landing gave him a place in the history books. Yet in spite of that, he has a breakdown."

Topelius smiled approvingly. "And . . . ?"

Charlie shrugged. "And I suppose we have to find out the reason."

"Why?"

"Why?" Charlie looked at him uncomprehendingly. "Because you need to diagnose an illness before you can treat it."

Topelius shook his head firmly. "Not in this case. We already know the nature of the illness—nervous depression. The problem is not to find out what caused it—that is irrelevant—but to find out how to get rid of it."

"Quite. I wish I knew the answer."

Topelius smiled. "You do. Or at least, your instinct has pointed you in the right direction. You immediately seized on that comment by his sister. It indicates that Macy was not interested in churches or colleges. Yet he was a man who wanted to excel. What did he want to excel *in*? His career gives us the answer. He joined the Navy when he was seventeen, in spite of strong opposition from his parents. His sister tells us that his favorite reading as a child was a history of the first world war, and that he used to play secretly with toy soldiers in the attic . . . "

Charlie suddenly understood. "Of course! His great uncle, General whatsisname?"

"Cunliffe. Yes, I am convinced that he provides the clue." He took the automatic control and wound the tape forward. "I suspected it when I saw the interview with the old man, and it was confirmed by the photograph of Macy's room at Wright Field. This should be it." A still photograph of Macy appeared on the television. Topelius leaned forward and placed his finger on the screen. Clearly visible on the locker behind Macy was a photograph of a man in a military cap. "You would expect a young man to have a photograph of his girlfriend on his locker, or perhaps his parents. If he has a picture of his great uncle in uniform, it surely implies that he regards him with great admiration." He wound the tape forward again, consulting the notebook in which he had written the numbers of the digital display. "And when Macy is being interviewed after his first orbital flight of the earth, what do we see on the table behind him. . . ?" He placed his finger on the same photograph.

Charlie showed Topelius a page of the press cutting album.

"You're right. Look, they even look alike." A page of the *Mapleville Gazette* carried a headline: HEROES IN WAR AND PEACE. Underneath there were photographs of Roger Macy and General Cunliffe. There was a strong resemblance, but Macy's face was broader, the chin rounder, the eyes less aggressive.

They looked at one another. Both knew what the other was thinking. Charlie said, "So that looks like our answer. Let's look at that interview again."

The general was seated on a white garden bench, under a willow tree. He was in his mid-eighties, and the loose skin under his jaw made him look like an ancient saurian. His speech was slightly slurred, obviously the aftermath of a stroke. But the eyes still had the clear, straight gaze of a highly dominant individual. There was a dry humor in his manner of speaking. "When Roger was ten he used my favorite briarwood pipe for blowing bubbles. I knew then that he'd either do something amazing or end in jail."

The interview with the general was followed immediately by a speech made by Roger Macy at West Point. He was saying, "They say that in war, the heroes outnumber the soldiers ten to one. But in space there's no room for heroes. The astronaut needs the virtues of an old-fashioned accountant . . . "

Charlie froze the frame. "Notice that twitch of a smile at the corners of the mouth, exactly like the general."

Topelius picked up the telephone.

"Who are you ringing?"

"Alvin Rinkler. He told us to call him if we had any problems or queries . . . Hello, Alvin, this is Erik." They had ended the evening on first-name terms. "Fine, thank you, very comfortable. Alvin, we are rather interested in Macy's great uncle, General Cunliffe . . . Well yes, obviously I'd like to speak to him if that's possible, but it's not important . . . Yes, we have some ideas, but at the moment they are just speculations . . . Oh, before you go, could you find out if this young man McCaffrey is available during the next two days? I think we are going to need him . . . Thank you."

As he hung up, Charlie said, "You think the old boy's still alive?"

Topelius smiled. "No, I think it is highly improbable."

Charlie knew him well enough to guess at his thought processes. "You think his death caused Macy's breakdown?"

"Exactly. You see, I happen to understand what it is to model yourself on an older man. My uncle was the famous biochemist Olof Svedberg, the man who discovered hormones. He had tremendous charm and force of character, and he was responsible for my decision to become a scientist. I simply wanted to be as much like him as possible. It was the greatest sadness of my life that he died just before my first paper appeared in *Nature*." He used the control to rewind the tape. "Now look, compare General Cunliffe with Roger Macy's father . . . " An interview with Cunliffe Macy showed him to be a mild, white-haired old man with a hesitant voice, with an undertone that reminded Charlie of the bleating of a sheep. Topelius moved on to the interview with General Cunliffe on the garden seat. There was no need to underline the point. Even after a stroke, the general still had a force of personality, a racy directness of speech, that compelled attention. Topelius said, "Everybody has someone they want to impress more than anyone else in the world. It might be a parent, or a sister, or perhaps a pretty girl next door. In my case, it was my Uncle Olof. For Macy, it was General Cunliffe. If we assume that leaving NASA produced the 'homesickness effect,' then the death of General Cunliffe could have been the straw that broke the camel's back. Macy would suddenly feel like an actor playing to an empty theater."

Charlie stared at the face of the old man frozen on the television screen.

"In that case, we ought to think twice before doctoring that tape. If we make Roger Macy look like the general, it might revive some unpleasant memories."

Topelius shook his head."Yet it is a risk we have to take. I can see no other way. Can you?"

"Not at the moment."

Half an hour later, Charlie was cooking an omelette when the telephone rang.

"Erik?" He recognized Rinkler's voice.

"No, it's Charlie. Erik's in the bathroom. Hold on a moment."

"No need to disturb him. I've just managed to talk to Macy's sister Sam in New York. She tells me it probably won't be possible to speak to the general—he's very ill—but I can give you Samantha's number, if that's any good."

"So the general's still alive?" He said this for the benefit of Topelius, who had just come into the room.

"Only just. The old boy's had another stroke. She tells me there's not much chance he'll survive."

"I'll tell Erik. Thanks for taking so much trouble."

As he hung up, Topelius shrugged ironically. "So I was wrong. Pity. It all fitted together so perfectly."

Charlie was amused by his downcast expression.

"What difference does it make. You said yourself that it didn't matter why he got depressed, the real problem is to cure it."

"True. But it helps if you know the reason."

Charlie went back to the kitchen. "Anyway, that solves one problem. If the general's still alive, we may as well go ahead with the tape. I'll ring Pixell and see if we can go this afternoon."

They drove to the factory immediately after lunch. McCaffrey was waiting for them.

"Mr. McKeown said you'd be needing me for the next two days. Big job?"

"Afraid so. A ninety-minute tape."

McCaffrey looked taken aback.

"In two days? That's going to be a rush. It takes an hour to do five minutes."

"We don't need to do the whole ninety minutes, only the extracts where our patient appears. Ever hear of Roger Macy?"

"No. What does he do?"

They ran the relevant extracts showing Macy, then the interview with General Cunliffe. Charlie had also discovered a videotape with old newsreel material showing the general in his electioneering days. McCaffrey studied all this carefully, then projected an image of Macy on the screen and went to work. A few strokes of the stylus made the face thinner, altered the angle of the jaw, and made the nose more aquiline. The result was a kind of caricature of the general. Then, using the enlargement facility, he softened the lines and made subtle adjustments of light and shade. When the face was reduced to its original size, they agreed that the resemblance to General Cunliffe was now remarkable. But there was still something subtly wrong with the mouth. It was another half hour before Topelius said, "That's it! Leave it just as it is!"

Later in the afternoon, Boris Gorski joined them. He had been working on another project. With his help, a seven-and-a-half minute interview with Macy was transformed into an interview with a man who looked like a younger version of General Cunliffe. Gorski was satisfied, but this was mainly because the alterations were undetectable. The other three knew there was still something wrong. They played back the film extracts of the general, then compared them with the doctored tape. McCaffrey said, "It's the eyes. Look, you can see it in the newspaper photographs. Somehow the old boy's eyes are more aggressive." It was true. The general had the open, direct gaze of a man who does not expect to be contradicted. By comparison, Macy's eyes were clouded and introspective. This was obviously not due to any lack of self-confidence, it was simply that part of his attention was directed inside himself. The general looked as if he found the world around him endlessly fascinating. Macy looked as if he was driven by an obscure urge to find something else.

McCaffrey experimented with the eyes, enlarging them until they occupied the whole screen. Half an hour later, they still had to acknowledge that there was something wrong. Roger Macy's gaze still looked introspective, and attempts to make the eyes more assertive only gave them a menacing glitter reminiscent of Bela Lugosi as Dracula.

Topelius said, "What a pity you could not simply transfer the general's eyes into Macy's face."

McCaffrey and Gorski stared at one another, and McCaffrey slapped his forehead with his hand.

"Idiot! Why didn't I think of that? Of course it's possible; the damn thing's got a superimposing facility! Hand me that manual . . . "

It proved to be absurdly simple. A picture of Macy was projected on to the screen, and the erase facility—the stylus with an erase-head —was used to remove the eyes. This picture was then fed into the memory. After that, General Cunliffe's face was projected on to the screen, and the erase facility was used to remove most of his face, so only the eyes and eyebrows remained. Then Macy's face was again projected on to the screen, and the eyes adjusted until they were in position. The overlap between the two was made undetectable with careful strokes of the stylus. At the end of ten minutes, General Cunliffe's eyes looked out at them from Roger Macy's eye sockets. McCaffrey and Gorski slapped one another on the back.

Charlie looked at his watch. "I think that's about enough for one day. Why don't we go and have a drink?"

CHAPTER NINETEEN

As HE opened the door of the flat at ten thirty that evening, the telephone was ringing. It was Alvin Rinkler.

"Thank God I've got you at last. I've been trying to reach you all evening."

"Sorry Alvin, we took Boris and Dermot out for a meal. What's happening?"

"Roger Macy's flying into Heathrow at ten o'clock tomorrow morning, and leaving again at mid-afternoon. I want to bring him round there as soon as he arrives. Is that okay?"

"Tomorrow! You said Thursday."

"His sister telephoned to say the general's seriously ill. He wanted to fly direct from Geneva to New York, but I persuaded him he'd do better to take the Concorde from Heathrow. So he'll be in London for about four hours tomorrow."

Charlie made disgusted faces at Topelius.

"We can't do much in four hours."

"I don't expect you to. I realize the notice is too short. But when he's got back to Oregon, he may not want to return to Europe for a while. That's why I'd like him to meet the two of you before he leaves. I think that it's important for you to get acquainted. You may be able to persuade him to come back."

Charlie placed his hand over the mouthpiece. "Macy's arriving in the morning. We've got four hours." Topelius placed both hands round his throat and gave a comic imitation of a chicken having its neck wrung. Rinkler was saying, "Listen, have a word with Ben."

McKeown's voice said, "Hello, Charles. I just want you to understand I'm not expecting miracles. I only want you to try and make a start."

"We'll do what we can."

"Thank you, Charles. I know I can rely on you."

Charlie banged the phone back on its cradle. Topelius said, "What did he say?"

"Just that he doesn't believe in miracles." He gave a snort of laughter. "But I don't believe him. That's his trouble. He *does* expect bloody miracles."

283

"Never mind. Have a drink." Topelius had brought a bottle of expensive duty-free brandy.

"No thanks." Charlie sank into the armchair. "I've got to get up early tomorrow. If we start early enough, we might be able to get more of the tape done before Macy arrives."

"Why bother? He can't expect us to do much in a few hours."

"You think we ought to forget about the tape?"

"I intend to forget about it until tomorrow morning. I never make important decisions after ten o'clock at night. They are usually wrong."

Charlie was waiting outside Pixell Electronics when it opened at eight o'clock the next morning. He was alone. Topelius had flatly declined to get out of bed before daylight, and Charlie had a feeling that he resented McKeown's attempt to rush them.

The receptionist let him into the empty workshop. When Gorski came in an hour later, Charlie was watching the final moments of the space documentary.

"Hi. You're early."

"I came to collect the program. Macy's arriving later this morning."

"This morning! But that's terrible! We need another two days on that VTR. Can't it wait until tomorrow?"

"Unfortunately, no. Macy's flying back to the States this afternoon."

"So what do we do?" Charlie was grateful for the "we."

"I've been looking through the programs. I reckon there are two places that need altering. One is the meeting with Nixon in the White House, and Macy's speech on the lawn afterwards. The other is the last couple of minutes of the local TV program where he talks about the future of space travel. I've worked it out and it's about five and three quarter minutes altogether. Do you think there's any chance of doing all that before eleven o'clock?"

"That depends on how much he moves his head."

"Very little. He nods a couple of times—otherwise he's looking straight ahead."

"Okay, let's have a look at it."

Neither of them was happy about starting work without Dermot McCaffrey, but McCaffrey was not expected for another hour. He had to call at the BBC Television Centre on his way to Pixell. At least the superimposition technique simplified their task. Charlie had already chosen a number of stills of the general's face. They tried these one by one over photographs of Macy until they found one that fitted like a mask. Then Gorski used the superimpose facility to alter the eyes. When the finished result came on the screen, Charlie said,"Let's leave it at that. Those eyes make all the difference. If we try to change the mouth and the shape of the face, we might spoil it."

By programming the eyes into the remaining frames, they finished the White House sequences in what seemed a remarkably short space of time, but when Charlie looked at his watch, he saw that it was already ten twenty-five. McCaffrey had still not returned. He said,"Look, I'm going to have to get back. Macy's due at about eleven. Could you and Dermot finish the last three minutes of the other tape and send it over by taxi when it's done?"

"I'll do better than that. I'll bring it over myself."

"Marvelous. Just one thing. If Macy's there when you arrive, don't let him see you giving me the tape. I don't want him to suspect what we've been doing."

"Won't you tell him eventually?"

"I don't know. At the moment, I don't know what we're going to do."

Traffic in the West End was heavy and it was a quarter to twelve before he drew up outside the surgery. As he pulled into his parking space, he recognized McKeown's Daimler on the concrete ramp that led down to the underground car park. The car park attendant was arguing with a pretty redhead whom he recognized as McKeown's office manager and private secretary. The man was saying "I'm very sorry, Miss, but you can't stay there even for ten minutes. This is a private car park. If you want to go in, I'd advise you to get the driver to cruise around the block . . . "

Charlie said, "It's all right, Albert. They don't need to park." He looked into the back seat and recognized Roger Macy. "I'm Dr. Peruzzi. Would you like to come on up?"

The girl was obviously relieved. "In that case, I'll leave Mr. Macy in your hands. I'm due back at the office."

"Isn't Mr. Rinkler coming?"

"I'm afraid I don't know."

Macy got out of the car and shook hands. His face looked older and more tired than on the television programs, and he was carrying more weight. Charlie thought he looked tense and harrassed. Macy said, "You look very young for a nerve specialist."

Charlie was glad he had his back to Macy, locking his car.

"Er . . . yes, I suppose I am."

Macy said agreeably, "Well, I guess that means you're pretty good."

Charlie could think of no answer to that, so he smiled noncommittally.

As they entered the building, they met Sandor Kos, who was leaving the surgery. He said hello to Charlie, then looked at Macy with a penetrating, questioning gaze. Charlie decided that, since Macy was a patient, there was no need to introduce him. After exchanging a few words, they separated. In the lift, Macy said, "Is there something odd about my appearance?"

"Of course not. Why?"

"That man looked at me as if he thought I was crazy."

"No. Sandor's a psychiatrist, and he probably guesses that you're a patient, so he looks at you with professional interest."

Macy looked relieved. "I see." It struck Charlie that his fairly calm exterior concealed a great deal of insecurity.

Topelius opened the door. Charlie could see that, behind him, the flat was immaculately tidy. Topelius himself was dressed in a dark suit with a bow tie. Charlie introduced Macy. As he shook hands, Macy said, "I understand you and Dr. Peruzzi are partners."

"I suppose you could say that, yes."

From the way Macy's eyes wandered round the flat, Charlie wondered whether he suspected them of being homosexuals. Macy asked, "Are you a nerve specialist too?"

Topelius said smoothly, "No, my field is brain research. I am not a doctor of medicine but a professor of biology."

"That's a relief. I'm getting tired of psychiatrists."

"Coffee?"

"Er, yes, thank you."

As Topelius went to the kitchen, Charlie asked Macy, "What's wrong with psychiatrists?"

"They just seem to have rather weird ideas. Dr. Kronhausen thought I had an Oedipus complex, and when I told him he wouldn't think so if he met my mother, he seemed to feel I was being flippant."

Charlie laughed. "This is the doctor in Switzerland?"

"Oh no, that's Dr. Feldman, Kronhausen's in Los Angeles. Feldman's a Jungian. He thinks I've got a fixation on the moon."

Topelius, who could overhear the conversation from the kitchen, asked, "Did he explain what he meant by that?"

"Yes. He said the moon is the ancient mother goddess, and it's a primeval archetype, whatever that means. He says that when I landed on the back side of the moon, I probably felt I was seeing the moon goddess from an indecent angle."

Topelius laughed. "All psychiatrists are crazy. I've never met one who wasn't."

Macy said feelingly, "I'm glad to hear you say that. I was beginning to think there was something wrong with me."

Topelius brought in the coffee. "I doubt it's an Oedipus complex, either about your mother or the moon."

"Thank God for that!"

Charlie said, "Could we offer you anything to drink with your coffee? A whiskey or brandy?"

Macy looked slightly surprised. "Well, yes, that's a most appealing idea. I'd appreciate a whiskey."

Charlie placed the decanter and a glass on the table. Macy helped himself to a large whiskey. "Aren't you gentlemen going to join me?"

Topelius hesitated. "Well, yes, I don't see why not. How about you, Charles?"

"A small one."

Macy was already looking noticeably more relaxed. He looked at his watch. "Well, it's kind of you to see me at short notice like this."

Topelius smiled. "We're delighted. I've talked to Alvin, and he's explained the situation." Charlie felt relieved. At least Topelius was in possession of the facts. "But if I may, I'd like to ask you a few questions."

"Go ahead."

"Perhaps you could tell us how these periods of depression began?"

"Sure." Macy drank half his whiskey, as if to nerve himself. "I suppose it started with all the razzmatazz after the first Mercury mission. We went around the country, meeting people, talking to schools and colleges and women's meetings. It was fun at first, but after a week or two, I began to feel tired. I couldn't understand it. I wasn't overworked or anything, but I began to feel tired all the time. Then one night, when I was guest of honor at some banquet—I remember it was in Bismarck, North Dakota—I suddenly got a weird feeling as if I was dreaming. When people talked to me, it was as if they were talking in a foreign language. I could understand what they were saying, but it didn't seem to make sense. Suddenly, I got this frightened feeling as if I was losing contact with reality.

And it was some nice little blonde gal who saved me. She came over and said, 'You don't feel good, do you?' and I told her I felt lousy. She took me for a walk in the garden, and made me sit down on a bench and close my eyes and pay attention to my breathing. That made me feel better. She told me to go on home and she'd tell everybody I felt sick, but I couldn't do that. I went back in, and somehow I got through the evening. But as soon as I got back to the hotel, I called my boss at NASA, and said, 'You've got to get me out of this, I can't take anymore.' He tried to persuade me to finish the tour, but he called back the next morning and told me to go home and take a rest. I reckon they decided that I wouldn't do NASA a lot of good if I felt like throwing up all the time."

"You were supposed to raise money for NASA?"

"Sort of. Make people enthusiastic about the space program. Even then they were saying it was a waste of money that ought to be spent on helping real people." He poured himself more whiskey. "Anyway, back in Florida it was fine. I went back into training."

"You didn't experience any doubts or misgivings about the space program?"

"None whatsoever. You see, I knew President Kennedy—we all did—and when he was assassinated, we felt it was up to us to redeem his promise to put a man on the moon within the decade. I felt pretty bad in 1967 when Gus Grissom took my place in the capsule, and they all died on the launch pad. But that was just one of those things. When I was a test pilot, other pilots were always getting killed. My best friend died when his chute failed to open, and he landed at my feet on the concrete airstrip. Others died when we were training at Langley and Cocoa Beach. One poor guy lost his head and we never did find it. You simply knew that could be the price you'd have to pay.

"Once I was back in training, everything was fine. It was an exciting time. Most of us thought there was only a ten to one chance of a moon landing before the end of the decade. So many things kept going wrong that there seemed to be a jinx on the Apollo program. On Apollo six, there were three engine failures. On Apollo seven, just about everything went wrong; there were fifty malfunctions. And by then it was already 1968. But Apollo eight went into orbit around the moon, and we began to get the feeling that things were going to work out after all. After that, things began to move really fast. Apollo eleven was already on the launch pad while ten was on its way to the moon. And when Neil finally stepped out on to the moon, we all felt as if we were there with him. That was really a great moment. I was drunk for two days . . . "

As he talked about the moon landing, Macy seemed transformed. All the tiredness had vanished from his eyes. Once again, Charlie experienced the feeling that he was watching some kind of dual personality. It reminded him again of the remark that inside every fat man there is a thin man struggling to get out. The man who was struggling to get out from inside Roger Macy was a visionary optimist. It was like watching the movements of a chrysalis as it tries to turn into a butterfly.

Topelius said, "Did you have the same feeling when *you* landed on the moon?"

Macy gave a half shrug. "Oh sure. But that was different. It's different when you're involved in the action." He was silent for a moment. Then he said, as if overcoming an inner reluctance, "But it was a great moment."

Topelius said, "And how did you become involved in politics?"

Macy seemed to emerge from a daydream. "That was in 1976, just before I left NASA. An environmentalist pressure group wrote to me about the problem of air pollution from aerosol cans. There was a lot of fear about the ozone layer. I got interested, and when I left NASA in February '77, I worked with the US National Academy of Science on ozone monitoring. I sat on the Consumer Product Safety Commission, and I made a television program about the dangers of fluorocarbon sprays. As you may know, the state of Oregon banned this type of aerosol later that year. I seemed to be regarded as quite a hero by the environmentalists. After that I got involved in various Republican committees, including one to ensure that the governorship of Oregon went to a Republican in 1978. And that, as you know, was successful."

Topelius said, "I'm surprised they didn't ask you to run for governor."

"They did. I turned it down."

"Why?"

Macy shrugged. "I just did." He seemed to feel that this explanation was sufficient. "Anyway, the other big battle was about Proposition 13, the tax cutting initiative. It sounded like a good idea at first, because my family owns a lot of property, and property taxes were going through the roof. But the Californians, who started the whole thing, soon had to learn that if you pay less tax, you get less public services. I was on the committee to fight Proposition 13 in Oregon, and we finally succeeded in November last year."

"A remarkable record."

"I suppose so." But Macy's smile had a trace of weariness.

"What happened then?"

"Then?" Macy seemed to lose the thread for a moment. "Oh, then I was approached by a group of women who said that a certain herbicide spray was causing miscarriages, and I agreed to look into it. That was just before we defeated the tax cutting initiative." He lapsed into silence.

"When did the depression start?"

"It had started by then. I would wake up in the night with a feeling there was somebody in the room. Of course, there never was. I began feeling tired most of the time. The day after Proposition 13 was defeated, I was supposed to be guest of honor at a banquet. An hour before we were due to leave, I knew I couldn't face it. I made my wife call up and say I was sick. The next day I flew to Los Angeles to see a psychiatrist."

"Dr. Kronhausen? Who said you had an Oedipus complex?"

"That's right." The smile was ironic.

"Any idea what caused this depression?"

"No."

"You say it happened just before you were due to go to this banquet. Had anything happened that day that might have caused it?"

"No."

"It was a perfectly normal day, like any other?"

"Well . . . not entirely. That morning I received a letter from Governor Reagan of California, congratulating us on defeating Proposition 13, and asking if I'd support his campaign for the presidential nomination."

"What did you reply?"

"Yes, of course."

Charlie said, "Why of course?" It was the first time he had felt impelled to speak.

"Well, it was the kind of offer I couldn't refuse."

"You say 'offer.' What do you think you might get out of it?"

"I didn't mean it in that sense. That was just a manner of speaking."

Topelius took up the point. "But what *might* you get out of it, if Governor Reagan became president?"

Macy considered it. He said slowly, "Well, I suppose I might be in a position to do a lot of good to NASA."

"You mean you might be appointed the president's space advisor, or something of the sort?"

Macy was obviously reluctant to pursue the point. "Something of the sort."

Topelius changed the line of questioning. "Do you still get the attacks of depression?"

"Yes. I had one last night."

"What exactly happens?"

"I wake up with a feeling of tension and anxiety. Sometimes I'm sweating like a pig. Then I begin to worry about all kinds of things, and I want to get up and walk about. If I don't get up, my heart begins to beat too fast."

"Too much adrenalin flooding into the system?"

"That's right." Macy was suddenly looking very tired. His face was gray and unhealthy.

Topelius allowed the silence to lengthen. Then he said, "Mr. Macy, has it ever struck you that this depression is your own fault?" Macy looked at him with mild surprise. Charlie wondered what was coming. "While I've been asking you about depression, you've become depressed." Macy saw his point, and grinned sheepishly. "A moment ago you were describing the moon landings to us, and you were full of enthusiasm and energy. Do you realize what this means? It means that you *do it yourself. You* depress yourself. And if you can depress yourself, you can undepress yourself just as easily." He paused to allow it to sink in, then said, "Now it so happens that we have already solved your problem, in my laboratory in Uppsala. A few years ago, I was studying the problem of the chemistry of the brain—how brain cells know how to connect up with others to form a neural network. In order to do this, we inserted tiny electrodes into individual cells in the brains of leeches. Leeches are ideal for the purpose because their brains are so simple and their cells are so large. In this way, we were able to identify the cells that are involved in a leech's panic response, it's flight from danger. The next problem was to identify the same cells in the human brain. This took two years, and was finally accomplished in America, at Cold Spring Harbor on Long Island. What it meant was that we could place electrodes in the scalp and stimulate the panic function in human subjects."

Macy was listening with total attention. So was Charlie, to whom all this was new.

"Our original intention was to learn how to deactivate the panic mechanism. There are some psychotics who go into such a state of panic that it becomes a kind of vicious circle, and they reach a point known as 'exhaust status' and die. We were simply looking for a method of helping such people. And, with the help of our Long Island colleagues, we discovered it. This has not been widely publicized because our experiments are not yet complete. But we now know how to stop panic attacks before they begin."

Macy said, "That's sure good news." He spoke in a flat voice, but it betrayed his underlying excitement.

Topelius held up his hand. "But we soon discovered something even more important. When I tried the experiment myself, I found that the first bursts of electrical stimulation produced an irrational feeling of panic. If I made an effort, I could control this panic, so that I could increase the current. That would cause more panic, which in turn I could control. And this made us realize that we had not merely learned to combat the panic attack, we had learned to show the patient how to cure himself. Even in the most deranged patients, daily doses of panic would gradually increase their resistance. And with intelligent patients, who were willing to make a real effort to control the panic, it worked much faster and much more effectively. Within ten days, two weeks at the most, a depressive patient is well on the way to recovery."

Macy said, "That's unbelievable."

Topelius shrugged. "On the contrary, it is self-evident. If you can depress yourself by thinking depressing thoughts, you can undepress yourself by doing the opposite. So our electrode technique is really unnecessary. You will find that it is just as effective to deliberately set out to depress yourself, think the most depressing thoughts you can conjure up, then undepress yourself by an act of will. It is a simple exercise, a little like doing push-ups. And, like push-ups, it becomes increasingly easy with practice. We have found . . . "

He was interrupted by a ring at the doorbell. Charlie said, "I expect that's Boris." He opened the door and to his surprise, he found himself confronting two men in waiters' uniforms.

"Dr. Peruzzi?"

"Yes."

"The Belvedere Restaurant, sir. Mr. McKeown ordered lunch for three at half past midday."

Topelius said, "Ah, I forgot to mention. Someone rang up to say Mr. McKeown would be providing lunch . . . "

The waiters wheeled a trolley into the room. Charlie hastened to clear the table of books and videotapes. One of the waiters laid a starched white tablecloth, then set out plates and cutlery. The other began to carve slices from a smoked salmon.

"Shall I open the champagne now, sir?"

"Please."

"Steaks are in here, sir, and this dish contains roast duckling. These are the vegetables: new potatoes, peas, asparagus, French beans, celery hearts. The salad is below, with the sweets and cheeses. Shall I open the wine now, so it can breathe?"

Out of the corner of his eye, Charlie observed Roger Macy's expression as the champagne foamed out of the bottle. It was a beam of satisfaction mingled with undisguised greed. Again, he experienced the curious sense that there were two men who took turns using the same body.

Boris Gorski arrived while they were eating. As Charlie admitted him, he slipped the videotape into his hand.

"You're just in time for lunch."

"Thanks, I've already eaten."

But when he saw the food that was still on the trolley, he changed his mind and joined them. There was more than enough for all.

The cassette had been wound forward toward the end of the program. When no one was looking, Charlie pushed it into the video recorder, and switched on the television set. He moved it on its wheels so it was facing Macy. The image that filled the screen was of the lift-off of a spacecraft, lapped around by its sea of fire. Macy, who was eating a leg of duck, said, "Ha, Flash Gordon makes a hasty exit." But the flippancy was belied by the attention with which he watched the screen.

Charlie said, "We were watching it before you arrived this morning. It's the NBC documentary."

"Oh, yeah. Strangely enough, I've never seen it. By the time it was made, we were back in training."

It was clear that he felt constrained about watching the program while they were still eating and talking, so Charlie turned down the sound until it was scarcely audible. Macy resumed his conversation with Gorski. They were talking about communications satellites. Charlie pretended to listen intently. A few minutes later, he observed the sudden shift in Macy's attention that revealed he was watching his own face. Gorski said, "Hey, there's you."

Charlie looked round. It was the scene on the White House lawn. "Shall I turn up the sound?"

Macy smiled with embarrassment. "Oh no, not now."

Gorski said, "*I'd* like to listen to it."

Charlie used the automatic control to turn up the volume. Macy was saying, "I understand those people who think space exploration is a waste of money. But they are missing the point. The real motive in trying to reach the moon was not vanity. It wasn't even curiosity. It was a desire to show that man can do anything he really sets his mind to. If he can solve that problem he can solve any problem, from poverty, ignorance, environmental pollution, to war and crime. All these problems could be solved overnight, if we decided to make the same concerted effort we made to reach the moon."

Gorski had done a brilliant job of editing the tape. The eyes that stared out at them were bold and forceful. By contrast, the restraint of the voice produced an impression of iron control. Charlie knew the tape had been doctored, yet it still produced in him a shiver of excitement like cold water down his spine.

The narrator was saying: "The spirit of the Apollo missions was summarized by Roger Macy, in a speech he made in June 1974, when he opened the new Macy Hospital in Mapleville, Oregon." Charlie experienced a sense of satisfaction when he recognized the face of General Cunliffe immediately behind Macy. The face had that intent frown of concentration that seemed typical of the old man.

Macy said, "If you believe that science is about man's conquest of nature, you are mistaken. It is basically about man's conquest of himself. *That* is why space exploration is important, because it's the most recent and exciting episode in the story of human evolution.

"Man has evolved faster than any creature on this earth. In just over half a million years he has changed from something like an ape to something not unlike a god. That is why it is vital to continue exploring the universe. That is why we are sending rockets to study the surface of Venus, Mars, Jupiter, Saturn—even Pluto. When ancient man looked into space, he felt small and helpless, because he felt he would never understand its mystery. When modern man looks into space, he knows that we hold the key to the mystery . . . "

The telephone rang, making them all start. Charlie cursed under his breath. As Topelius reached out to turn down the volume, he said, "Don't bother. I'll take it in the other room."

Alvin Rinkler's voice said, "Is that you, Charles?"

"Yes."

"It's Al. Charles, I've just had a phone call from New York. General Cunliffe died this morning."

Charlie said, "Oh Christ."

"I know. It couldn't be at a worse time. How are you getting on with Roger?"

"Very well."

"Well, I'm sorry, but there it is. You'll be getting a call from Samantha during the next ten minutes, so I'd better get off the line. I leave it to you whether you break the news to him before she calls."

"Yes. All right."

"Ring me back later, if you would, and let me know what's happening. Does he want us to cancel his flight this afternoon?"

"I'll do that."

He hung up and stood there, staring out of the window, wondering what to do. The decision was taken out of his hands when the telephone rang again. The operator said, "Hold the line. I have a call for you from New York." A moment later, a woman's voice said, "Could I speak to Roger Macy? It's his sister."

"Hold on a moment, please."

He went back into the other room. The program was just finishing, the credit rolling across the screen against a backdrop of the far side of the moon. Charlie said, "Your sister wants to talk to you, Mr. Macy."

"Ah." The expression on his face showed he anticipated bad news.

When the door had closed behind him, Charlie switched off the television.

"General Cunliffe died this morning."

Topelius said savagely, "Damnation."

There was a silence. Gorski said, "I'd better leave you."

Topelius nodded. "It might be best."

"Thanks for the lunch."

When they were alone, Topelius said, "We must try to persuade him not to fly back today."

"Why?"

"Because it would be the worst thing that could happen; flying back with the knowledge that he is too late."

Charlie poured himself a glass of wine. He was normally cautious about drinking at lunchtime, but his throat had suddenly become dry.

Macy's conversation seemed to go on for a long time. Topelius said, "If only we'd been able to work on him for another day . . . "

Charlie said nothing. He shared the feeling.

Macy came back into the room. His face was expressionless. Instead of returning to the table, he sat in the armchair.

"That was my sister. My great-uncle died this morning."

Topelius said, "I am sorry to hear that. You were flying back to see him?"

Macy nodded. The silence lengthened. Charlie said, "Will you still be flying back today?"

Macy shook his head. "What's the point? I may as well get back for the funeral on Sunday."

Charlie and Topelius exchanged glances. Both were experiencing the same hope. Charlie said, "We have an interview with the general on tape. Would you like to see it?"

Macy said, "Oh sure, I'd like that."

As Charlie found the other videotape and inserted it into the machine, he again caught Topelius's eye. Both had the same thought; that a man who is willing to watch a dead relative on tape is not too shocked by the death. A man who was deeply upset would prefer not to be reminded.

He found the interview with General Cunliffe. The old man was saying, "When Roger was ten, he used my favorite briarwood pipe for blowing bubbles. I knew then that he'd either do something amazing or end in jail."

Macy laughed. "I can still remember that pipe. He nearly twisted my ear off."

As the interview proceeded, Charlie watched Macy's face out of the corner of his eye. The smile of affectionate reminiscence reassured him, confirming that Macy was not unduly upset. Trying to place himself in Macy's position, he thought he could understand why. Macy knew the general was dying. It could not be a particularly pleasant experience to fly seven thousand miles merely to stand by a deathbed. Now the race was over. No matter how sad Macy felt about his great-uncle's death, he must also be experiencing a certain relief.

The interview came to an end. It was followed by the speech Macy made at West Point. This was the section of tape that McCaffrey and

Gorski had doctored the previous day. Technically speaking, it was less impressive than the previous tape. Staring at the areas around the eyes, Charlie could detect a certain amount of double exposure. Fortunately, lack of definition in the recording made this look like shadow. He glanced sideways at Macy. He was watching with an air of absorbed concentration.

When the interview came to an end, Charlie reached out for the automatic control. Macy said, "Would you mind letting it run a little longer?"

"Of course not."

What followed was an interview with Macy's old headmaster, then with the principal of the Sunday school at which he had taught before joining the navy. Then, suddenly, Macy's own face appeared again, and Charlie experienced a sinking sensation. This section of tape was unedited. The eyes had Macy's own preoccupied, inturned look. Again, Charlie glanced at Macy. He seemed to have noticed nothing. Charlie said, "Have you definitely decided to stay on in London?"

"Oh sure. There's no point in rushing now, is there?"

"Of course not. I'll ring and get your flight canceled. Will you be needing a hotel?"

"No. I can stay with Alvin."

Charlie telephoned Rinkler from the laboratory, and explained the situation. Rinkler said, "Does he seem depressed?"

"No, not at all. In fact, I'd say he's fairly cheerful."

"Good. Of course, you can never tell. It may hit him later. Anyway, I'll get that flight canceled."

"He says he can stay with you. Is that all right?"

"Oh sure, no problem."

As Charlie hung up, Topelius came into the room. He said, "He wants to watch the rest of the program."

"I thought he might. It's a pity. We've only doctored the first ten minutes."

"He may not notice."

Charlie said, "By the way, do you remember Alvin telling us he hardly knew Macy?"

"Yes."

"It seems strange they refer to one another by their first names, and Macy takes it for granted he can stay in Alvin's London flat. He must have done it before."

Topelius said, "From which you infer . . . "

"That Alvin and McKeown must have planned this in advance."

"I had assumed that anyway."

"Then why not tell us so?"

Topelius said patiently, "They want Macy to support Reagan in the primaries. If Reagan becomes president, it could mean a great deal to Alvin, and to McKeown Enterprises. After all, it can do no harm to have a friend in the White House. When the stakes are as high as that, it's natural to play your cards close to your chest. We might get anxious and nervous. We might even refuse, because, after all, we've been hired as researchers, not psychiatric nurses."

"And in the meantime they hope for a miracle."

Topelius laughed good-naturedly. "It does no harm to hope."

The door opened. Roger Macy looked into the laboratory.

"Hey, fellers, I think I've seen enough."

Charlie said, "I canceled your flight, and Alvin will be expecting you later."

"Thanks." He wandered over to the window, and looked toward Tower Bridge. "It's a beautiful view."

Charlie said, "Yes."

Without looking round, Macy said, "You know, I'm grateful to you two."

"Why?"

"You've helped me a lot."

Charlie and Topelius exchanged glances. Topelius said, "I'm glad to hear it. But I don't see how."

Macy said, "I suppose . . . you've made me realize that depression is a form of self-indulgence."

Topelius said, "When you know that you are already cured."

Macy turned round. "There's one question I'd like to ask you."

"Yes."

"What did you do to those tapes?"

Topelius's face remained non-committal. "What makes you feel we did anything?"

Macy said, "I saw Charles take it out of his pocket after he let Boris in. I know it wasn't in there before because it's too big not to show. I know Boris is a computer expert. That suggests he'd been doing something to the tape."

Charlie said, "Have you any idea what?"

Macy was silent for a moment, then shook his head. "No."

Charlie said, "Come on in, and we'll show you."

He rewound the tape to the speech at West Point. He allowed it to play for several seconds, then asked, "Do you notice anything?" Macy watched it intently. "No. I look pretty good . . . " Charlie froze the frame. "Take a good look at that." He touched the rewind button on the control, then stopped the tape halfway through the interview with General Cunliffe. Again, he froze the frame. "Can you see it now?"

Macy stared at it for several seconds before shaking his head. "Are you telling me . . . you've made me look like the general?"

"Exactly. We've used a computer to superimpose some of his characteristics on to you." He wound the tape forward to the West Point speech, and again froze the frame.

"But why?"

Charlie said, "I'll try to explain. Have you come across the term 'threshold' as it's used in psychology?" Macy nodded. "A person with a high pain threshold is a person who can stand a lot of pain. A person with a high noise threshold can stand a lot of noise. And all men have what you might call a 'worth doing threshold.' When it's high, they don't give a damn about problems and difficulties; they take them in their stride. When it's low, life turns into a series of hurdles and obstacles. They feel things are just not worth doing. That's another name for depression.

"Now we're not concerned about why a patient becomes depressed, whether it's an Oedipus complex or guilt feelings, or just bad digestion. All that matters is to find how to raise the 'worth doing threshold.' It's just a matter of persuading the patient that it really *is* worth making an effort. Depression is a kind of short-sightedness, a kind of tunnel vision, and the problem is simply to find out how to widen it.

"In your case, we came to feel that your great-uncle was one of the most important figures in your life."

Macy said, "You're damn right."

"That's why our aim was to make you see that you've already achieved everything he could have wished. If your aim was to become more like the general, we wanted to show you that you've succeeded."

Macy looked at his own image on the screen and smiled wryly. "A kind of brainwashing."

Topelius said, "You could call it that. But this is positive brainwashing. The aim isn't to enslave you, but to give you more freedom of action."

Macy said, "Let me see some more."

They played him the interview that followed. After that, they showed him again the final scenes of the documentary. As he watched the scene on the White House lawn, Macy said, "Yes, now I'm beginning to see. That's really amazing."

When, a few minutes later, the credits rolled across the shots of the far side of the moon, Charlie switched off. For a moment, no one spoke. Then Macy said, "Well, I have to acknowledge that you gentlemen are pretty brilliant."

Charlie said, "Unfortunately, so are you. It's a pity you caught on so quickly."

"Why? How long does it normally take to . . . brainwash somebody?"

Charlie shrugged. "We don't know. Our researches are only just beginning. You are one of our first subjects."

Topelius asked Macy, "You still feel this is a form of brainwashing?"

Macy grinned with a touch of embarrassment. "I guess no more than most education is."

It was then, for the first time, that Charlie knew they could stop worrying. Until that point, he had been afraid that Macy might feel angry and resentful about being manipulated. But his grin made it clear he was concealing nothing.

Topelius said, "Could I now ask you one question?"

Macy said, "Sure."

"Why do you hate politics?"

Macy looked at him an astonishment."I don't." He hesitated, then added, "I don't hate it." When Topelius said nothing he asked, "Why do you say that?"

"You told me the breakdown began when you received the telegram from Reagan asking for your support. That came after a hard political battle about Proposition 13. You were tired and you wanted to relax and forget about politics. Am I correct?"

"Yes, I was tired all right." Even admitting it seemed to make him tired.

"And that telegram was the straw that broke the camel's back. It lowered your 'worth doing' threshold to a point where you felt you had to escape."

Macy frowned. "Reagan's an old friend of mine."

"I realize that. And this increased your sense of responsibility about helping him." When Macy made no reply, he said quietly,

"You say that you don't hate politics, yet two years of political campaigning produced the same kind of depression as your publicity tour after the first flight. Is that not true?"

Macy met his eyes. "Yes, I suppose that's true." There was an honesty about him that Charlie found very appealing. At the same time, he was aware that this honesty was connected with Macy's vulnerability.

Topelius continued to probe. "Your publicity tour must have seemed an anticlimax after that first orbital flight. Didn't you experience a similar feeling when you retired from NASA?"

Macy shook his head vigorously. "No, I didn't, because when I retired from NASA, I felt I knew what I wanted to do with the rest of my life." He hesitated, and the eyes took on the familiar, in-turned look. "You see, when you've been up there, looking down at the earth from space, it makes you see certain things in perspective; like how small we are, and how it wouldn't make any real difference if the earth disappeared. They say travel broadens the mind. Well, space travel broadens it until you feel dizzy."

Topelius nodded. "I can understand that."

"You see, when we left earth on that final mission, we all felt we might never get back alive. In 1970, Apollo 13 was almost destroyed, and in 1971, three Russians died during re-entry. For all we knew, it was our turn next. It's a strange feeling traveling away from earth at more than two thousand miles an hour. Somehow it violates your deepest instincts. You find yourself wondering why you should do anything so crazy; leave behind every human being you love. But the strangest moment of all was a couple of hours before the module landed. As we went round to the far side of the moon, we watched the earth sink behind the horizon. It was a weird sensation, watching the earth sink behind the moon instead of the other way round. And I suppose it was then that I suddenly realized that I had to do something . . . "

"Do something?"

"About the earth, about the problems of human beings. There's something frightening about the moon. It's just a dead hulk, like an old junkyard full of used cars. And then you look back at the earth, and it's blue and alive, yet it's also very small. And you realize it could easily end up the same way.

"As we were flying back toward the earth, I was thinking, If I get back alive, I swear I'm going to spend the rest of my life trying to make people aware that we've got to take care of the earth. We've got to stop taking it for granted, because it's all we've got. There's just one earth, and a hell of a lot of empty space. As we splashed down in the Pacific, Ed Volkov said, 'We're back.' And I knew what he meant. He meant, we're back *home*, this is our home. And you don't know what that means until you've been a quarter of a million miles away."

For the first time, Charlie began to understand. Oddly enough, it brought a sense of shame. Shame for the inadequacy of his imagination, which until now had been incapable of grasping the reality of Macy's journey to the moon.

"Well, I guess there's a lot of my parents and grandparents in me. My grandparents were religious, so they built a church. My parents made a religion out of education, and they built a school. Until I came back from the moon, I'd never understood what it meant to be religious. Then, suddenly, I felt I understood what it was all about. I wanted to get out there and preach. I wanted to get up on platforms and tell people what I'd seen. All the time we were in decontamination, I was thinking about what I was going to say at the press conference. And when we got in there, in front of the television cameras, I got up and said it; all the things I'd been thinking, about how we had to forget about political divisions and build a new society. And when I sat down, they all clapped politely. And some people came up to me afterwards and said, "That was great stuff, Roger." But what really made me understand was one inoffensive little guy from my hometown paper. He was very nervous, and he said, 'Don't mind me asking this, sir, but should we conclude from your remarks that you're thinking of running for congress?' Then suddenly it hit me; that nobody understood what I was talking about because they all thought they knew already. For them, I was just making the right noises. Every one of them was convinced that he already agreed with me."

Topelius said, "Nevertheless, you decided to go into politics?"

"Sure, because when this ecology group asked me to help get CFC aerosols banned, I was glad to go along. It seemed like the kind of thing I ought to be doing. And in a way, it was one of the most satisfying things I ever did. I talked on platforms all over the country, and I met plenty of people who felt just as I did about the environment. Finally, we were convinced we had the whole country behind us. Every congressman we talked to said he agreed with what we were doing. Yet at the end of the day, the only state that voted to ban fluorocarbon sprays was Oregon. It was quite a disappointment."

"Then why did you go on?"

"Well, the aerosol campaign got me noticed, and I made a lot of friends. Then the next thing that happened was they wanted me to run for governor. I just didn't feel I could go along with that, so I refused. But I campaigned on the Republican platform, and we won."

The glint of satisfaction in his eyes made Charlie ask, "Did you enjoy campaigning?"

"Oh, sure. It's always exciting to fight an election. What I didn't enjoy was all the other things you have to do in politics; the infighting and the wheeling-dealing and the string-pulling and lobbying. Besides, and I'd rather you didn't quote me on this, I found I didn't really give a damn whether we had a Republican or Democratic governor. The real issues don't divide along party lines."

Charlie asked, "So how can you support Reagan?"

Before Macy could answer, the door buzzer interrupted them. Charlie pressed the intercom switch. "Hello."

"It's Alec, sir. I've come to collect Mr. Macy."

"He'll be down in just a moment."

Macy heaved himself to his feet.

"Just one more thing. That machine you mentioned—the thing that can prevent panic attacks. Could I make use of it if necessary?"

Topelius said, "Of course. That will be no problem."

"Thanks. And would it be possible to get copies of those videotapes?"

Charlies said, "Certainly. I'll get Boris to make them for you tomorrow."

They accompanied him to the lift. As Macy stepped into it, Charlie repeated his question.

"Will you support Reagan?"

"I honestly don't know. Right now I feel I never want to make another political speech. But maybe I'll feel different next year."

Topelius said, "Don't let them try and rush you into any decisions. It's your choice."

"I know. Thanks again for everything." He smiled at them as the door closed.

They stood a moment, listening to the lift descending. As they walked back to the flat, Charlie said, "Have you really made a machine that can prevent depression?"

Topelius smiled. "Not quite. That was a slight exaggeration. We are still working on it."

"What if he wants to take up your offer to use it?"

Topelius said with quiet confidence, "He won't."

Later that evening, McKeown rang up.

"Charles. I just thought I'd ring to congratulate you."

Charlie asked with surprise, "What for?"

"Alvin tells me you've done wonders with Roger Macy. He says he's a hundred percent better."

Charlie asked cautiously, "Does he say what he intends to do about supporting Reagan?"

"Well, no, he says he doesn't want to make a decision yet. But that doesn't matter. Alvin can talk anybody into anything."

When Charlie repeated the comment to Topelius, Topelius said, "Poor devil. Now he'll really find out what it's like to be brainwashed."

"I'm not so sure. I've got a feeling that Macy can take care of himself."

He proved to be correct. Two months later, when they met Roger Macy again in London, he was on his way to join an anthropological expedition in central New Guinea. He was still there in November 1980, when Ronald Reagan was elected President.

CHAPTER TWENTY

I MET Charlie Peruzzi in the summer of 1981. We were introduced in the bar of the Admiral Nelson, the pub that has figured so often in these pages, by Petra Friedmann, a lecturer in psychology at State College, Pennsylvania. Within an hour of being introduced, I knew that I was going to have to write a book about him.

Petra Friedmann had introduced herself to me when I was speaking at Bristol University a couple of months earlier. The attractive, red-haired girl who approached me after the lecture asked me if I had ever heard of Charles Peruzzi. The name seemed to ring a bell, but I couldn't remember why. She explained that Peruzzi had created a completely new kind of "self-image psychology," and that it was going to cause a revolution in psychiatry. He had, for example, invented a form of personality classification which he called the "personality identikit," which some of America's largest companies were now using for selecting personnel.

This jogged my memory. I had heard the name Peruzzi recently from a friend in the Seattle Police Department. He had told me, in confidence, that an English doctor called Peruzzi had helped to trap a criminal who had become known as the Seattle Strangler. He had done this by means of some new method of "personality identification" similar to fingerprinting. Peruzzi had helped them, my friend added, on condition that his name was kept out of the newspapers. He wanted to be allowed to finish his researches without the distractions of publicity.

I was excited at the thought that I had tracked down the mysterious doctor Peruzzi, and asked Petra Friedmann for his address. The next morning, I wrote to him at the flat above the surgery in Southwark. There was no reply. Ten days later I wrote again, this time registering the letter. Again, there was no reply. I decided that the doctor was probably determined to avoid all forms of publicity, and shrugged my shoulders.

But I kept in touch with Petra Friedmann. A few weeks later, just as I was about to leave my home in Cornwall on a visit to London, she rang me and asked if I would like to meet Dr. Peruzzi. He had apparently just returned from Uppsala, and found my two letters

305

waiting for him. They had been opened by his part-time secretary, but she had decided to do nothing about them, just in case Peruzzi classified writers with journalists as undesirable nuisances. Now it seemed that Peruzzi, who knew my work, was stricken with guilt, and wanted to meet me next time I was in London.

There was only one condition, and I knew what she was going to say before she said it. Peruzzi and his colleague Topelius wanted to complete their researches before they published their results, so I would have to treat anything they told me as confidential. Naturally, I agreed immediately.

So at half past midday on July 9, 1981, Petra and I walked into the Admiral Nelson in the Old Kent Road. A squarely built young man with a round, good-natured face, walked across the bar to meet us. I found it hard to believe that Charlie Peruzzi was a brilliant research psychologist. If I had seen him in a hospital, I would have taken him for a medical student. He had a pleasant smile, a faint trace of a Lancashire accent, and the kind of hair that looks as if it needs plastering down with water to keep it in order.

After ordering bar meals we sat down and without any kind of reserve, Charlie launched into an account of that weekend at the Park View Hotel, and his meeting with Sharon Engstrom. I could understand what Petra meant when she said he was "one of the nicest men I have ever met." There is a frankness and enthusiasm about him that never fails to remind me of a schoolboy. Neither then, nor at any other time, was there any suggestion that what he told me should be treated as a secret. My own impression is that it was his employer, Ben McKeown, who wanted to avoid publicity. Like all good scientists, Charlie seemed to regard his work as public property.

The story of Sharon fascinated me, and when he had finished telling me about Lesley Engledow and Nicky McKeown, I interrupted to say, "You ought to write a book about it."

"I don't have time. Why don't you?"

"Are you serious?"

"Of course. I'd be flattered."

It was arranged as simply as that.

After lunch, we walked the hundred yards or so back to his flat. The laboratory now housed a computer, the "digital paintbox," and a great deal of video equipment. There was also a desk and a filing cabinet. As we came in, a tall, rather good-looking woman with shoulder-length black hair was seated at the desk, filing letters. With her sensual mouth and jutting breasts, she was the kind of woman any man looks at twice. Charlie introduced us to her as Mabel. She was cordial to me, but struck me as distinctly cool towards Petra. A few minutes later, when she had left, I asked Charlie if she was the woman who had ignored my letters.

"Oh yes. Mabel's a bit overprotective. But she means well."

He asked us to sit down, and made us coffee.

"Now, where would you like to begin?"

I said, "I'd like to see one of these tapes of yours, the original and the doctored version."

"Of course. I know just the thing."

He drew the curtains and switched on the enormous television set. A moment later, a woman's face appeared on the screen. She was a rather ugly, overweight woman, and the television showed clearly that she had some complaint which gave her skin a coarse texture. She was talking about her father, and describing his insanitary habits. There was something familiar about her, and I asked Charlie, "Who is she?"

"You've just met her. That's Mabel."

I found it unbelievable. The difference was astounding. The Mabel I had just met had high cheekbones, deep-set dark eyes, and the ravaged face of a woman of strong passions. This woman had a round face. Her hair, which was short, was of an indeterminate brown color. She gave the impression of a woman who is self-centered to the point of being mildly psychotic.

Charlie said, "I'll wind it on a bit. This next sequence is what Boris and Dermot did with the digital paintbox."

This was, in a way, the most surprising change of all. The face of the woman on the screen was thinner and the mouth was redder, more sensuous; although, looking closely, it seemed to me that it had not been actually enlarged. The eyes were somehow more attractive, as if she had put drops in them. She was saying exactly the same words as before, yet they seemed quite different. This was because this woman's face was no longer tight and bad tempered. It was a calm, rather sympathetic face, and she said things with a slightly self-mocking smile.

I said, "Are you telling me that's the same tape as before?"

"Exactly. You'd be amazed what the digital paintbox can do. Mind you, that represents hours of work, as well as months of experience. Once you get used to the paintbox, you begin to see how the expression can be changed. We couldn't have done this at the beginning."

I found it almost impossible to believe that this calm, attractive woman was the Mabel of the earlier videotape and the Mabel I had just met.

"But how on earth did you change her appearance—I mean the *real* Mabel?"

"Ah, that's the incredible thing. We didn't. When Erik first saw her he made an interesting comment. He said she was obviously a deep hypnotic subject, and therefore highly suggestible. Now as soon as we showed her these doctored tapes, it caused a change in her personality. She seemed to gain more self-control. We kept on subjecting her to doctored tapes about once every ten days, and, believe it or not, it turned her into a far more agreeable person. Of course, this was partly a matter of feedback from other people. Because she had a nicer personality, people found her more likeable and showed it. This made her nicer still . . . the ordinary reinforcement mechanism. Then some eighteen-year-old boy fell heavily for her—I suppose he saw her as a sort of mother figure—and moved in with her, and it was at that point that she also began to change physically. She began to lose weight, her skin complaint vanished, and the shape of her mouth seemed to change. I'm not sure it's really altered, it's just that her face has become thinner, so the mouth stands out more. She also grew her hair longer, and dyed it black because this boy had a thing about black-haired women. It was quite amazing. She suddenly seemed to exude sex. She's not my type at all, yet even I found I was beginning to feel attracted to her. Now if you'd seen Mabel as she was when I first knew her, you'd know just what that means. Now she's separated from the eighteen-year-old and she's living with a reporter on our local newspaper, but she's certainly never looked back. Incidentally, I asked her if she'd gone on a diet to lose weight. She said no, it just happened. I think it's an incredible case of suggestibility. Seeing herself on the screen was exactly like being hypnotized."

Petra, who had seen none of this film material before, became immensely excited. I was also excited but, being English, preferred to conceal it. Petra, on the other hand, could hardly keep still. "My God, do you realize you're going to change the whole world?" She pointed out of the window. "When this gets into the newspapers, you're going to have hordes of screaming women, as far as the eye can see, all begging you to transform them into goddesses."

Charlie looked dubious. "I know. That's why we want to keep it a secret for the time being. Once we've got it all worked out, clinics all over the world can use the method and there'll be no problem. But until then, we have to keep it to ourselves."

Petra said, "Come to think of it, perhaps I ought to reserve my place at the head of the queue." She was joking but we both sensed in her the undertone of seriousness. What I was observing in her was the peculiar excitement, the starry-eyed fascination, that I was later to see again and again when people were watching "transformed" versions of themselves on the screen. It was what Charlie called "the magic effect."

I noticed a bookcase containing a dozen or so large files labeled "Personality Identikit." He allowed me to look through them: hundreds of pages of photographs of faces, all with different expressions. At the beginning of the first volume, each had a description underneath: worried smile, self-deprecatory smile, discouraging scowl, puzzled frown, suggestive leer, and so on. But later in the volume, most of them were simply labeled with a letter and a number. I could see why; it would have taken half a page to describe some of the expressions.

"But what exactly do you intend to do with all these?"

"They've already been fed into the computer. That's been our main task during the past two years."

"But how do you intend to make use of them?"

"Have you ever come across this?" He handed me an old Victorian volume entitled *Lavater's Physiognomy*. There were dozens of plates, each one containing eight or ten heads. Most of the book consisted of descriptions of each of the heads. "Choleric type. The beetling brows and outthrust lips denote impatience and a tendency to self-righteousness. Such men are at their best within a rigid disciplinary system."

I said, "But surely this is just pseudo-science?"

"In a sense. But there is more to it than that. After all, every one of us knows how to read people's moods from their faces. How do we do it? You might say that it is too subtle to put into words. But it's not too subtle to put into a computer."

"But what do you *do* with it once it's in the computer?"

"I'll show you."

He took a large box from the top of the filing cabinet and opened it on the desk. It contained photographs—several hundred of them. "These were sent to us by a large corporation. They're looking for two managerial types; one for their chain of service stations and restaurants in England, another for their operation in Nigeria. They know roughly what they want, of course; enterprise, imagination, dominance, and so on. Honesty is also important. But for their African operation, they don't want a man who is as rigidly honest as their English manager. He'll have to get used to giving and accepting bribes, because it's normal practice there. Now we've evolved what we call a 'managerial profile,' and put it in the computer. So all we had to do was to feed these photographs into the computer—you notice there are three of each, full face, profile and half-profile—and it came out with a selection of half a dozen applicants for each job. And these are the two final applicants who were selected." He handed me two photographs.

The men certainly looked as if they would be ideal for the job. But so did dozens of other photographs in the file. I found it all rather disturbing.

"How can a computer judge from photographs? The face doesn't reveal everything about a man. I've known men who looked like total crooks and were rigidly honest, and vice versa."

"That's the astonishing thing. It *does* work. We start from the assumption that certain parts of the face reveal a person's character: the mouth, the eyes, the lines on the forehead. A man with a weak, self-indulgent mouth probably *is* weak and self-indulgent, and a woman with a bad-tempered glare and a tight mouth probably *is* bad tempered. As a person gets older, his character gets imprinted on his face, and there's no reason why those imprints shouldn't be read, just like fingerprints. It's merely a question of classification."

"But does a photograph contain enough information?"

"It seems to contain the basic information. The final selection of those candidates was done by interview, because the computer couldn't decide between them. In Uppsala, my colleague Topelius is developing a method of getting the computer to read short extracts from filmed interviews, and that should be much more accurate. More like a lie detector, in fact."

"Can it do it the other way round; give an assessment of a person's character based on a photograph?"

"Oh yes. In fact, we did that with Mabel, and the result was rather interesting. When we fed in that early picture, while she still had the skin complaint, the computer told us she was highly dominant, egotistical, sex starved and unsure of her identity. When we tried it again the other day with the latest photograph, it said she was highly dominant, egotistical, self-confident and sexually active. So her main characteristics haven't altered, she's still dominant and egotistical. To change that would take far more radical personality surgery."

"It could be done, though?" It sounded disturbingly like brain-washing.

He seemed to read my thoughts. "Oh yes, but *she* would have to want it. That's the whole point of personality surgery. The easiest way to change people is to get them to change themselves. All we can do is to try to show them the kind of person they might like to become, like a hairdresser showing a woman a brochure full of hair styles she can choose from."

I thought of that sentence from *Lawrence of Arabia*, which I had quoted in my first book: "I did not like the 'myself' I could see and hear." This is one of the central "outsider" problems: Self-dislike. If Peruzzi and Topelius had found a way of dealing with *that* problem, then it would be a privilege to write about them.

That is why, in the autumn of 1982, I began assembling material for this book. I could see that it demanded a completely different approach from my biographical studies of Abraham Maslow and Wilhelm Reich. There my main task was to place them in the mainstream of the history of psychology. In the case of Peruzzi, this would be unnecessary. He was a loner whose ideas owed nothing to anybody but Topelius. Besides, the story of the development of his ideas, from that weekend in the Park View Hotel to "the case of the disheartened astronaut," was so naturally dramatic that all I had to do was to tell it, as closely as possible, in his own words. I have accumulated thirty cassettes of interviews with Peruzzi, Topelius and other leading characters in this story.

During those early days of research, it looked as if the main problem was going to be the question of professional etiquette. Charlie naturally felt that it would be unethical to discuss the case histories of his various patients. The only solution was for me to approach them and persuade them to tell me their stories. At first it looked as if there was a jinx on my research. I rang Dr. Morton-Jones and found myself speaking to his wife Martha. When I ex-plained what I wanted, she told me briskly that her husband had no time to talk to journalists, and hung up on me. When I tried contacting Sharon Engstrom, I learned that she had married an air traffic controller and moved to Houston, Texas. I wrote a letter to Ben McKeown, and received a reply from his secretary saying that he would be in America for the next three months and would therefore be unable to see me. But gradually, with Charlie Peruzzi's help, the obstacles were smoothed away. I succeeded in ringing Morton-Jones at his club, and he invited me to lunch. I entered into correspondence with Roberta Seneca in New Mexico. I succeeded in interviewing Sharon Engstrom (now Healey) in New York. And when I spent an afternoon with Lesley Engledow, in the flat she shared with Duncan Baron in Lavender Hill, she talked with such breathtaking frankness that I at first assumed it was 'off the record.' But when I asked her how much I could print, she looked at me with mild surprise and said, "Whatever you like." It was then, for the first time, that I knew beyond all doubt that this book could be written.

There remained only one minor obstacle and that, oddly enough, was caused by Charlie himself. When I asked him about the case of the Seattle Strangler, he shrugged and said that it was not worth including. I pointed out that most people are interested in a murder case and argued that it would make the logical conclusion for the book. It took a great deal of persuasion to overcome his reluctance—I have the impression that he regards some of the details as too unpleasant for the general reader—but I eventually brought him around to my way of thinking. What follows is based on the four-part account of the case by Murray Salk, published in the *Seattle Examiner.*

On December 4, 1969, a young sociology student was making her way from the library on the campus of the University of Washington, Seattle, when she heard a noise behind her, and caught a glimpse of a man in running gear who was bearing down on her. A moment later she was hurled on her face on the grass. When she tried to scream, her face was jammed into the damp ground. The man said in her ear, "Okay, you know what's going to happen?" He yanked down her jeans so hard he tore off the waist button. When she struggled, he punched her until she stopped. She lay still, allowing him to rape her. She said that he smelt of aftershave, and that when he kissed her afterwards, his chin felt smooth. Ten minutes later, he bound her hands with her own belt and ran into the darkness.

During the next six months, similar rapes occurred at intervals of approximately three weeks. In several cases, the victims were themselves early-morning joggers. The attacks occurred over a wide area, from Tacoma in the south to Lynnwood in the north. Extra police patrolled all areas that were popular with joggers. They were afraid that, sooner or later, a victim would resist and be killed.

This happened on June 8, 1981, between half past six and seven in the morning. Donna Goodman was a twenty-three-year-old married woman whose husband worked for the city waste disposal department. He usually left the house while she was still asleep. A neighbor who was awakened by a woman's scream looked out of her window but saw nothing. When Ross Goodman came home for lunch, he was alarmed to find that the house was still locked. The screen over the kitchen window had been slashed with a knife. Donna was lying on the bed, naked. She had been strangled with a pair of tights. Clutched in her hand, the police found a thread of blue nylon cord that had probably come from a pair of jogging shorts. The room had been wiped clean of fingerprints, indicating a man who was in no hurry.

On June 25, an eighteen-year-old student, Karen Jones, disappeared from her room in the students' residence. Another girl who had looked out of her window early that morning had seen a man in blue jogging shorts and a white shirt walking across the lawn behind the residence. Karen's body was found in a cellar a block away. She had been manually strangled and raped.

The case was deliberately played down in local newspapers. Seattle has a fairly high crime rate, and the various cases lost themselves among other reports. Three more rapes occurred during July and the first week of August, one of them among the tombstones in a churchyard. In each case, the victim described the man as a powerfully built white male in jogger's uniform. Then, for some reason, the rapes ceased for nearly two months. Police began to hope the man had left the area. This hope vanished in the last week of September when a thirteen-year-old girl was attacked by a jogger on her way to Sunday school and raped.

The police now began a massive operation to try and trap the strangler-rapist. The rapes had occurred over such a wide area that they were reasonably certain he drove a car. Residents' committees were asked to take the numbers of any strange cars left parked in their streets at dawn or dusk, and to take special note if they saw joggers leaving or entering their cars. They interviewed over a hundred suspects. In mid-October, police in a patrol car heard a woman scream and saw two figures struggling on a lawn. As they drove up, the man, who wore a jogger's outfit, broke away, leapt a garden fence, and vanished at high speed. A police net was thrown round the area, and the owners of all cars parked within a square mile were interviewed.

In October 1981, the girl who lived in the room next to Lynda Sue Gerhardt, in a two-story frame house not far from the campus of Seattle University, heard muffled noises from the next room. She called to ask if anything was wrong, but received no reply. Half an hour later, she happened to be looking out of her window when she saw a man in jogger's outfit running across the lawn behind the house. She called the police. Lynda Gerhardt was found under her bed. She had been manually strangled and raped. The killer was evidently a man with cool nerves, who had not taken alarm when the girl called to ask if anything was wrong.

On November 7, 1981, Mildred Dobrovolny, twenty-seven, the wife of a university lecturer, was found strangled and raped when her husband returned from classes at mid-morning. She had been dead about two hours. This indicated that the rapist had broken in shortly after her husband had left the house, and that he must therefore have been watching it. This suggested a man who either knew the area well, or who knew that Dr. Fred Dobrovolny had classes that morning. Dozens of male students were interviewed, and many agreed to lie detector tests.

On December 2, 1981, a campus guard at Mapleville College, Oregon, discovered that a back window of a sorority house had been forced. He hurried to a telephone to summon a second guard to cover the other entrance, and on his way back saw a dark figure running hard towards the sports field. He gave chase, but the man was a fast sprinter and vanished in the darkness. In a downstairs room, Kathy Ziegler, eighteen, was sitting on her bed, apparently dazed. Her nightdress had been torn from the neck to the waist. Marks on her throat showed that she had been strangled into a state of unconsciousness before being sexually attacked. She could remember nothing except waking up and feeling hands round her throat.

Roger Macy, who was on the board of governors of Mapleville College, interviewed the girl in the hospital later the same morning. She was badly shocked and very emotional. Macy was deeply disturbed by her condition—he had known her parents all his life.

He spent the rest of the morning talking to the sheriff, John Calissi, and was shocked to learn that five rapes had taken place in Mapleville during the past two months. None had been reported in the newspapers.

Sheriff Calissi had heard of the Seattle Strangler. At Macy's suggestion, he contacted the Seattle Police Department to see whether any connection could be established between Kathy Ziegler's attacker and the Seattle Rapist. (In fact, there was none. The Mapleville rapist, a school janitor, was caught three weeks later.) Detective Ira Goldman, who had worked on the Strangler case from the beginning, flew down to Mapleville. Macy invited him to dinner the same evening, and they discussed the Seattle case. And it was when Goldman mentioned that his own file contained over three hundred photographs of suspects that Macy thought about Charlie Peruzzi. They had kept in touch since that first meeting, and Macy had called to see Peruzzi and Topelius on a visit to London a few weeks before. During that visit, Charlie had demonstrated his computerized method of selecting administrative personnel for an international chemical company. As far as Macy could see, the same method ought to be applicable to identifying a sex killer from among three hundred photographs.

The Seattle Police Department was desperate; anything seemed worth trying. So a large envelope containing duplicates of the photographs was dispatched to Charlie in London.

What Macy had not taken into account was that Peruzzi and Topelius had evolved their system to select managerial applicants. Their computer had been programmed to look out for such qualities as enterprise, imagination, adaptability, persistence, honesty; none of them characteristics usually associated with criminals. On the morning the photographs arrived, he and Boris Gorski were working on a program to help universities to select applicants for places. Turning his attention to criminals was the last thing Charlie wanted to do. His first impulse was to return the photographs, explaining that his program was not designed to identify "criminal types."

In the event, he decided to sleep on it overnight. And, lying awake an hour before dawn, he was struck by the thought that his computer could already identify certain "criminal" characteristics, for example, dishonesty and laziness. The idea began to intrigue him. Immediately after breakfast, he went to the local library and looked through the criminology section. By chance, one of the first volumes he laid his hand on was called *Mental Deficiency* by A. F. Tredgold, and it contained many photographs of people suffering from feeble-mindedness, idiocy, syphilitic imbecility, and so on. Studying these, it struck him that such faces lacked *character*, as if the spirit behind the eyes, so to speak, was too feeble to stamp its force on the lines of the face. He began to look through volumes of the Notable British Trials series, with photographs of murderers. Once again, he noticed how often the faces seemed to lack character, although character had often been replaced by a certain shiftiness, a kind of animal cunning. It was then that he recognized that criminality was not irrelevant after all. It was an integral part of his study of human personality. He had even fed into the computer the faces of Beethoven, Newton, Leonardo and Bernard Shaw, so surely it was illogical to deliberately avoid criminals?

Before he left the library, he talked to the chief librarian and arranged to borrow every volume on crime containing a photograph. The following day, with Gorski's help, he collected them all in his car. He also recalled that Guys Hospital had a fine criminological collection, much of it accumulated by Professor Keith Simpson. He spent a day at the hospital and arranged to borrow whatever he wanted.

It took nearly six weeks. During that time, Charlie and Boris Gorski—and later Topelius, who joined them after Christmas—looked at criminal photographs all day long, and applied what they had learned of the Chinese science of *hsiang shu*. New Scotland Yard was also helpful. One morning toward the end of the project, Commander Bob Markham of Criminal Records arrived with two large packing cases of photographs and other materials.

It was in the third week of January, 1983, that they decided to put the program to the test. Charlie had no idea of how efficient it might prove to be. He had merely fed into the computer an enormous amount of raw data. The computer's job was to observe similarities. On the morning of January 23, at 9:30, they started feeding into the computer the 332 photographs sent by the Seattle Police Department. By 10:30 it was all over. The computer, asked to identify the face of a man capable of sexual abuse and murder, had ended by selecting just three photographs. Four more were rejected on grounds of "insufficient data" (i.e. the photographs were poor). Charlie sent the Seattle Police Department a cable, giving the serial numbers of the three photographs, and also mentioning those on which there was insufficient data. It was received by Detective Ira

Goldman when he started work at nine that morning (Seattle being eight hours behind London).

When Goldman checked the numbers against his own copies of the photographs, his first reaction was incredulity. The first of the three photographs was of a good-looking young man with short-cropped blond hair and a firm chin; the inscription on the back said "Gary Wiseman, Jr." Wiseman senior was one of the most respected members of Seattle society, a businessman and property owner whose investments were worth millions of dollars. His mansion on Mercer Island, in Lake Washington, had been built by one of the "robber barons" who created the Pacific railroad. It was regarded as one of the showpieces of the northwest. A check revealed that Gary Wiseman had been included in the collection of mugshots only because his car had been among those parked within the square mile on the day the police patrol had interrupted the attacker. The police department had already been subjected to strong criticism for inducing male students from the University to submit to poly-graph tests, some of them alleging that they had been threatened with harassment if they refused. This is why Ira Goldman's first reaction to the photograph of Gary Wiseman was to drop it in the wastepaper basket and forget it. But he checked on the other two photographs, and what he discovered made him thoughtful. Neither of the men had police records in Washington state, and both had produced alibis that cleared them. One was a middle-aged door-to-door encyclopedia salesman, the other a short-order cook. The salesman had given his last address as Kansas City, the other as New York. Both had been fingerprinted. A check with the Kansas City police department revealed that the salesman had spent five years in prison for a long list of sexual offenses against boys. The short-order cook had been confined in a mental home after convic-tions of rape and sodomy.

Understandably, these results made Detective Goldman decide it was worth conducting a closer investigation into Gary Wiseman. A check revealed that Wiseman had a police record, but it contained only one item. About a year before, a girl had reported that her car had been stolen. She also mentioned that her boyfriend had stormed out of her apartment in the early hours of the morning after a drunken quarrel. The boyfriend was Gary Wiseman. When the car, badly damaged, was discovered at the side of Highway 90 on Mercer Island, Wiseman was questioned and charged with its theft and with causing willful damage. A good lawyer had secured Wiseman's conditional discharge, on the grounds that he had only intended to borrow the car. Wiseman agreed to pay for the damage.

Detective Goldman traced the girl through the delicatessen where she worked, and interviewed her. She explained that she had known Wiseman for about a year before their quarrel. He had paid repeated visits to the store until he persuaded her to go out with him. She was divorced, with a two-year-old son, and at first she could hardly believe her luck. This clean-cut young man from a wealthy family insisted he wanted to marry her. She quickly became his mistress. Then she began to discover he was not all he seemed. He told her he ran a radio station owned by his father, as well as an engineering supply company. It was true that he *had* held both jobs until his father was forced to remove him for drunkenness and incompetence. She finally had to recognize that Wiseman was a fantasist, whose tales about his heroism in the Vietnam war, his sporting achievements and his business empire were pure wishful thinking. She also found his sexual tastes disturbing. When sober, he was usually impotent. When drunk, he wanted to dress in her underwear and perform abnormal acts on her with a cucumber. It was after her son had walked in on one of these sessions that he had left the house in a rage and stolen her car.

The girl was also able to tell Goldman that a schoolfriend of Wiseman's was a member of the police department. George Drew was a detective sergeant in Everett, north of Seattle, and had been a neighbor and playmate of Gary Wiseman's in the days when the family lived in Kirkland. They had been fellow students at Northwest College, and had kept in touch ever since. Goldman drove up to Everett, and spent an afternoon talking to George Drew. Without too much prompting, Drew admitted that Gary Wiseman had always been obsessed by sex. He had a large collection of pornographic magazines and books, and from the age of fourteen, spent most of his pocket money in seedy "massage parlors" where girls dressed only in bra or panties would administer "relief massage" after a sauna. But although Wiseman claimed to be a formidable seducer, his track record with girlfriends seemed to be poor. At least three of them had told Drew that Wiseman became clumsy and embarrassed as soon as he found himself alone with a girl in the back of a car. The only girl with whom he seemed to have a sexually satisfying relationship was a little Indian girl from a slum family, and she was generally regarded as an "easy lay."

For Goldman, the picture was beginning to build up into the kind of man he was looking for. Obsessed by sex and pornography, he was nevertheless unable to achieve satisfaction with girls who might be regarded as his "social equals." His sexual tastes were "peculiar" and seemed to involve humiliating both himself and the girl. He was a fantasist, with a compulsion to impress his sexual partners with bogus achievements. The girl in the delicatessen was typical of the kind of woman with whom he could be more or less sexually potent; a gentle, rather shy girl who gave the impression she could be used as a doormat, and who believed everything he said.

Goldman reasoned that, for such a man, rape might well be the only means by which he could achieve successful sexual contact with more glamorous and dominant types of women. The rape victims who had survived had all described how he would force them to lie face down, threatening to kill them if they tried to look at him, and had entered them from the rear. He cursed and swore all the time he was committing the rape, telling the victim that all whores ought to be treated like this. It did not take a psychiatrist to see that this fitted into the picture of a man who needed to boost his self-esteem by playing games of sexual dominance.

The delicatessen girl still had many photographs of Gary Wiseman. He loved posing in front of the camera. Goldman borrowed these pictures and sent copies of them to Charlie Peruzzi, asking him to put them through the computer. By now, Peruzzi, Topelius and Gorski had evolved a far more elaborate program of "character assessment," and they submitted the result of the computer analysis to Dr. Emil Gurwitz, the author of a standard work on sexual psychopaths. Gurwitz's report read, in part, "The subject shows signs of the fatal weakness of character that is a basic characteristic of the criminal. He has probably been spoiled from early childhood by an overindulgent mother who is convinced that he can do no wrong, and that he is brilliant and talented. Unfortunately, he has been unable to live up to this exaggerated estimate, for he lacks any kind of persistence or determination. He compensates by living a rich fantasy life. An abnormally strong sex drive has turned this fantasy life into channels of sexual deviance associated with domination."

Meanwhile, Gary Wiseman was being shadowed night and day by a team of detectives, which included three women. One of these, Officer Marilyn Daly, was herself an enthusiastic jogger, and often followed behind Wiseman as he jogged in the area of the University of Washington campus. On the second occasion when this happened, she turned a street corner to find that her quarry had vanished, but as she passed the lawn of a public building, she saw him lurking in the bushes, apparently watching her. It dawned upon Officer Daly that the Seattle Strangler had probably selected her for his next victim. She reported back to Ira Goldman, who asked her to continue to run in the same area at the same time every morning. Officers placed at various vantage points, such as the university car park and the Burke Museum, would try to watch her continually through binoculars.

On the morning of February 14, the rapist walked into the trap. As Marilyn Daly turned into a quiet, tree-lined street near the Arboretum at 6:45 a.m., she saw a figure in blue running gear jogging ahead of her. Then, as she turned right, along the route she usually followed, she realized that he had vanished. As she passed a lawn surrounded by rhododendron bushes, she was grabbed from behind, and a hand clapped over her mouth. Although terrified, she followed her instructions, and allowed herself to be dragged on to the lawn. The man seemed to be in no hurry. He told her that if she submitted, she would be unharmed. He smelled of expensive aftershave. As he squeezed her throat hard, from behind, to convince her he meant business, she managed to nod and say, "Don't hurt me." Although she had been trained in karate, the man was far stronger than she had expected, and in her present position, she felt helpless.

Convinced that she meant to cooperate, the man stopped squeezing her throat, and tugged down her running shorts. From reports of previous rapes, she knew that he had often taken as long as twenty minutes, so she felt that her best hope of remaining unharmed was to lie still. Meanwhile, she prayed that help was on its way. But as she felt the man's attempt to enter her, she experienced an uncontrollable revulsion, and tried to twist away from him. At this he grabbed her by the throat and began to bang her head on the ground, squeezing so hard that she was unable to cry out. Then, as she felt consciousness slipping away, she heard a shout, and the pressure was suddenly released.

The patrol car that was supposed to follow her at a distance had turned into the street and found it empty. Their timing was so accurate that they knew she should still be visible at the far end. The two policemen, Detective Pete Coleman and Patrolman Jeff Adams, realized that if they drove down the street or sounded the siren, they would warn the rapist. So they stopped the car, turned off the engine, and then cautiously proceeded down either side of the street. Coleman was the first to hear sounds of a struggle from behind the rhododendrons. He shouted a warning and aimed his revolver. Like an Olympic runner the man was on his feet, leaving his jogging shorts behind, and running across the lawn. The shot fired by Coleman struck a tree. Patrolman Jeff Adams arrived in time to see the man vaulting a garden fence, and took a pot shot with his revolver. He saw the man stagger. Moments later, Detective Coleman heaved himself on to the fence, took careful aim at the running figure, and fired. The man staggered, then dropped. As the policeman ran toward him the rapist screamed, "Don't shoot again, I'm dying." His hands were handcuffed behind his back. Detective Marilyn Daly, who had now had time to recover, joined the two men in escorting the man to the patrol car. He walked with a limp. The last bullet had gone through the soft flesh of his thigh.

When it was announced that Gary Wiseman was the Seattle Strangler, many local residents were convinced that the police had made an absurd mistake. They had known him as a charming if rather reckless young man, a fine tennis player and an expert water-skier. The celebrated lawyer who was hired by the family succeeded in getting Gary Wiseman released on bail, but the publicity caused other witnesses to come forward. One was a young married woman who said that Wiseman had raped her when she was a maidservant in his father's house. Other victims recognized Wiseman's photograph as that of their attacker. One girl who had accepted a lift from him, and been raped in the back of the car, admitted that she had allowed the family lawyer to buy her off for five thousand dollars. Another victim who knew his identity said that she felt it was not worth reporting the rape because Wiseman's family connections would ensure that he was never convicted.

At the trial, the defense maintained that Wiseman had been "entrapped" by Detective Daly. Wiseman's story was that they were not strangers. He claimed that she had accepted a lift from him on a previous occasion and allowed him to kiss her. He insisted that she had gone on to the lawn with him voluntarily, and had only started to struggle when they heard the police running towards them. Asked why, in that case, he had run away, he said that he was convinced he would be shot to death if he stayed.

Wiseman's demeanor in the witness box was so convincing that it took the jury two days to reach a verdict, and even then it was not unanimous. But the eventual verdict was guilty. In sentencing Gary Wiseman to two consecutive life terms in prison, Judge Manfred Cleckley said, "I have no reasonable doubt that you have been getting away with rape for more than ten years, and that you would continue preying on women for as long as you were at liberty."

Now that I have finished this account of the discovery of personality surgery, I have only one regret: that this book could not have been twice as long. To my mind, the six months of laboratory work that followed the "case of the disheartened astronaut" are more dramatic than anything that went before. But I agree with my long-suffering editor that they belong to another book. And that is also true of many other cases that occurred between 1979 and 1984: the case of the Peeping Tom headmaster, the case of the schoolgirl who loved cobras, the case of the masochistic millionaire, the case of the terrified clairvoyant, the case of the honest forger, the case of the permanent victim, and, perhaps strangest of all, the case of the "reincarnated genius"—which revealed Topelius's psychological insight at its most dazzling.

Peruzzi and Topelius are themselves engaged in writing a book about the medical implications of personality surgery. I have not seen any of it, and all that Charlie will say is that it is based on the conviction that the human mind has reached a turning point in its evolution. The mind, he says, has so far been conditioned to regard itself as a product of nature, essentially passive. He believes that personality surgery can provide actual disciplines to reveal to us that the mind itself is the fundamentally creative force in human existence. This is why they intend to call the book *The Mind Itself*.

I admit that I find it frustrating to conclude this book without presenting the reader with at least some basic outline of its ideas. It is equally frustrating to have to remain silent about some of the amazing practical developments that have taken place in the past two years. I console myself with the thought that this is not really the end—only the beginning.